PRINTHOUSE BOOKS PRESENTS

Hidden Agendas

You Never Know Who Has One

2nd Edition

A Novel by

Lorenzo "EL GEE" Gladden

VIP INK Publishing Group; Incorporated
Atlanta, GA.

PrintHouse Books, Atlanta; GA.
Published 9-7-2013

www.PrintHouseBooks.com

VIP INK PUBLISHING GROUP; INCORPORATED

Cover Art, designed by SK7.

Isbn – 978-0-991-1719-1-0

Library of Congress Cataloging-in-Publication Data

LORENZO 'EL GEE' GLADDEN

Hidden Agendas; *You Never Know who has one.*

1. Fiction-African American-Romance
2. Fiction-African American-Urban Life
3. Lorenzo 'El Gee' Gladden

PRINTED IN THE UNITED STATES OF AMERICA

Silhouettes of two lovers are cast upon the walls by the flickering light of the spiced apple scented candles. The ambiance is intensified by the soothing voice of your favorite songbird. Chocolate dipped strawberries and champagne on ice are the chosen consumptions for the occasion. As you pull away the bitten strawberry from the lips of your lover, you gaze into his eyes. A warm sensation fills your body because you now feel that you have found your soul mate. If you could look deeper into those eyes you love so much, you would not find the love you've been so desperately seeking. You would find a hidden agenda masked by what you thought was true love.

Hidden Agendas takes you on a journey with André Marshall, a smooth talking, lady's man trying to go straight and find the one piece of the puzzle that his life is missing and the women searching for more than just love. After his reign as a super senior comes to an end by graduation, he accepts a position as head writer with a Georgia based television network. André has to relocate his life from a small city in South Carolina to Atlanta leaving behind Alicia Burroughs, his best friend since the fourth grade and the only woman that ever truly loved him but never told him for fear that he would pass up on his dream to stay with her. On the day he arrives in Atlanta, Alicia expresses her hidden love for her best friend and tells him that she will come to him after graduation in the spring.

A promotion pushes André to a higher position and into a higher tax bracket. As he begins to rub elbows with another class of women, how can he maintain focus on Alicia? Old habits begin to creep up on him and he allows himself to fall weak to the desires of the flesh. When a man has an abundance of quality women to choose from, what can the outcome be? Who will he choose? Will his selected woman be true?

Dedicated
In Loving memory of
Gloria Cortez Johnson
"I love you, Lola!"

LORENZO 'EL GEE' GLADDEN

Hidden Agendas

You Never Know who has one

FICTION

VIP INK PUBLISHING GROUP; INCORPORATED

Atlanta, GA.

Table of Contents

André's Intro

When it comes to life, there is one thing that almost every man and woman strives to obtain on a daily basis. To capture it would surpass success in itself and make living life a little easier. That one thing is love. *Webster's Dictionary* defines love as a strong affection or a liking for someone or something or a passionate affection for someone of the opposite sex. This four-letter word embodies a power that men and women have known for centuries. How can a word so small carry so much explosiveness? While in college, a professor asked me what I considered to be the most powerful spoken word universal to any language. To everyone's shock and disbelief, my reply was love.

Look at it like this. *Love* possesses the power to emotionally break down the hardest man and return life to the coldest woman. It has been the root of many arguments and discussions, as well as the cause of eternal unions between two people. Does love hold true as a triumphant expression of one's sincere inner being and display? It can be considered as the giver of life because lack of this feeling could bring death, physically, emotionally and mentally. Knowing how it feels to be loveless and dead is a feeling that no man or woman should have to experience due to the lack of knowledge, respect, and understanding of this complex emotion.

I used to feel that I had to have a woman in my life to complete me. During my journey, there were escapades with a few women but there seemed to be no future in any of them. From first love to new love, I learned that love is something you cannot control no matter how hard you try. It just has to happen. Alicia Burroughs, my best friend, helped me realize that in order for me to have a whole relationship, both parties involved must be two whole individuals.

With all the joy and happiness love brings, in some cases, it can also be accompanied by a few uninvited or unexpected guests—lies, tricks and deceit. For every success story, dealing with relationships between men and women, there is an underlying story that often goes untold. I don't believe that there is no such thing as a good man. If this is true, then there is no such thing as a good woman. When the elements of money, power and respect come into play, the dating game leaps to a whole new level. When the individuals involved possess all three, or at least two of the three, you sometimes find that someone may carry hidden motives and agendas. The lives that they present are new ones built to cover old ones.

"What's up wit' you and ol' girl?" Alicia asked one night out of the blue as I helped her study for a final.

"Her name is Melissa."

"You knew who I was talkin' about," Alicia laughed.

"To tell you the truth, I don't really know. Our paths are going in two different directions. You know what I'm sayin'?"

"No I don't know what you're sayin'."

"Look at me. I don't have a clue what I want to do with my life or where I wanna go with it. Melissa seems to have it all together. She wants to go to Maryland for law school next year and after grad school she wants to live in New York."

"But that ain't what you want," she interjected as she shuffled her note cards.

"It's not, but at the same time, I don't wanna lose her."

"Can I ask you a serious question?"

"Sure."

"Are you actually trying this time?"

"What kinda question is that Alicia?"

"I'm serious, Dré. I've known you for how

long? You never do right by women. Even in a relationship you still continue to play the field."

"Wait a minute!" I laughed.

"I thought you were supposed to be on my side."

"This ain't about sides André. This is about right and wrong. How can you concentrate on one woman when you keep trying to add more into the equation? That's why your relationships don't work."

"Can I get a little credit here? Maybe I've grown up a little. Since me and Melissa been together, she has been my main focus. To be honest with you, since you got me all on blast, I used to think that the reason why some of my relationships didn't work was because of you."

"Me?" Alicia responded with a surprised squeal.

"You."

"What do I have to do with you and your failed relationships?"

"How many men and women do you know that are as close as we are and aren't dating or have ever dated?" Alicia paused.

"That's exactly my point. I've never told

you this but a lot of the girls I dated felt threatened by you."

"Why are you just telling me this?"

"Because I know you, had I told you that you were the reason for a girl breakin' up with me; it might have caused you to push away from me. You've always considered my feelings and well-being before you considered your own."

"No I do not."

"Yes you do. Does the name Victoria ring a bell?"

"Now that is a low blow. We were 14 years old back then."

"True enough but that was the first time it ever happened. You knew how I felt about music so you backed off because you didn't want to stand in the way of me and what I liked to do. It wouldn't have been a problem if I was in a rap group with another dude."

"That's bullshit André Marcellus Marshall and you know it. Victoria was your girlfriend."

"Me and Vickie didn't start going together until after you cussed me out the night we won the talent show at Heat Waves…"

"For the record," Alicia interrupted. "I did

not cuss you out."

"Can I finish please? The only reason we started dating was because you weren't around anymore. All the things that we used to do together, like go skating, go to games and to the dances at Union Station were the things that you and I used to do. Even though I was with Victoria, I would have given her up just to enjoy those things with you. I never wanted anything to come between our friendship. If I was ever put in a position where I had to choose between you and them, I'd choose your friendship over a relationship."

"Have you ever had to choose?"

"Once."

"Who?"

"Tommy Girl."

"Are you serious? I thought you and Tommy Girl broke up because of her attitude."

"It was because of her attitude towards you. When we started dating after I came back for the summer, it was just me and her. Granted she knew about you and how close you and I were back in the day, she never had to experience it because you and I had not come back together. Once you came back in the picture, she felt threatened because we were so close. When it started becoming a major problem, I felt that I had to cut her loose because you meant more to me as a friend than she meant to me as a girlfriend."

"Dré, that is so sweet. Now can I be honest with you?"

"Okay."

"I look at you and how your relations are with other women and I'm thankful that when it comes to me, you've always been straight up and honest with me. That means more to me than you'll ever know."

"That's because you're not just some random female. You've stood beside me whether I was wrong or right. You don't find that in a friendship between a guy and a girl."

"Wait a minute. Is that what this is about? Are you and Melissa having problems because of me?"

"Not this time. She's one of the few that don't feel threatened by our friendship. There's a lot more to it."

"Then what's up?"

"I just don't know if I'm the right man for her. Sometimes I don't know what she sees in me. Melissa has it all together. She's independent, has a good job that is going to pay her way through grad school and she has a dream. All I have is a room at my grandfather's house, a probation officer, and no clue."

"Stop being so hard on yourself; in less than a month you'll be the first one in your family to graduate from college. That's an accomplishment in itself. I know things aren't good for you right now but it'll come. Trust me. It takes time. You're a good man and any woman would be lucky to have you in her life. I know I am."

The entire time I lived in South Carolina, I was not together. My incomplete state of mind followed me across the state line into Georgia. Now I can see how I blamed Atlanta for my trials of lost love and downfalls. Don't get me wrong, I love the ATL but it was a love that had to grow on me. When I first arrived, my mind was so mixed up I took out my frustrations on a city that had done nothing to me. A wino I had given some change to told me that: "A city is just a city. It's the people that makes it what it is." He also told me that only I could control how my life would turn out. In my heart, I still believe that *Hotlanta* had a little to do with how my life turned out. If nothing else, it helped lead me to the life that I now live.

Reflecting on the condition my life was in when I first moved to Atlanta was a scary sight. Looking at my life now, one never would've thought that I went through a lengthy period of pure hell before everything managed to come together. Now that I think about it, I must've looked like the biggest man-whore that ever lived and it started with a mysterious lady I met on the first night I arrived in the city. From that innocent meeting I knew that living in Atlanta was not going to be an easy task. Never in a million years did I think I would go through the things that I did. Through it all, I overcame adversity leading me to be young, black, and successful. I have everything I ever wanted and more. Finding the woman that would love me for me was the hardest part. There were so many to choose from.

When asked to describe myself, I was told that I was being too modest. The best description that I can recall was when I was introduced at the Mr. Black Greek Pageant I entered while in college. The Mistress of Ceremony's card read:

Standing 5 feet 10 inches tall, he hails from the city of Fayetteville, North Carolina. The women of Franklin Memorial voted this Adonis the school's sexiest senior. From his razor sharp haircut that match his wits, to his chinky eyes and full lips, this man can easily qualify as any woman's fantasy. His muscular frame is covered by a mocha cappuccino complexion that can make a female melt when pressed against it. Representing the men of the

Royal Blue and White, I present to you André Marshall.

I was born André Marcellus Marshall, friends and family call me Dré, a humble, young man raised in the Carolinas by his grandparents. I know my parents loved me but they were young when I was born. My grandparents wanted me to have stability in my life so they took the responsibility and raised one more. Over the years I learned to understand things I could not or did not want to accept as a child. Now it's okay because all things happen for different reasons.

If my life could be summed up in a few words, I would need a few more. Through all of the sudden turns, ups and downs, and not to mention all of the loops, the words, roller coaster ride come to mind. However, I am content with my current position. I am the reigning champion of my own destiny. No victory comes easy; so believe me when I say *to hell and back* is an understatement.

When I arrived in Atlanta, I was in a bad situation. I was hurt because I felt I'd left a piece of me behind. Putting this country boy in the big city was like throwing a little lamb to the wolves. It was hell trying to keep from being consumed. Looking at my current life, I think I did a damn good job maintaining.

The day I saw my probation officer for the last time marked the first turning point in my life. I was out from under the thumb of the judicial system and ready to get the hell out of South Carolina. I had several family members scattered up and down the East Coast. My cousin, Jerome, lived in Atlanta and had been begging me to come to stay with him. It seemed like a good idea so I started to search for jobs in the area.

Out of all the résumés I sent to the various companies, there was one job that really caught my attention. The position was for a writer at a television network. This was perfect because it was in my field and I had done an internship as a news writer for one of the local news stations. I must have sent their human resources department my résumé about ten times in two weeks. My persistence paid off when they contacted me for an interview. I took two days off from work and shot down to Atlanta for my interview with one of the Executive Producers for the show I would be writing for if hired.

I was thirty minutes early for my interview. When I arrived to the fourth floor, I was instructed to have a seat and Ms. Union would be with me. There was a grey leather couch sitting on the wall adjacent to the door leading to Ms. Union's office. By the right side of the doorway, was an arm chair sitting against the wall; which is where I chose to sit. While clearing my head and gathering my thoughts and information about what I'd researched about Black Reign; a woman stepped off of the elevator and walked toward me.

"Mr. Marshall?" She inquired.

"Yes Ma'am," I replied as I stood.

"It's a pleasure to meet you." Ms. Union looked at her watch after she shook my hand. "You're early. I like punctuality."

"Thank you. My grandfather used to tell me that you're late if you're on time; if you're 10 minutes early, you're on time."

Ms. Union gave me one of the fakest laughs I'd ever heard.

"You can follow me right this way."

Karen led me into her office. Of all the interviews I'd been on to that point, Karen's office was by far the most memorable. As you walk in, to the left was a round conference table surrounded by six dark blue, high backed chairs. The entire office was laid out in different shades of darker blues and three different shades of grey. To the left was a wall of windows that looked out over the lot of Black Reign. Directly in front of me was Ms. Union's desk. Behind it were two large bookshelves separated by shorter shelves that stood just above the top of the desk. On the shelves I could see awards. On the wall above the shelves was what looked like a movie poster but it was of their number one rated television show, *Tryin' Times.* I took a seat in one of two grey armchairs positioned in front of Karen's smoked glass desk.

"This is a really nice office," I admired.

"This office was earned by long days and many sleepless nights."

"Hard work is its own reward."

"Yes it is Mr. Marshall. Are you ready to get started?"

"Yes I am."

The interview began like every other interview. The beginning was the learning about me part intertwined with small talk. That lasted for about twenty minutes. There was a moment of silence when Ms. Union started to read my sample pieces.

"This is amazing," Ms. Union raved as she looked over my sample scenes. "I find it hard to believe that you've never worked for another network."

"I just like to write," I modestly replied.

As Ms. Union continued to marvel at my writings I began to notice something about her. She was a beautiful woman. Aside from her beauty, there was something else about her. From the moment we made eye contact when I entered the room, she treated me like we'd met somewhere other than at an interview. She made me feel like I wasn't just an applicant.

Before we could get into more of her thoughts and comments about my samples, two large men walked into the office. They were twins that looked like two dark skinned Suge Knights.

"Ms. Union," one of the men began. "We need to talk right now."

"I'm in the middle of an interview, Jonathan. Can you give me; maybe thirty minutes?"

The other of the two men turned to me, "Young man could you excuse us for a minute?"

"Yes sir."

"Just have a seat outside. Ms. Union will be with you momentarily."

I exited the office and returned to the same seat that I sat in while waiting for Ms. Union the first time. I pulled the door behind me but it didn't shut all the way. It opened up enough for me to hear the conversation. I didn't notice it when I walked in but to the left of the door, was a small window. I had just now spotted through the mirror on the wall across from me. Through the open blinds, I could see everything that was going on.

"This is an outrage!" Jonathan roared as he slammed a stack of papers onto Karen's desk.

"Please calm down before you pass out," Joseph pleaded with his twin.

"Have you seen these numbers Karen?" Again we have failed to surpass or even come close to our competition in the ratings."

"You can't expect to surpass a network like B-E-…"

"Stop!" he halted Karen in mid-sentence. "That name is not to be used on these premises, even in comparison."

"I believe what Karen was trying to say is that we can't expect to obtain such a feat in just two years on the air. We are Black Reign and they are Black Entertainment…"

Jonathan gave his brother a horrible scowl before he could say the last word.

"I'm sorry. They are the competition. They have established their audience and we have to establish ours. We have to find out what they are doing and do what they are not in an attempt to capture their audience as well as audience members they have yet to acquire. What we need is new blood."

"Especially in our writing departments," Jonathan interjected as he stared directly at Karen. "What we have now is a bunch of the competition's rejects that have been brainwashed by their previous employers. Now they are trying to pass off ideas to us that have already been shot down." Jonathan walked over and gazed out of Karen's 4th story office window.

"Come see this." Joseph walked over to the window and joined his brother. "Look past our lot and tell me what is out there."

"The city of Atlanta," Joseph answered.

"Exactly! Somewhere out there are people who can help this network rise to greatness. I want them."

"And how are we supposed to do that?"

"You know human resources is not my field. I'm not the people person. Remember? I deal with business management and finances."

"But I know just the person that can do that for us. Right, Karen?"

"Yes Sir." Karen remarked.

"You can't be serious?" Jonathan laughed in

disbelief. "She's run away every good writer and producer we've had due to her inability to work well with the opposite sex."

Karen was sitting at her desk while the two men stood at the window talking like she wasn't in the room. I saw Ms. Union's complexion turn bright red because of Jonathan's statement. The look on Karen's face that day could have been described as the face of a woman trying to withhold how terrified she was. By the way she was acting; it was evident that there were a couple of blemishes on her slate. Her demeanor was like that of a sheep pulled away from the flock knowing one of two things was going to happen. Either it will be shaved for its wool or it would be slaughtered so that some fine dining establishment can boast of having the best lamb chops in town. Nevertheless, she remained calm.

"That's not completely true. Karen is good at what she does and I stand by her decisions. Since you go by the numbers; she is the one responsible for the success of *Tryin' Times*."

"That's just one show in a lineup of several." Joseph walked back over to Karen.

"Karen, I'm going to be honest with you. The network is not doing so well in the ratings. Jonathan and I feel that it is time to revitalize our staff." Karen sat up and straightened her blouse.

"We need new blood at this network. We need fresh, new ideas that can help give Black Reign the boost that it needs to have a fighting chance against our adversaries. We're placing that responsibility in your hands. Since you are the Executive Producer of our most popular show, we want to start with that one. You need a new team of writers because quite frankly, the ones you do have are not cutting it anymore. Granted you are in a tough time slot competing with The Young and the Restless and All My Children; still, there is no excuse why our soap opera does not have a larger audience."

"I'll do everything that I can to get the ratings up."

"That's the same thing I told my brother. For some odd reason he feels that you don't have what it takes to do so. I beg to differ."

"Ms. Union," Jonathan interjected. "What my brother is trying to say, in the ever so nice way he says things, is that we have a problem. I'm saying fix it or we'll find someone who will."

"I know that I've done some indiscretions in the past but we all agreed that we were going to let the past be the past. I've been on a good path as of late and we've been making some progress. The young man that was just in here has talent and an extraordinary writing ability. See for yourself." Ms.

Union handed my samples to Jonathan. "I think he has what it takes to take us where we want to go."

Jonathan handed the samples to his brother. Joseph scanned through them then tossed my samples back onto the desk.

"You have my word that I will do everything I can to rectify the situation."

Jonathan leaned toward Ms. Union, "I'm sure you will. Good day."

"Good day, Gentlemen."

The men turned and walked toward the door. I sat up straight in my chair. Joseph walked through the door but Jonathan paused and turned back to Karen. I couldn't believe the words that came out of his mouth next.

"Oh yeah…and Karen, please do make sure that the decisions you make are in the best interest of the network…and not your own uterus."

Jonathan walked out of the office. Both men strutted down the hall and got on the elevator.

After about five minutes, Miss Union came to the door.

"Mr. Marshall, shall we continue?" I followed her back into her office. "I apologize for that."

"No apology necessary. I know how it goes when the bosses come in."

Karen took her place behind the desk again. I could tell by the way she was acting; she was really shaken up by the previous meeting. She shook it off and continued with the interview.

"After what I've seen so far and talking with you, I believe you are *exactly* what I need."

"I am?"

Ms. Union's tone added a little more to her words than what was said. I'd heard those words before and the times I'd heard them, they were coming from a woman that was ready for me to become a part of her life. Maybe I was overreacting as I had the tendency to. Maybe I wasn't.

"Yes you are. It is unreal how your words jump off of the page. You make it easy to bring them to life. The subject matters you expound on and the way you play with words is unbelievable. I bet the women just throw themselves at you."

"*Where in the hell did that just come from*?" I thought to myself. "I choose subject matters that I have experience in and retell the stories through a different cast of characters. When I write, I don't see things as they are but through an objective but very detailed set of eyes. This allows me to capture many different audiences."

"And that is what I see."

"Before we get too excited," I paused and took a deep breath. "I have to be up front with you. I've been to this point on every interview I've been on. I do well in the interview and they want to offer me the job…"

"So you have a lot of offers," Ms. Union interrupted. "I'm sure we can make it worth your while to join our team."

"The offers are not the problem. My background is."

"I don't understand."

"A few months prior to my graduation last year, I got into some trouble and as a result I have a felony on my record. It wasn't drug related and it wasn't a violent crime. It was actually a white collar crime but still a crime."

"Well," Ms. Union sighed a little as she spoke. "I appreciate your honesty but we do have a strict policy dealing with a candidate's personal background. If it were up to me, I would turn the other cheek and hire you but a matter like this has to go above me. I have to speak with the network owners and the board of executives and I will get back to you. How about you do this, go get yourself something to eat then come back in about an hour and a half."

“Okay,” I replied in a semi-confident tone.

I stood up and walked towards the door. I knew I was sunk. Ms. Union went from talking to me as if we were at the club to treating me like another applicant. She actually called me a candidate.

“André,” she called.

I stopped and turn to look into those piercing gray eyes.

“I don’t usually go through what I’m getting ready to endure for just anybody. Your honesty says that you’ve learned your lesson and want to move on with your life. I feel you’d be an asset to the show and the network. The men that were just in here are the owners of the network. I’m going to go to bat for you. If I can pull this off, you better not let me down.”

Judging by what I heard during their meeting, I knew I was getting ready to go back to square one. I was too nervous to eat so I sat in the parking lot for an hour and a half. My mind raced as the time approached. I had come to the final ten minutes before I had to be back upstairs to receive my verdict. Reaching out, I grabbed the rear-view mirror and adjusted it so that I could see myself. When I looked into my own eyes, I was reminded of my determination and desire to overcome. My mind brought Ms. Union’s last words back to the front as reassurance. This woman didn't know me from any other but she was going to her superiors on my behalf. At the same time, confidence began to rise, doubt began to rear its head. Doubt reminded me of my previous attempts and failures. It also brought to my attention that people in positions of power, also have the tendencies to tell you what you need to hear, in order to make you feel at ease. Time wound down. I had five minutes to return to the 4th floor. I inhaled and stood tall.

"You are a talented writer and she knows it," I told myself as I stepped onto the elevator.

The ride to the 4th floor seemed to take forever. When I arrived Ms. Union had not returned. I was asked to have a seat. I sat in the exact same chair as before. Five minutes passed and no passengers made their way to the 4th floor. Ten minutes went by followed by twenty. After thirty minutes of waiting the bell went off and the fourth floor symbol above the threshold of the elevator lit up. The door opened and on the other side was Ms. Karen Union.

"André," she called as I stood up upon her entrance onto the floor. "I sincerely apologize for keeping you waiting this long."

"No apologies necessary. Business is business."

"Please, step into my office."

I took a seat in the same chair that I sat in during our initial interview. Instead of assuming her seat, Ms. Union positioned herself on the front edge of her desk and crossed her firm, light-complexioned legs.

"If I were to sit here and tell you the past two hours of my life weren't pure hell, I'd be telling a huge lie."

"That bad, huh?"

"Here at Black Reign we have a strict set of rules and policies that we follow and adhere to. After careful consideration and a great deal of begging and pleading, I cannot offer you the writing position you applied for." I tried not to let it show but I knew Ms. Union saw the disappointment in my face.

"I understand. I appreciate your help and consideration." I stood up, shook her hand and turned to walk toward the door.

"On behalf of the owners of the network, Jonathan and Joseph Conrad, I'd like to offer you the position of Head Writer for our highest rated program, *Tryin' Times*. Would you be interested in that?"

As I turned around, a huge smile lit Ms. Union's face as she watched my facial expression change from despair to utter disbelief.

"Are you serious? Interested would be an understatement! This is like a dream come true. Thank you so much."

"There is one thing you have to remember. This is in the strictest of confidence. Let's just call it our little secret."

"What secret?" I laughed.

"The fact that we hired you…"

"I know that. It was a joke."

"I knew that," she replied and let out a fake chuckle.

"So when do I start?"

"How soon can you be in Atlanta?"

"Is two weeks asking too much?"

"Two weeks it is."

"Welcome to the Black Reign family." Ms. Union slid off of the desk to meet me face to face. I extended my hand to shake hers but instead, she hugged me.

Success! I was offered the position of Head Writer for their hottest soap opera, *Tryin' Times*. I couldn't wait to get back home to tell my family and friends the good news. As I traveled eastbound on Interstate 20, my newfound excitement began to wear down and reality allowed new thoughts to surface. Every time I closed my eyes I could see Ms. Union's face. The faces I saw were not images usually found in a fantasy or daydream. In this case, they were photographic impressions from our interview. Each face carried a different expression but in every image, her eyes were the same. My grandfather used to tell me that a person's eyes were the windows to their soul. If a person could not look you in the eyes while speaking or being spoken to, meant that they had something to hide. On the other hand, a person's eyes can also tell you things that they cannot or will not allow their mouths to say. I don't know what it was about her eyes but they looked familiar to me—as if I had seen them before.

When I came off of I-20, the first stop I made was at Franklin Memorial University, to tell Alicia of my journey to *Black Mecca.* She came out of her apartment when she heard the rumbling bass of my stereo system.

"So?" she asked with a hint of anticipation in her voice. "How'd it go?"

"Not so good." I replied trying to keep a straight face as I got out of the truck.

"What happened?"

"Everything was going good until they

asked me about my criminal background."

I sighed heavily as I put my head down. Deep down inside I wanted to burst with laughter because of how Alicia expression changed.

"It's okay," she said while pulling me into her arms. "There are plenty of jobs in Atlanta. Something will come through."

Alicia hugged me as a mother consoling her child that had just failed at something he had tried so hard to succeed at. I couldn't take any longer.

"I got the job," I mumbled as my face was buried in Alicia's shoulder.

"What was that?"

"I got the job."

"Oh my Gosh!" she squealed. "That's what's up! I am so happy for you." Alicia let me go and punched me in the arm.

"You play too much."

"They are starting me off with $45,000 a year plus benefits including one week paid vacation."

"Look at you. Grandma's baby boy done finally growed up."

"You should have seen me in the interview. I had her eating out of the palm of my hand. She was all on ya boy."

"Shut up, Dré! Contrary to popular belief, every woman doesn't want you."

"I'm serious. She didn't talk to me like I was interviewing for a job. She was talking to me like I stepped to her at Shooters."

"She probably did it like that so you would be yourself in the interview and not feel uptight."

"I'm telling you, she wanted me."

"You know what? You're getting ready to get on my nerves. When do you start?"

"In two weeks."

"Two weeks?"

"They are giving me time to give my job a notice and to tie up any loose ends I need to tie up. Goodbye fish shirt, hello business suit."

I yelled at the top of my lungs. "Goodbye, Florence! Hello, ATL!"

"What about Melissa?"

"Melissa who?" I answered in a serious sounding voice.

"I guess I got two more weeks to put up with yo' retarded ass." Alicia joked.

"You better be nice to me or I won't let you come visit me, shawty."

"Negro please! I'll be right there, breakin' it down at Club 112."

Alicia playfully did the *hoochie mama* dance—that's when you bend over slightly and put your hands on your knees, stick your butt out, and pop it up and down as you turn your head to look at it.

"Not dancin' like that you won't." We laughed as we hugged.

"I knew you could do it. I'm proud of you for not givin' up."

"I couldn't give up if I wanted to. Not with you pushing me like you do."

"You got that right," she laughed and kissed me on my cheek.

2

Alicia

The fashionably high-tech city of Atlanta, Georgia can be a beast. One can be consumed without the proper frame of mind. In a city with so many inhabitants there is an array of people with a variety of different stories, motives and agendas. Throughout my time spent in Atlanta, I met a menagerie of individuals. A few that had a real impact on my life, most of them being women. I know you're wondering what that has to do with anything but as you get to know me, you'll understand.

With spring approaching, love would soon be in the air. The broken-hearted from the previous year will soon crawl out of their caves of depression and despair to see the budding of new life. As the season of love approaches…so do the hunters. These are people, both male and female, who prey on the weak individuals like the ones still trying to get back on their feet from that Yule Tide heartbreak. They will do and say any and everything they can to tear down those walls of protection around the heart.

Every day in Atlanta, young people fall in

and out of love. Seeing this happen raised a couple of questions: Can a relationship thrive and be successful in a city that throws more curveballs than major league pitchers? Do people really know how to be in love? Seeking the answers to these questions; the complexity cause many to second-guess their past, present and future relationships. It is not right, but for some people, they have to cast the blame somewhere other than where it belongs, so Atlanta is a perfect target.

Through the eyes of this country boy, Atlanta was just like any other metropolitan city. It was fast paced and an all-out fashion show. If it wasn't the ladies trying to out-do each other with clothes, shoes, hair and nails, then it's the guys trying to conquer as much booty as possible. I'd seen this type of thing throughout my school years in the Carolinas but it was nowhere close to the game that was being played in the ATL. For some reason, things seemed to be a little more twisted in the A. I can't explain it. Maybe it was the city. Maybe it wasn't.

I graduated from Franklin Memorial University, in Florence, South Carolina, in the fall of 2001 not knowing that I would end up in that God forsaken land of the lost. Through the constant begging of my cousin, Jerome, and becoming employed by Black Reign Networks, I moved. Jerome helped me realize that a person of my nature should not allow himself to be suppressed by an ass backward town as the one I lived. He also convinced me that if I wanted to be happy, then I had to unleash my true inner self that had been burdened down over the past few years.

I didn't go to Atlanta right out of college (because of a legality that I don't want to go into detail about.) Instead, I hung around the Carolinas because of a couple of people that I just could not let go. My grandfather, Louis Henderson, and Alicia were the two people that meant the most to me in the world. Through my grandfather's prayers and Alicia's advice, I always managed to get back up after being knocked down. I must have been the luckiest man in the world to have two people like that playing major roles in my life. I loved my gramps with all my heart and soul but Alicia was the hardest to let go. She and I had experienced so much together. If there was ever a model for what a true friend was, it would have to be Alicia. She embodied the very rare essence of a female that you do not find in many women. Most of all, she was always straight up with me.

It is difficult to explain what kind of person Alicia was or what kind of relationship we had. She was the type of girl that was so true to me that if she told me a fairy tale in the right way, it was hard to believe that it was just a tale. When we went out it was just like being with one of the guys but the only difference was that she was better looking and had a much better body.

Hanging at the clubs was the best. I used to get a kick out of her putting simple-minded men in their places after being approached in a disrespectful manner. One time, while we were out at one of our regular spots on a college night, I had to go to the bathroom to get rid of a few Coronas that I had consumed. The table we were sitting at was right across from the bathroom. When I came out, I saw this guy leaning on the table talking to her. I didn't get upset, nor did I get jealous. I slowly walked up behind him and leaned on the pool table that was in earshot of the conversation.

"I'm out with my best friend," she yelled over the loud music. By his next statement, he must have assumed that by saying her best friend, she had to be referring to a female.

"That's cool," he began. "The more the merrier. Shit, if she's down, we can all bounce and get into something freaky." Alicia laughed because she peeked over his shoulder and saw me suppressing my laughter by holding my hand over my mouth.

"You can ask her yaself," she said calming her laughter. "She's standin' behind you."

He turned around to see me leaning on the pool table. I gave him the traditional *what's up*? head motion. He must have felt about two inches tall as he hurriedly walked away from the table.

That was my Alicia. We truly had some great times together.

The bond between Alicia and I dates back to grade school. We were students at Westchester Elementary School in Fayetteville, North Carolina, in two different fourth grade classes. I always knew who she was but never spoke to her. My grandmother used to say I was fast because I was gaining interest in girls at such a young age. She would always joke about me growing up to become a pimp—little did she know.

Westchester was the typical elementary school nestled in the middle of a suburban community. When the boys and girls were all together, the boys played with the boys and the girls played with the girls. Every time the guys and I were playing tag, I always managed to run past or near where Alicia and her friends were sitting. Alicia always seemed to be a prissy little girl. I never saw her running around or participating in any playground games. She was *Little Miss Perfect.* Before adolescence had arrived, I'd developed my first crush. In my eyes, Alicia was the prettiest girl at Westchester Elementary.

In comparison with the other girls in my class, Alicia was a step above them. Her hair was always prettier than the other girls and her white socks always seemed whiter than everybody else's. Mrs. Burroughs was a beautician, so her daughter's appearance was always top notch. Her hair was like black silk thread. It was wavy and extended down the middle of her back. That was one of the things I liked the most about her. The other two things, besides her personality, were her beautiful almond-shaped, hazel eyes that later on made it hard for me to lie to her and her award-winning smile. Every time I saw the pearly whites and those dimples, for the moment, Alicia had the power to make me do any and everything she wanted me to do. If she ever found out that bit of information, I'd be in bad shape.

My friends were the worst when they found out that I had a crush on Alicia—not that they were worse than any of the other boys. They used to do the typical boy thing by going up to Alicia and telling her that I liked her. You know how we used to do. Alicia never seemed to pay them any attention. No matter how hard I tried to get her to notice me, nothing worked until that one day.

It was a warm Friday afternoon and because everyone passed the weekly spelling test, we were allowed to go outside. When we got on the playground, my friends and I joined some other boys in a game of *King of the Hill*. Though we were on the far end of the playground, I could see Alicia sitting with her friends wearing a pair of dark blue jeans and a red windbreaker. During the game, I noticed some sixth grade boys picking on the group of girls. I got the attention of my friends, Eric and

Ty and we started towards the altercation.

We were about twenty feet away from them when one of the boys pushed Alicia to the ground. At that point everything went blank and all I could see was the boy, and Alicia on the ground holding her wrist as tears streamed down her face. My fast paced walk turned into an all-out sprint. Before I knew it, I stepped off of a bench and dove on the sixth grader. To this day, I do not know where the strength came from. When the other boys tried to break up the fight, Ty and Eric thought that they were trying to gang up on me, so they jumped in. It was an all-out brawl on the playground of Westchester Elementary. There were so many kids standing around that it took a few minutes for teachers to get to us. It took three teachers to pull me off of him. He had put his hands on the wrong girl that day.

After everything was cleared and all of the classes were sent back inside, I was sent to the Principal's office. Sitting on the bench in front of the office was like waiting to see the dentist. As I waited to be sentenced, Alicia came out of the nurse's office with her arm in a sling. Her face was still flushed from crying but she was still beautiful. When she saw me, she smiled and sat down beside me. For some reason, I wasn't nervous anymore.

"Hi, André," she said. "That boy has been pickin' on me since we got on the bus this morning."

"Why was he messin' with just you?"

"Because I won't be his girlfriend."

"Well, if he bothers you again, tell him that your boyfriend is going to beat him up, again."

"I don't have a boyfriend."

"Want one?"

"Maybe." Alicia stood up and started back to her classroom. She got about five feet away and turned around.

"Thank you, André." She blew me a kiss and scurried off down the hall.

More years went by and the early nineties were in full swing. We were all in the ninth grade at Springville Junior High, getting ready for the world of senior high school. Salt-N-Pepa, Big Daddy Kane and Kid-N-Play were the hype. All of the guys were rockin' flattop fades, two-toned jeans and polka dot outfits with patent leather shoes. The girls were wearing bamboo earrings, lip-gloss, ponytails, Jellies and all white Keds. My crew consisted of Alicia, Eric, Monica, Ty, Danielle, and Me. It was funny to see how we all looked like a group of couples but none of us went together. We were all just good friends that loved to have a good time in each other's company. Every party or game, the UE Crew was in the building.

Friday was skating rink night. All of the junior high students in the city gathered to see who they could see. You know the UE Crew was in the rink every Friday. One particular Friday night, the girls went to a slumber party at Monica's house leaving us to go skating with-out them. At that age, skating was strictly forbidden to anybody that was considered to be popular and cool. Skating was for kids, nerds, scrubs and old heads with Jheri curls. All the cool kids just walked around the building all night.

With Alicia and the rest of the girls always there, we never had the chance to notice the other girls until that night. You should have seen us. We thought we were the finest brothers in the whole place because we had finally convinced our parents to buy us all matching Starter coats that displayed the logos of our favorite sports teams with the hats to match. Being the huge NWA fan that I was, naturally, I had to represent the Oakland Raiders, which were the Los Angeles Raiders at the time. In the immortal words of MC Lyte, we were *funky fresh dressed to impress and ready to party.*

Just as we were making our first round, we saw three fly girls coming out of the bathroom dressed like triplets. One of them was about 4'11" and light-skinned. She was wearing the high ponytail that started almost in the middle of her head and fell down to the base of her neck. She was the one I had my eyes on. The other two were twins that were around 5’ 1”, brown complexions and wore their hair in a Mushroom. The words on their shirts revealed that they were from our rival school, Oak Forest.

“What’s up, ladies?” I greeted as we approached.

They stopped in order for us to talk to them.

“We’re da UE Crew. I’m Dré Smoove, this is E-Nicety, and that’s Ty Boogie.”

One of the girls looked at our matching outfits and asked, “Y’all a rap group or somethin’?”

“Somethin’ like that,” answered Eric. “Dré does the rappin’ and me and Ty do the dancin’.”

“I’m Victoria a.k.a. Sweet V, and that’s Tina and Tonya b.k.a. TNT [Twins-N-Tight]. Together we form Da Bad Gyrlz, the hypest female crew to hit da scene. J.J. Fad and 3.5.7. ain’t got nuttin’ on us!” Simultaneously, the three girls touched their index fingers to their tongues and then touched their backsides while making the sizzling sound.

“SSSSSS!”

“That’s fresh,” I replied.

"I know y'all in the talent show next week at Heat Waves?" Victoria asked after she pulled the Blo-Pop out of her mouth. How did she know sour apple was my favorite?

"We didn't know nothin' about it," Ty stated.

"What!" Tina exclaimed. "Only the freshest of the fresh and the flyest of the fly are gonna be in it!"

"How do we get in?" Eric asked.

"We got the number at home," Tonya stated as she adjusted the charm on her necklace. "Remind me to give you my number before we leave."

The six of us spent the entire night together. We had so much fun, I almost wanted to come without the girls all of the time. It was convenient that there was an even number of guys and girls so nobody got bored. Victoria and I hit it off like we'd known each other for years. Soon it was time for the Friday night disco. For the last two hours of the night, the skaters were cleared from the floor. That's when it became Club Eutaw. That's when we took over. It was tight to see Eric and Ty battle Tonya and Tina with dance routines. We all danced the night away. At the end of the night, while we were all exchanging phone numbers, Victoria came up with an idea.

"Check this out," she said. "Since we already got a spot in the talent show, why don't we all perform together? That way, y'all don't have to audition."

"What y'all think?" I asked Eric and Ty.

"Sounds def to me," replied Eric.

"Fresh," Victoria approved.

"Dré, call me tomorrow so we can start practicing."

When we got back to school on Monday and told the girls, you would have thought they would have been excited but not *Three the Hard Way*. They were jealous that we spent time with other girls besides them. I was confused because they were acting like we were three couples. They knew as well as we did, that it wasn't like that. Alicia didn't speak to me for the rest of the week. She really knew how to get on my nerves.

After much anticipation, Friday crept up and it was show time. By the time we got there, the club was damn near packed. There were kids from all over Fayetteville as well as students from, Spring Lake, Raeford and Hope Mills—outskirts towns of Fayetteville. I had never seen so many people. I was a nervous wreck and nobody seemed to be able to calm me down. I was backstage pacing back and forth going over my rhymes when Victoria came up to me.

Victoria put her hand on my shoulder and asked, “You ready to do this?”

“As ready as I’ll ever be.”

“We got two more acts before us and then were on.”

“Let’s do this.”

We stood behind the curtains and waited for the MC to introduce us. Our clothes were the tightest. We were laced in our matching black and white outfits looking like a collaboration of Big Daddy Kane, with Scoob and Scrap, and Salt-N-Pepa. Since me and Victoria were the MC’s, we wore white t-shirts, black jeans and white Nikes. The dancers, Ty, Eric and TNT wore white jeans, black t-shirts and black Nikes. On the front of the T-shirts, “Smoove-N-Sweet” was airbrushed in fancy cursive letters. On the back, we each had our individual stage names in iron-on letters, thanks to my grandmother. Everybody was there to support us except for our best friends. When the curtain opened, I searched the crowd for Alicia and the rest of the crew but to no avail. The music started and the crowd went bananas. Victoria and I went back and forth while the other four danced their hearts out. Five minutes later we were done and the performance was flawless.

After all had performed, I realized that the competition was tight. We were all called back to the stage for the announcement of the winners. As we waited for the MC, I saw someone making his or her way to the front. Because of the lights, I couldn't see who it was. When the mysterious figure pushed through the crowd and made it to the stage, I saw that it was Alicia. Though I had performed already, I finally calmed down. She mouthed the words *I'm sorry* and blew me a kiss.

The MC interrupted, "May I have everyone's attention?"

The crowd brought their load roar down to a low rumble.

> "Tonight's winner of the Annual Heat Waves Talent Show is...Smoove and Sweet!"

The club erupted and I could not believe that we had won. We managed to keep our composure until we walked off stage and into the wings. After we got there, we were jumping around and acting like we had just won a Soul Train Music Award. There was a tremendous amount of emotion running wild backstage. Just when I thought the situation between Alicia and I was mended, it got worse. Alicia walked backstage just as Victoria pressed her lips to mine. When the kiss was over, I opened my eyes. Over Victoria's left shoulder, I saw Alicia rushing out of a backstage door. I followed Alicia out of the club and into the parking lot. When I caught up to her, she was crying.

"Alicia," I said as I tried to wrap my arms around her from behind.

"Don't touch me Dré. How could you do that?"

"Do what?"

"Kiss another girl."

"What do you mean? We got caught up in the excitement. Besides we're just friends, right?"

"Honestly," she paused. "I don't know what we are. All I know is that you are the only guy that I spend all my time with. Maybe I need to meet new people."

I watched her walk away. It felt like we had just broken up but how can you break up when you are not together? Now I was really confused. I guess she felt betrayed after coming to the show to apologize and support me. After that night, Alicia and I were never quite the same.

For the next year, we didn't talk like we used to. We spoke and had short conversation but not like normal. Victoria and I saw more of each other. We won more talent shows and became a hot team but it was murder to run into Alicia when Victoria and I were together. Sometimes, I wanted to just get away from everything. Be careful what you wish for.

Around the middle of December, right before our Christmas break, I received the worst news of my life. I was moving to South Carolina. How could this be? I was a local celebrity and now all of this was going to be taken away from me. Most of all I was going to be taken away from all of my friends that I grew up with. The UE Crew as well as Smoove-N-Sweet was getting ready to be disbanded. I had not been given any warning. It was Thursday and my last day of school was Friday. The only person I cared about telling was Alicia. Though we were not on terms like that, we were still friends.

That Friday was a morbid day for everyone. For some reason, Alicia wasn't in first period when I told the rest of the crew. Normally, we sat in English class and joked around the entire period but not that day. I didn't see Alicia until we all gathered in the cafeteria during our lunch period. I was reluctant to tell her then because it was going to be an awful sight. When I approached the table where she was sitting with her new boyfriend, I felt a lump form in my throat.

"Alicia," I said as I approached. "Can I speak to you outside for a minute?"

"Excuse me for a minute baby," she told her boyfriend. He watched as we walked out of the cafeteria and into the commons area.

"Now what is so important that you had to bring me outside?"

"I don't know how to tell you this, but..." Tears began to form in my eyes.

"Dré, what's wrong?"

"I'm moving."

Alicia asked as her emotions were starting to race and the tears developed in her eyes, "Movin' where?"

"My grandfather opened a church in South Carolina and now we're movin'."

"When?"

"Over the break."

Alicia collapsed in my arms and cried. No matter how things seemed to be between us, we still couldn't throw away the fact that we were still best friends. At that moment we settled all of our differences. In an instant, we were okay again but it might have been too late. I spent the rest of the day sitting in the gym with Alicia and the rest of my crew. When the final bell rang, I knew it signified the end of our rounds together. I could not help but feel that when I walked Alicia to her bus, and it drove off of the lot, that was going to be the last time we ever saw each other. In order for us to spend a little more time together, we decided to walk home. We knew there was no way we could make up for our lost time. Somehow, we tried.

At Alicia's house, things got worse when my grandmother arrived to pick me up. It took Mr. and Mrs. Burroughs about five minutes to pry Alicia away from me. As we rode off, I watched the bond between Alicia and I snap for what I thought was going to be forever. At that moment, I didn't give a damn about anybody else but her. Victoria was not even an issue and she was supposed to be my girlfriend.

The move was painful but after a-while, I got over it. Two years later I graduated high school and was college bound. Because I was in a new state, scouts were no longer looking at me for football, so I quit the team and enjoyed my senior year. The plan after graduation was for me to accept a scholarship that was offered by a two-year junior college. There, I would get an Associate's degree and finish at a four-year university. Obviously, God had another plan for me.

Upon completion of the first year of my collegiate career, I lost my grandmother. Her death was more devastating than leaving North Carolina. When I look back on my life, I realized that my grandmother's death had a deeper effect on me then I thought. When a man that was raised around a lot of women or one particular woman loses that woman, sometimes his views and actions towards women have a tendency to change. Some men find it hard to get close to another woman or let one woman all the way into his heart for fear that that woman will not always be there for him. With the loss of Alicia and my grandmother, I felt like I had no one.

Anger and pain made me want to give up and move back to Fayetteville to find Alicia because I felt that if no one else would be there for me, she would. After several talks, my grandfather convinced me that running away would not solve my problems. After gathering my senses again, I spent that summer working and running wild. When the fall semester came around I still wasn't ready to go back so I waited until the next fall. Instead of going back across the state to Greenville, I chose to go to the local university.

That fall semester, I started my sophomore year at Franklin Memorial University. When I moved on campus, I saw a few familiar faces from high school but there was one face I saw that took the life out of me. The memory of that day will forever remain burned in my mind. I was walking into the administration building to get a copy of my schedule when I saw her. She was the angel that had come back to me. I could not believe that this being was walking towards me. Was it her?

"André!" she screamed as she dropped her backpack and ran into my arms.

Over three years had passed and Alicia Burroughs had not changed a bit; except for a noticeable scar on the right side of her face that started at the middle of her ear and extended to directly under her eye. I later found out that she had been in a car accident about a year prior. That blemish still couldn't hinder the natural beauty that she had. Once again I was face to face with the only girl that ever mattered to me. When she smiled at me and I saw her dimples and those beautiful, white teeth peek from behind those full and sexy lips, which were a shade of natural brown that day, my mind immediately told me that I could never be apart from her again. Reunions like that one only came once in a lifetime.

She asked as we were still hugging, "Oh my God, what are you doin' here?"

"I transferred in from junior college. What about you?"

"I changed my major to marketing and came here cuz the program's better."

"This is a trip. I thought I'd never see you again and here you are. You never cease to amaze me."

"What are you getting ready to do?"

"I just need to run in and pick up a copy of my schedule from the Registrar's office. Then I'm free. What's up wit you?"

"Nothin' really. I just haven't seen you in so long, I'm anxious to catch up on old times."

"Give me two minutes and we can go back to my place."

"I'll be waiting right here."

"You promise?"

"I've waited this long for you. Two more minutes won't kill me."

I walked to the Registrar's office in disbelief. I wondered how time had affected our friendship. Granted Alicia and I weren't on the best of terms prior to me leaving, I believed that what we built in the years that led up to my departure was still there. I would soon find out. When I returned to the front entrance, I could see Alicia looking at herself in her compact mirror. I stopped for a brief moment and basked in the moment of seeing my best friend again.

"You ready?" she asked with a huge smile on her face.

"Willing and able." I grabbed Alicia's

backpack and hoisted it over my shoulder as we walked towards my apartment on campus.

"I see you're still a gentleman."

"I guess I'm still used to carrying your books," I laughed.

"So how you been?"

"I'm doing better now that I'm back in school."

"Back in school?"

"Yeah. I sat out last year after my grandmother passed away." Alicia stopped in her tracks.

"Your grandmother died? Oh my goodness, Dré, I am so sorry."

"I'm cool. I'm just glad she lived to see me graduate high school and start College. Now I have to finish; because I promised her I would."

"That is so sweet. You were always grandma's baby boy."

"And I still do everything as if she were still here." As we neared my on-campus apartment she asked the question I was anticipating.

"So who's the lucky lady?"

"Her name is Chelsea but everybody calls her Tommy Girl."

"Is she black?"

"What kinda question is that?" I asked.

"I know you and you don't discriminate. Besides, how many black girls named Chelsea do you know?" We laughed as we entered my apartment and went into my room.

"Yes, she's black."

"She's light-skinned, ain't she?"

"Do you know her?"

"No but I see you are still color struck."

"I am not color struck."

"Negro please. Every girl you ever went with since I've known you has been light. If not light, she was white."

"Can I please continue?"

"My bad. Please, continue."

"Tommy Girl was the first girl I met when I moved to South Carolina but she had a boyfriend at the time. We got together the summer after we graduated but we broke up that August when I left to go off to school."

"You didn't want to do the long distance thing?"

"We had it made up in our minds that it wouldn't have worked so we didn't even try. She came to my grandmother's funeral and we've been together ever since."

"That's interesting. She caught you while you were vulnerable and reeled you in."

"What?"

"I'm sorry, I was just thinking out loud."

"You were being judgmental."

"I am not a judgmental person."

"Yes you are or at least you are when it comes to the women I date."

"Cuz' all you date are skeezers."

"Excuse me?"

"Nothing has changed, Dré. When it comes to you, no girl is ever going to be good enough for you in my eyes."

"Then why were you never my girl?"

"You never asked. Did you?"

I paused for a moment and gazed into Alicia's eyes then laughed, "Just promise me you'll never leave my side again."

"You left me, remember?"

"I promise not to let anything come between us again."

"Not even distance?"

"Not even distance."

"André Marcellus Marshall, I've always been there for you and always will."

"Promise?"

"I promise."

It is funny how your life turns around when you least expect it. Never in a million years did I think that I would reunite with my best friend at a school in South Carolina. Because her emotions were just as strong as mine were, we vowed that we would never let the other get away ever again. It was a strong promise but we believed that we meant every word of it.

3

New Horizons

The closer it came for me to leave the closer Alicia and I became. In the public eye we were perceived as an item. For us, we were nothing more than best friends. The day before my departure for Atlanta, she told me some extremely good, yet odd, news. It was a Thursday night and I was taking Alicia back on campus after the club.

"I want to come to Atlanta after I graduate," she said as she ran the back of her hand down the right side of my face.

"Seriously?" I inquired as I turned down the radio.

"Since the day you came back into my life, I've gotten so used to us being together. I can't let you go to the ATL and have all of that fun without me."

"Whatever you decide to do, you know I got ya back. We down like fo' flats on a Cadillac. We go back like rockin' chairs. We're…"

"Dré!" she yelled as she put her hand over my mouth. "I get the point."

After I dropped her off and was on my way home, I thought about what she said. If we were only friends, then what would make her want to throw caution into the wind and move down to Atlanta? Would it be just to be with me? I know there is a lot of opportunity there, but she never once said anything about a job or career. That sealed our friendship.

You should have seen us on the day I left for Atlanta. I thought that new beginnings were supposed to be happy occasions but my departure could only be described as pitiful. Alicia latched onto me as if I were just drafted and on my way to Vietnam. I couldn't believe that after all of these years, Grandma and Grandpa's baby boy was finally leaving home. With Alicia by my side, I stood in the middle of my backyard and surveyed everything that I was leaving behind.

The house that held so many memories upon my arrival to South Carolina, despite its flaws, had never looked more beautiful to me. To my left was the very reason that brought me to this town: One Faith Church of God in Christ Jesus. If it were not for the church, my life may have never changed in the direction it was now headed. It played a major role in my life meaning my spirituality and faith, my manhood and my desire to achieve despite all that stood against me. Through my move I acquired an education at one of the state's top universities and numerous friends and associates.

While dwelling on all of the memories that I had obtained living on the corner of Millwood and Patrick Lane, emotions over took me. This was supposed to be one of the happiest days of my life. Melancholy managed to dampen the joyous occasion. The more Alicia tried to help me look on the bright side of things, the harder it became for me to leave. I knew that day was inevitable. No matter how hard I tried to prepare myself, all of my preparation went out of the window. It was like I was getting ready to leave a piece of me behind.

Just when a person thinks he or she has his game plan together, doubt always seems to come lurking around trying to destroy what could possibly be. As I looked at my SUV, packed with all my possessions, I could not build up the courage to get in and drive away. The feeling was indescribable and very new to me. It wasn't like I was going off to school for the semester or moving to another spot in town. I was leaving the state of South Carolina to start a new life. It took me a while to gain the status that I had in the area but once again I was getting ready to go from well-known to unknown. Is that really how life was supposed to be?

Getting on the road that day was a very

difficult task—not just because it was hard to drive with tears in my eyes. I knew I was leaving a piece of me behind. The first hour of my drive was very hollow and vague. I had no recollection of the songs that played on the radio or cities and towns I rode through. I could not help but think that I would never see Alicia again. In the back of my mind I could hear what she told me but I felt that my absence in her life would have a serious effect on our tightly bound relationship. Who knows what will happen over a year's time? What and who will Atlanta hold for me? Who will she meet while I'm gone? Only time would tell as my head swelled with blueprints of a new life.

When I arrived into the city limits it was about 9:30 p.m. The lights were almost blinding to my sleepy eyes. I had never witnessed a more beautiful sight. Being from a small city, the buildings seemed enormous. Where I was from, the tallest building in the downtown area, if that is what you want to call it, was the city-county complex, which was only eleven stories tall. Maybe the fact that this was the place that I would be calling home contributed to the city's beauty. I learned very quickly that looks could be deceiving.

My cousin used to tell me how *off the hook* the Buckhead area of Atlanta was on Friday nights. I could tell that by the way the people going in and out of restaurants were dressed that the party scene was getting ready to unfold. As I rode through the bustling streets of the downtown area of this urban jungle, I saw an array of things. The first thing I saw was a white dude staggering in front of a building as others stood laughing at him. He was severely intoxicated. My attention was drawn to a bright sign that read: *The Drunken Monkey*. Under that in small, indigo letters was the bar's motto: "*We don't close up, until you throw up!*" Just as I was reading the last two words I heard an awful sound. The same guy had begun to vomit into a trashcan on the sidewalk.

The sight of this situation embedded a mental note into my wondering mind. I had to be careful about where I went and whom I associated myself with. Back home, a scenario such as this would have never happened. I'm not saying that we didn't allow our friends to get drunk, but at least we had the decency to take care of them, and not let them make complete fools out of themselves while we stood around laughing.

Traffic became hostile because I allowed my speed to decrease as I watched what was happening. I had never been called so many *jerk-offs* and *assholes* in such a short period of time. I gathered my thoughts and continued on to my destination. Until I got my own place, I would be crashing at my Cousin Jerome's crib. I don't know why but it seemed like 'Rome lived in the busiest part of downtown Atlanta. On the left of his building was a liquor store and across the street was an old burlesque theater. As I parked my car and walked towards the building, I felt as if I was on the runway at a fashion show because it seemed like every available eye was on me. It couldn't have been because of my clothes because all I had on was a pair of light blue, denim shorts, a pair of all white Air Force Ones and a white shirt that displayed my fraternity letters across the chest. Maybe it was because no one had ever seen me before.

I'll never forget the first person I met when I arrived. She was a tall and slender woman with curves in all of the right places. Standing in a pair of calf laced wedge heeled sandals; the short, navy blue Baby Phat dress she wore, clung to her body until it got to the bottom of her hips and flared until it stopped mid-thigh. I managed to draw a smile out of her as the newness of my face caught her attention. I don't know what it is with my infatuation with eyes, hair and smiles, but those are the first things I notice on a woman.

"You must be new around here," she said as she waited for me to open the door.

I nodded as I examined her appearance. She was a very attractive, young black woman who was slightly taller than I, due to the heels of her shoes. The stranger seemed to be in her early to mid-twenties. Her hair was braided in cornrows that only extended to the middle of her head leaving the rest of it in spiral curls that dropped down to her shoulders. I was never into women with thin lips but hers were sexy. The one thing that I found the most alluring about her was the fact that she had a small beauty mark above her upper lip on the right side of her face. As I looked closer, I could tell it was real but slightly accented with an eyebrow pencil.

"What brings you to Atlanta?" she asked as she shifted the bottle of liquor into her other hand.

"My cousin, Jerome."

"J-Rock on the 12th floor?"

"I guess."

"Are you referring to the same J-Rock that runs that Club Ebony?"

"Yeah, that's him. What about him?"

"Humph." In saying that, she crinkled her face and turned up her nose.

As we waited for the elevator I could feel her looking me up and down. Her soft brown eyes seemed to burn every spot of my body that she investigated.

"She's a pretty girl," she said as she looked towards my hips.

"What girl?"

"The one on your key chain; is she your girlfriend?"

"She's my best friend," I replied looking at the picture of Alicia and me at the winter formal. "We grew up together."

"She must be crazy to let a fine man like you leave her behind."

"If everything goes according to plan, she'll be here in about a year."

"A lot can happen in a year," she said as she extended me her hand.

"My name is Vanessa." The look in Vanessa's eyes told me that a lot would happen in a year if she had anything to do with it.

"I'm Dré."

We shook hands as the elevator doors opened. There was complete silence as we rode to the 12th floor. When we arrived we began to part ways. We were no more than ten feet away from each other when she called to me.

"Dré," she called as I turned. "I live in 1216. Come by and see me if you need anything, want a home cooked meal or if you just want to talk to someone."

I watched as Vanessa's long legs walked

down the hall and turn the corner. If all of the ladies of Atlanta were as friendly as she was, then it was going to be a long year without Alicia.

When I got to my cousin's place and knocked on the door, another woman that was built kind of like the one I had just met, greeted me with a smile and open arms. She knew who I was. I had no clue who she was. I walked in and saw Jerome sitting on top of the kitchen counter talking to another woman while she was cooking. When he saw me, he ran from the kitchen and greeted with one love—a traditional male hug using a handshake and one arm around the back.

I love everyone in my family but Jerome was my ace. He was three years older than I and did not look like he belonged in our family. On my father's side of the family, we are from Filipino decent and most of the grand and great-grandchildren had chinky eyes except for Jerome and his older brother. Even though he did not have the family eyes, he had the family chin and wide face.

Growing up, Jerome was always the ladies-man. When we were young I used to envy him because of the way girls went crazy over him. By the looks of things now, nothing had changed. J-Rock was still the man-whore that he had always been. He introduced me and we all exchanged greetings as the half-dressed ladies sat on the couch with me. Was this the life that I was going to be living?

For about two hours we caught up on old times and they gave me the run down about life in Atlanta. This was the first time I had seen Jerome in about three years and I quickly learned that the two girls were two of many that called *Apt 1200* their second home. The crazy thing about it was that they all knew about each other. I guess this was their selected time to spend with Jerome. I had not been in town for a half a day and already I was in the company of women. I knew it was coming, but not this soon.

Just as one of the girls came back from the kitchen with drinks for everyone, I noticed the time and sprang from the couch. They looked at me strange as I rushed into the back. I had been at my destination for almost three hours and had not called to let Alicia or my grandfather know that I had arrived safely. The moment she answered the phone I felt a chill in my body. She sounded like a new woman. This was not the same person that was crying and carrying on before I left. My voice seemed to have given her new life. I hadn't been away for a whole day and Alicia was already trying to plan a road trip. Before I brought her here, I had to have my own place. I could not bring her to Jerome's with half-naked women running in and out day and night.

"When I find a place and get settled, I promise I'll fly you in."

"How long is that going to be?" she whined.

"My job starts Monday, so give me about two weeks after that. Can you wait that long? Besides, Club 112 is closed." I was trying to make her laugh to ease the situation.

"I guess I have to," laughed Alicia.

"It'll fly by, I promise. I gotta go. I'll call you tomorrow night. Okay?" There was a long pause before anything else was said. I did not know that Alicia's next words were going to be crucial.

"Dré, I love you."

I was caught off guard. Alicia had done it again. Just when I thought I had her figured out, she throws me for another loop. I didn't know what to say. Do I say it back? So I said the first thing that comes to a black man's mind when thrown off like that.

"Huh?" I mumbled.

"I said…I love you, André Marcellus Marshall."

"I love you, Alicia Renee Burroughs."

What had I done? Was that a good thing or a

bad thing? Did I mean what I said? Only time would tell. I had to gather myself before I went back into the living room with the others because I could not let on to Jerome that anything was wrong, especially something of that nature. Since we were teenagers, Jerome and I had always been about the ladies no matter what but at some point, every ladies man has to play his final Ace and get out the game. A lot of time had passed since my cousin and I had really spent an extended period of time together. The last time we chilled together was in a hotel in Fayetteville with another cousin and four females. I enjoyed those times but it was time to grow up. If I knew my cousin like I did, he wasn't trying to hear that. Jerome would try to convince me to push Alicia to the back burner to simmer and experience my new environment to the fullest. That was the plan until my conversation with Alicia. Between J-Rock and company, Alicia and Vanessa, my first moments in Atlanta were eventful. Only God knew what would happen next.

Living in Atlanta, I felt like a face in a sea of many. I remember my first morning in the city. I walked outside and stood in front of the building I was temporarily calling home. On the busy sidewalks there were people walking, street vendors, homeless people begging for change and an assortment of other things I had never experienced. Every kind of car you could think of whizzed up and down Peachtree Street. For a country boy like me, this was going to take some time to adjust to. This was almost like the busy streets of Philadelphia, in which I had spent a few summers.

In the midst of all the goings on, reality started to set in. I lived in Atlanta, Georgia. Wow! This was huge for me because I'd never lived in a city that I didn't know. I had no idea where anything was or how to get there if someone didn't tell me where it was. I had a thing about being lost. If it wasn't for mapquest.com, I probably would have never left the house. The only place I did know how to navigate to was Black Reign Networks, my job.

New life in a new city became monotonous. I didn't know where anything was. When my cousin was home, I was at work and vice versa. To work and back home was my daily routine. I no longer had places to stop after work. No friends' houses to drop by or family to run in and get a hot meal from. For the first time since I moved to South Carolina, I felt alone. Though I had my cousin J-Rock, somehow he didn't count.

It was hard for me to cope with being just another face in a large city. There was no more entering the mall and being hailed by everyone as if I was a superstar. Being blessed with many friends and associates was something that I was proud of but when I left the Carolinas, all of them stayed there. The only time I came close to hooking up with someone from back home when I first got to Atlanta was when a classmate, from college, called me and said she was on her way to Chattanooga but we never could catch each other.

For five days straight, I walked around like a lost puppy longing for the comforts of home. As I experienced those feelings from day to day, Alicia was the only thing that kept me from losing my mind—thanks to free nights and weekends. Every night before we got off of the phone, she would tell me that everything was going to be okay. It helped for a little while, or at least until I fell asleep. There had to be a better way, but at that time, I just couldn't find it. I needed other ways to release my frustrations of loneliness and homesickness.

One afternoon, while driving home from work, I noticed a gym. I figured that while I was dealing with being alone in a big city, I might as well stay in shape. After going in to inquire about a membership, the guy running the desk gave me a tour of the facilities. As we were walking around, I noticed some familiar faces. If I wasn't mistaken, the faces I saw belonged to Black Reign employees. I guess they had seen me around work because I was getting waves and head nods. After the tour was over and I was on my way out, I was stopped by a guy.

"Don't you work at Black Reign?" he inquired.

"Yeah, I do." We shook hands.

"Troy."

"Dré."

Troy was an average height, brown-skinned male with a slim build and long dreadlocks that were pulled back into a ponytail. By the look of his arms, I could tell that he had been going to the gym for a while. As we conversed, I learned that he was head of all of the network's camera crews. Before I left, he took me back inside and introduced me to Alex, Zack and Smoke. Alex and Zack were first cousins and reminded me of El and Chico DeBarge, you know, those pretty, high-yellow brothers with good hair. Zack was the taller and more slender of the two making him El. With the goatee, Alex had to be Chico. Smoke looked like Cedric the Entertainer. He was dark-skinned, short and stout. Just like Ced, he was always clowning. The four guys reminded me of my boys from college. Talking to them started to make me feel like I was home again. After I loosened up, I asked them about the hot spots in Atlanta.

"Club Ebony!" they answered simultaneously.

I had been in Atlanta for about a week and I still had not been to my cousin's club. I didn't want to go by myself because I did not want to seem like a freak or a pervert. Around my way, going to the strip clubs was something you just didn't do by yourself. They were more for guys' night out.

"As a matter of fact," Troy started. "We're going tonight. You wanna roll?"

"I'm not really feelin' a strip club just yet. What about regular clubs?"

"What about The Honey Hole?" Smoke asked like he knew he was going to get rejected.

"Man, hell no!" Alex interrupted. "Not that teeny ass hole in the wall."

"But it be bumpin' tho'," Smoke defended.

"What about Club Blaze in Buckhead?" Troy suggested. The other guys paused and thought about it but before they could answer Troy sealed it.

"Tonight is Ladies Night."

"Club Blaze it is," Zack answered.

"What's the dress code?" I asked while leaning on one of the stationary bikes.

"Dress to impress, Shawty!" Smoke said with a deep southern accent. "No tennis shoes, no jeans and no athletic gear. No Thro'backs, no big ass baseball caps, no wife-beaters…"

"Ok, Smoke, Damn!" Troy said cutting him

off.

"I think he got the point," Alex laughed.

"Ho-Hol' up, dawg. Don't be cuttin' me awff. I ain't finish. No wind suits and church shoes, no socks and sandals and definitely no Jheri curls." Smoke was a big, big, big, DUMB ASS but he was cool as hell.

Once all of the particulars were out of the way, Troy said he would pick me up for the club. After our conversation, I headed to the crib. The evening was kind of chilly for an August night. Though it was cool outside, I knew it would be hot in the club. I had to choose my apparel accordingly. It was hell because I did not have my own place; I was living out of my suitcases. I sifted through many outfits and pulled out about seven different ensembles. Alicia and the rest of my friends used to tell me that I was worse than a woman when it came to selecting an outfit for the club.

After an hour of changing clothes, the reflection in the mirror finally revealed perfection. I settled on a cream linen pants outfit. I was going to wear the shirt open with no T-shirt under it but I decided to put on a tank top. A pair of dressy sandals would have accented the outfit. Since that was not my style, I chose a pair of leather, chocolate brown loafers with a small gold ornament across the top of the shoe. Now it was on.

That night Alex and Troy picked me up around 10:30. When we pulled up into the parking lot, it was nothing like I had ever seen. There was nothing but big body SUVs, Lex' coupes, Benz's and BMWs. Nobody was parking lot pimpin' because anybody who was anybody was inside the club or own their way in. A major difference I noticed about the club in comparison to the clubs back home was the way the partygoers were dressed. In the clubs I was used to attending that had a dress code, they only enforced it for the men. It was apparent that here, it was for everyone because the bouncers turned away two ladies that were wearing the strings of their thongs exposed over the waistline of their low cut, hip-hugger Capri pants.

While we stood in line, it felt good to not be standing among guys in throwback jerseys or white T-shirts and doo-rags. As Alex, Troy and I stood in line checking out the ladies that walked up, a black Lincoln Navigator with twenty-two inch, chrome rims pulled up front for valet parking. The windows were so dark, that I could not see inside of the vehicle. When the doors opened, my mind was blown because out stepped four of the finest ladies I had ever seen. Back home, if a girl was pushing a ride like that, nine times out of ten, it belonged to her man or her brother. As I examined a bit closer, I saw a personalized front license plate that read: *Natalie's Navi.* I couldn't believe it. Even the women of Atlanta were holding it down for themselves.

Fifteen minutes of standing in line was over and we were in Club Blaze. The inside was like nothing I had ever witnessed. The only time I saw a club like Blaze was on TV or in a movie. The dance floor was packed and the DJ was rockin' the house with some down south music I'd never heard. As we shuffled through the crowd on our way to the bar, my surroundings seemed to pass me in slow motion. The colored lights that danced around the club amplified the mixture of synthetic fog, cigarette and Black & Mild smoke. When we got to the oasis of alcohol, all I saw was people buying all sorts of exotic drinks, bottles of champagne and pitchers of mixed liquor.

"Dré," Troy called as he leaned on the bar. "What you sippin' on?"

"Hennessy."

"Bartender," he called. "Two pitchers of Henny and Coke."

After we got our drinks we found a good table and began to post up. The club was jumpin' and the ladies were looking good. Just as we were getting settled at our table to wait for Zack and Smoke, the four ladies from the Navigator sat down at the table beside us. I was in a new spot so I had to put on my game face.

Heaven would not describe this place. This was a club that we only wish we had back home because all of the clubs we had was either a haven for youngsters or holes in the wall. While surveying the scene, my eyes managed to catch the eyes of one of the ladies sitting at the table beside us. It was hard to look past her because every time I looked at her she was looking at me. I had to say something.

"Hey," I spoke loudly over the music. "What's up?"

"Just chillin wit' my girls."

"Ok. Can I get that dance later?"

"Maybe."

That was unbelievable—a beautiful woman that was not too stuck on herself to at least acknowledge a brother. I continued to look around but made a point to keep making eye contact with her. Just as we were pouring drinks, Smoke came up, loud as ever.

"What up, folk!" he yelled as he noticed the ladies. "What's the deal? Now I know y'all ain't gonna let these fine ladies sit here with no drinks."

The ladies seemed to be annoyed by Smoke's approach to their table. One girl thought she could get Smoke to leave them alone when he asked them what they wanted to drink by ordering something expensive.

“Ladies, excuse my friends. They’re rude. Can I interest you in a drink?”

“Cristal,” said one of the ladies. Smoke walked to the bar and in five minutes, came back with a glass of water containing four straws and sat it on the table.

“What is this?”

“Cristal-clear water,” he laughed.

The ladies got up and left. Smoke seemed to have a way with the women. I could only watch as my mystery lady walked away. I wanted to follow, but I didn’t want to seem eager. Smoke sat down and informed us that Zack was on lock down with his girl for the night and was not going to make it.

Our four-man crew sat and drank but as always, I had to walk around. I excused myself in order to explore the club. In my mind, I wanted to find my mystery lady but I didn’t want her to think I was searching for her. I descended from the second level to find the mystery lady and company seated at the bar talking to three guys. I leaned against the stairwell and discreetly watched. Before long the DJ kicked it in high gear with Uncle Luke and three of the four ladies grabbed the guys and rushed the dance floor leaving the one I wanted behind. It was time for me to make my first impression. She saw me approaching but before I had time to get to her she got up, walked towards me, grabbed my hand and led me to the dance floor.

Watching her was pure elegance with a touch of freak. She was more than a dime piece, in my eyes. For the most part, monetary value would have done her no justice. She was about five feet, six inches tall. Her shoulder length hair brushed across her bare caramel shoulders. This woman had a small oval-shaped face that fit her small, yet well-toned, body. Just like with all women, I paid close attention to her hair, eyes and smile. From what I could see, she was good to go. The smile was the last thing that I had to check out before we left the floor. Being the clown that I was, I made a comical gesture towards her causing her to laugh. She had a smile that lit up our area of the crowded dance floor. The thing I found the most attractive about her was the small but sexy gap between her two front teeth.

She was so seductive in her dancing. It was hard for me to keep my composure. After about three songs, we left the dance floor and she led me upstairs to another room. It was obvious that she had been there before. The room we entered was called *The Network* and from the entrance I could see why. It had a very soothing ambiance. Couples sat all over the room making connections over glasses of champagne as smooth R&B music lulled out of the speakers. We found a cozy corner and sat down for conversation.

"It is a pleasure to meet you," I said as I extended my hand. "I'm Dré."

"I'm Natalie," she obliged as she shook my hand.

"So you're the driver of the Black Navigator."

"How did you know that?" After asking that question she sat back on the leather couch we were sitting on and crossed her muscular legs.

"My friend and I were in line when you pulled up. Everybody's not able to have VIP status."

"I'm far from a VIP but I am Natalie's Navi."

"So, what do you do to be driving a truck like that?"

"Before I tell you what I do, you tell me what you do first."

"Okay. I am head writer for Black Reign Networks.

"The same network that does *Tryin' Times*?"

"Yes ma'am. Now what about you?"

"I'm starting point guard for the Atlanta Diamonds."

"The WNBA expansion team? No you're not. Not with pretty feet like that."

"I'm for real. I signed the contract this morning and just because I'm an athlete don't mean I have to have jacked-up feet." We both laughed.

"Well, congratulations, Ms. Natalie…"

"Simms."

"Natalie Simms. The pleasure is all mine."

"I don't usually go out but my girls thought it would be a good way to celebrate the occasion."

"Indeed it is. I think a toast is in order." We raised our glasses.

"To the Diamonds."

"And Black Reign."

Our glasses clanged together and we continued to get well acquainted. During our conversation I engaged a thorough scan of Ms. Natalie Simms. I listened to everything she said and watched her every move. It had been a minute since I met a genuine person. It was almost like Natalie and I were old friends as opposed to new acquaintances. Everything about her was sexy; from her smile, the way she slid her hair behind her ears and the soothing tone of her voice. I noticed her noticing me as I checked her out.

"Why do you keep staring at me?" Natalie inquired. "Do I have something on my face?"

"Yes," I responded. "True beauty."

Looking as if she had never received a compliment, "Excuse me?"

"Sorry if this sounds forward but you are the most attractive woman that I have met since I've been in Atlanta."

"You trying to make me blush? I'm too light for that." We laughed as she placed her hand on my knee.

"You're pretty cool yourself, Mr. Marshall."

"Listen, I'm not one for picking up women in clubs but there's something different about you and I'd like to do this again sometimes."

"I'd like that," Natalie reached for her cell phone that she had tucked in between her breasts.

"That's a good place to put it."

"This way I don't lose it."

As we were exchanging numbers, her

girls found us and crashed our private party. We said our good-byes and I watched her friends haul her off. I could not believe it. I was talking to a future basketball star, and she was feelin' me. I guess that meant I had to attend a few WNBA games.

4

Black Reign

The more I hung out with Troy and the rest of the guys, the more comfortable I became at the network and in the city. Black Reign was one of the few black owned television networks. It felt great to be a part of something of that caliber. With all of us working in different areas of the network, we didn't get to see each other unless we ran in to one another in the cafeteria.

One morning, I went down to Studio B to talk to one of the actresses about a last minute script change when I ran into Smoke and as always, he was clowning.

He asked as he gave me a pound, "What's the deal, pimpin'?"

"Nothin' much, just looking for Sheila Goodman. Have you seen her?"

"I just saw her going to wardrobe."

"Good lookin' out. I'll catch up with you later."

"Before you go, I gotta ask you about ol'

girl from the club." I knew Smoke wasn't going to let me just be on my way like that.

"Who?"

"The short chick I saw you dancin' with the fat…"

"That was Natalie Simms," I interrupted as he was making the typical ass gesture.

"Not the Natalie Simms that the Diamonds just signed." I was amazed that he knew who she was. Then again, he was a sports fan.

"True indeed. As a matter of fact, we are supposed to hook up this weekend."

"What's up wit a friend?"

"I'll see what I can do."

The more I tried to get away from Smoke to do what I had to do, the more he wanted to talk. I finally convinced him I would set him up with one of Natalie's friends and he let me go about my business.

Sheila was in wardrobe when I caught up with her and gave her the script changes. She was an incredible veteran actress. It took her a while to land a steady acting gig until she did her first season of *Tryin' Times*. Before coming to Black Reign, she had done several appearances on other highly rated soap operas.

Her beauty was amazing and she was so down to earth. Shelia's attitude and personality accented her outer appearance. Drucilla from the *Young and the Restless* had nothing on this woman. Through years of extensive make-up you could see the age in her face but it was not overbearing. If I were into older women I might have tried to step to her on a different level.

Talking to Shelia made me realize a couple of things: Actors and actresses are real people and that I had someone real back home. I know you're wondering what that had to do with anything. It's simple. After talking to Sheila, I learned that she was also in a similar situation. When she came to Georgia for her first season of *Tryin' Times* she had to leave her boyfriend behind in California. She had been in Atlanta for almost eleven months and her relationship was at risk every day. Just like me and Alicia, she and her man had been friends since high school. They moved to Los Angeles together for her to pursue her acting career. Because of his job, he couldn't leave California when she did. When she got to Atlanta and started mingling with people in her industry on a daily basis, reality made her second-guess her relationship with her blue-collar boyfriend.

After my conversation with Shelia, I returned to my office. I stared at my computer screen thinking about Alicia and our situation. We exchanged *I love you's* but a commitment was never established. I felt that Alicia was someone that I could be happy with. It was hard to grasp that concept when you're separated by miles in a city with more beautiful and successful women than a little bit. While those thoughts raced through my head, I realized where I was at that point, Alicia had been there to help me every step of the way. I would be a fool to let her go. Wouldn't I?

I wanted Alicia to be there with me and at the time, I didn't care about any other female in Atlanta. That was a bold statement, bearing in mind the type of women I had met so far. I could easily go back to my days before she and I reunited in college or I could patiently wait to see what the future had in store for us. It was unclear to me what Alicia expected of me. That was something we never discussed. Go figure.

My thoughts were mixed up and then interrupted by an email. I had to attend a mandatory meeting after work concerning some possible episode changes. The day came to a close and I found myself in a meeting held by the Executive Board of Producers. While the meeting was going on, I looked over the crowd. Troy brought to my attention that every person sitting on the board had all started off in positions like mine. That further confirmed that if I worked diligently, a seat on the executive board could one day belong to me.

The meeting adjourned and I went home. While I sat in my room and rummaged through old college photos, I came across pictures of the first play I ever wrote, directed and produced at Franklin Memorial University. There I was playing the lead role with Alicia as my leading lady. She was always there supporting me in everything I did. When half of my cast walked out on me and I had to recast three weeks before opening night, she was right there. When it came to matters of the heart, she knew how to deal… That was it! *Matters of the Heart* was the last play I was working on before graduation. Because I graduated a semester earlier than expected I never completed it nor did it go into production.

I jumped up and began to look through a trunk that all my writings were in, searching for the script. When I found it, I thumbed through it and realized with the proper work it could be developed into a series. With the story line, and the fact that I used *Tryin' Times* as a model, it could serve as a spin-off of the soap opera. I needed to run the idea by someone that would not try to steal it. I called Karen Union.

"Hello," answered the voice.

"Hi, Karen," I said. "This is André Marshall."

"Hi, André, what can I do for you?"

"Remember in my interview you told me that Black Reign was always looking for new ideas?"

"Yes, I recall telling you that."

"Well, I have an idea for a primetime soap opera. It is still in the developmental stages but I think with the right minds together, it could be a success."

"Well, if you feel that strongly about it, put together a treatment and a presentation and I'll see about getting you a meeting with the Conrad Brothers and the Executive Board. How much time do you need?"

"I need about three weeks."

"I'll try to pull some strings and see if I can get you set up."

"Thanks, Karen."

"If you need to talk to me, call me. I'm here for you."

I was confident that I'd sold Karen on the idea but selling her wasn't enough. I needed her to believe in it. I needed to put some major time and charm into it. This meant cutting out clubs and parties for a while. For a couple of weeks straight, I was going to have to be a hermit. Every spare minute had to be devoted to my project even if it meant no Natalie. *Matters of the Heart* was my number one priority and possibly my ticket to the top.

At the beginning of the first week of work on my presentation, no matter how hard I tried to stay focused, nothing worked. Living at *Casa de J-Rock* was a nightmare for concentration. Everyday women ran in and out of the apartment but these were not ordinary women. Due to the industry they worked, let's just say they were very giving and straight to the point. Among the women were two regulars, Monique, also known as, Vixen and Jordan, known to the adult industry as Jada.

Vixen was one of the ladies that had danced for J-Rock the longest. Jada was new to the game. She was Vixen's best friend. They were considered as the Salt-N-Pepa of Club Ebony. Vixen was the lighter and the shorter of the two and thick like hot grits in the morning with the bacon and eggs. Jada was twenty-one years old and believe me when I say she was a grown ass woman. She had a bronze skin tone with hazel eyes. She was an exotic dancer but the funny thing about it was the fact that she had no breasts. I guess it was her ass that was her moneymaker because she had a tabletop—the type of ass you could sit a drink on.

On the first night I brainstormed ideas, Jada and Vixen were at the apartment watching a movie with my cousin. It was a Monday and things were slow at the club. *Apt 1200* was their chill spot for the evening. I sat at the dining room table in front of my laptop surrounded by a mound of papers. Jada excused herself from the movie and joined me. I don't know where my cousin found these women but he was good at what he did.

Jada said nothing as she sat and stared at me tick away at my computer. Occasionally, I glanced at her while she was poking around at some papers. Like the majority of the women in Atlanta I'd met, she was a *Tryin' Times* fan because she recognized the characters names in the script. The impression I got of the women of the city was that working for Black Reign meant money. I won't say all of the women were like that; just the few that I had come in contact with because every time I told someone that I worked at Black Reign, their eyes lit up.

Now, back to Miss Jada. After about fifteen minutes of silence, she decided to strike up a conversation. In a short time, she managed to tell me a great deal about herself. Jada had only been in the strip club game for six months. Because of Vixen, she had always been curious.

I asked, "What made you start dancin' as opposed to a regular 9 to 5?"

"Well," she started. "I've known Vix' since I was eighteen. She used to come and get me to go shopping with her on Sundays. I used to see all of that money she had and I wanted to know how she made it."

"I guess curiosity killed the cat."

"Something like that. I wasn't ready at eighteen because I had a boyfriend that wasn't havin' it."

"Let me guess. Y'all broke up about six months ago."

"Exactly. I'm used to it now but you shoulda seen me on my first night. I was scared as hell. I felt so cheap and dirty but after the money started rollin' in and I learned how to use all this ass I got…I got over it. Now I got tricks tryna to buy me houses and shit."

I sat and listened to Jada ramble on and on about things that were of no concern to me. She was tight but I could never see myself involved with a stripper. I had nothing against what they did but it just wasn't my style. I liked my women classy; not showin' all the assy. Feel me? The more she talked, the faster time moved and I had to get up for work in the morning. I excused myself from the conversation, gathered my things and put them in my briefcase. Jada seductively watched me move around the table. I said good night to everyone and retired to my room. For some strange reason, I felt that she was not going to just let me walk away from her. While setting my alarm clock, I heard a quiet knock on the door. On my command of *come in*, Jada walked in and sat down on my bed.

"Why you goin to bed so early?" she asked as she rubbed her hands in a circular motion on my comforter.

"Midnight is not early for me. I have to be up early in the mornin'."

"But the party don't start until after twelve. You know what they say; the freaks come out at night."

For those of us that had nine to five jobs, anything after midnight was past our bedtime. For a couple of minutes I studied her as I listened to her ramble on about nothing. Then it hit me and her motive indirectly rose to the surface. She was a stripper and was used to having the full attention of her chosen man. Jada didn't know how to react to me walking away from her like I did. She was persistent, as well as provocative. Alicia's distinct ring tone exploded from my cell phone before Jada had a chance to get too comfortable. WHEW!

"Could you please excuse me," I told Jada as I answered the phone. "Hello."

"Hey Baby!" Alicia squealed with excitement in her voice. "What you doin'?"

"I was just getting ready to get in the bed." In more ways than one if Alicia hadn't called.

"You okay?"

"Yeah. I'm cool now that I'm talking to you."

"Well, I know it's late and I just wanted to hear your voice before I went to sleep. I'll talk to you later. I love you."

"I love you, too."

Deep down in my heart I loved Alicia. The problem was I didn't know whether or not I was in love with her yet. Nevertheless, she'd saved me from doing something I might regret later. If I knew J-Rock's crew like I did, that night was the first advancement of many more to come. I needed my own place as soon as possible.

The next morning came and another workday was on the horizon. The ladies were still in the apartment. Vixen was in the room with my cousin and Jada was on the couch. Jada gave me one of the nastiest looks as I walked pass the couch. Whatever her problem was, she'd get over it. Until she did, I needed a place to work in peace. That's a damn shame when a man had to leave his own place to have some privacy even though it wasn't my place. I thought about the situation as I tore through rush hour traffic on my way to the network.

Black Reign could be described as a Mecca for African-American talent. Whether it was acting, music, writing or production, it was all at Black Reign. This was the first place I had ever worked where whites were the minority. I was in a comfortable element where my abilities could be nurtured to their fullest potential. All through school I worked in restaurants where the only place you really saw a lot of blacks was in the kitchen or on dishes. I never thought that I could ever find myself submerged in a place that was 95% black and *legit*.

Gathering in the company parking garage in the mornings reminded me of high school. Me and the boys met up to crack jokes and talk about typical man stuff before we went our separate ways for the day. It felt good to have a crew again. Out of all of the members of the crew, I was closest to Troy and Smoke. We didn't see Alex and Zack much because they both had live in girlfriends that they had to get home to at night. I guess it ran in the family. Smoke was a clown like me and Troy was going through a similar long-distance relationship. We could relate to each other. In a brotherly way, he helped me deal with my situation.

As far as the women of the network were concerned, walking through Black Reign was like being at a live taping of BET's *Comic View* back in the days. There were light ones, dark ones, slim ones, thick ones, short ones and tall ones. Whatever a man's heart desired, she was there. Because of this, a lot of people dated within in the network. The sweet thing about it was that, the network was so big; you didn't have to always be in each other's faces unless you worked in the same department or area.

Being the handsome and debonair fellow I was, it did not take long for me to catch the eyes of a few of the network's prime ladies. In the romantically confused state I was in, I could not bring myself to make a move. It was hard to casually converse with these women because they all looked so good. I think that was on the application in capital letters...*MUST LOOK GOOD.* From the parking garage to my building, I walked with some of Black Reign's angels: producers, make-up artists, wardrobe techs and many others. Even the female security guards were attractive.

There was too much going on around me at such a critical time. It was critical for two reasons: Alicia and my presentation. I was trying to be a good man to a woman that was not with me physically. Her commitment to me was solid but I wasn't sure of mine. On top of that, I was trying to better my pockets and myself. I wanted to be known for my work and not my relations. Three weeks was my deadline and I had to make it.

When I arrived to my office I was greeted

with a surprise visit from my supervisor. Karen came by to inquire about my idea for the new show saying that she needed a little background information before she set up my meeting. I gave her just enough info to present to the board without giving her a full idea. Just because she was my supervisor didn't mean I fully trusted her. I didn't think that she would stab me in the back but business was still business. After she gathered the necessary information she left.

Writing for the network was a fun job because of things like collaboration. This was when all of the writers got together to read the next episode's script. The group sounded like a room full of bad actors. That wasn't the funny part. The funny part was that some of them tried to get into their assigned roles with hopes of being discovered. After collaboration came the critical session for editing and cutting out parts before the final copy went to the print shop. Since I was the new writer, they insisted that it was my duty to take the script over to print. I thought it was a bunch of bull. It was later brought to my attention that my writing associates were trying to play matchmakers.

One of the girls in the print shop conveyed to one of my peers that she was interested in me. The ill thing about it was that she knew who I was but I had no clue about her identity. It was like one of those Internet dating sites that hosted personal ads and profiles. A woman with no picture on her profile was feeling you because she saw your picture but you couldn't feel her back because you didn't know whether she was attractive or looked like a sea duck. I know that sounds shallow but that's just life. Anyway, the mystery lady remained a mystery. When I found out I informed my colleagues that I wasn't interested in participating in their elementary school, *she likes you* games and gave the duty back to the Associate Producer so she could do the full description of her job. That was Black Reign, a bunch of gossip folks running around trying to play cupid so they could have another relationship to talk about.

Over the next few days I worked more on my presentation in every spare moment. I even convinced my cousin to ask his lady friends to stay away for a couple of days unless it was just one coming to see him and him only. I managed to make some major progress which was more than I had expected. It was amazing to see how much work I could get done without any interruptions. Once the presentation was a success, the first thing I had to do was get my own place.

The first week of pounding out the developmental stages of my presentation was over and I was drained. I needed a break. It was Saturday night and Atlanta was in full swing as it always was. I tried to get in touch with the guys but that was a no go. J-Rock was at work (if that's what you want to call it) and I was stuck in the house. Even

Alicia was nowhere to be found. Was everybody out that night but me? Maybe I needed to catch up on some lost sleep. Just when I started to doze off my cell phone rung and startled me.

"Hi, Dré," she said in a sexy tone. "This is Natalie. Did I catch you at a bad time?"

"I was just sitting here working on a couple of things. What's up?"

"I was calling to see if you were busy tonight."

"Not really. Why?"

"Sorry for the short notice but one of my teammates from Tennessee is in town with her new husband and I was wondering if you would like to go out to dinner with us."

"That's cool. What time we talking?"

"We'll be by to pick you up at about eight-thirty."

"Okay. I live in the Bridgeford Arms apartments on Peachtree. Call me when you get here and I'll come down."

"See you soon. Buh-bye."

I got up, showered, and got dressed. While I was putting on my shoes the house phone rang. I looked at the Caller ID and it was Alicia. The answering machine picked up.

"Hi, Dré, it's your baby girl calling to let you know that I'm thinking about you. I'm out with my girls but I'm bored cuz you're not here. When you get this message; holla at ya girl. Love you."

Alicia knew how to make a man feel guilty. There she was out with her girls not having a good time because I was not there and I was on my way out with another woman. Now my mind was going to be occupied with thoughts of her. I could not afford to let that bother me so I kept telling myself to shake it off. You know what happens when you are out with one woman thinking of another. You are vulnerable to calling her the wrong name. I had never done it but I'd come pretty darn close.

Half past eight crept up and Natalie was calling from downstairs. I grabbed my keys and we were out. The four of us had a cozy dinner at a Japanese restaurant in Downtown Atlanta. It was one of those places where they cooked the food in front of you. We laughed and had a good time reminiscing about our college days when I learned that Leslie's husband was my fraternity brother. The fun started when we began to trade war stories about our pledging days. The ladies laughed as we talked about the long road searching for Phi Beta. During dinner, Leslie brought up the subject of marriage. That was not a conversation that I wanted to get into.

She asked, “Nat, when are you going to settle down?”

“Whenever I find the right man,” she said looking directly at me.

“What about you, Dré?”

“One day, when my career is where I want it to be and I’ve found the woman I’m happy and satisfied with…I’ll jump the broom. Until then, I’m focusing on my career.”

“You and my girl should hook up and see what happens.”

“If it is meant to be, it’ll happen. I just don’t want to rush into anything.” I was trying to discreetly show my interest in Natalie without coming straight out with it.

“It’s all about what you put in it,” Natalie emphasized.

You wanna know something? I’m a dumb ass sometimes. I was already putting more on my plate than I could handle. Between trying to keep Alicia in the picture and developing the new show, I did not have any more room. It was like fixing your plate during Sunday dinner. It is already full when someone mentions that there is something else that you have overlooked. It was sort of like pushing the collard greens over just enough to make room for some macaroni and cheese. I guess Natalie was trying to be the cornbread that everyone manages to strategically place on top of everything.

The further the night went the more Leslie tried to push Natalie and me together. At first, Natalie was not buying into what Leslie was doing. The more she pressed the issue, the more Nat gave in. By the end of the night, she was all over me as if I was her man. She was feeding me, we were wiping each other's mouths with the napkins and because we were sitting on the floor, she would put her legs across mine. The four of us looked like two couples in love. When we left and got back to my place, Natalie excused herself and walked me to the building.

"I had a great time tonight," Natalie said putting her arms around my neck. "We need to get up and do this again, just me and you."

"Just call me."

"You know I will."

Natalie kissed me on the lips then I watched as the sexy Atlanta Diamond climbed back into her Navigator and drove off. In one evening Natalie displayed that she had the makings of a good woman that needed a good man in her life. I didn't know whether or not I could be that man. That was something only time could reveal.

Me being me was something that concerned me. I had never been in a situation like this before. Relationships were considered to be my area of expertise when it came to others. Now that it was me, I felt as if I was new to the dating game. Look at my situation. I had a woman in South Carolina willing to devote her life to me in every way. Alicia was every real man's dream woman. She was head strong, beautiful, intelligent and independent. To her, a man could only be an asset to her life. He would be viewed as the piece of a puzzle that would complete the romance section of her life but first he must be whole himself.

The thing that bothered me the most were the questions of: Was I whole enough to complete that part of her life? Could I be that way within a year? All I knew was that I had to come to a decision within myself to either walk away while I still had a friend, or step up to the plate and take my pitches. Since my arrival to Atlanta, I added a rarity to the mix of the city. I found that the ratio of men to women was about sixteen women to every one man. Had I come here immediately after college, those would have been some sweet ass odds but now it doesn't stack the deck in my favor. Like most men, when it came to women, I was weak.

On the other hand there was Natalie. She seemed balanced in every way. She had not reached stardom yet, so she was still down-to-earth, easy to talk to and a lot of fun to be around. Her looks only added to everything. Even if she hadn't chosen basketball as her career, she could have had a successful career in public relations. Natalie had it all but still couldn't manage to outweigh Alicia. The history between Alicia and I is what gave most of her weight on the scales.

I felt that my first year in Atlanta would either make or break me. I did not know at that time but the rest of the women I was going to meet were going to be placed, one by one, on a scale to see how they measured up with Alicia and the first real candidate was Natalie.

All of these thoughts passed through my head as I was gathering my game plan for the completion of my presentation. With a hurdle of this magnitude standing on the track field of my life, I had to approach it with the correct footing and proper respect. Time ticked away as I approached the closing stages, getting ready for the editing phase. Since I worked during the day, the only time I had to work on the presentation was at night and living in *Apt 1200,* it was more than a chore.

When I walked into the apartment, Jerome was sitting on the couch counting money. He informed me that I had a couple of messages on the answering machine. One was Alicia and the other was Karen. She was calling to tell me to see her first thing Monday morning. I wondered what for. Sunday came and went and before I knew it, Monday was on the horizon. As soon as I arrived to the network, I dropped my briefcase off and went straight to Karen's office. I knocked on the door and waited for her to answer.

"You need to see me?" I asked as poked my head into her door.

Karen was standing by the window looking out over the city of Atlanta. Her long legs jutted out from under the black skirt that was hugging her lower half. The Sun rays illuminated her light complexion as they poured through the window.

"Yes, Dré. Come in and sit down." I walked in and sat in the same chair I did when she interviewed me.

"We have a problem with your presentation. You have to be ready by next Monday or you'll have to wait until the Conrad's get back from Europe."

"How long will they be gone?"

"Six weeks."

"I guess I'll be ready on Monday. I have to make some sacrifices but I can do it."

"That's just the kind of attitude you need to

have," Karen raved.

"It's the only attitude I have. This is not just a job for me. I want this to be my career but I don't want to spend it all in the writing department."

Taking her seat behind her desk, "Tell me André, what is your five year plan?"

"Over the next five years I want to solidify myself as a writer with all intentions for advancement. In addition to my degree in English, my minor was Mass Communications. Being at Black Reign I feel I can put all my talents to use."

"I hope so," Karen smiled. "Just let me give you a bit of advice. Black Reign Networks is a very reputable operation but just like all companies, it can become very high schoolish."

"I'm not quite following you."

"I'm talking about people that date within the company. I've worked with some talented people that are no longer here because they couldn't separate business and pleasure. I'm not saying that you can't date a co-worker, if you so choose, just be careful and remember why you come to Black Reign every morning."

"I don't think I'll have that problem. I'm kinda involved with someone."

"Really now?" Karen inquired with surprise in her voice. "Is she from Atlanta?"

"She's from my hometown but she's back in South Carolina finishing up her senior year in college."

"She must have been crazy to let you come to Atlanta without her."

"I think I can manage for a year."

"A lot can happen in a year."

Karen stared at me with a look in her eyes that signified something brewing under those soft sandy, brown locks. There was a moment of awkward silence.

"What I guess I'm really trying to say is that focus is the key. If you want to advance you have to put all your effort and energy into it. There's no doubt in my mind that you can be successful. Just remember the task at hand."

"I'll remember that," I replied as I stood up.

"Thank you for your time and words of wisdom. I guess I'll be getting back to the bullpen."

I couldn't figure out where Karen was coming from with her sudden lecture about inner-work relations. I couldn't allow that to cloud my mind. It was crunch time and the pressure was on. Over the next week, I put every waking minute into my presentation. Once again I had to put Natalie on hold. Every spare moment I got I worked on the treatment and presentation for my new show. That had a nice ring to it—my show. When Friday came I was burnt out again just like the week before but I was almost finished. All I had to do was run through it on Saturday and Sunday and I was good to go. I deserved a break. What could I do? I didn't want to go out with anyone so I decided to hit up the spot of all spots, Club Ebony.

5

Deja

Being in a new city had its advantages especially when your cousin ran the hottest strip club in the city. Club Ebony was where all the high rollers, players, pimps and hustlers came to ball out of control and trick off. I remember the first time I went to the club with J-Rock. I felt like I was with the *Ghetto Hugh Hefner*. You should have seen the way men and women were hailing and approaching him. He had male and female groupies. As I was introduced to everybody, attitudes changed when they found out that I was J-Rock's number one man. Maybe they thought that if they wanted to get in good with him, then they had to be nice to me.

A good friend of mine used to manage a strip club back home. Between going to the club when he was working and out to other gentlemen's clubs across the Carolinas with him and the owner of the club, I had spent some time in strip clubs. Club Ebony was not like any club I'd been to in my area.

When you walked in the entrance of the club, you stepped into a hallway that had pictures of the dancers on the wall displayed in the lighted frames you find at movie theaters. After you pay the girl at the window and proceed through the curtain, you step into a whole new world. Directly in front of the entranceway curtain was the main stage with a pole in the middle that went about fifteen feet into the air and secured to the ceiling. Off of the main stage, a lighted runway jutted out about two car lengths. To the left of the main stage, against the wall, was a smaller satellite stage with mirrors behind it. Behind the main stage, in a corner, was an area that contained leather couches and a couple of small tables. The entire area was encased in glass. That was the VIP section that was reserved for anyone that had the money and wanted to look important. The only time it was used was when celebrities were in the club. The bar was on the far right wall and was always packed.

The patrons of the club were both male and female, which was something I could not get used to seeing. I had been to clubs where there were females sitting at the bar getting gullible men to buy their drinks. At Club Ebony, women sat at the stage and tipped the dancers. Some of the lesbian and bi-sexual clientele paid to have lap dances and private shows. I guess that just goes to show you how different things are across the board.

That night, I sat in J-Rock's guest VIP section like a superstar. I didn't know whether it was me or the bottles of Moet that brought women to me. Out of all the women that came my way, there was one particular girl that stood out from the rest. She wasn't like the others in and out of the

VIP. She sat directly in view of me and had this look of disapproval on her face—as if to say, "Nigga please." It was almost like I disgusted her. When the time came and I was by myself, I asked one of the bouncers to ask her to come and join me. At first, she was reluctant to come over. After I sent her a drink, she decided to join me. Once she stepped into my domain, I told the bouncer that I wouldn't be accepting any more company for a while.

She seemed shy at first but after she saw I wasn't the average strip club hopper, she loosened up. It was hard to talk in a civilized manner because we had to practically shout at each other. Through the shouts I managed to find that her name was Liberty and she was a Biology major at Spelman College. Liberty was a very interesting young lady. She seemed to have a level head on her shoulders and knew what she wanted out of life. In a short time, I found that we had a certain compatibility but I wasn't trying to push the issue.

Liberty was not a girl that guys would consider to be a drop-dead gorgeous girl. She was an average looking female. Her body was the killer. The short, backless top of her chosen ensemble revealed her slightly muscular mid-rift and well-defined back. She had a small, perky chest and an hourglass figure. You know, slim in the waist and thick in the hips. I'm not into feet but she had the prettiest toes that wore a French pedicure, to match her hands, and a toe ring on the middle toe of her left foot. I know you're wondering: What about the eyes, the hair and the smile? Her true eyes were hidden by gray contact lenses. She wore a short cut, quick weave that was flipped in the back. She did have a pretty smile with full and thick lips. I'm always a sucker for pretty lips.

The only thing about her that was out of my norm was the fact that she was dark-skinned. I used to have a complex about only dating light complexioned women. As I got older and away from Alicia, I realized that all women are unique in their own way. A woman's complexion did not define what kind of person that she was. As far as Liberty was concerned, she was beautiful and smart.

At about 1:30 a.m., the mixture of alcohol, testosterone, estrogen and g-strings moved the club into a chaotic state. Just as I poured Liberty and I another glass of champagne, a fight broke out between two dancers. Remembering what J-Rock told me about the dancers; it was probably a dispute over either money or clothes. That is the difference between dance clubs and strip clubs. When you put so many diverse women with different attitudes together, in competition, you're bound to have some dispute. Nine times out of ten, it was over something petty.

By the end of the night, Liberty and I had finished a bottle of champagne and I was in high gear. I wanted to leave the club with Liberty but I couldn't bring myself to bring it up. During a conversation about what brought me to Atlanta, J-Rock came over to me and said that he needed to see me in his office. I excused myself and followed him to the office. When we came to the end of a long corridor, we entered a room. J-Rock's office looked like a pimp's heaven. There was plush furniture, dim lights, autographed celebrity photos and figurines of women everywhere. I sat down in amazement as J took his place behind his desk.

"What's the deal, cousin?" I asked while I thumbed through a magazine.

"I need a favor," he answered.

"I have to go out of town to pick up a couple of dancers for a show we're doing on Sunday. I need someone to run the club tomorrow night."

"I don't know nothing about runnin' a club."

"You're my cousin, aren't you?"

"Yeah, but..."

"Then, that's all you need."

"What about paperwork and clerical shit like that?"

"Deja will handle all of that. All you have to do is walk around, talk a little shit on the mic, collect money from the private shows and the bar fee from the girls. At the end of the night, get the numbers from the bar and the door and match them with the money. Lock up and take the report and the money to da crib and put it under my mattress. Can you handle that?"

"Sounds simple enough. If you can do it, I know it should be a breeze for me." I laughed as I mocked my cousin.

"You got mad jokes. But on the real, if you have any questions, Deja's there or you can hit me on the hip."

"When in the hell are you gonna get rid of that old as 2-way and get a real cell phone?" J-Rock still had his Motorola Timeport from the late 90's.

"How much do I get for this?"

"You chargin' me? Your own cousin…"

"Absolutely."

"I'll give you thirty dollars per girl up front. Tomorrow is Saturday so you should have about twenty-five to thirty girls. You should make about seven to nine hundred. Sound good?

"That's what's up."

After we got all the particulars out of the way, we walked back into the club and J-Rock announced that I would be runnin' the show in his absence tomorrow. When I returned to the VIP section, Liberty was gone. I couldn't remember if I had given her my number or not. The champagne had my memory distorted. I needed to go home while I was still able to drive. I walked to the front, told J I was leaving and I headed home to the crib. I had gotten lost in the night and it was already 5:30 in the morning. I drove straight home and went to bed.

The next day, J-Rock left town. The final quarter of the Georgia versus South Carolina football game came to a close when someone knocked on the door. When I opened it, I saw two familiar faces but I didn't know their names. They said they were supposed to clean the apartment before they went to work. I let them in and the two sexy ladies went about their duties. I was amazed. I knew Jerome had it going on but I didn't think he had it like that. He had women doing shit for him and he wasn't even in town.

I watched them as they cleaned the apartment and realized who they were and where I had seen them. The two ladies were White Zin and XXXplosive, dancers from Club Ebony. XXXplosive was the sexier of the two and I noticed she was giving me crazy rhythm as she completed her tasks. I think because she knew I was looking, she bent over and exposed her chest and backside a little more than usual. The eye contact was electrifying. I tried to ignore her but it was like trying to pull a big man away from a buffet.

One thing I learned about women in the adult industry was that you never knew how she was going to look from one day to the next. While at the club, women portray a fantasy for men and have to be able to change characters on demand. When I first saw XXXplosive, she was dressed as the naughty schoolgirl. She had on a red and black, plaid skirt that looked like it could be a part of a private school uniform. In addition to the skirt, she wore white, knee socks with black heels with her hair in two pigtails. Later on that night she was the sexy soldier girl as she wore the camouflage g-string, matching hat and bra top.

When she came to the apartment that day she was dressed down wearing a tank top that was tied in a knot between her breasts and a pair of cut-off denim shorts. Her hair was hanging long from under a white bandana. At first, I thought it was a wig or extensions but as I took a closer look, it was her real hair.

Because I watched a lot of TV and movies, I like to use stars to describe the people that I meet from time to time. XXXplosive looked like Ronnie from the movie, *Player's Club* (Lord knows I loved me some Ronnie). She was tall, thick and high yellow. White Zin reminded me of Chrissy from *Three's Company.* She was a very chesty, bleached blonde with blue eyes and legs for days.

I tried to watch the pre-game show for the next game but XXXplosive made constant, seductive sachets in front of the television. When she finally made her way to where I was sitting, I was in full lust mode, waiting for her to say something.

“Weren’t you in the club last night?” she asked while she straightened the magazines on the coffee table.

“Yes I was.”

“I thought so. You were in the VIP section. I wanted to come over and speak but I had a lot of my regulars in the club last night.”

“You gotta make that money.”

“J-Rock told us he had family in town but he didn’t tell us his family was this fine.”

I couldn’t speak as she came on to me. My mind raced as I fought my primal urges. The distinct ring of Alicia on my cell phone broke my silence. I ran to the back to catch it before it stopped.

“Hey Mami,” I said as I answered the phone.

“Hola Papi,” Alicia said with a sexy Spanish accent.

"How's my boo?"

"I'm okay. I'm just trying to relax before tonight."

"What's happening tonight?"

"Jerome asked me to run the club for him because he had to run out of town."

"Don't he run a strip club?"

"Yeah." She didn't say anything, but I could tell by her silence, she disapproved.

"Listen, I'm only doing it for the money and the money only. This way I don't have to dip into my account in order to get a place. Understand?"

"I guess so."

Though she said everything was okay, I still don't think she was completely comfortable with the idea. Hopefully, she'd get over it. XXXplosive must have been listening outside of my door because as soon as I hung up she knocked.

"Dré," she called through the door. "Are you busy?"

"Come in."

"We wanted to know if we could ride with you to the club tonight."

"Who is we?"

"Me and White Zin."

"That's straight."

"Okay. We'll be back around six."

"Don't be late because I have to be at the club at seven."

The two brick houses left and I laid down for a nap. Time flew by and before I could get into my sleep, the ladies were back. I got up, took a shower, got dressed and we were off to the club. The three of us arrived at the club to find that there were already six girls waiting. J-Rock had an all-star squad waiting for me. It seemed like every nationality was represented and there was still more to come. About twenty minutes after I got situated in the office, Deja came to work. When she knocked on the door and came in I realized that the dim lights did her no justice on the first night we met.

I looked at Deja standing a sexy five feet even. Her bodily dimensions were half-woman, half-amazing. She had a cocoa skin tone with a reddish undertone and a small but well developed body. Deja looked like a well-built teenager, especially with her hair in Shirley Temple Curls. J told me she was twenty-six. If he hadn't, I would not have believed her when she told me. Behind a pair of designer glasses that were slightly tinted, I could see that she had brown eyes and long eyelashes. You know how I go. I had to make a joke in order for her to smile revealing one dimple in her right cheek

She let me know early that she didn't take shit from anybody. Deja had the mentality that, even though she worked in a strip club, she was going to be respected. After we got all of that out of the way she proceeded to give me the low down on all the girls. While she was speaking, I couldn't help but notice how her child-like voice flowed out of her full-grown body. I can't front. She was sexy as hell but she and I had to have a working relationship.

Eight o'clock rolled around and it was show time. I stood at the front with Deja while customers began to pour into the club. Just like with the girls, she started giving me the scoop on the regulars. There was one geeky-looking guy that came in that looked just like Myron from the *Player's Club*. Deja told me that just like Myron, he sat in the same spot, every dancer knew who he was but the majority of his money was spent on one dancer. He would sit in the club from open to close. Some nights that wasn't until five or six in the morning. Nevertheless, he was right there.

The club population continued to escalate and around eight-thirty the rest of the bouncers and security rolled into position. Ten minutes later, the DJ fell into the groove. He piddled around in the booth while he was getting his rotation together and in no time he had the club jumping. Everything was running like clockwork and for the first few hours I sat back like a kid in a candy store and monitored the activity of the hottest club in Atlanta. Through all of the activity, I managed to graze by the front a couple of times so I could flirt with Deja.

"What's up, Deja?" I asked as I leaned on the counter.

"Everything is good. Having fun yet?"

"I'm having a ball. This is definitely a change from my 9 to 5."

"Where do you work?"

"I work for Black Reign."

"Wow! I bet that's fun. What do you do?"

"I am the Head Writer for *Tryin' Times*. Have you ever seen it?"

"Seen it? I watch it faithfully. I'm really feeling the relationship between Christine and Raymond the millionaire."

"That was my idea."

"Stop lying!"

"I'm serious. I've only been at the network for a short time but I was brought in to shake things up a little bit."

"So what's going to happen?"

"I can't tell you that. You have to watch."

"That is so foul," she laughed.

"What about you? What's your story?"

"Where do I start? I'm a single mom working and going to school. I'm a senior at Georgia State majoring in Psychology."

"Uh oh. You're one of them."

"One of who?"

"One of those female Psych majors, that go around trying to get into men's heads."

"I am not like that."

"I'm just messin' wit you. So what do you wanna do after you graduate?"

"I plan to continue on to get my Doctorate because I want to do private practice as a therapist. Since I've been working here a lot of the girls come and talk to me and I believe that some of the advice I have given them has helped them."

"That's what's up. Good luck to you."

"Thank you."

"You're welcome. I guess I better go see what the bartenders are up to. I'll talk to you later."

"That was the lamest excuse for wanting to go get a drink that I ever heard," Deja laughed.

"Wow! I guess your analysis of me says that I'm an alcoholic."

"Maybe."

I could see she picked up on my vibe because she started to treat me like a person and not a customer. I also noticed the way she observed me as we talked. Though we were just shooting the breeze, she seemed to hang on my every word. Maybe she was interested and knew that I was only going to be there for one night and wanted to feel me out. I didn't know. Around midnight Deja's relief came in for the late crowd. She discreetly became my shadow. Everywhere I went she managed to find her way to me. I wanted to post up in the VIP but one of the area's most popular rap duos had it occupied. I told one of the bouncers to keep an eye on things while I went to the office to get away from the madness for a minute. When I got there and sat down behind the desk, in less than two minutes, Deja made her way to the office. She came in, sat on the couch and stared at me.

“Can I help you with something?” I asked.

“Depends.” Deja said with a seductive look in her eye.

“On what?”

Deja didn’t answer my question. Instead, she stood up and walked behind the desk where I was sitting. I watched as she picked up a remote control that dimmed the lights and turned on music. Deja began to dance for me. Her motions were mystical and I was mesmerized. I rolled back in the chair and leaned back to enjoy the show. She slowly removed her clothes as she danced to the soulful voice of Jaheim. I could only stare as she advanced towards me wearing nothing but a g-string and a beautiful smile. She climbed on my lap and began to dance for me. It was like no lap dance I had ever experienced.

I leaned my head back and closed my eyes as she kissed me on my neck. I became quite aroused. I knew she felt it through my khakis because when she rocked back on it, she let out a soft ooh. Here I was with a nearly naked woman on my lap, an erection and an opportunity. I couldn’t do it. It was hard for me to stop Deja in the middle of her escapade but I could not allow her to continue. Deja looked at me strangely as I admired her assets on my lap.

“This is a place of business,” I forced myself

to tell her. "I don't feel we should conduct ourselves in this manner."

She looked at me as if she didn't understand the words that were coming out of my face. I told her that doing something like we were beginning was not my style. I wasn't the type to go out like that on the first night. I wanted to take the time to get to know her as a person before we got to that level. My words sank deep in her but still she felt rejected. I guess a girl like her had never had a man to turn her down. She got up and silently started to get dressed. I didn't want her to stray away from me. I assured her that it was nothing wrong with her. Her mouth said that everything was cool but her eyes revealed hurt. What else was I to do?

The remainder of the night went smooth. Before I knew it the last few customers left and we were closed. Once again our duties led Deja and I to be alone in the office. She said nothing to me as we counted the money and did paper work. I wanted to ease the situation but I was at a loss for words. After we were done, Deja gathered her belongings and walked towards the door. It seemed like she was waiting for me to say something.

"Deja," I called. "Wait a minute."

"Yes," she answered as she turned around.

"I don't want you to think I'm not interested in you or find you unattractive because it's not like that. My mind is occupied with a lot of things and I can't think straight right now. I think you are a very attractive and sexy girl. Believe me when I say my mind was telling me no, but my body was telling me yes."

"Maybe I was feeling the same way and reacted a little over zealously. I've been through a lot since I've been in Atlanta and it is hard for me to express myself with words. That is why I speak with actions."

I looked at Deja as she stood in front of me with pain in her eyes. Club Ebony was not good for her or her mentality but who was I to tell her that? From my understanding, besides J-Rock, she was the backbone of the club. I couldn't tell her to quit or think about doing something else. It was not my place. I hoped that, for her sake, she would see it for herself and find another way to make her living. I hugged Deja and kissed her on her forehead. She turned to walk away. I could tell that our experience had not turned her away from me. If anything, it made us a little tighter. I finished up and left with security. When I got to my car, Deja was waiting for me.

"Thank you, Dré," she said as she hugged me once again. "It's nice to meet someone not like the rest of the guys here."

"I'm glad everything is cool between us.

Maybe one night we can get together and go out for drinks or something."

"I'd like that."

We exchanged numbers and I watched her as she got in her car and drove away. I didn't know what else Atlanta had in store for me but if it was like anything I've experienced thus far then I was in trouble. I needed to hold tight because this was going to be a bumpy ride.

6

Vanessa

I'd been in the ATL for almost a month and things had not gone as planned. Because of my presentation, and an occasional club, here and there, I had yet to attempt to find a place of my own and it was almost time for Alicia to come visit. Honestly speaking, that was the last things on my mind. Through it all I still managed to keep things straight between us. She thought that her ticket was going to be in the mail any day and that was my intention. I had to find a place to live first.

That morning, as I got dressed for work, a funny feeling came over me. It was that feeling of having to do something but not being able to remember what it was. I hated when that happened. I hoped that it would've come to me, as I continued to put my clothes on. While I was buttoning my shirt I heard a muffled electronic tone. Where was my cell phone? I searched through scattered clothes that were thrown across the bed. I managed to find it before the musical tone ended.

"Hello," I answered holding the phone on my shoulder as I continued to button my shirt.

"Hi, André," said a sexy but unfamiliar voice.

"Who is this?"

"Were you that drunk that you don't remember who you gave your number to?"

"Maybe I was. Who is this?"

"This is Liberty. We met the other night at Club Ebony in the VIP."

"I don't remember you."

"How many girls did you give your number to that night?"

"Three that I can remember."

"I must've been your fourth. Anyway, I was calling to see if we could get together on a more one on one basis."

"Now is really not a good time for me. I have a lot of things going on right now. Hit me back in a couple of days. Maybe we can work something out."

I had no idea who that was and a voice in the back of my mind was telling me that all of the attention I was getting from the females was going to lead to nothing positive. Staying focused on Alicia became more and more difficult as the days went on. It was hard being in the company of other females, especially Vanessa.

After I managed to get settled in, Vanessa found her way to me. I believe she saw me going into the apartment one night as she was getting off of the elevator because twenty minutes after I got in the house, she came knocking on the door. I did the gentlemanly thing and invited her in. We sat and talked for a long time and that was it. I don't know what I said to her throughout the course of the conversation but she started making it a point to stop by frequently. Don't get me wrong, baby girl was blazin' but I was not trying to get involved with her or anybody. I believe that this vixen had her eyes set on me and she was like the stealth hunter stalking her game, waiting for the exact moment to strike. I believed that she could have any man she wanted. Why had she chosen me? What had I done that was so special? Did I possess something that other Atlanta men didn't? At first, I thought she was just being hospitable until her actions and conversations started saying otherwise.

Temptation is really a bitch sometimes and I don't know how I managed to keep Dré Jr. in my pants through some of the situations I was put in. After Deja, things got more and more hectic. I fought with myself about Alicia. There was no relationship established between us but knowing how she felt about me made me act as if we were together. Go figure.

I can't explain it but my attraction to Vanessa was different. Even with her being as straight up as she was, sex seemed to not be her motive. The more I talked to her, the more I found out what had taken place in her life that caused her to be the way she was. Vanessa was like me in a lot of ways. She was a country girl turned loose in the big city but for her, it was at age sixteen. She moved to Atlanta from Tupelo, Mississippi to live with her aunt. From what she told me, her aunt was a wild one. She used to take Vanessa to all of the spots that she had no business being in at that age. Being young and naïve, she shadowed and mimicked her aunt's behavior until the day she met Polo—every young girl's worst nightmare.

Polo was the guy that all mothers warned their daughters about. He was a notorious pimp that had girls running every strip club and track in Atlanta. Because Vanessa was as young and beautiful as she was, Polo figured that the streets were not for her just yet. He started her career as a lady of the night, in strip clubs. In a short period of time, Polo managed to brainwash her into believing that he was the only man that would ever give a damn about her. The only thing other men were good for was to give her money.

Vanessa stayed with this man through five years of pure hell and torture. If it had not been for him wanting to flaunt her and the rest of his stable at a Player's Ball in Chicago, she would have never gotten away from him. Prior to their trip to the Windy City, someone dropped a bug in her ear, forcing her to wake up and see what was really going on. In every city, no matter how evil, there was at least one Good Samaritan. In Vanessa's case, his name was Claude.

Claude used to be one of Vanessa's regular tricks. After an emotional breakdown one night in a hotel room on the eastside of Atlanta, Vanessa realized that she wanted out of the life and asked Claude to help her. When Polo, Vanessa and three more of his top choice females left for Chicago, he was right behind them. When they got settled into the hotel, Claude posed as a Chi-Town native, wanting to do a *date* with Vanessa. If you don't know what a *date* is, I'll tell you. A *date* is the coined term that prostitutes use to refer to the solicitation of sex.

After everything was established and the two went back to the hotel room, he waited for about ten minutes and then fled with Vanessa. Now the heat was on and she knew she could not go back to Atlanta for a while. Lucky for her, Claude had a very down to earth aunt that lived in St. Louis, Missouri. When she got to St. Louis, she was a mess. Vanessa was twenty-two years old, her body was badly abused and her state of mind was in shambles. It took about two months for her thought process to be reconditioned to that of a normal woman. It wasn't long before she was cooking, cleaning, doing laundry and other survival skills essential for a woman to know. Thanks to a man she met in that lifestyle, she had been delivered out of a life of evil and he wanted nothing in return. Periodically, he would call or fly to St. Louis to check on his aunt and Vanessa.

For two years, Vanessa called St. Louis home until she caught the urge to return to Georgia. Skepticism was automatic because she didn't want to run into Polo again. Her woman's intuition convinced her to hold off for a little while longer and it paid off. One Saturday afternoon, she got a call from Claude. He told her that Polo was brutally murdered by one of his own girls. The streets of Atlanta were now safe for her return. After her turbulent period, her job allowed her to transfer to a branch office they had in Downtown Atlanta.

When I first met Vanessa, she had only been back in town for about six months. I guess when my association with Jerome came up she cringed because she had worked in Club Ebony before. J-Rock's lifestyle reminded her so much of Polo but she didn't hold the fact that we were family against me. My difference from Jerome revealed itself in no time. If one were to just look at Vanessa, he would never be able to tell that a woman that beautiful had been through so much and was still able to function as a normal person.

I learned more and more about Vanessa. I

managed to figure out what my role in her life was. I was the first man, outside of her former lifestyle, that she had associated with in any way other than sexually. She found favor in me because I paid her no mind and went on about my business. Though she was no longer in that lifestyle, she still had some outstanding habits from it, persistence and aggression. She saw what she wanted and set out to get it. Only this time, she was not using her body as bait. Every now and again, another old habit crept in on her. I noticed that sometimes when we talked, she called me *daddy*. It was a common term that a prostitute called her pimp.

Vanessa and I spent a little time together talking over casual drinks and an occasional dinner—when she felt like showing off her cooking skills. I also learned that just because she was a grown woman, her mind was not fully grown up. In some ways she still possessed a small piece of a sixteen-year-old girl's mentality. Because I was cordial to her, she grew an attachment to me. That made things a tad bit harder. If I told her I was going to call or stop by at a certain time, and didn't, she acted like a high school girl in the matter of pouting or giving me the silent treatment. All she really needed was a good man to be there for her. Unfortunately, at that time, I could not be that man.

Alicia was no secret but Vanessa still tried to pretend that she did not exist. She was living by the rule of *out of sight, out of mind*. The more I talked about Alicia, the stronger Vanessa's feelings became for me. I kept Alicia in the equation in order to keep from digging a deep hole. It seemed to do more harm than good. Dealing with Vanessa was like fighting an uphill battle with skates on. The more I tried to resist, the more she tried to get into my head. She was like a twenty-four hour virus that was taking seventy-two to get out of my system. Battling temptation was hard because I knew that all I had to do was say the word and Vanessa would have been all mines. I knew this for a fact because I decided to test her level of desire. Don't ask me why. I just couldn't help it.

It was a Thursday night and Vanessa and I were on the telephone having one of our evening conversations. Jerome had left for the club and I had the apartment all to myself. During our conversation, the subject of fantasies and crazy things we would like to do but lacked nerve to do had come up. She was in the middle of telling me about wanting to arrive to her man's place wearing nothing but a trench coat, when someone knocked at the door. When I asked who it was, there was no answer. I opened the door to find Vanessa standing in front of me in an overcoat. Because of our conversation (and the one button holding it closed) I knew I was in trouble.

Speechless was not the word to describe what I was at that moment. She stepped into the apartment and closed the door. Vanessa leaned against the door with a seductive grin on her face as she bit down on the fingernail of her index finger. I told myself that if she reached for that one button that stood between me and all of her nakedness, I was jumping out of the window. At the close of that thought, she reached. The coat did not open fully but I could only imagine what was going to be revealed. As she took two steps forward, I took two steps back almost tripping over the end table. At every stride the trench coat played a crucial game of peek-a-boo with me.

"Nervous?" she taunted.

"What would make you ask me that?" I asked as my voice cracked.

"You seem as if you don't want to further our conversation."

"The conversation wasn't the problem. It's the acting part that's got me."

"I just wanted you to know that I'm not just talk," she said as she put her arms around my neck.

Vanessa pressed her body against mine and then pushed me back onto the couch. I was wondering whether or not all of Atlanta's women were as straightforward as Vanessa. As bad as I wanted to see everything that was under that coat, I couldn't handle it.

"Look, Vanessa," I said as I grabbed her hands. "This is too much. I can't lose focus."

"What are you talking about?"

"You see this girl?" I asked picking up my keys and showing her Alicia. "She loves me."

"Do you love her?"

"That part, I'm not sure but it feels as if I do."

"Then say no more," she said as she buttoned her coat and walked towards the door. "I hope this doesn't change anything between us."

"Of course not. You've been through a lot in your life and you deserve more than just a one-night stand or a sex partner. You need a man that is going to be there for you and only you; someone who can appreciate these kinds of things. I'm not saying that I don't but I can't give you what you need. Not right now." I walked to the door where she was standing.

"I understand. If you ever change your mind and can be that man, you know where I am. I just hope it's not too late."

Vanessa hugged me and kissed me on the cheek. I wanted to kick myself in the ass repeatedly for passing up that opportunity but something in my heart still kept Alicia on a high pedestal. I just couldn't let J-rock find out. As much as he had been pushing me on Vanessa, he would have revoked my *Player's Card.*

As I was getting her out of my mind, Vanessa must've sensed that I was just thinking about her because as I headed for the elevator, she came around the corner. I gazed at the long-legged stallion as she walked towards me with a smile that was lighting up the very dimly lit hallway. She was perfect in every way—outside of her past. Even the shadows in which she was walking couldn't manage to darken her butter cream complexion. Every stride she took screamed *take me, I'm yours*. The red, body dress she wore hugged every curve like a NASCAR driver. Her silky curls bounced off of her shoulders as she moved. Her walk seemed to be in slow motion and I began to realize that she was, by far, the finest woman that I had met since my arrival. When she stopped in front of me, I couldn't help but notice how perfect her C-cups sat in the V of her dress.

"Hi sexy," Vanessa called as she pressed the elevator button. There was a brief pause. I couldn't speak for a moment. I felt like a peasant boy gazing at the King's daughter, feeling unworthy to speak to her. She called to me again.

"Dré!"

"Hey, what's up?" I answered as I gathered

my thoughts and tried to stop lusting.

"You must be on your way to work."

"Yes I am. I have a presentation to do for the executive board and the owners of the network." The elevator door opened.

"All this time I've known you, I still don't know what you do."

"I never told you?"

"Nope. You didn't."

"I am Head Writer for one of the shows produced by Black Reign Networks"

"Isn't that the same network that produces *Tryin' Times*, which happens to be my favorite soap opera?"

"That's the show that I write for."

"So are you the reason Tina had an affair with Ryan and the whole story about Lauren being the illegitimate daughter of Raymond the millionaire?"

"I can't take the credit for the Lauren and Raymond incident but Tina and Ryan is all me," I replied with egotistic pride.

The elevator stopped and we exited the

building. I hope I didn't make a mistake by telling her what I did for a living because you know how some women are when they find out a man is making a little bit of change.

I thought about Vanessa as I rode to work. How could it be? Thoughts of another woman were occupying my mind. I had not forgotten about Alicia but for some reason, that day, she had been pushed onto the back burner.

7

Boss Lady

Half past noon found me pacing back and forth in the canteen like a mad man. I hadn't too long finished my presentation. I was a nervous wreck because I wanted to know how it had gone over with the Conrad Brothers and the rest of the board. It wasn't like my job was riding on it but it sure felt like it. This was just an opportunity to write for my own show. I managed to calm myself enough to sit down. I grasped my hands together and put my head down in between them. As I sat there I heard someone enter the canteen.

"André, there you are," said a familiar voice. "I have been looking all over for you."

I raised my head and locked eyes with a light complexioned, mulatto woman in her late twenties. It was my boss lady, Karen Union. Karen was very attractive, as well as single. I tried not to look at her in that way. It was the strangest thing because in a lot of ways, she reminded me of Alicia in physical appearance. Karen was a tad lighter than Alicia, as she was bi-racial, but the two women had the same lips and smile. Karen did not have dimples but did have a slight cleft in her chin that was adorable. Because of her light complexion, she wore natural shades of lipstick but very little other facial make-up. Her hair was bone straight and sandy brown. At a glance or from a distance, she could pass for a white woman.

"Hey Karen," I replied straightening myself in her presence as she sat down at the table.

"Are you okay? You look a little flustered."

"I'm alright. Just anxious to know how the presentation went over with the big dogs."

As I began to explain how I was feeling at that moment, I could feel Karen's piercing, gray eyes examine me as they did during my first interview.

"I just want the opportunity to give this network another highly rated program."

"Well, I believe that you have the mind to do it. You are sharp, intelligent and witty. You already have my vote but we have to wait and see what the rest of the board decides. Why don't you take the rest of the day off and I'll call you as soon as I get the results."

Karen excused herself and walked away. I sat for another fifteen minutes or so before I went to my office to get my briefcase and laptop. On my way, I passed the conference room where the

Conrad Brothers and Karen were in deep discussion. I could not tell whether they were discussing the future of the show or if she was pleading a case for me. I tried to put it out of my mind.

The ride to the apartment was just as hollow as my first ride to Atlanta. I stared into the horizon as my instincts led me to *Apt 1200*. I was about twelve blocks from the crib when I noticed an apartment building that I had overlooked. It was amazing. The building rocketed about sixteen stories into the air and had a very high-class appeal. It looked exclusive in every way. Coming from a small city, the building looked like something I had only seen in the movies—including the doorman. I pulled over to inquire about a vacancy. As I approached the entrance of the building, the doorman nodded hello as he opened the door for me. A friendly voice greeted me as I stood in awe of the lobby.

"Hello," greeted a pleasant voice with an Asian accent. "May I help you?"

I turned around to see a short Asian woman standing behind me wearing a beige skirt and a white blouse. Her nametag read: Mei Li.

"Yes you can. I need to know whether or not there are any apartments available. If so, I need info and prices. Nothing to elaborate but nothing to simple."

"Two bedrooms, one bedroom, or a loft?" I'd always wanted a loft but something told me to go against it.

"At least two bedrooms. I need a place to use as an office/study."

"What do you do for employment?"

"I'm an associate producer and head writer for Black Reign Networks."

"Is that the network that puts on *Tryin' Times*?"

"The very one." Damn! Does everyone watch our show?

"It would be an honor to have a celebrity in the building."

"I'm not a celebrity, just yet. Give me some time."

"Well anyway, I have the perfect place."

She explained all the details and particulars and we were off to the 10th Floor. Me Lei was right. The place was perfect. It had enough space, was the right colors, and most important it was the right price. After the tour of the rest of the facilities we went to her office and did the paperwork. I couldn't wait to get to the crib and tell J-Rock the good news. On my way to the apartment, I glanced down at my phone and noticed that I had a voicemail message.

"Hi, André," she began in a voice that didn't seem professional. "This is Karen. You and I have a lot to talk about. I would like for you to meet me at Justin's for dinner at seven. Call me back to confirm. Bye."

I was confused. Was this going to be business or pleasure? From the tone of her voice it sounded like pleasure. Because she was my boss, it had to be business. I called her back to accept her invitation. Once again her voice sounded like it was not going to be a business meeting.

I continued my journey home to relax and tell J-Rock the good news before my meeting with Karen. When I walked in the apartment, my cousin was lying on the couch being messaged by a girl I hadn't met. Vixen was in the kitchen cooking. I sat down in the recliner and told him the good news. We started talking and before I knew it, I only had two hours before my appointment.

That evening, I decided to take a hot bath instead of a shower to loosen me up. I was so tense. As I sat in a hot tub of water with plenty of bubbles, a soft knock came through the door. On command, a sexy, young lady entered the bathroom and sat down on the side of the tub and swirled her fingers in the water as if to test the temperature. I let my eyes focus on her soft, round bottom that hung over the edge of the tub.

"What in the hell was going on?" I asked myself.

"You look relaxed with not a care in the world. Mind if I join you?"

"Say what?" I asked with confusion.

"You heard me. Can I join you?"

This being was about 5'5". She had smooth, brown skin and a small round face. Her hair was in a ponytail that started high off of the back of her head and stopped between her shoulder blades.

"Did Jerome send you in here?"

She shook her head no. Now I was in trouble. It had been a while since my last sexual episode. If she started something, I did not know if I had the willpower to stop her. I was doing so good.

A million and one thoughts raced through my head at that moment. Do I let her? Do I reject her? What do I do? It wasn't a normal thing to be taking baths with women you didn't know. Before I had the chance to answer, she stood up and pulled her shirt over her head and exposed two nice breasts that looked like two large, juicy oranges sitting in a black push-up bra. She inched her skirt to the floor to reveal a black satin thong and then reached for her bra fasteners. I wanted to stop her but I could not nor did I want to. When she was fully in the flesh, I examined her body in every way. I noticed a few stretch marks around her abdominal area, signifying that she had a child. Other than that, she was good to go.

She approached the predestined pool of sin and stepped into the water. With a look in her eyes that silently screamed *I'm going to eat you alive*, she knelt into the steaming water. I watched in amazement as the water engulfed her lower body leaving her breasts atop the bubbles. Once in the water, she cupped her hands and seductively poured water over her brown sugar coated flesh. My eyes followed the streams of water as they ran down her body back from whence it came. This drove me crazy and I did not know what to do. My lower man knew because I felt him rise. Her hands explored the depths of the water in search of the sunken treasure below the water's surface. Deep in my mind I wanted to jump out of the tub and run out of the bathroom soaking wet, erect and butt ass naked. My body told me that Alicia was a few hundred miles away but I had needs that needed to be met.

The unknown creature of beauty slowly moved towards me and pressed her soft, full lips against my chest. I know I keep saying slowly but that's just because everything seemed like it was moving in slow motion. I was caught and there was no turning back. She started to kiss and lick my neck as I took both of her soft breasts in my hands and rubbed her erect nipples with my fingers. She let out soft, passionate moans. She stood on her knees and leaned forward placing her breasts in perfect height of my mouth. With breast in mouth, I explored her slick skin as she moaned even louder when I let my fingers run south of the boarder. Feeling that the time was right she repositioned herself and before I knew it, I was face to face with twice-wet southern hospitality. I was no longer in control of my actions.

I rose to my knees to accept her offer. As I slid into her soaked flesh, she bowed her back and braced herself with one hand on the wall and the other on the side of the tub. I started with a slow jog and before I could blink, I was sprinting inside of her. She tried to contain her noise but she could not. From the other side of the door I knew Jerome could hear a menagerie of moans and *yes's* because I heard the music get louder. The entire time we were making waves, not one thought of Alicia crossed my mind. Her body trembled from the oncoming orgasm as I felt mine coming to my shaft's exit. A scream of ecstasy came from her mouth as I pulled out and exploded into the bath water. She fell back onto my chest. I wrapped my arms around her trembling body and held onto it.

At that moment I felt as if I was lost in time. Our bodies pressed against each other; unaware the world around us was still there. As she lay there with her head on my chest, a million more thoughts filled my mind. Was I a bad person for my previous actions or was I a victim of circumstance? Those were questions that would go unanswered. It was what it was. I had an appointment to keep that concerned my future. All other things were meaningless to me.

I managed to ease myself from the lust filled water, as she lay motionlessly submerged in the memory of what had transpired. It was a damn shame. I didn't even know her name. As I exited the bathroom, J-Rock was sitting on the floor getting his hair braided.

"Have fun?" he asked with a smirk on his face.

I shook my head as I walked into the darkness of my room. The clock glared the red numbers of 6:15 p.m. I had less than an hour to be in place with Karen. I had no clue where time had gone. The night was special, so I had to dress for success. Time was ticking and I did not have the time to be indecisive about what I was going to wear. Quickly but very carefully, I selected a navy blue, double-breasted suit, white collarless, shirt and black dress shoes. Upon completion of my task of getting dressed, I splashed on a hint of Burberry cologne and left the apartment.

When I drove off, I noticed that there were three missed calls and another voicemail message. I was hesitant about checking it, but it might have been Karen. Nope. It was Alicia.

"Hi, my love. I was just calling to see how your presentation went and to tell you that I love you and I miss you. Give me a call when you get a chance. Love you. Muah!" Her words pierced my soul and numbed me as if each word was a shot of Novocain. I knew she had no clue of the situation, but it disturbed me to know that in her time of loneliness, I was engaged in hot, nasty sex with a woman I didn't know. All of this came at the wrong time. I needed to have my mind free because I did not know what the evening was going to unfold for me.

I arrived at Justin's to find Karen waiting in the lobby. I had never seen her in this way. From business suit to eveningwear, she was gorgeous. Her shapely body looked as if it had been poured into her navy blue, V-backed dress. We exchanged casual greetings as we were notified of our ready table. Walking behind her, I could not help but notice how her dress amplified the contour of her body. Her presence alone made it hard for me to see her as just my *boss lady*. For a moment, my eyes were locked on her every move. I caught the flex of her legs when she walked, the switch of her hips, and her body's overall sway. She was poetry in motion…phenomenally.

When we got to the table, I pulled her chair out for her and she seemed surprised. She was a hard one to read, but I was concentrating. Her motions and facial expressions gave no clues of what we were there for. We engaged in some small talk as we were getting acquainted on a more personal level. Karen asked me every question under the sun. Maybe she was trying to get to know me in order to have a better working relationship. Karen's *away from work newness* soon wore off and I became anxious about the outcome of the presentation. She must have tapped into my mind because she changed the course of the conversation.

"You know, André," she said in a low, sexy voice. "There are two reasons I asked you here tonight." Here it came. The moment I was waiting for. "The first reason was to tell you that the Conrad Brothers loved your concept for a new primetime soap opera."

"Wow! This is unbelievable. Do you know how long I have waited for this? I have the first ten episodes outlined and…"

"Wait a minute, calm down," she interrupted. "There is a catch."

I paused for a moment.

"What's the catch?"

"Because you are new to the network, the board knows your work, but does not know if you can handle a project of this magnitude by yourself. They stipulated that in order for this to go into effect, this project had to be a team effort."

"So who is the team?"

"You and I," she smiled. "You are to be the head writer for the show and we will share the position of Executive Producer. You don't mind sharing a position, do you?"

"If I'm sharing one with you, it's not a problem." My words came out faster than I was thinking. That sounded so sexual. I was feeling awkward, so I tried to clean it up before it was taken out of context. "What I meant was…"

"I know what you meant," she said as she cut me off.

"That brings me to the second reason I asked you here tonight."

"And what is that reason?"

"As you may know, putting a new show on the air takes a great deal of time and effort. For an extended period of time we are going to have to live for the show, and when I say live for the show, I mean live for the show. When we leave the office for the day, our work can't stop there. We are going to have to spend a lot of time outside of the office to get this show on the air. The network has given us clearance for a full season, but if we fail within the first six episodes, they are going to pull the plug. It would help for us to get to know each other on a more personal level so we can have a good working relationship. Ten months is all we get. It was a take it, or leave it type deal. I told them we could handle it. Can we?"

"Without a doubt." I answered confidently, staring into her glassy, gray eyes.

"Then let's show them what we got. The first thing we have to do is assign the crew, and I think you can handle that. First thing in the morning I'm going to get on the phone and get us the best director within our budget. After that, all we need is a cast. It sounds easy, but it's not."

"We already got it under control. I'll have the crew complete by the end of the week."

"If you can do that, give me two weeks and I'll have us a director."

"Then let's do it."

"That's exactly what I had in mind." With that statement she gave me a devilish grin.

Karen and I were in the middle of conversation when a strange feeling came over me. Our business dinner seemed like more than just a business dinner. After all of the particulars were over, so was the professionalism. The way Karen looked at me, spoke to me, and frequently touched my hand and arm made me feel like there was something more to it. From the little I knew about her, she seemed to be quite the professional. The more we talked, the more she fell into a comfort zone with me. Was I buggin'? Did Karen have something else on her agenda for me? It was too early to tell, but like my grandfather always told me: *what happens in the dark will eventually come into the light.*

Those thoughts aside, I felt my dreams beginning to come into full manifestation. Like I said before, as a child, I watched a tremendous amount of television and movies. When I got to college, I wrote and produced plays with the help of my friends at FMU. It was hard because we were black students. The predominately white fine arts department wanted no part of what we were doing. They said that my works lacked substance. I went to some of the plays that the department put on to gain ideas. The plays that the school thought had substance were of no interest to the black students or the African-Americans of the community. In my opinion, they were full of bullshit. I did my own thing without the help of the school. It took a lot of hard work, dedication and sleepless nights to put the plays in production. On the collegiate level, I received rave reviews for my stage presentations and more people from campus, as well as the community, came to see my productions.

With all of that in mind, I set my sights on a much larger venue, either television or motion pictures. It was just my luck that the executives and director of human resources at Black Reign Networks found me worthy to write for their number one show. That was a great point in my life, but I'm not one that will accept that and that only. Since my first days at the network, I had been brewing up something but did not know exactly what it was until the night I ran across my unfinished script. I guess that hard work and perseverance does pay off. The one thing that I appreciated the most was having a superior like Karen that had my back. From day one, she believed in me. Every time there was doubt about an idea, she would turn it over to me and let me work it through. Because of that, a few of the other writers that were there before me started letting jealousy rear its ugly head. I tried to please everyone by backing off of certain assignments. It was Karen that convinced me to maintain my focus. When I stopped letting others bother me, the executives noticed my work.

I remember my first encounter with Joseph and Jonathan Conrad. It was about my third day on the job when they decided to pay the writing department a surprise visit. The mood of the office was tense and edgy that day and I could see why. The Conrad brothers were twins and both very tall and stout men. Jonathan, the older of the two, by five minutes, wore a full beard on his round, dark face. Joseph only wore a very thin mustache. I think I would have been okay if no one had identified the two men. I was a little more than nervous that day.

There I was sitting at my desk working on a scene when I sensed a large figure standing over me. I wanted to turn around, but fear had me stuck. Mr. Joseph Conrad asked me if he could look over what I was writing. After I printed out the scene, I watched him reading. He was a hard man to read; his facial expressions did not give me any indication on whether he approved or not, because there were none. When he had completed reading the scene, he tossed the paper back on my desk and walked away. He had said nothing. I didn't know what to think. Five minutes later, Karen came in and told me that Mr. Conrad was impressed with the scene. She went on to tell me that if I kept up the good work, I would go far with the network. That just added more fuel to the fire burning inside me. From that point, I put one hundred and fifty percent into every task that I was given. I knew that it would pay off.

I had only been with the network for a short while, and already I had become the head writer for my own creation and an Executive Producer. Up until that point, everything else had become a blur.

Everything had left me. That night marked a new beginning in my life. Life in Atlanta moved fast, and I intended to be careful enough not to get thrown off or run over. I could not afford to let the angels of temptation get the best of me in Alicia's absence. I did not want to hurt or lose her, but I didn't know whether she was the right one for me. Only time would tell. As I laid myself down to sleep, I prayed that the Lord would keep me sane and lead me to the right decisions. I also thanked him for giving me the opportunity to prove that I was more than just a first time felon.

8

Matters of the Heart

Once everything was locked and bound by contract, I thought that the hardest part had passed. Getting the green light to put the show into action was the easy part. The next thing we had to do before we gathered our cast was to designate our crew. Since Troy was my homeboy, I put him down with the show and had him gather his best camera crew. Though Smoke was a clown, he was the best set technician Black Reign had. I placed him over all of the set designs. When it came to lights and sound, Zack and Alex had it on lock, making them the right men to handle those affairs. I know it seemed like I was playing the same role that MC Hammer played when he was making it big by putting all my friends in such positions. By qualifications, they were the best. This was a new project, and that was exactly what I wanted, the best.

Besides the cast, all of the positions were filled except for the position of director. Karen and I wanted someone who would soak it all in and, as we gave it to him, add his genius then give us back a masterpiece. Through some careful selection and some of the Conrad Brothers pull, we managed to get Shane West. Shane had served as assistant director for the *Young and the Restless* for seven years before leaving CBS to pursue his independent filmmaking career. Due to lack of funds, his newfound career was about to hit rock bottom. We managed to reel him into the network before anybody else could get to him. He was a perfect addition to the Black Reign family.

Being a young gun, I wanted actors like Shemar Moore and Susan Lucci, but our budget would not allow it. We could only afford a few well-known actors and a host of unknowns. On the brighter side of things, for an up and coming actor or actress, this was the perfect opportunity to rise up the ranks to stardom. Since it was a spin-off of *Tryin' Times*, there had to be several cameos and guest appearances by some of the original show's leading cast members, with a couple of them with permanent roles.

When we started contacting agencies to notify them of the auditions we had coming up, Karen came up with an idea. It sounded far-fetched, but proved to be lucrative. She wanted to host an open audition to see if we could find a hidden star of our own. We knew that announcing something like that to the entire city of Atlanta and other parts of the country would bring every drama queen and wannabe Denzel Washington from miles around. Through commercials on our station and the help of the city's radio stations, we managed to gather a huge turn-out for the audition. The first three days were the funniest of the entire process. It was murder trying to compose myself and hold my laughter. I thought I was going to have to go to the hospital from Karen elbowing me in the ribs for laughing out loud. Out of the hundreds of people who showed up, we only selected one hundred of them to audition, and out of those, we selected twenty-five to advance to the next round. Among those twenty-five, Karen and I had our eyes on three. One of them was a seasoned off-Broadway thespian by the name of Kayla. Kayla flew in from New York to make her dreams come true. Of all of the women that auditioned, Kayla was the only one that caught my attention and kept it. Besides her acting skills, she was a stunning young woman. Her physique was like that of a model, though she was not tall like most supermodels. Her hair hung straight and sat atop her shoulders. Kayla had the prettiest and the biggest brown eyes that sat under perfectly arched eyebrows.

On the fourth day of auditions, Karen and I made our final cut. We selected five out of the twenty-five to audition with the professional actors. After the selections were made and all the hype died down, we decided to have a little informal dinner celebration with the selected group. During the limousine ride to the establishment we had made reservations for dinner, I picked up on a few vibes that a couple of the ladies were sending me. For a moment, I lusted for one of the girls, but I had to get it out of my system. I tried to remain professional, but her beauty and body were making it very difficult. She was the girl from New York and I did not know what it was about her. All I knew was that I had to have her on the show. At the beginning of the dinner, we had everyone introduce themselves. The five selected were: Khalid Ivy, Jefferson Fitzgerald, Alexis Rhodes, all from Atlanta, Shanice Spears from Miami, and Kayla Moses from Manhattan. These five young men and women seemed to possess the raw talents that we were looking for.

I tried to keep the conversation going with everyone. Because of my attraction to Kayla, I found myself talking to her the most. At one point in the evening, Karen pulled me aside and pointed out that the excessive attention I showed Kayla was causing others to feel uneasy. In order to maintain professionalism, I stopped talking and Karen carried the remainder of the conversation. I could tell that Kayla had a little something for me because even though I wasn't talking, her attention was still focused on me. Since it was Friday, we all went to Classics for some drinks and dancing. Karen used her Black Reign pull to score us a VIP section so we could all socialize together and not be bothered if we did not want to be. As a special treat to the group, I paid the DJ a little visit. Over the microphone he announced to the entire club that there were five people in the building that were selected to audition for a new television show. I stood in the DJ booth as he shined the spotlight on our VIP section. Before I could get back to the area, it was swarmed with wolves and wolfettes. From the bar, I watched as Karen excused herself from the group and joined some friends at another table so the five could have their time to shine. A couple of them would probably have to get used to it. The bartender and I were engaged in a conversation when Kayla slid up to the bar.

"Are you enjoying yourself?" I asked while turning to face her.

"Mr. Marshall, you don't know how much this means to me."

"Please, call me Dré."

"Okay. Well, Dré, what's the next step?"

"Next, you will do a formal audition with the professional actors for the casting company so they can see what kind of screen appeal you have, how you act with others, and if there is a certain chemistry between you and another actor."

"What if I don't make it?"

"I'm sure you won't have a problem, but if, by chance, you don't get chosen for the cast, we have decided to cast the five of you as extras just for making it this far."

"Are you serious?"

"I wasn't supposed to tell you yet, so let's keep that between us for now."

"Don't worry, I will."

"Come on, let's dance." Kayla and I went to the dance floor just as the DJ slowed things down. I felt a chill when she wrapped her arms around my neck and pressed her body against mine. There was definite chemistry between her and me. As we danced to *Let Me Love You Down*, by Ready for the World, I felt Kayla's body tremble every time I squeezed her tight or slid my hands up and down the white silk blouse that covered her back. Her body was so soft, and her fragrance had me momentarily in another realm. On the last note of the song, we returned to the VIP to partake in some champagne, courtesy of the club owner. When the others saw Kayla and I returning together, the hating began.

"Looks like somebody is trying to get a lead role," Alexis remarked as she sipped her drink.

Kayla asked, "What are you talking about?"

"What better way to secure a spot than by seducing the Executive Producer."

"It's not like that. Dré and I were just dancing."

"Now you're on first name basis," added

Shanice.

"You three stop it," Karen interjected. "Mr. Marshall, may I speak to you for a moment please?" Karen and I stepped to the bar.

"What are you doing? I told you, No showing favoritism."

"I'm not. I was sitting there talking to the bartender when she came over."

"So then you take her to the dance floor and grind on her?"

"We were not grinding. It was merely a slow dance."

"Dance or no dance, you cannot get involved with any of them in any way. It will cause a conflict of interest. I see the same potential in Kayla that you do, but if she gets selected for a role and the others don't, they are going to think something funny was going on. That could lead to a messy situation that we don't want to go through."

"I see what you're saying. I didn't realize that it was being viewed that way. Would it make things better if I grinded on the other two girls and you back that ass up on the two dudes?"

"Dré!" Karen playfully scolded. "No grinding, no backing that ass up, and no dropping it like it's hot either."

"You are such a white girl," I laughed. "What about shakin' what my mama gave me?"

"Stop it," she giggled. At the close of the night, the limo took us back to the network to get our cars. Since I was there, I decided to run in and get my laptop, just in case I had any ideas pop into my head over the weekend. When I returned to the parking lot, everyone was gone except for Kayla. She looked as if something was bothering her.

"What's wrong?" I asked as I unlocked my truck.

"I don't know if I can deal with this type of pressure. This is more than I'm ready for. Stage plays are one thing. This is national television."

"Sure you can. All actors and actresses are nervous in the beginning. You have it easy compared to the weight Karen and I are carrying.

"I know this is a big deal for you. I don't want to screw it up for you. I think I'm just going to head back to New York."

"No you're not. Listen…everybody has to have someone believe in what they can do. Karen believed in me from day one. I started as a writer and now I am the creator of a new show. She believed in me and I believe in you."

"You do?"

"Yes I do, but you have to have faith and believe in yourself. If you don't, it doesn't matter how much I believe."

"But what about the others?"

"I know it seems like they're hatin' on you because they are. Do you think you are the first person to get this type of reaction from someone you are competing with? No, you're not. I'm sure actresses like Vivica Fox, Gabrielle Union, and Meagan Good all got hated on by other actresses that just couldn't cut it."

"I guess you're right. I'm glad I talked to you first, because I was just going to leave without saying a word."

"I'm glad you did too." I reached into my back pocket, pulled out my wallet and handed Kayla my business card. "Here is all my information. If you have any questions, doubts, concerns, or just need someone to talk to, call me."

"Thank you." Kayla responded while putting the card in her handbag. "I will."

"Now go back to your hotel and get your head right. You have some serious auditioning to do."

When Kayla got into her car, she had a look of confidence on her face that I had not seen to this point. Her face was that of a winner. I was thankful that she waited around to talk to me instead of just leaving. I saw the same potential in her that Karen and the Conrad Brothers saw in me. Who knows? Maybe she could become the next Vivica, Gabrielle, or Meagan. If I could only get Shane and the casting company to see what I saw, then she was good to go. When the final auditions came around, that next Thursday, our selected five were nervous wrecks. They were among a host of professionals. Karen and I sat on the set, along with the casting company, even though we had little say in who got selected. Though she was nervous, I knew Kayla was going to do fine.

I was amazed at how natural acting came to Kayla, once she got in front of the camera with other actors. Khalid also did very well when his segment came around. As for Alexis, Shanice and Jeff, the only things they would ever be were extras. After all the harassment and ill comments they made towards Kayla, I thought they were going to blow the audition out of the water. The theater really paid off for Miss Kayla Moses because everyone was just as impressed with her as we were.

All of the madness of the auditions ended on

that next day, but we still had three spots open that could only be filled by people currently on *Tryin' Times*. To my surprise, the casting director chose Kayla for a significantly large role; but there was a problem. Kayla did not have an agent, nor was she affiliated with an agency. Something had to be done and fast or her big break was going to be toast and I was going to lose a piece of the puzzle I was trying to put together. Karen and I met with Kayla to tell her the good news and bad news. Lucky for her, Karen had a good friend that worked with an Atlanta-based entertainment agency and they picked Kayla up based on our recommendations alone. Hard work and determination had paid off for the little flower that we discovered in a field of weeds. Kayla was on her way to stardom. No matter how happy Alexis and Shanice were to be selected as extras, I believe that they still thought that Kayla put in a little *back work* to get selected for her role. As long as we knew the truth, that's all that mattered.

9

Too Close

I spent the remainder of that weekend getting everything moved into my new apartment. In as little as three hours, I spent several thousand dollars on imported furniture and appliances. It took a great deal of effort from J-Rock and the rest of the guys to get me to spend that amount of money. It was well worth it because I had a fly crib. In the living room I had a cream leather sofa and love seat set. My coffee and end tables were made of the same color marble and glass. The dining room held an eight-guest-capacity, dark cherry wood table and the China cabinet to match. The table sat on an Oriental rug imported from Singapore. In the breakfast nook was a tall bistro table with a dark, smoked glass top and two chairs. The kitchen was done in black and white with an island stove and a long bar counter. From the ceiling hung a rack that held shiny, stainless steel sauté pans of all sizes. I even had a miniature version of my office set up in the spare bedroom. That way I could have the flow of the office with the comforts of home. The grand finale was the Master bedroom. In the center of the room was a California King-sized sleigh bed, which was also made of cherry wood, bedded with the finest of satin and Egyptian cotton. To the left of the bed was the matching dresser with the oversized mirror. On the wall to the right, beside the door to the closet, was the chest of drawers that completed the set. To either side of the bed sat the matching nightstands. On top of each one was a Tiffany lamp.

As a reward for helping me move in, I bought a bottle of Hennessy and ordered some Chinese food. We sat and watched the last college game of the night on my new 52" HDTV. I was just getting settled in good and the guys were already planning a party.

"When is the house warming?" Troy inquired.

"As soon as we get the show along a little further, I'll think about having one, but for now, I got too much going on."

"Just let me know and I'll get the butt-naked girls," Smoke said hungrily rubbing his hands together.

"No disrespect Smoke, but I've seen some of the girls that you deal with. I think I'll let my cousin, J to da Riz-ock handle da hiz-oes."

"You know I got you cuz. Who you want, XXXplosive, White Zin, Jada or Vixen? You name 'em and I'll get 'em. As a special guest, I'll even get Deja for you and you only."

"Yo cuz, this is just a house warming, not a bachelor party."

"Wit' these girls, you better believe it's gonna get warm in here. But any way, fellas, let us toast to my cousin and the success of the new show. To Dré."

"To Dré!" they all said as we clinked our glasses together.

After the weekend was over, Karen and I got a rude awakening concerning *Matters of the Heart*. Because we had consumed such a considerable amount of time selecting the cast and crew, we had neglected our writings for the show. Whoever said progress was a slow process could not have been talking about what we were doing. It seemed that the less we got done, the faster time moved. Karen and I were in the office that afternoon when she suggested something that seemed innocent, but would later on have a great impact on my life outside of Black Reign Networks.

"André," she began. "Do you realize how much time we spent to get the cast and crew together and how much more work we have to do to get ready for taping?"

"I didn't think that we used as much time as we did, especially with that first audition. At least we got Kayla."

"That's true, but if we don't get on track, Kayla is not going to do us any good with no scripts for the show."

"Then what do you suggest?"

"Extreme sacrifice. For the next few months, we have to live, eat, and breathe this show, inside of the office as well as outside. You put more work on us because you waived a writing team because you wanted to write all of the episodes."

"I didn't think it would be a problem. On the *Dick Van Dyke Show* they only had three writers."

"What does Dick Van Dyke have to do with us?" she asked with a look of confusion.

"Buddy, Sally, and Dick were the only writers for the *Allen Brady Show*. The show aired every night and was a live broadcast. Our show airs once a week and it's pre-recorded."

"Once again, I ask you. What does that have to do with us?"

"Together, the three writers had half a brain. You and I have all the talent that is needed to do the job. We can do it."

"André Marshall...I need you to do me one favor."

"What's that?" I knew something smart or

sarcastic was coming, but I entertained her anyway.

"I need for you to stop watching so much TV." she laughed. "Where are we going to meet in the evenings to write?"

"When I furnished my apartment, I set up an office that is designed as a combination of my office here and the writing room. We could use that."

"That sounds good to me. We can get started on it tonight." That afternoon, Karen and I left the network and headed to my apartment. On the way, we stopped and picked up some take-out because I hadn't gone grocery shopping yet. When we pulled up to my building, Karen was shocked to see that I lived in the Royal Winds. She joked about the network paying me too much money. With no major bills to pay, I could afford to live lovely.

"Make yourself at home," I told Karen as I put the food down on the coffee table and Karen gave herself a tour of the apartment.

"This is nice. It looks like a woman decorated in here; doesn't look like a single man lives here alone."

"Wait until I get with my Dad so he can help me hook up my plants and flower arrangements."

"Oh my God," she gasped as we entered the

bedroom. "This is the bed I've always wanted. Do you mind if I lay on it?"

"Not at all."

Karen looked so sexy as she sprawled across the huge bed. For a quick moment, I envisioned her naked. I had to quickly shake that thought out of my head.

"How does it feel?"

"Like heaven. I could really get used to this."

"Oh really?"

Karen gave me a sly look and a devilish grin.

After Karen had her fun in my bed, without me in it, we sat down to eat before we got started on our writing session. Karen went on about how nice she thought my place was and tried to give me some suggestions that she thought would really bring the place out. Though I disagreed with everything she was saying, I just smiled cordially and took it all in. About an hour into our writing, Karen and I both got blocked and were at a temporary loss for ideas. Nothing we said was to the other's liking. No matter what we tried, our creative juices just would not flow. After about fifteen minutes, I realized what was wrong—at least for me. The room was too quiet. I walked into my bedroom and into the closet to find a special box. When I found it, I returned to the study.

"What is that?" Karen asked as she rolled her neck around trying to loosen it.

"This is my box of inspiration. Whenever I used to write back in college, these were the CD's I would listen to."

"Back in college? Then you mean eight tracks, don't you?"

"Oh, so we got jokes. Let's not forget who the oldest is. Wasn't Moses your senior class President?"

"Shut up!" Karen gasped as she threw a crumpled piece of paper at me. When the first notes of Lenny William's song, "*Cause I Love You*" came through the speakers of my laptop, Karen almost lost her mind.

"Oh, Dré," she said swaying her body to the melody. "This is one of my favorite songs of all times."

"Didn't Lenny write this song about you?"

"Okay, enough with the old jokes, we have work to do." Before we went back into our writing session, I noticed that Karen pulled a bottle of prescribed medication out of her purse.

"What is that?" I asked with concern.

"This is my blood pressure medication."

"Does your blood pressure bother you often?"

"Sometimes. If work gets too hectic, my stress levels rise, and so does my pressure. Once it gets up there, I have awful headaches. My doctor told me that I needed to be careful, because it could lead to serious complications if I don't keep it under control. Now, enough about my health, turn the music up and let's get back to work."

Since the show was based on romance, what better way to help us write about it than to write while we listened to slow jams? Our favorite old school ballads inspired us, and before we knew it, Karen and I churned out quality material. It usually took the average team of six writers a while to decide on material for one scene because there were so many different ideas to be considered. That first night, we almost completed an entire episode.

"Oh my Gosh!" Karen shrieked when she noticed the time. "I didn't realize it was so late.

"Damn! It doesn't feel like its 1:30 already."

"I have to go home and get some sleep."

"Next time; just bring a change of clothes and a sleeping bag and you can crash under this table."

"You are so silly."

After we gathered our things together and put them away, Karen left. I sat at the table and thought about all the things that had led me to this point, and was truly thankful. If the show became a success, I was on my way to the top. For a split second, a thought of Kayla crossed my mind, but was very short-lived because of my cell phone.

"Hello," I answered while I was walking into the bedroom.

"Hi Dré, this is Kayla. Did I wake you?"

"Not at all, I was just doing some late night work. Why, what's up?" I didn't want to tell her that I was just thinking about her.

"I was just lying here in my hotel room and couldn't sleep, so I decided to give you a call."

"Is there something wrong?"

"Not at all; I just wanted to tell you thanks for everything that you have done for me so far."

"I didn't do anything. You landed that role on your own because you're just that good."

"Yes you did. If I hadn't talked to you, I would have gone back to New York and missed out on the biggest break of my life. Thank you so much for believing in me."

"It's all good. Like I said before, someone had to believe in me in order for me to get to this point."

"Well, I know it's late, so I'll let you get some sleep, plus my flight leaves for New York in the morning. I'll get in touch with you when I get back to Atlanta. See you soon." Now that was weird. I had just been thinking about her and she called. At first I wondered how she got my number, but then remembered that I gave her my card after we left the club. I was thinking that women and men don't just call each other in the middle of the night to say thank you; or maybe they do and I was thinking with the little head instead of the big head. Regardless, I was sleepy and I was trying to catch the 1:55 train to dreamland.

That night I had the strangest dream. It started with me sitting at my desk at the network. I was going over some scenes when Kayla came into the office wearing a black, skintight cat suit. From what I could see, she had a very seductive look in her eyes. She approached me. Before I knew it, she climbed on top of my desk and started dancing very sensuously. I leaned back in my chair and focused all my attention on the being of intrigue; dancing for me. The twisted part about the dream came when I noticed that Karen was standing outside of my office window looking in at Kayla dance for me. When I looked back up, thinking that it was Kayla still dancing for me, she was no longer there. Standing in her place was another woman wearing a black veil over her face. When she removed the veil, it was Alicia. Needless to say, that was the point I woke up in a cold sweat.

All that next day, I tried my hardest to decipher the dream, but I kept coming up with nothing. When I told Troy about it, his dumb ass said that maybe it was suggesting some group activity. That is why you do not discuss certain things with your friends. Later on that day, Karen and I were having lunch when she told me that she, too, had a strange dream the night before.

"It was the oddest thing," she said after wiping her mouth with a napkin. "I was pregnant."

"Pregnant? By who?"

"That was just the thing. There was no man anywhere in the entire dream."

"Maybe you're going to be the next Virgin Mary."

"Do you always have to say the first thing that comes to your mind?"

The more Karen and I worked together, the more I noticed how attractive she really was, beauty and personality. Even so, she was a hard person to read. One minute she was all about business, and the next she was laughing and joking about everything. Many times I wanted to compliment her on qualities other than those that were professional, like her smile, her eyes, or her overall beauty, but I kept it to myself. The complexity of her entire demeanor made it hard to figure her out. I knew that there was a fine line between business and pleasure that I didn't want to cross. If there was going to be anything initiated on a personal level, I was going to let Karen do it.

Another day at Black Reign came to a close, and it was time for us to start phase two at my place. She told me that she had to make a couple of stops before she got to my place, but assured me that she was right behind me. The night before, I joked about Karen bringing a change of clothes and a sleeping bag. I didn't know she was going to take me seriously. When she arrived to my apartment that evening, she had everything but a sleeping bag.

"I hope you don't mind," she said putting her bags in a corner. "I brought a few things just in case we run late again tonight." Karen had an overnight bag, a suitcase and a hanging bag.

"I know I told you last night to make yourself at home…but damn girl. Do you need me to go park the U-haul and get the rest of your things?" Karen pushed me aside as she walked past me towards the kitchen.

"What's for dinner?" she asked. I heard her open the oven and the microwave.

"I thought you were going to bring it."

"You didn't tell me to stop, so I thought you had it covered. That's okay because I passed a supermarket on the way over. We could take a little time, and go shopping for groceries, so that we will have food in the house." She was really making herself at home.

"That sounds like a good idea because I'm tired of take-out."

We walked about three blocks down to the local grocery store. Karen and I were like two kids because neither of us had gone shopping for groceries in a while. I never thought something so simple could be so fun. The moment we got there, we argued about who was going to push the buggy. Since she was persistent, I decided to let her win. I couldn't stand to see a grown woman pout. For an hour straight, we went up and down every aisle. I tried to grab and go, but not Miss Union. She was the bargain hunter. Everything we bought was off-brand except the cereal. She and I both agreed that Froot Loops and Fruit Rings are not the same thing.

After we burnt up an hour and a half, we went back to my place to start writing. At least that's what I thought. Since we had gone shopping, Karen insisted that we cook something. She looked so at home in the kitchen, unlike many new millennium women that didn't know a pot from a pan. I had to remind her of the time so she wouldn't cook anything too time consuming. We decided on Hamburger Helper. When she finished cooking, I tried to fix my plate and go into the study, but she wanted to eat at the dining room table. Once again, I obliged her request and sat down with her to eat.

"Tell me Dré," Karen started. "Do you think we are going to make our deadline?"

"Honestly? Yes I do."

"How do you figure?"

"Because I am willing to do anything that it takes to get this show on the air."

"Anything?"

"Anything."

I wasn't sure what Karen was getting at with her questions. By the look in her eyes, I felt she had something brewing under that soft, brown hair. When we finally sat down to write, it was around eight-thirty or a quarter to nine. Karen popped in one of our inspirational CD's, and our creative process started in motion. I didn't know what Karen had riding on this show. I had my entire career and reputation on the line, and when I told her that I would do anything to get this show on primetime television, I meant it.

At the close of our fourth CD, around 1:30 A.M., I excused myself to take a shower, and Karen did the same thing. Twenty minutes later, she came out of the bathroom in her pajamas, if that's what she wanted to call them. She had on a pair of black, satin lady boxers and the matching top with spaghetti straps. Now, from business suit to sleepwear, she was still a showstopper. I tried to keep from staring, but it was so hard to see those firm thighs uncovered and her breasts unleashed, nipples erect and barely covered. Only a fool would have believed that I was not thinking what I was thinking when I saw Karen damn near in her bare essentials.

I had to stay focused and tell myself that just because we were getting ready to go to bed didn't mean that things were going to get freaky. To keep myself from temptation, I tried to offer her my bed and take the couch.

"Well, you sleep tight," I said pulling a blanket out of the closet.

"What are you doing?"

"I'm getting ready to go to sleep."

"Where at?"

"On the couch."

"Come on now, Dré. We are both adults. I believe that we can sleep in the same bed. Besides, what kind of woman would I be to put a man out of his own bed?"

"An ugly one," I thought to myself as we walked into the bedroom. "Karen, hold on a minute."

"Is there something wrong?" she asked.

"This doesn't feel right to me."

"I know where this is going, André. I just want to let you know that what we are doing is strictly professional. This is just a small sacrifice to make in order to get this show off of the ground. Just trust me. Everything is going to be just fine."

Even though I heard everything that Karen said about professionalism, I still felt that this was the beginning of trouble. Maybe I was overreacting. I had butterflies in my stomach and my heart started to flutter. It had been a while since I had just non-sexually slept with a woman, if you know what I mean. The more I thought about it, Alicia was the only woman that I had ever slept with that I didn't engage in anything sexual with. I was just glad I bought the king-size bed so that there was plenty of space between Karen and me, because if her skin touched any part of my skin, I was done.

For the first hour, I fought off my urges as hard as I could. The newness of my bed caused Karen to toss and turn, inching her towards me with almost every movement. There was really no place for me to go but on the floor if she came too close. The more she moved, the closer she came. I felt beads of sweat form on my forehead when she was finally close enough for me to feel the warmth of her body next to mine. I wondered whether or not she was doing it on purpose.

Right before Karen got too close; I got out of the bed and went into the bathroom. I looked down at myself and noticed that he was still at ease but somewhat heavy. I ran some cold water and splashed it on my face to cool me down before I went back into the bedroom.

"Are you alright?" Karen asked as I slid back into bed

"Yeah, I'm okay. What about you?"

"I'm still trying to get used to your bed. You know how it is when you sleep some place other than home."

"Would you like to switch sides?"

"I'm fine over here. I would feel more

comfortable if you came a little closer."

Why did she say that? I did not want to be embarrassed if she tried to spoon with me, but she got somewhat persistent in her request, and once again, I gave in to her. We were both lying on our left side with about a foot of space in between us. In one sly movement Karen moved her knees closer to her chest, pushing her soft behind into my stomach and pelvic area. **Oh My Damn!** This was not happening. I began to silently beg my little soldier not to wake up, but he was trying to be hard headed in more ways than one. When I felt him rise, I tried to ease back. Every time I moved, Karen moved. Maybe that was what she wanted. I stopped fighting it and let her back into it. Not once did she try to move away or make any further advancement. She and I fell asleep and I must say that was some of the best sleep that I had in a while.

10

Proceed with Caution

Every day for a month, Karen and I worked around the clock to get our episodes written. When Karen said we had to eat, sleep, and breathe *Matters of the Heart*, she was not lying. Due to our intense workload, I started to neglect Alicia. We went from talking every night to talking maybe once a week, and then it was just hi and bye. This was not on purpose. I believed that Alicia understood the situation, though the promised two weeks were long gone and she still had not been to visit me. The bond between us weakened more and more as the days went by.

On the other side of things, Karen and I built a pretty strong working relationship and a friendship—which wasn't a hard thing to do when you're with the same person damn near twenty-four hours a day. We had fallen into a daily routine as if we were married. The only things we didn't do were to have sex and argue. Every now and then we would have a little squabble, never anything serious. It was always something minor like someone eating the last of something and not replacing it, or me leaving the toilet seat up at night. The situation was cool, but I wondered if Karen was developing feelings because we were spending so much time together. I noticed that she would give me these nasty looks whenever I would talk to another female on the telephone.

One night, Natalie called and I left the room to talk to her. We must have talked for a good thirty minutes before I returned to my work. When I walked back into the room, Karen seemed to be upset with me. Before the phone rang, she and I were laughing and talking. After my phone call, there seemed to be a high level of tension in the room. Karen did not say a word to me for twenty minutes.

"Karen," I said to her as I stopped typing. "Is something bothering you?"

"No. Why do you ask?"

"Because you haven't said a word in almost half an hour."

"I was concentrating on something, plus I have a terrible headache."

"Oh, okay. I was just wondering, because, this is a collaboration."

"André, nothing is wrong."

Right then, I knew something was wrong because the only times she called me André was when we were having a dispute. Eventually it passed and we were talking again until I got another phone call. This time it was Vanessa. Once again, I excused myself to have a short conversation. Five minutes later I walked back into the study, as Karen was packing up.

I asked, “You’re closing up shop kinda early, aren’t you?”

“Well, it’s obvious we aren’t going to get any more work done tonight.”

“Why is that?”

“Because you have a regular hotline going on, and it is not conducive to the writing process. Good night!” Karen walked out of the study, into my room and slammed the door like a child having a tantrum. Wait a minute. How was she going to get mad at me and go into my room, in my house, and slam the door, like I was supposed to be sleeping on the couch? It seemed that jealousy was starting to become a factor. How could that be when we were only friends and co-workers? She reminded me of Alicia when we were back in school. I dare not tell her that. She started acting like we were a little more than two people making a sacrifice to make a deadline. I told you, Karen was a hard one to figure out.

Because Karen was bothered by something, I found myself creeping into my own room so not to disturb her. When I got in the bed, Karen did not come towards me as she usually did. Instead, there was enough space in between us for about three more people. Normally, she and I would talk until one of us fell asleep on the other. Silence filled the room, and I could tell that the shift in our normal routine had affected her.

"André," she said rolling over to face me. "We cannot afford to lose focus. We've come too far."

"What are you talking about?"

"Two times tonight, I lost ideas because you were on the phone and I couldn't run them by you."

"Why didn't you write them down and we could have gone over them when I came back in the room?"

"Is that how we normally do things? No. We get them out as they come. We have a little while longer before we can both get our lives back. Please, let's not forget about where we are trying to go."

"Then I guess now is not a good time to tell you that I made plans for Saturday."

"Plans? What kind of plans?"

"My friend Natalie, the pro ball player, asked me to play on her team in a charity basketball game."

"If that game is more important than our careers, then go and have fun."

Why do women say things like that? She knew that taking one day off —or even a piece of a day—was not going to affect us that greatly. If nothing else, it would help us out. She and I had not been anywhere other than the network and my place. The space would have done us some good but to keep the peace, I canceled my day with Natalie. I told her that I had a lot of work to do that was going to keep me confined to the house. Karen seemed to be overly happy when she found out that I put an end to my plans. After that night, I made it a point to let my cell phone go unanswered until we were finished for the night, unless it was Alicia.

That Saturday came and I'd cancelled my plans for the day. Karen did not arrive at my place until six o'clock that evening. Needless to say, I was livid when she arrived. My mouth had to stay closed to keep from going off on her. At first she did not notice the mood I was in or the look I had on my face, but as the evening progressed and I hadn't moved from the spot that I was sitting in for an hour, she suddenly became concerned.

"Is something bothering you, Dré?" she asked as she sat on the arm of the chair I sat in.

"Nice of you to notice," I sarcastically

replied.

"What's wrong?"

"Please tell me that you did not ask me that question. I cancelled my day, which would have been over by now, in order for us to get some work done. You left here this morning and said that you were going to your place to get a couple of things then you don't get here until eight hours later, but then you ask me if something is wrong."

"I got tied up. I'm sorry."

"It's called a telephone. You are one out of three that have my home number, not to mention my cell phone number. I don't think that there is any excuse. If you did not want me to go to the game, you should have just asked me not to go to the game."

"It has nothing to do with the game, Dré. I told you, I got tied up."

"You know what? Just forget it." I was disgusted at that point. I grabbed my keys and left. How in the hell can a woman that I was not dating drive me to leave my own house? My grandmother used to tell me that it was always best to just walk away, and that is exactly what I did. I had no destination in mind when I left. Minutes later, I found myself at J-Rock's place. He immediately sensed that something was wrong just by the look on my face.

"Uh oh," J-Rock said as I sat down. "Who done pissed in ya cornflakes?"

"Remember when I told you that me and Karen were working on the show at my place after work?"

"Yeah, I remember you tellin' me dat."

"Well, we just got into an altercation."

"See...that's why they should never give a colored man a degree in English."

"What are you talking about?"

"How many black people do you know that say the world altercation?"

"My bad, Cousin."

"It's all good…but on the real, how long you and ol' girl been doing this at-home shit?"

"Over a month now. We've fallen into a routine."

"Is she sleepin' there too?"

"Yes."

"In the same bed?" I nodded my head yes. "Uh-oh."

"What da hell is uh-oh?"

"Sounds to me like somebody is catchin' feelings and I don't believe it's you."

"How you mean?"

"Let me ask you another question? Have you had sex with her?"

"What is this, 21 questions?"

"Just answer the question."

"No I haven't."

"Do you hold her at night?"

"Sometimes…but what does that have to do with anything?"

"It has everything to do with everything. You and baby girl spend all of your time with each other. Y'all sleep in the same bed, but have never got busy. She's comfortable with you and she trusts you. Now what caused the argument?"

"I told her that Natalie asked me to play on her team in a charity basketball game today."

"Another chick was gettin' ready to get some of her time. It's the same thing that happened wit you and Alicia back in the day. Does the name Sweet V ring a bell?"

"Now that I think back, it is the same situation, but more like a catch twenty-two because we have a deadline to meet, plus she knows about Alicia and her plans to move to the ATL next year."

"None of that matters. She's with you now and to her that's the only thing that matters."

"So what should I do?"

"I don't know what to tell you, bruh."

"All that diagnosis and no answer. Thank you, Dr. Phil."

"I guess you just gotta proceed wit' caution like you do all matters of the heart. No pun intended."

While I was talking to my cousin, Alicia called. The conversation started off like our normal conversations. Then she got sensitive on me. When God created woman, I wish he had not have tuned her intuition to be so sensitive.

"How is everything going'?" she asked.

"Everything's cool. Why do you ask?"

"I'm just concerned about us. It seems that we are driftin' apart."

"I know this is a hard time for us, baby. I just need you to have my back now more than ever."

"You know I've always had your back, but we need to be in touch a little more. I gotta be honest with you. I'm having some security issues."

"Alicia, there is not a day that goes by that I don't think about you. Even this project that I am working on reminds me of you because you inspired the original play and made me stay on top of it until senior semester started gettin' hectic."

"There is no doubt in my mind that you are thinking of me, but I know you've been meetin' women."

"True, I have, but you are still my number one angel."

"Once again, I don't doubt that. I just want you to keep it real wit me. If you start feelin' somebody else, please let me know."

That would have been a perfect time to tell Alicia about what was going on with Karen, but I couldn't bring myself to tell her. "Always. We promised each other when we came back together at FMU that we were never going to let go of each other, no matter what. Our friendship exceeds anything that two people could ever possess."

"I know, and I hold that and you closer to my heart than I hold anything else. That is why I am tellin' you this. All I want to do is love you."

"Just hold tight. We'll be together soon."

"I know."

When dealing with insecurity issues with women, one has to handle the situation with care. If a man knows he has a good woman, he will do anything and everything to keep her—at least a real man would. In my situation, I knew I had a good woman in Alicia, but dealing with women like Natalie and Vanessa made it hard to maintain. To add more difficulty to the situation, Karen's feelings were sneaking up on me. What does a man do when he has three or four quality women to choose from?

Usually, when a man has more than one woman to choose from, it's only one or two qualities in each woman that kept her around. With the ladies I was dealing with, they all possessed similar qualities, as well as unique qualities of their own, that made it hard to lean towards just one. Karen and Alicia were a lot alike in many ways, and Natalie was just phenomenal in every way. In the comparison of Natalie and Alicia, the two were very evenly matched, especially in the department of having a good time. Though Vanessa was beautiful and charming, her past life was a major strike against her. Honestly, I could never have her in my life as a companion.

I really needed some time to myself. With

Karen constantly around, it was hard for me to just drift away. If she was at my place when I returned, then I would just have to be a man and ask her to leave so that we could have a little space in between us for at least one night. Surprisingly enough, when I got home she was not there. I wondered what she could have possibly been thinking or doing on our first night apart in a month, but Karen was a headstrong woman that I believed could shake it off and see the reality of the situation. At first, I was going to try to do a little work, but I decided that I needed to let my brain take a break. Slow jams floated through the apartment while I engaged in some quality time with myself—no phone calls, no television, and no distractions. It was just my slow music, my fish, and me.

A while back, my father told me that watching the fish in his aquarium relaxed him if he had had a stressful day, or if he just wanted to ease his mind. Like father, like son; I had an aquarium. Watching my fish made me notice something that I had never noticed before. In the tank there were ten fish, and as I studied their actions, they seemed to mimic the accounts of my life. There was one particular fish that was always being chased by the same four fish. After being chased by any of the given four, he would huddle with five other fish, and the other four would not come near him. As a metaphor of my life, the lone fish represented me and the four that pursued him on a regular basis portrayed Alicia, Natalie, Karen and Vanessa. The other five that he huddled with represented my boys and my cousin.

As I looked deeper into the matter, they represented my life in more ways than I thought. Look at it like this. The aquarium, as a whole, represented Atlanta. The first two fish I bought and put in the tank were J-Rock and me. I started off by adding one fish at a time. The next fish I added, after the initial two, I viewed as Alicia. Those three fish were cool with each other and there were no problems until the Vanessa fish came. After the Vanessa fish, I added four more fish, all at one time—Troy, Smoke, Alex and Zack. Once I added them, the Alicia fish started to shy away and only came near me when I ventured away from the others, then she would chase me. Later on, I put the Natalie fish in, which by price was the most expensive; and last but not least came the Karen fish. Karen's fish was a little discreet in her pursuit. She did not chase me as Natalie and Vanessa did, but only followed me when I was away from the others. If I turned and noticed that she was there, she quickly changed directions and ducked behind some rocks. Another thing I noticed was that the four fished who chased me never congregated together. They always stayed to themselves. Alicia's fish used to hide in some plants I had in the tank. Sometimes I would forget that she was in the tank, just like in reality.

That night, I realized by watching the fish

act out my life that I had to keep Alicia on my mind at all times if I wanted to maintain what we had. Up until that point, every time a new fish came into my life, I forgot about her and the fact that she was there from the beginning. There my life was right in front of me. Now what was I going to do about it? I did not know right then. Hopefully, the morning would hold some answers for me.

That next day, I looked at my phone and noticed that Karen had called me twelve times between the night before and that morning. If she called me that many times, maybe she had something heavy on her mind. I called her back.

"Hey, Karen," I spoke as she answered the phone. "What's up?"

"Do you know how worried about you I was last night?" she asked with a concerned tone in her voice. "You leave upset and I hear nothing from you until now? That's not how you treat people."

"I was here at home taking some time to be by myself."

"But you were gone for at least three hours! I know this, because that's how long I stayed there hoping you would return so we could talk."

"I'm sorry. I just needed to be alone."

"Well, next time, could you just call me

back and let me know something?"

"I didn't think you wanted to talk to me for a-while after the way I acted yesterday."

"But you were absolutely correct in what you said."

"I was?"

"Yes you were. Look, over the last week, you and I have said some things to each other, and things got a little out of control."

"What do you suggest we do to keep us on track?"

"I was going over our work last night, and we have done more work than I thought. We have six completed episodes, four more outlined and ideas and material for at least ten more."

"We did that much work?"

"Yes we did. How about this? We work around the clock Sunday through Friday. After work Friday, we don't pick back up until Sunday evening. We can't completely get our lives back just yet, but we can get a little."

"Sounds good to me."

"I guess I'll see you tonight."

"Can you pick up some more Cap'n Crunch on your way over, since you ate the last of it?"

"Bye, smart ass."

Well, I managed to get a small portion of my life back. Now I could catch a club or two, a football game, or something. Life really had a way of working itself out. Since it was Sunday and football season was going on, I watched the game until Karen arrived. Once she got there, it was back to work until next weekend.

11

What Goes Around, Comes Around

After we decided to use the weekends as refreshers, things became a lot better between Karen and me. You would not believe the amount of tension that was lifted off of our shoulders. We had become friends again. Karen and I opened up to each other, and after a while it seemed as if we were becoming best friends. No longer did she care who called me or whom I went out with. I believe that it had something to do with this new guy she had been talking to. In my eyes, Allen was an arrogant, self-centered son of a bitch that was considerably older than Karen. True, the dude had money, but he wanted the whole world to know it, as if the Mercedes and the Jaguar were not enough. The thing that Allen failed to realize was that Karen was a person who could not be bought. She was too independent and headstrong. Every situation has two sides. The good thing about the situation was that her attention was diverted from me to him. The bad thing was that everything had to be on his time.

"André," Karen started. "Would you mind if we took Thursday night?"

"Why?"

"Because Allen has tickets to this play he wants me to see with him."

"Can't it wait until Friday night or Saturday?"

"He has to leave town on Friday."

"Well, if that play is more important that our careers…"

"I know where you are going with this, so stop it."

"I'm just kidding. Do what you like. I'm sure I can find something to occupy my time."

"Thanks, Dré," she said kissing me on my cheek. "You're a sweetheart."

"I know I am."

"And don't go runnin' off to your cousin's lil' nasty strip club."

"Who me?"

Thursday night came and I was Karen-free. I tried to call up the homies to see if they wanted to go to the sports bar, but all of them were occupied. I forgot that in order for them to go out on the weekends, they had to spend quality time during the week. While I was trying to figure out what to do, I got a phone call.

"Hello," I answered.

"What's up, sexy?" asked a strangely familiar voice.

"Not too much. Who is this?"

"Who do you want it to be?"

"Gabrielle Union," I said picking up on the voice.

"What!"

"Stop playin' Natalie."

"How did you know it was me?"

"Because you have a little voice and just then you sounded like a little girl trying to be grown and sexy."

"Anyway... I was calling to leave you a message. Didn't think you were going to pick up. I thought you worked at night until Friday."

"I'm off tonight because Karen has a date."

"What? You couldn't go to the game with me on a Saturday, but she has a date on a Thursday. You should kick her in her forehead."

"You stupid," I laughed. "Sounds like you're driving. Where you at?"

"Just got to Buckhead. I was on my way to your side, so I thought about you. Can I come and pick you up since you are free tonight?"

"Where are we goin'?"

"Let's go to the Silver Dollar. I feel like shootin' some pool and having a couple of drinks."

"That's what's up. Call me when you get downstairs." Natalie picked me up and we went to the Silver Dollar to get our pool on. On the way to the sports bar, she joked about me wearing blue jeans. If I was not going to work or to the club, I had on khakis because in my eyes, those were my jeans.

When we got there, all of the tables were full. We sat at the bar until one became available. While we were laughing and joking around, I noticed a guy walk in with a woman. I could not tell who he was from a distance, but he looked familiar. I paid him no mind at first, but there was something about him that kept bothering me, and Natalie noticed it.

"Stop lookin' at that man's woman," Natalie joshed.

"I'm not lookin' at her. I'm lookin at the guy."

"Is there something you need to tell me?"

"You got jokes. I think that's the guy Karen is supposed to be out with, but that's not Karen."

"Want me to go over and find out?"

"That's okay. If it is that asshole, I'll find out in a minute."

"Come on, Dré, a table is open. Later for him."

I had only seen Allen once, but I was almost one hundred percent positive that was him. It was around ten-thirty, so maybe he had dropped Karen off already. I tried to call her to make sure she was okay, but her voicemail kept picking up like her phone was off or her battery was dead. I bothered not to call her house because even if she was there, she was not going to answer the phone. For a split second I thought maybe that wasn't Allen and I was overreacting.

At the close of our second game, the guy and the woman he was with (who looked like a prostitute) took the table beside us. I could not remember exactly how Allen looked, but that dude looked a hell of a lot like him. While I was shooting, he confirmed my thoughts when I overheard him say something about his house, a Mercedes, and a condo in Florida. That had to be him. I wanted to find out for sure.

I said approaching their table, "What's up,

man, wanna shoot one?"

"I'm always game for a little competition."

"Marcellus." I extended my hand.

"Allen Long. Nice to meet you." Identity confirmed.

"Do you want anything from the bar, while I'm going?" Natalie asked.

"Drinks on me," Allen interrupted. "Just go up there and tell the bartender to put it on my tab."

Once I had confirmed his identity, I couldn't just come out and ask him about Karen. I had to figure out a way to make him bring it up. Before I did, I had to figure something else out. What in the hell did Karen see in this dude? He did not look like the type of guy that Karen would be interested in. He was shorter than she was, he wore too much jewelry, and he talked too much. Then again, maybe it was his mouthpiece that got him in the door with Karen. She was a sucker for some sweet words and attention.

"So, Allen, What kind of work do you do?"

"I'm in commercial real estate. What about you?"

"I work for Black Reign Networks."

"No shit? I was dealing with this freak that works out there."

"Oh really?" I tried to control myself. "What's her name?"

"You probably wouldn't know her. She's big time over there. As a matter of fact, we were together tonight."

"Oh, that wasn't her that went to the bar with my lady friend?"

"Hell naw! I dropped that bitch off right after dinner."

"What happened?" I asked, tightly gripping my pool stick. "If you don't mind me asking."

"Through the entire dinner she kept talking about some dude named André. It was André this and André that."

"Damn. That must have been some ol' bullshit."

"You know? If she wanted to talk about André so much, she shoulda gone out wit that nigga, instead of me."

"I feel you, dog."

We were in mid-game when the ladies returned from the bar with the drinks. I don't know what it was about a man that had a gang of money that made him think he could talk to people any way that he felt.

"Damn, girl!" he said as he started to raise his voice towards his lady friend. "What in the hell took you so long?"

"It was crowded around the bar," she explained.

"I don't give a damn. When Al Long is in the building, everybody is on his time. You almost as bad as that bitch I was with earlier." As soon as he used that word, Natalie looked at me as my facial expression was rapidly changed.

"Please," I pressed. "If you don't mind, I would rather you not use that term in the presence of my lady friend."

"And who the fuck are you supposed to be?"

"Let's not take it there. We're havin' a good time. Let's not ruin it."

"André, let's go." Natalie grabbed my arm and tried to pull me away.

"André? I thought you said your name was Marcellus?"

"It is. André Marcellus Marshall, Executive Producer at Black Reign Networks."

"Oooh, now I see. You're the guy that Karen couldn't stop yapping about. Now I can see why she chose to go out with me."

"André," Natalie urged. "Just walk away."

"Yeah, André, walk away. Listen to your bitch."

That was the one that did it. I carefully pushed Natalie aside and tried to knock Allen's head off. We rumbled in the billiard room for at least five minutes before security pulled us apart. When they pulled us apart, I begged the bouncer for five more minutes. After I calmed down and my vision came back into focus, I saw Allen sitting in a chair holding napkins up to his nose, which was bleeding something awful. Natalie took me out of the bar and drove me home. When we got to my place, she accompanied me upstairs so that she could tend to my hand and make sure I was okay before she went home. Karen was sitting on the couch in the dark when we walked in.

"What happened to you?" she asked when she noticed that I had blood on my shirt and I was holding my hand.

"You know your friend Allen? Send him a get well card. By the way, this is my friend, Natalie Simms." The two ladies shook hands and Natalie asked me where the kitchen was so she could get some ice for my hand.

"What did you do?"

"Let's just say that with all of the money and mouth that he has, Big Money Grip shoulda bought a bodyguard."

"How did all of this come about?"

"Natalie and I went down to the Silver Dollar to have some drinks and shoot pool. Shortly after we got there, ya boy came in with another woman. I didn't know who he was at first, but I knew he looked familiar. We started shooting pool against each other so I could make sure that it was him. When I mentioned Black Reign, he brought you up and what happened between you and him tonight. To make a long story short, he said some outlandish things, called you and Natalie both bitches, and I lost it."

"Well, Dré, I'm going to call it a night, I have a team meeting tomorrow." Natalie kissed me on the cheek and told me to call her when I got some time.

"This is all my fault," Karen sighed as Natalie left.

"How is it your fault?"

"I was selfish," she said as she slid closer to my end of the couch. "You going to the game with Natalie had nothing to do with work. I just didn't want you to go. Don't ask me why, because I can't answer that question."

"Whether I went to the game or not, I'm not going to stand there while someone blatantly disrespects any of my friends."

"I'm sorry Dré. I guess this was a case of *what goes around, comes around.* You think?"

"Not really. It was just a case of Allen should have just kept his mouth closed and played the game. If he would've done that, he wouldn't have caught an unnecessary ass whoopin'."

After I let my hand sit in some ice to bring down the swelling, Karen and I turned in for the night. While Karen showered, I called Natalie to let her know everything was okay and to make sure she got in safely. As we were lying in bed, Karen tried to tap into my head to see whether or not it was feelings for her that caused me to react the way I did. Ten minutes of probing passed and she came up with nothing. She gave up and went to sleep. If it was feelings, I could not let her know that. Some things are better left unsaid.

I was always told that violence never solved anything. In the case that had transpired between Allen and me, it may not have been right, but it felt so good. Two days after the incident, word about the fight got back to the network, and my boys were curious to know how everything went down and why I did not tell them about it. Like I said before, some things are better left unsaid. Had I told them, they would have been ready to start an unnecessary war, and George Dub-ya had already done enough of that. If Jerome had found out, he would have taken it so personal that one would have thought Allen had disrespected him. That's just how tight J-Rock and I were. In the eyes of the women that found out about the incident, I became some sort of hero to them. This brought more attention to me than I was already getting. I tried to down play the entire situation because in reality, it could have wound up as bad publicity for the network. How would it look if one of Black Reign's executive producers would have gotten arrested in the aftermath of a bar room brawl? I had to be more in control of my actions. It wasn't like I was a violent person, but you can only push a man so far.

Through some extensive convincing, I finally got Karen to stop apologizing because she felt that it was her fault. She kept going on about the fact that if she would not have been selfish and told Allen that his Thursday night invitation had to be declined, then I would have never got into the fight. The altercation did add a little more to the feelings that Karen had been developing for me because I had defended her honor. I didn't see it as a big deal. Karen acted as if I'd saved her life and she was in debt to me. She had flowers delivered to the office for me, cooked every night, pampered me like I was the King of Atlanta. If I told you that I did not enjoy it, I would be telling a lie. The attention was nice, but after a while, it started to get a little annoying. As bad as I wanted to see exactly how far she would go, my conscience would not let me.

Karen carried on like that for about two weeks, and then she finally brought it to a screeching halt after I took a Tuesday night off to celebrate Natalie's birthday with her. Once again, she got a little jealous but did not react like she did before. She pouted a little bit before I left and gave me the silent treatment when I returned later that night. It was okay because I know how some women can be sometimes, and I do emphasize the words…*some women.*

12

King of Diamonds

Since the success of my presentation, my new position of Executive Producer/Head Writer and the accompanying pay increase, I became one of the big dogs. I made history at Black Reign Networks by advancing in the company in the shortest period of time. I'd become the youngest executive producer since Karen. My salary jumped from five to six figures. I was on my way. My dreams of being a part of the upper class were coming true. Grandma's baby had made something out of himself.

If I was going to be a-part of the upper class, I had to look the part. Being 26 years old, I still had a Cash Money mentality. I had it, so why not show the world. Alicia wasn't there to celebrate with me, so I called on the one person I knew I could have a good time with, Natalie Simms. One Saturday afternoon, Natalie and I were on our way to lunch when I spotted a Cadillac dealership and pulled in.

"What are you doing?" Natalie asked as I pulled into the dealership.

"I'm going to buy a new car."

"You don't just up and decide to buy a new car just because you see a car lot."

"Let me tell you something. For years I've dreamed of the day that I could walk onto any lot and buy the car of my choice. I can do that now."

"On the way to lunch? Come on now, this is a little too spontaneous."

"Now is just as good a time as any. Besides look at this truck, it's old."

"But it's paid for."

"It's time for change."

"Okay, okay. Just be careful. You know what happened to MC Hammer."

When we got out, I began to walk around. There were so many cars that I liked, I just couldn't make up my mind until I walked down one particular row of cars. There it was—the new Cadillac Escalade with factory chrome wheels. To me, this was the Sports Utility Vehicle of all times. My grandfather told me when I was young that every black man should have owned at least one Cadillac in his lifetime.

The salesman asked as he approached, "Can I help you two with anything?"

"Yes sir, you can. I'd like to purchase a

vehicle today."

"Okay. If you could just follow me, I'll show you some nice used cars." Because Natalie and I had just come from playing basketball, he took one look at our apparel and thought that I couldn't afford the car I was looking at.

"I don't think you understand." I said as I laughed. "I want a new car."

"A new car?"

"One of those," I said pointing to the row of Escalades.

"You do know the starting price of a sports utility like this, don't you?"

"Do you see concern on my face?" Natalie began to get disgusted at the way the salesman was acting, so she decided to join into the conversation.

"You know what, André? Maybe we should take our business across the street to Lincoln. I think a Navigator would be better for a Black Reign executive."

The salesman realized that we meant business and changed his tune. He promoted the Escalade as if he was in a commercial. The more he tried to sell the car, the more Natalie and I played with him. At one point in the conversation, we got in the car to leave. The salesman did everything but jump on the hood of my truck to keep us from going across the street to the Lincoln dealership. After we made him sweat and make a complete ass out of himself, I took the car for a test drive. I had to have it.

Once the paperwork was completed and the sale was final, I was the proud owner of a Cadillac Escalade. If only Grandma could see her baby now. Nat and I decided to go home and change because we were going to paint the town red in my new car. I was riding nice, living lovely, and had a Diamond by my side. My initial plan was to go to dinner and then hit a couple of clubs. All of that went out the window when Natalie told me that her team was having a banquet and a press conference to introduce the team. She asked me to be her date for the night and I obliged her request. I was getting ready to be surrounded by basketball players, the team owner, some Atlanta big wigs, and a host of other important people. The night began with a press conference at the all-new Freedom Arena, and we were dressed to impress. It was not planned, but our outfits coordinated perfectly. I had on a black, tailor-made, Italian silk suit that was accented with gold buttons. Natalie's apparel was a form fitting black dress that fell to the ground with a split on both sides that rose to mid-thigh. The straps that criss-crossed her back started at a gold ring in the middle of her chest and came together at two separate gold rings on each of her hips. Her long hair was swept up, which allowed the diamond earrings that dangled from her lobes to sparkle when the light struck them. If I must say, we were the sexiest couple in the entire place.

When we pulled up to the arena, cameras and reporters were everywhere. Thinking inside the box, I forgot that the Atlanta Diamonds were a nationally known, professional basketball club. The cameras were not just from local news networks. Reality started to set in as I was tried to avoid all cameras that could possibly broadcast Natalie and me to the world, especially with Alicia being the sports fan that she was. She watched *Sports Center* every night during football and basketball season.

That night, I found out that Natalie was very modest in her role on the team. Natalie was the main person that the management built their team around. She was like the *Michael Jordan of the ATL.* From the time we stepped into view, every reporter and cameraman tried to shove a microphone or a tape recorder in Natalie's face. I was cool as long as I was seeing local cameras. When I saw the ESPN camera, I got extremely nervous. The entire time she spoke with the press, she was holding my arm. All I could do was smile and maintain composure.

After the press conference, we found ourselves at the banquet. I sat with Natalie at the team table with the other players and their dates and companions for the evening. Out of all of the guys that I talked to, I was one of the few actually doing something with his life. Most of them were leeches holding on to the girls to get what they could. That was my perception of the situation. One guy that was dating one of the players didn't even work. He just lived off of her.

Through dinner I laughed to myself as these barbarians attempted to be the perfect dates. Natalie kept nudging me because I was commenting too loudly. I didn't care if they heard me because everything that I said was true. If they could not handle the truth, then that was their problem. In reality, I was the one who had no business being there. Alicia was supposed to be my superstar. I realized that I was allowing myself to get caught up already. How could I focus on one woman when I was allowing others to reel my attention and focus away from my main objective? My only defense for it was that at least I was dealing with high quality. I know that sounds like a sorry excuse, but that was how I thought at the time. Most men that have good women step out on their companions with scrubs. I was dealing with women of stature. Other than the history that Alicia and I have, she cannot compete. Knowing that, I still couldn't let go. We continued to have a fun evening until it was time for the banquet to come to a close. Natalie and I left with the night still very young. After about fifteen minutes of discussion, we decided to go to the sports bar to shoot some pool and have a couple of drinks. I knew right then that I was setting myself up. Though we had only known each other for a short while, Natalie and I were pretty tight. We were so alike, yet so different, that it was scary.

Once again at the Silver Dollar, Natalie and I opened up over Hennessy and Coke with a little Grand Mariner on the side. She told me about her last boyfriend and how he used her because she was getting ready to turn pro. Some people are a trip when it comes to money. After a couple of drinks, Natalie asked me about my love life. I decided to keep it real and tell her about Alicia. Natalie shocked me in her reaction when I told her the story behind Alicia and me. She asked while setting up for her next shot, “Do you think she’s the one?”

“I really don’t know. There was no true commitment established. She told me she loved me and I told her I loved her. Other than the fact that she’s supposed to move here after she graduates, nothing has been made official. Now with me meeting new people, it’s hard to maintain.”

“It’s not hard. You just have to want it as badly as she does. You strike me as the type of guy who has always been with his girl. When you left, you knew you wanted to be with Alicia and she knew it too. She just confirmed it when you got here. She didn’t want to tell you how she really felt while you were home, because she knew if she did, you would have second-guessed your move here.

She made a sacrifice so you could make it. She cared more about your well-being than her feelings for you."

"How do you know that?"

"Because the guy I was with before the last asshole was my best friend as well as my first love. He meant the world to me. He had an opportunity to go to Europe on international business. As bad as I did not want him to go, I couldn't stand in his way just because I couldn't go with him."

"So what happened?"

"He left without me telling him how I really felt. Now he is married to some French bitch, and every time I think about it, I want to just kill myself for not telling him how I really felt." Everything Natalie said to me that night made perfect sense. The more I thought about it, the more I realized how much Alicia really loved me. Natalie went on to tell me how she would understand if nothing more came out of us than a friendship. Because of her mistake, she didn't want to see me make one I'd regret. That turn of events really put an interesting twist on the evening. There I was thinking that after drinks, we were going to be so hot and bothered for each other that we'd go back to her place or mine. I guess that's what happens when you think with the little head instead of the big head.

The next morning I got the surprise and

shock of my life. There I was on *Sports Center* with Natalie. I couldn't believe it. In less than two minutes, my phone blew up. Every time I answered the phone, I prayed for it not to be Alicia. When I say everybody called, I mean everybody—Vanessa, Troy and the rest of the fellas, Karen, and a host of others. The only person that really mattered was Alicia. By the grace of God, she didn't call. Either she saw it and was too mad to speak or she missed it. I knew that if she hadn't caught it that morning, she had a few more times throughout the day to see it. All day long I was a nervous wreck. Somehow, God saw fit for me to ease by, because when she called, she said nothing about it. We casually conversed as we normally did, but it was no conversation that I had ever experienced with her. It was a good thing for me we didn't have videophones. If we did, my actions would have told on me.

Later on that day, I decided to go to the car wash over in Decatur to show off my new ride. You should have seen how thick it was. On Sundays in Atlanta, the car wash might as well have been a car show. When I pulled up, I realized that I was missing two things: rims and a system. Though the Escalade stood alone, for a man, they were essential. Once again I was the new face in the crowd, and all eyes were on me. The ladies were pushing Hondas, Infinities, and a few SUVs. The guys went all out with big bodies and old schools' sitting on 22's or better.

While I was waiting for an empty bay, I vacuumed the inside of my car, even though there was nothing to vacuum. I wanted to make it look like I was doing something. All the stares and pointing made me feel like a superstar. Countless girls pulled up to the vacuum beside me just to get a closer look at what I was doing. Not one person said anything until a midnight blue Range Rover pulled into the lot. Despite me being the man of the hour, even my attention was caught. The car door opened and out stepped the longest pair of legs attached to a brown-skinned woman. I was never into girls that wore basketball shorts and tank tops other than Natalie and Deena, a basketball player that I went to college with. She made them look good with the mid-top Air Force Ones. She wore a hat with her ponytail pulled through the back and a pair of Chloe shades with the heart in rhinestones at the bottom of the right lens. I wasn't normally attracted to women that tall, but it was something about her. Her exterior was kind of rugged and tomboyish but still sexy. The more I gazed at her, the more I started to feel as if I had seen her before. I couldn't picture it, but I had that feeling.

When the bay I was waiting for became available, I almost missed it because I was watching her. An excuse was needed in order for me to walk near her general vicinity. I could not find one reason until I pulled into the bay. I needed more change, and she just happened to be in the bay beside the change machine. It was time to make my move. As

I neared the machine, she was walking around to spray the front of her car. It seemed like it took ten minutes for me to get my dollar into the machine because by watching her, all of my motor skills were temporarily impaired. She noticed that I was watching and waved at me. It was time to strike. I managed to drum up a friendly conversation when I learned that she, too, was having the same feeling of de ja vu. The two of us tossed around a few places where we could have possibly seen each other, but still we came up empty.

"How long have you been in Atlanta?" she asked.

"Not long."

"What's your name?"

"André but you can call me Dré"

"I'm Shawna."

She was amazing. With a bronze complexion, Shawna stood a towering 6'5"—a true Amazon. Standing that tall, and with her build, she should have been a basketball player. I paused and took a good look. That was it. Standing in front of me was Shawna McKenzie, power forward for the Atlanta Diamonds. I knew I'd seen her somewhere before. She was at the table with Natalie and me.

"Now I know where we've seen each other.

I was at the banquet for the Diamonds last night."

"You're the guy that was with Natalie, right?"

"That was me."

Shawna was the player I was talking about that had the boyfriend that didn't work and was living off of her. The one thing that lingered in my mind was how a woman that fine and successful could allow herself to fall victim to a man like that. I wanted to ask her, but I did not want to intrude into her business. From the look in her eyes and her facial expressions, she seemed like she wanted to ask me about Natalie but, she refrained. Once we figured out how we knew each other, it affected the entire moment. It wasn't awkward to continue to talk to Shawna. It just put a damper on things because we were vibing with each other. The only barricade that stood between us was Natalie. Teammates they were; friends, I didn't think so, at least not yet. For me to ask her out wouldn't be violating anything because Natalie was not my girlfriend. Would it? Thoughts of Natalie and me, and how good things were between us curbed me from asking her teammate out. Shawna gave me her number anyway, and told me to call her if I changed my mind. It was obvious that she didn't care much about the man she was with, or should I say was with her.

All of this attention was not good for the ego of a small town guy. I'd never had this many women worth being with at one time in my life. I started to feel like I was in a real life episode of Flavor of Love. It started out with Lil Bit, Hometown, Diamond, Saditiy and Girl Next Door competing for me. The only difference was that I looked a hellavah lot better than Flavor Flav. Due to circumstances, Lil Bit and Girl Next Door were eliminated. Deep inside, I held a special place for each woman. I knew the day would come when I would have to choose one. Until that day came, I enjoyed the attention.

Following the car wash, I stopped by Smoke's house to show him the new wheels and tell him about my situation. Why did I do that? Smoke said that I was a jackass for not playing the role of the *The King of Diamonds*. I don't know why I bother telling my friends about my situations and encounters. While it's happening to me, they wished it was happening to them. Between Smoke and J-Rock, I was a saint and you and I both know I'm far from that. I left Smoke's and went home, and that's when the drama started. The first contestant on *As the Drama Goes Down* was Natalie. When I heard the stress in her voice, right then I knew she had talked to Shawna. I wanted to hear what she had to say, so I called back. As soon as she answered the phone, I got blasted.

"So what, now you trying to talk to

Shawna?" she asked in an ill voice,

"We met at the car wash. Besides, she knew who I was and my affiliation with you."

"Don't give me that bullshit, Dré. She told me that you tried to talk to her."

"I admit I stepped to her, but as soon as I realized who she was, everything changed."

"Yeah right."

"That is the truth." I had to be quick off the tongue to suppress the situation before it got too out of hand, and judging by Natalie's attitude, it was on its way.

"Look, Nat," I said in a soothing voice. "Why settle for a role player when I can have the star? Shawna is cool and all, but she can't handle me like you handle that basketball."

"Save all the smooth talk André." Why do women call me André when they are upset with me?

"I admit it. I did step to Shawna. Why? Because technically I'm single and she caught my eye, just like you did. When I realized who she was, that was the end of it. She's your teammate, and that would be disrespectful. Shawna is not worth me losing you as a friend. You and I have a special connection, and that bond gets tighter as the days go by. I don't know what the future holds, but if we're going to have anything, we have to have trust. Feel me?" For the remainder of the conversation, I knew I had her right where I wanted her. She still tried to act like she was upset but once again, the snake charmer had calmed the cobra waiting to strike. The *gift of gab* was something that I am thankful I inherited from my grandfather. If he knew I was using it the way that I was, I would immediately be rebuked as the devil that I was.

The second contestant was Karen. Instead of calling, she came by. Just like Natalie, she had an attitude. Apparently, seeing me with another woman caused some jealousy to rise. I thought that because Karen and I were just colleagues, it did not matter to her. I was wrong in that assumption. Karen tried to make it seem like me spending time with Nat would take my concentration away from my work. Like J-Rock said, she was worried about my focus being taken away from her. She had a good argument, but she was weak in her approach. This let me know that she could never be a prosecutor. Her feelings got in the way, and made her vulnerable to my defense. Karen was a hopeless romantic that masked feelings because of her position on the scale of social classes. She did not want to be taken advantage of by someone she felt to be beneath her.

Knowing this, my argument was powerful,

yet subtle. I had to play on her emotions in order to calm her. We went back and forth for about an hour. From the amount of emotion in her prosecution, I could tell that she wanted to be more than what we were. The situation was strange because of the amount of time that we spent together; in a way I grew accustomed to it and didn't want anything to take that away. Now my feelings were starting to weaken my own arguments of defense. Finally, we came to our closing arguments and we both agreed to try to keep our personal feelings out of involvement and focus on what was best for the upcoming show. Though nobody won the case, the prosecution and the defense got a little bit closer.

The final contestant was the reigning champion of my heart. Alicia called shortly after Karen fell asleep while I was watching the late game.

"Hey boo, what's up?" Alicia asked like nothing was wrong.

"Not much, just watching the replay of the late game," I said as I walked into the front room.

"I saw something interesting on *Sports Center* tonight. Does the name Natalie Simms mean anything to you?" I knew I wasn't going to just skate by that easily.

"Natalie is just a friend. She and I met at a club and she invited me to be her escort to the banquet. Besides, she knows all about you and our connection."

"Is that what they are calling it in Georgia?"

"I wouldn't exactly call it a relationship."

"Then what do you call it?"

"Two people trying their hardest to hold on until the day when they can finally be together physically, mentally and emotionally." Damn! I'm a smooth ass dude.

"You think you're a smooth talker, don't you?"

"I'm serious, Alicia. I know this is a rough time for me and you, but you have to trust me."

"It's not you I'm worried about. It's all the sluts and whores running around Atlanta with more hidden agendas than a little bit. You're living the life you've dreamed of and you deserve it. All I'm asking you to do is be careful."

My words struck a nerve and her whole demeanor changed. I convinced Alicia that she was number one in my life and it was hard being away from her holding those kinds of feelings. Whether I wanted to believe it or not, my bond with Alicia was stronger than I thought it was. I couldn't let go if I wanted to. The close of our conversation, along with the close of another day in Atlanta, had me reflecting on a host of things. The major thing that came up was the fact that I was confused as hell about which female I wanted, what I wanted, and how I wanted it. People (mainly my cousin and male friends) saw me as a man with a stable of beauties that was maintained rather well. They couldn't see inside my life and how mentally tormented I was trying to choose the right one without losing or hurting any of them. I didn't feel as if I could do it on my own. I felt that something major was going to have to happen in my life to make me choose. Until it happened, I had to hold on to what I had.

13

To Whom It May Concern

When we began to lay the foundation for the new show, I knew it was going to be hard work. Karen and I experienced an abundance of sleepless nights working on the show. It seemed like we were the only ones that put in excessive overtime. Every night, we stayed up until four or five writing. There were only two perks I saw in the whole situation—everything that went in to the show, I put there; and the fact that I was working side by side with the networks sexiest woman. Every hound that worked for Black Reign would have paid good money, or even killed, to be in my shoes. At that time, I didn't look at it like that. As far as Karen was concerned, she was merely a friend, colleague, and project partner. It was hard, but I tried my absolute best to keep it at that.

Karen was a phenomenal woman. Alicia was always my muse, but Karen became my inspiration in Alicia's absence. Whenever we sat down to write, the words came out like it was nothing. I thought it was just coincidental until the day came when I had to write alone due to a meeting that took her out of town for two days. I was pitiful. It took me two days to complete the dialogue for one scene. For most writers, that was average, but not for me. With her around, I cranked out at least three scenes a night. There were many nights that Karen and I fell asleep in the study at my place. Whoever happened to wake up first would wake the other for bed. Some nights we woke up just in time to get ready to go back to work. At the network, we used to take naps on our lunch hours instead of using them to eat. Due to the amount of time Karen and I were spending together, our colleagues started getting suspicious of what was going on between us. Plenty of rumors floated around that they thought we did not know about. At one time, I thought these rumors would take a toll on us and our working relationship, but they didn't. We paid them no mind, and kept on with our daily routine.

I also noticed how the attitudes of some of the ladies changed towards me. The ones that never looked at me twice went all out of their way to speak and do things for me. One day I walked into my office and there were a dozen red roses sitting on my desk from a secret admirer. Attached to the roses was a note that told me to check my email. The mysterious email told me that if I wanted to meet my admirer, then I should go to the lounge on the fourth floor during my lunch hour. This had to be somebody who knew that Karen hardly ever went to the fourth floor unless the Conrad Brothers were at the network. My admirer made it seem like she did not want to interrupt anything between

Karen and me. Maybe she just wanted to play her cards in private. I tried to pay it no mind.

The more I thought about it, the more my curiosity built. At about one o'clock, I called Karen's office and let her know that I wouldn't be joining her for lunch because of an errand I had to run. I made my way to the fourth floor just as a woman was walking into the lounge. I couldn't tell who it was, but I was getting ready to find out. I was nervous. When I walked into the lounge, I got the shock of my life. My secret admirer turned out to be my secretary, Melanie Isley. Melanie had never looked twice at me since the first day the temp agency sent her. She was sexy, sophisticated, and hard working. With eyes brown like Reese's Peanut Butter Cups and a little pug nose, she was a hot number at Black Reign. She had men with no business being on our side of the network breaking their necks just to get her to notice them. Melanie came from a family of money and was just working to have something to do. She could have had anything in the world. I guess it was me that she wanted.

"What took you so long?" She asked as she leaned on the table.

"I had a couple of things to take care of before I came."

"Surprised?"

"That's an understatement. The thing that puzzles me is that you never showed any signs of interest."

"I come from a professional family and that is what I try to be while I'm at work, but you make it very difficult."

"How so?"

"When I first came to the network, I couldn't believe that I would be working for such a handsome man. Most of the jobs that the agency sends me on are for old white men. Hopefully, my temp days can come to a close and I can work for Black Reign on a more permanent basis. I believe you are the man that can make that happen. Believe me when I say that I am willing to do anything to make that happen."

What in the hell was going on? Standing in front of me was the daughter of L.J. Isley, one of Atlanta's wealthiest stockbrokers. I was in a situation because I had a tremendous amount of money invested through her father's firm. If I rejected her, I could stand to lose a lot of money. On the other hand, if I accept her and her request, I was playing with fire. I didn't know how Karen would react to Melanie and me, even though Karen and I weren't together. I had to think quickly and come to a wise decision.

"This is what I'll do," I began. "I'll go to

personnel and tell them that you are the one that I want to be my permanent secretary. How does that sound?"

"That sounds good, but I was hoping to put in a little more work, if you know what I mean."

"I'm flattered, but I have a lot going on right now. It is not a good time. Maybe we can get together some other time." I ended the conversation and went back to my office. That was a close one. It would have been like playing with matches at a gas station had I dealt with Melanie. She seemed like she was a storm waiting to erupt. Despite her eagerness and straight-forwardness, she was good at her job. Melanie had me timed like clockwork. She knew what I needed and she knew when I needed it. If I had to go to a meeting, she had me on time. When I had deadlines to meet, she helped me keep on track. She was a great asset to me. I just hoped that she would not try to put her assets on me anymore. Right before my lunch hour ended I received a call from The Isley Firm. Apparently a long shot investment paid off and I had made one hundred and seventy-five thousand dollars. Was it coincidence, or did she have a hand in it? I didn't care because I had just made a heap of cash. I almost wanted to take Melanie across the street to the Hilton and give her what she wanted. That was just a thought.

I thought Melanie was the only one. It

turned out that she was just one out of many women that wanted to use me to get them into different positions—on the job as well as off the job. One would have thought that I was the owner of the Network the way the women approached me. It was funny because they were doing it so discreetly. I think that they thought Karen was still above me and didn't want to jeopardize my job. For a month straight, it was something and someone different. My email box had about twenty new messages a day from different women. One woman took the cake. Jody Raines was the bold one. Jody was a thirty-one year old, white woman with curly, brown hair that she wore long. It seemed like she didn't care about taking the precautions that the others took. She started dropping by my office almost every day. It may not have seemed like much, but Jody was the receptionist and her desk was on the first floor. That didn't stop her. Every chance she got to get away, she came right up to the fifth floor to see me.

One afternoon, Karen and I were in my office going over an idea that popped into her head while she was in her office. Jody came in and openly flirted with me like Karen wasn't even in the room. It was an awkward situation because of how Karen paid it no mind. Jody was new to the network, and I don't think that she knew who Karen was. I guess she saw me as someone she was attracted to and she wanted to see what was up. Jody hung around for about five minutes. Within in those five minutes, she managed to ask me out. I was nervous because I wanted to accept her invitation, but I could not bring myself to do so. I could tell that Karen was starting to get very aggravated with Jody's actions and behavior. After I turned her invitation down, I asked her to excuse Karen and I. Karen tried to ignore the situation, but it was eating her up. I knew she wanted to say something. After we had finished what we were doing, she got up to go back to her office. She turned at the door and said something to me that I never thought I would hear this professional woman say.

"André," she said before she opened the door to my office, "tell these gold digging whores of the network to concentrate on their jobs and leave you alone."

I was shocked to hear her talk in that manner—not Karen Union. She didn't even wait for me to reply. How had I gotten into this position? All I had done was get promoted and be myself. I didn't flaunt my position, nor did I use it to my advantage. Well, maybe once. There was one woman at the network that I had my eyes on since the first day I started working there, but never thought I could get next to her. This wasn't an average employee. She was an actress on *Tryin' Times*. Her name was Estacia Morgan. Estacia was a Hispanic woman from California. Smooth beige skin and dark eyes made this woman incredibly irresistible. Her smile was bright and her accented words were like magic spells that reeled me closer to her every time I heard her speak. I had been attracted to Latino women since the Puerto Rican girl I dated in high school when I first moved to South Carolina. Estacia was brought in for the new season. We were unsure on whether we were going to make her a part of the regular cast. Because of my new status, I now had a chance to get to her. I could approach her like a real man, or I could use my position to entice her into what I wanted. The fact that a new show was in the making would catch her interest, but I was going to do it the real way. Incognito is what I had to be to keep Karen from finding out.

One Monday morning, I went down to the set as she was just getting there. I introduced myself and it seemed like that was all I had to do. She invited me into her dressing room for a cup of coffee and conversation. We talked while make-up and wardrobe were getting her prepared for the day's taping. There she was sitting in a chair in a white satin robe. Only God knew what that robe was covering. Estacia was like no actress that I had ever met. She was so cool and levelheaded. I had made the right decision in my approach of just being myself. All she wanted was to associate with a normal person on a one to one basis. During the course of our conversation, Karen called me on my cell phone to inquire upon my whereabouts. I ignored the call because I didn't have much time left to see where Estacia's head was. The close of our conversation told the entire story. I invited her to spend an evening with me out on the town. She gladly accepted, and I left.

When I returned to my office, Melanie handed me an envelope. When I sat down at my desk and opened it, I almost fainted. The envelope contained two tickets to a comedy showcase for Karen and I but I was supposed to be going on a date with Estacia the same night. How in hell was I going to break this engagement with Karen in order to go out with Estacia? I had to think, and I had to think fast. I know; I'll just tell Karen that I had a prior engagement already scheduled. I quickly called down to her office and asked for a rain check. Karen was hesitant, but she didn't sound suspicious. I told her that I had to meet with my broker about an investment, which was technically not a lie because I did have a meeting with Mr. Isley during my lunch hour on that day. I didn't want to lie, but I had no choice. I didn't know why, but I was treating Karen as if she were more than a colleague.

That night, Estacia's Mercedes Benz limousine picked me up in front of my building. She wanted to have a simple evening. How in the hell was that possible parading around Atlanta in a limo? I found out; that is what all actors and actresses wanted. Because they were constantly in the public eye, they want to be seen as little as possible when they are out in the streets. Our evening led us to the neighboring city of Smyrna, a city on the outskirts of Atlanta. We started at this Italian restaurant called Vito's. It was the perfect place. It had dim lighting that made it hard for anyone to recognize us. From Vito's we went to a movie, and then back to her penthouse in Midtown. Once inside, she let it all hang loose, and I do mean everything. She left me sitting in her living room while she went into her bedroom. When she returned, she had shed the green dress, which drove me crazy the entire night, and slid into a colorful oriental bedroom ensemble. Estacia was beautiful. Her long, curly brown hair complimented her complexion. She walked into the kitchen and came back with a bottle of wine. We began to drink as we reminisced over the evening's events. She went on to tell me how she had never spent a simple evening out since she started gaining recognition for her acting. Everywhere she went; there was always a group of people in her face.

"Jew wanna know somesing, André?" she began with that sexy accent. "Jew are thee first man I've met seence I've been acting that treated me like a normal person."

"In my line of work, I work with celebrities every day. I know how it can be, so I try to remember that you all are normal people just like me."

"Thees is what people tend to forgit."

"Even with me just being an Executive Producer, you'd be amazed at how much attention I get." Oops. Didn't mean for that to slip out.

"Executive Producer? For what show?"

"I created a new show entitled *Matters of the Heart*. The show is a spin-off of *Tryin' Times* and is going to be a primetime soap opera that is supposed to air in September. You would be surprised at how many people approach me about being on the show." I did not mean to entice Estacia's interest in the show, but I had to. She seemed like she wanted to ask me how she could get on the show but didn't know how to ask. She asked seductively sipping wine. "Do jew have the cast completed?"

"Not yet. We have three lead roles open. One of those roles has to contain a woman from the *Tryin' Times*."

"I'm from *Tryin' Times*."

"Are you telling me that you are interested?"

"Jes I am."

I played devil's advocate for a minute. "How interested are you?"

"Thees interested." Estacia stood up and opened her robe to reveal to me a sexy beige body that was totally nude. She walked over to me and straddled my lap and looked me directly in the eyes. Desire and lust shot out of her coffee brown eyes as she grabbed my hands and placed them on her breasts. She rocked her head back and sensually bit her bottom lip as my hands cupped her soft chest.

I asked as I caressed her soft bottom, "Are you doing this because you want to or because you think that I have the power to get you a role on the show?"

"Both. Even eif my efforts are in vain, at least I will have received some enyoyment."

I continued to caress her chest, along with the rest of her body, as she called me *Papi*. (I love it when they call me Papi.) Estacia was a woman that knew what she wanted and how to get it. For the moment, I was her desired want, and I was going to give her what she desired. She bombarded me with an array of kisses to the neck and lips while I was taking of my shirt. Impatience was building because I was not coming out of my clothes fast enough for her. Estacia practically ripped me out of my pants and boxers. Before you knew it, she and I were making a real life love scene on the couch of her Midtown penthouse.

The next morning when I arrived to work, I received a horrible scare because sitting in my office was Karen holding a bouquet of fresh flowers. From the look on her face, I could tell that they weren't from her. She threw the card at me and stormed out of the office. When I read the card, I learned that the flowers were from Estacia and she was thanking me for a lovely evening. The P.S. was the killer. It read: "Hope to see you on the set." My lie had caught up with me and I had to react quickly. I had to mend things with Karen in order to maintain a smooth working relationship. I walked down to her office and found her at her desk crying. When she looked up at me, I wanted to just die right there on the spot.

"Why did you lie to me?" she sniffled.

"I don't know," I answered. "I thought that if I went out with someone else from the network, you'd get upset."

"I'm not upset about you and Estacia going out, I'm upset that you lied to me. You and I are not together no matter how it looks or seems. I just want you to respect me and not feel that you have to run around behind my back."

"I'm sorry. I didn't realize it meant that much to you. From now on, I'll be totally honest and straight forward."

"Thank you. That's all I ask. Now if you'll excuse me, I have to get myself together. We have work to do." I left Karen's office feeling as if I had just been in with the principal at elementary school. She was really latching onto me.

Karen called a meeting with the casting company in order to fill those last three roles open in the show. We all were tossing around suggestions about ideal people for the roles. When I brought up Estacia's name, Karen gave me a look that would have slain me if looks could kill. Though she didn't want her on the show because of our outing, Estacia fit the role, and she was selected for an audition. On our way back to my office, Karen asked me a serious question.

"Are you going to see Estacia again? And before you answer, I want you to think about it and be honest."

I paused for a moment. "If it means possibly destroying the working relationship that we have built, then I won't see her again."

"Honestly?"

"That's the truth. Estacia's cool and everything, but I don't see myself involved with an actress like that. They're too unstable. Every event in their life is like a scene from television. It's too dramatic for me."

Karen did not respond; she just smiled as we parted ways. I felt as if I had made the right decision. One thing I did have to hold on to is the fact that I had Estacia Morgan. She was one notch in the belt that I would never forget. I don't mean to sound like the average man, but I have to be real.

Most men only dream of sleeping with a famous actress; I had done it, and done it well. Now all I had to do was maintain while she was on the set and I'd be just fine.

14

Crosswords

"I am so drained," I said as I stretched. "This show is really kickin' my ass."

"You aren't the only one," Karen responded.

"I never thought, in a million years, that putting a show together from scratch was so much work."

"Wish you would have told me what I was getting myself into."

"You act like I knew. I've never done this before."

"Wanna take a little break?"

"What time is it?"

"9:30."

"Feel like playing a quick game of Scrabble?"

"Let's do it."

I went to get the Scrabble board while Karen cleared the table. How in the world could we play a word game, as hard as it was for us to concentrate on what we were previously doing? I never cared too much for playing the game with certain women because they liked to put words on the board that signified different things. At least I know Alicia used to do that. Sometimes we used to have an entire conversation without saying a word. That's just how tight Alicia and I were. Karen drew the lower letter giving her the opportunity to go first. From the first word she put on the board I knew it was going to be a long game. The word was *COMMIT*. After placing the word, she looked at me with a devilish grin on her face. I refused to respond; I was not going to get into that with her. No matter how I tried to avoid it, I couldn't because the only word that I could play for a good amount of points explained my answer. Using the I in COMMIT, I placed the word *AFRAID*.

"Punk," she mumbled.

"What was that?" I asked, placing my hand to my ear.

"Oh nothing. Just thinking out loud."

"Yeah right."

It took about ten minutes for Karen to study the board and make her next play. Playing off of the F in AFRAID, she spelled FAIL. I had no response for her word. I wanted to tell her that failure had nothing to do with it. Normally, in a game of Scrabble, you have difficulty seeing words using the tiles that you had. It was like Karen had a knack for seeing the words she wanted to see. In my next play, I used the L in FAIL to make the word *LOVE*. Once again, she gave me that devilish grin. This was supposed to be a game of strategy for points, but it was evident that Karen was more concerned with conveying a point than gaining points. Using the entire word of LOVE, she added an R to the end to start her word that spelled *REGRET*. From what I read in her play, she was trying to tell me that if I had a good *LOVER*, then there would be no *REGRET,* and that is totally true. I wondered if she was insinuating that she could be that lover for me.

I wanted to change the subject, so I took a couple of extra minutes to survey the board before I made my next play. It needed to be a word that had nothing to do with nothing. From the C in COMMIT, I played the word *COW*. Immediately after my play, Karen added ARD and made *COWARD* as if to tell me to stop trying to change the subject. I hated when people added letters to my words in order to make bigger words.

"Will you stop it?"

"Stop what? I'm just playing the game."

"No you aren't. You're trying to be funny."

"What's wrong? Truth hurt?" She started to get on my nerves and I almost quit but I didn't. That would have been the same thing as admitting that she was right. The more I tried to change the subject we were on, the more she kept it going. Eventually the hint was taken and Karen let it go, but just because she had stopped putting it on the board did not mean that she stopped talking about it.

"Why are you so afraid of a commitment?"

"I'm not afraid. I just don't know if I'm ready."

"When it comes to something like that, you're never going to be completely ready. You have to go with it."

"I understand that, but I would like to be a little more ready than I am."

"What about Alicia, do you think she's ready?"

"Don't know."

"If she's willing to move to Atlanta to be with you, I think that in it 'self says she's ready."

"True, but I'm not completely sure that it is her I want to be with."

"Then who do you want to be with?"

"Don't know that either. Right now, I'm going with the flow." I wondered what Karen was getting at since she never talked about Alicia unless

I brought her up. I believed that she was trying to see where my head was at so she could plan her next move. At the close of the game, I was the victor by twenty points. Karen's satisfaction was fulfilled without the victory. Getting up in my head was victory enough for her. After we put the game away and called it a night, my mind raced a mile a minute with random thoughts. I knew that Alicia was ready to commit to me. For some reason I could not bring myself to tell Karen how I really felt. I guess that was the coward in me. A man confused was a bad thing to be with a woman that had her sights set on you.

After that night, Karen really started to dig into me. Almost every day, she found some way to bring up Alicia's name. She was determined to find out exactly how I felt about my distant lover. The real question was: Could she accept the answer that she received, if I decided to give her one? No matter what, I stuck to my guns and kept her wondering, regardless of how persistent she became. A couple of days went by and she still had not received the answer she was looking for, so she ended whatever it was she was trying to do. I was glad, because at one point, I thought I was getting ready to cave in.

It only seemed that Karen had stopped her search for an answer. Since the night we played Scrabble, she started using words to pose different questions hoping for a response. When we would be at my place working, she would scribble a word on a piece of paper and slide it towards my laptop. The first time she did this, she wrote the word *CHANGE*. My interpretation went in two directions; she might have meant that change is what I needed, or she might have meant that things had changed between Alicia and me.

The next time it happened was at the office. She left an envelope with Melanie, my secretary, to give to me. Upon opening the envelope, I found an index card with the word *WILLING* written in bold, capital letters. Was she telling me that she was willing to be my lover, or was she telling me that I had to be willing to accept change or a commitment? I did not understand why Karen was playing word games. Maybe she was trying to get me to face my fears of a commitment. If that was what she was trying to do, then why was she beating around the bush? Why wouldn't she just come out and tell me what was on her mind?

At first Karen's word games were annoying me, but after a while, I became quite intrigued by the situation. She was going through a heap of trouble in order to see where my head was. One night, Karen confused the hell out of me. We were at my crib doing our nightly writing when she asked me some uncomfortable questions.

"Why hasn't Alicia been to Atlanta to see you yet?"

"We've been so busy with this show, it would make no sense for her to come and I not have time to spend with her."

"I don't think you want her to come."

"What would make you say something like that?" I asked as I stopped typing.

"I'm just saying that if it was me, and I had someone that felt the way she feels about you, wanting to come see me, I would've had them here to visit by now."

"What are you getting at?"

"I'm not getting at anything. I'm just stating the obvious."

"Well, it's obvious that you do not know what you are talking about."

"I think you are just afraid that if she does come here, she might mess up something between you and somebody else."

"Somebody else like who?"

"I don't know. It just seems to me that you are trying to keep her away from something or someone."

"Can we just drop this and finish up for the night?"

"Fine by me."

I have to admit that what Karen said to me started to hit home. Maybe I was trying to keep Alicia away from something, although I could not quite put my finger on what it was. Then again, this might have been Karen's way of helping me keep her away. In reality, I believed that it was Karen that did not want Alicia to come to Atlanta out of fear that I seeing her would make me realize what we had and both strengthen and reinforce our bond.

We continued to work until twelve o'clock that night. While we were getting ready for bed, I decided to give Karen a little chin check of my own to see how she would react and to see if what I was thinking about her was true.

"I think you're right," I began as I walked out of the bathroom. "I'm going to call Alicia and see if she can come down next weekend."

"Next weekend?"

"Yeah. Won't that be fun?"

"Next weekend is not good. We have to meet with Shane to go over the first five episodes."

"You can't do that by yourself?"

"Is this my show, your show, or our show."

"Our show, mostly mine."

"Okay then. I think that we both need to be there."

"But that's on Friday and we don't work over the weekend anymore. I think I'll still call her."

"It's still not a good time because I am scheduled to have my apartment painted Saturday and I have no place to stay because Charlene's going out of town."

"I guess I have to shoot for the following weekend."

My theory was confirmed. Karen did not want Alicia to come. She knew that her coming was not going to interfere with the meeting with the director on Friday. As for her apartment, if it was not already scheduled to be painted next weekend, it would have been. Now I really did not know about Alicia coming to see me because I was unsure of how Karen would act if she did come to Atlanta.

15

Unexpected Guest

December was in full swing and Christmas was right around the corner. I wasn't in the spirit of the holidays that year because it was the first time I was away from home and my loved ones. As a matter of fact, this would be the first Christmas that Alicia and I would be spending apart, outside of the couple we missed when I moved to South Carolina. For me, the holidays had not been the same since the death of my grandmother, but Alicia always managed to make them bright for me. How in the hell was I supposed to be happy without her around?

Another workday ended and Karen and I were on our way to my place. We began to go through our nightly routine of getting comfortable so we could continue working. As we came in and put our briefcases in the study, we proceeded to start preparation of our evening meal. The routine was simple. One would start the meal while the other took a shower. On this particular night, I really wished I could take all of it back. Usually, Karen would take her shower first and then me. For some reason I took my shower first and threw the routine out of sync. Why did I do that? I came out of the shower with a wife beater and basketball shorts on, feeling refreshed and ready to take over preparation of dinner. I felt funny. It was like the feeling that a person would have in a scary movie when they knew the monster was coming. When Karen left the room to get into the shower, everything started to move in slow motion. I tried to shake it off and continue to cook, but it was not working. While I stirred the spaghetti sauce, someone knocked on the door. I turned to the door and walked slowly towards it. The knock came again. I looked through the peephole and my heart dropped to the floor and I couldn't move. Alicia had finally come to town, at the wrong time. There was nothing going on between Karen and I other than a working relationship, but would Alicia see it that way at the moment, or even worse, would she give me a chance to clarify the situation?

When I opened the door, Alicia rushed in, grabbed me, and latched onto me like a child not wanting to leave his parent on the first day of school. Her emotions stabbed my soul every second she held onto me. On the inside, I was the happiest man in the world, but the situation wouldn't let me show it. When she let go, we moved to the couch and sat down. She started telling me how much she missed me, but her words lost my comprehension because at any moment, Karen was going to come out of the bathroom and the shit was going to hit the fan—twice. Sure as I thought it, the shower cut off and it became a waiting game. Was Karen going to come out in a towel, in one of my T-shirts, or in my robe? My mind became an oasis of thoughts and I was losing myself. As the bathroom door unlocked with the turn of the knob, I felt my entire body go numb. Karen approached and I watched Alicia's entire emotion change. When Karen finally came into full view, she was wearing short night shorts and a T-shirt that Alicia bought for me on my birthday last summer.

Alicia asked in a voice of confusion, "Who is that?"

"I'm Karen," she said as she extended her hand. "I've heard so much about you." I felt as if I was shrinking.

"That's funny," Alicia said with a scowl on her face. "André never mentioned anything about a roommate"

"Karen is not my roommate. She is my project partner for the soap opera I told you about."

"Looks like y'all makin' a soap opera," Alicia replied with much sarcasm.

"Please don't get the wrong idea. André and I are just co-workers who have been given a deadline. We have to spend day and night together in order to make it. I assure you that he and I have nothing going on. I know this looks odd and all, but we have to work outside of the office in order to make that deadline. I do hope you understand."

"How does your man feel about the situation?"

"I don't have a man." Karen's explanation started to have an impact on Alicia until she said that she was single.

Karen decided that we could take the night off and make it up tomorrow at the office and went home. Alicia and I sat down and caught up on lost time. While we were talking, another knock came at the door. I wasn't expecting anyone and the only other person besides Karen, Natalie and Alicia that knew where my place was J-Rock. When I opened the door, the nightmare continued. It was Vanessa. Obviously, my dear cousin had given her directions to my new place.

"Did I catch you at a bad time?" she asked.

"Yes you have."

"Baby, who's there?" Alicia called.

"Look. I'll have to holla back at you," I said, rushing her away.

"Call me."

Alicia was coming towards me just as I closed the door. "Who was that?"

"Jehovah's Witness."

"This time of night, yeah right."

"It was nobody, honest."

"Okay, nobody."

Mixed emotions ran through me the entire night as we sat and caught up on old times. I wondered if being in Atlanta had changed my views towards Alicia. One half of me was ecstatic that she had come to visit, but the other half was asking me why I was holding on to the past. I felt as if I was being sucked into a vacuum of confusion. As I spun around in this spiral of good versus evil, I wondered when this was going to end. Everything may be fine while she was there, but what would happen after she left and it went back to Karen, Vanessa, Natalie and God only knows who else? I should have never put myself out there like that. I made a mistake when I didn't stick to my game plan. I allowed myself to be drawn in by my temptations, my bachelor mentality and old habits.

The night grew old fast, and we retired to the bedroom. The scene was set, and the mood was right. It had been months since we had been with each other and I believed that I was getting ready to find out exactly how much she cared about me. I sat up in my bed, waiting for her to finish her shower and nightly primping. It seemed like she was taking forever; or maybe I was a little too anxious. When the door finally opened, the magic began. She appeared before me as an angelic being. The dim lights and the steam of the bathroom made Alicia seem more and more like she was heaven sent. I had never seen her in this way.

For the first time, in a long while, her body was in full view to me. Alicia approached the bed wearing a royal blue lingerie ensemble that would have made a preacher say Damn! If this was Victoria's Secret, then I wish she had told me this a long time ago. The flickering lights of the candles reflected off of her smooth, cream-coated skin. Her body was so perfect it looked unreal. I was afraid that at any minute I was going to wake up and the dream was going to be over.

I didn't awaken, and it wasn't a dream. Alicia crawled into bed like a panther stalking its victim. From the first kiss she laid on my lips, my body temperature rose—along with my lower man. The ends of her hair tickled my chest as she ran her tongue from my neck to my stomach. I thought that I would be a fool to let her slip away. She easily pressed her firm yet soft D-cups against my chest, allowing us to see eye to eye. When I looked at her face, I took a good look at the scar she had gotten from the accident. I usually wanted my women to be completely flawless, at least in the facial area. For some reason, that scar didn't matter. She kissed me once again and then asked me a fatal question.

"Dré, do you love me?"

I had been put on pause. Each of those words stabbed me in my heart, one word at a time. I thought back to the movie that Vanessa and I watched about two weeks ago and I could hear Della Reese speaking directly to me. She was saying: "Dré, you better be careful about the consequences of your actions. One night of passion can cause you a lifetime of pain. There's a thin line between love and hate." It was time to place all of my cards onto the table and call. I carefully rolled Alicia off of me and sat up in the bed.

"Look, Alicia," I said as I stood up. "I care a great deal about you. More than you can imagine. I know I told you that I loved you. I was caught up in the moment and it seemed like the right thing to say. I do love you, but we haven't been together long enough for me to be in love with you."

"Dré, I know, because I feel the same way. At that time, I missed you and it seemed like the perfect thing to say."

"I gotta be real with you. Since I've been in Atlanta, I've met a couple of people of the female persuasion and…"

"I know," she said as she cut me off. "I would be a fool to think otherwise."

"We have to be honest with ourselves in a

situation like this. True, everything might be fine while you're here, but what's going to happen in May when you graduate and are ready to move here? What if things have changed?"

"All I ever wanted was for you to be straight up with me. I can only imagine what life is like for you here. You're practically a celebrity. A successful brotha living alone in a big city like this is bound to attract some attention. I just trust that you'll follow your heart, and if it leads you in a direction other than me, then it is what it is. We're not kids anymore and break-ups are a part of life. I just hope we can be adult enough to remain friends. Just show me the respect that I would show you."

That conversation between Alicia and me sank deep into my soul, and I leaned back against the headboard. I did not know what to think, nor did I know what to do or say. The sexual mood that had begun was brought to a screeching halt. All I could do was put my arms around her and lay there. I had a lot to think about. Lying next to me was a beautiful and intelligent black woman that knew me almost better than I knew myself. All I had to do was say the words and she would be mines forever. The question was: Could I tell her that I was totally hers? Atlanta had laid the bait, and I believed that I was hooked. Now, I could do one of two things. I could let it reel me in or let the ATL tell the story of the one that got away. Only time would tell as my head swelled with thoughts of a new day.

The next morning as I drove to work, my mind wandered and I started to reflect on my first couple of months in Atlanta. I had one question—what was wrong with me? As hard as I fought to remain as faithful as I could, with the exception of the *bathtub boricua* and Estacia, I couldn't make love to the one that I really wanted to make love to the most. I felt that while Alicia was alone at my place, she was questioning whether or not I had slept with Karen. If there was any belief that Karen and I were just colleagues, it's probably gone now. When I got to work, Karen was waiting in my office. She had the same look on her face that I had been carrying all morning.

She asked, "Is everything alright between you and Alicia?"

"Why do you ask?"

"Because; you have on blue jeans and sneakers."

"What does that have to do with anything?"

"You never wear jeans and sneakers unless you are going to the car wash or over to your cousin's apartment. Now what's wrong?"

"Honestly, I don't know. Some things happened last night that may have tremendously affected the relationship between Alicia and me."

"What happened?" As if she really wanted to know.

"Nothin'."

"Now you are confusing me."

"Nothing happened. She wanted to make love to me, but I couldn't. As hard as I fought to let opportunities pass me by in order to be true to her, all my fighting was in vain." Why was I discussing this with Karen?

"So what now?"

"I don't know that either. I feel like she's at my place right now, questioning everything that I have told her since I've been here. To top things off, our working relationship didn't look like a working relationship, at least not last night."

"Well for your sake, I'll stay out of the way. We'll just have a lot of work to catch up on when she leaves. Besides, we could use a little break from each other. You were starting to get on my nerves."

"Ha ha, very funny. I guess that'll help a little."

"Listen, I have to get to a meeting. Will I see you for lunch?"

"Not today. Alicia and I are getting together for lunch. Can I catch you tomorrow?"

"Okay."

Somehow, I don't think that those were the words that Karen wanted to hear, but that was just how things were. It really got thick when Alicia came to the network to meet me for our lunch date. I was standing at Karen's car when she pulled into the staff lot. I could tell by the look on her face that our first day was already starting off on a bad note. Alicia and I ate lunch at a café about two blocks from the network. Why is it that when you are with someone, people that don't normally pay you any attention go out of their way to speak to you? Every woman that worked at the network seemed to come through that particular café that day. If they had just come in, eaten, and then left, I would have been cool. But no, they wanted to speak and wave. This didn't do anything positive for my current situation. I looked like quite the ladies' man at the wrong time. Every woman that spoke seemed to upset Alicia even further.

"Aren't you quite the ladies' man?"

"It's not like that."

"Yeah right."

"Look, I know you might be feeling like your trip to Atlanta was in vain, but you have to believe me when I tell you that I am not involved with anyone here."

"Why should I believe that? First, I see you on national TV with another woman and then I come all the way here to surprise you for Christmas and find Karen barely dressed in a T-shirt that I bought you. To be honest, I don't know what to think right now."

"Have I ever lied to you?"

"No you haven't, but you do have a tendency to not tell me the whole story."

"I know what you're gettin' at. Whether you believe that Karen and I are just colleagues is to be determined. She and I are strictly friends that have been placed on a critical assignment."

"Can we just drop it and eat?"

I couldn't tell if I was helping or hurting the situation. When Alicia dropped the entire situation completely, she only dropped it until Vanessa started blowing up my Blackberry. She was relentless in her attack. Common sense would tell a person that if you text someone and they don't get back with you, they are busy. That's what I get for dealing with people who don't have a normal thought process.

My lunch hour flew by and I was back at the network. Karen didn't say too much to me for the rest of the day. The only conversations that we had were about work. There was none of our usual joking and casual talks about anything and everything. It was strictly professional, just like before my presentation with the Conrad Brothers.

Upon the end of business for the day, I returned home and found the shock of my life. From the front door to the dining room, were red rose petals and the apartment was dimly lit with candles. I stepped back into the hallway in order to look at the number on the door to make sure I was in the correct apartment. Alicia had set the scene, and I was anxious to see what was next. When the petals came to an end, I found Alicia sitting at one end of the dining room table looking so beautiful. I tried to speak, but she motioned for me to not say a word as she pointed at the chair for me to sit in. To be real, it looked like a *Basic Instinct* scenario, but I didn't think Alicia was like that—I hoped. We ate dinner in silence as a certain mood built up, but it wasn't a sexual mood. It was more emotional. Our meal ended and Alicia broke the silence. This time, she laid all of her cards on the table.

"I'm sorry, Dré," she apologized. "I didn't mean to jump to conclusions. I lost sight of who you are and who you've always been. People like you, and most of the people who have liked you over the years have been women. It's just that I care so much about you. I can't imagine you being with another woman."

"I understand, because I feel the same way."

"I just have to get past a few things."

"Like what?"

"After you left Fayetteville, me and Shawn got closer. Regardless of how things were while you were still there, I couldn't let him in because of the feelings I had for you."

"You've been having these feelings about me since then?"

"I've loved you since the fourth grade, but I could never tell you. I figured if we got into something while we were young, it would've ended in disaster and we would have never had the friendship that we have now."

"But what does Shawn have to do with anything?"

"Shawn put me through so much shit after you left. I started to fall in love with him and he used my emotions against me. He started runnin' around on me with girls from other schools and I had no idea. If it had not been for him, I would have never gotten this scar on my face."

"What do you mean?"

"The night I got into that car accident, I had just found out that he was cheating on me. I was home from A&T for the weekend, planning to surprise him for his birthday. Me and Danielle were in the mall when him and some girl walked past the store we were in, holding hands. When I walked out to confront him, he acted like he didn't know who I was. I was so hurt and pissed off. I shouldn't have been driving, but Danielle couldn't drive a stick. We were on the expressway heading back home and I was driving like a maniac. This car started coming into my lane and I jerked the wheel and lost control of the car, ran off the road, and hit a telephone pole. The only thing I remember after that was waking up in the ambulance. From that moment, I promised myself that I would never let my emotions cloud my judgment concerning men and trust."

"But what about me?"

"André, you have always been the exception to all of my rules. I hold you higher than I hold any man besides my father. I can't help but to trust you, because you know more about me than anybody. That's why I was so calm last night—emotions versus reality. I know you would never do anything to intentionally hurt me, but I'm still careful."

"I never knew you felt this strongly about me. My bad for not telling you everything."

"It's okay because I know you. Did all the girls you messed with or dated back home know the extent of our relationship?"

"Not all of them. It's not that I was trying to

hide you from anyone, but I know how some women can be when you tell them that your best friend is a female."

"I'm a female, Dré. I know all too well."

"So what now?"

"If we are going to have anything solid in the future, I have to trust you. I have to trust that if I am not the one you want to be with, you will tell me. The same goes for me, even though you are the only man that I've ever wanted to be with."

In one romantic evening, Alicia and I reconciled and went back to the way things were before I left to come to Atlanta. Alicia and I spent a wonderful week together. It was like old times again. Chillin' at the club, late night talks, shopping together and reminiscing about old times made me think that if I held on tight enough, I could keep her, but my new life was just as good. I didn't know where those new thoughts came from, but it was reality. Maybe it was me mentally preparing me for Alicia's departure.

Christmas break was coming to a close and spring semester was on the horizon. It was time for Alicia to return for her final term as an undergraduate student at Franklin Memorial University. After she got back home, I had five months to either let her go and move on or keep what we had together and tighten the seams. In my heart, I honestly felt that this was going to be the last time I saw Alicia before the summer due to her cruise plans for spring break with her sorority sisters and friends.

16

What Are We?

The drive to the airport brought on a familiar feeling. It felt like the feeling I had when I left for Atlanta. When Alicia boarded the plane, I couldn't help but feel like that would be the last time I ever saw her. When Flight 704 flew out of sight, it took a piece of me with it. It sounded strange, but an uncle told me that you always want something more when you can't have it right then. He also told me that if you felt strongly about someone and you let them go, if they come back, that shows how strong it was to begin with. The ring of my cell phone interrupted my thoughts.

"Hi, Dré," said an unfamiliar voice. "You are a hard man to catch up with."

"I'm sorry, but I don't know who this is."

"This is Liberty. We met at Club Ebony a while back."

"It's still not registering."

"The last time I talked to you, you were on your way to work and you said you would get back with me."

"Oh. Your number must have been the one in my phone that I didn't recognize."

"You should have called. I would have refreshed your memory. Anyway, what are you doing tonight? It's been a while since I've seen you and I was wondering if we could get together or something."

"Well, at this moment, I'm free. What did you have in mind?"

"How about dinner and a movie? There is a new movie out by Alonzo Gladston called *Two and a Half Years*. I've been dying to see it. They say he's gonna be the next Tyler Perry."

"That sounds good," I said as I began to walk to my car. "So how do you want to do this? I could pick you up, or do you want to meet me at my place?"

"How about I come to your place around seven?"

"That's straight. I live in the Royal Winds. Just ask for 1026. I'll tell the front that I'm expecting you."

"The Royal Winds in Buckhead? Damn, Mr. Man."

"What?" I asked.

"Only doctors and lawyers live there," she said with a hint of excitement in her voice.

"What do you do?"

"We'll talk about that later. See you at seven."

Look at me. Alicia was barely out of sight and I was already on the prowl. I couldn't help it. I craved female attention. I shouldn't be that way, but that's just me. With a new night ahead of me, I felt that a new outfit was in order. I shot by the Lennox Mall and then back to the crib. Karen had been there and had slid an envelope under my door. I opened it to find a note.

My Dearest Andre

I know your friend was in town and I know the two of you had some catching up to do. I don't know how to tell you this but my life has been miserable this past week without you. Even though we saw each other at the office, I'm not used to it being like that anymore. Do you know how hard it was for me to be at my place alone? I've gotten so used to being with you. I really need to see you ASAP. I miss you like crazy.

Karen

Now shit was starting to get thick. The way things were going, I expected something like this to happen. I tried to give it the benefit of the doubt because of what Karen and I were trying to accomplish for Black Reign. What was I to do?

I called Liberty and broke our engagement for the evening with ease. After that, I called Karen over so we could talk. At about 6:30 she arrived looking as lovely as ever. Even in jeans and a sweater, she was sexy. Before I had a chance to say a word, Karen wrapped her arms around me and pressed her soft lips against mine. When she pulled away I looked into her eyes. I could see the chains of depression release from her mind and soul. She was free again now that she was in my presence. The more we talked, the happier she became.

"I didn't know what to do," she began. "It was hell being in my apartment by myself. I couldn't even get comfortable in my own bed."

"It couldn't have been that bad."

"You just don't understand. I felt like I was in prison. While we were at work, it was like recess time when I was allowed to see you. At quitting time, I was hauled right back to my cell, where I waited for the next day." I was shocked that she felt this way and had said nothing before.

"It's time for me to stop beating around the bush and tell you how I feel."

"And how is that?" I inquired.

"Since October, you and I have been with each other a lot. It was more than I was used to. I found strong favor in you because you are so much fun to be around and so easy to talk to. When I first interviewed you, I knew there was something special about you just by the way you spoke. You had me hanging on every word. That's why I bent over backwards to get you this job."

"What do you mean?"

"After I read your sample pieces, I knew you were a talented writer. The only thing was our policy about felonies. Yours was still fresh. Remember when I asked you to come back after lunch?" I nodded yes.

"I called the Conrad Brothers and cashed in on a favor that they owed me. They said if I was willing to stand behind you, then I could hire you. I don't want you to feel like you owe me anything, because you don't, and I don't expect anything. I just wanted to give you an idea of how deep this is."

"I don't know what to say."

"Why do you think I made every excuse to keep you from asking Alicia to come here? I have nothing against her, but I wanted all of your time. I tried to be discreet, hoping you wouldn't see it. That's also why I got mad about Natalie and Estacia. I have grown to care a lot about you and if given the opportunity, I can make you a happy man. I know you have a strong tie to Alicia, but I just had to let you know where I stand."

I knew her feelings were genuine because if you look at the situation, Karen and I had begun the beginning phases of a relationship—the getting to know each other to see if we were compatible part. It was obvious that we were good together because we followed a perfect daily routine. One shift in the balance threw her life off track. Now I know what Usher meant in *You Got it Bad.* It didn't affect me because Alicia's presence shifted my mind from the absence of Karen. I believe that if the tables were turned, I probably would have felt the same way Karen did.

Karen bombarded me with feelings like the Japanese on Pearl Harbor. That night she said everything except *I love you.* Once Karen opened up to me, I realized that I shared some of the same feelings. I didn't know how it was possible to care for two women. I knew that I was going to have to choose. It was like placing two perfect women on a scale. In some ways, each out-weighed the other; but they were still damn near equal. Both women were the cream of the crop, and the harvest was drawing near.

I saw a familiar look in Karen' eyes as we talked that night. Her piercing, grey eyes screamed sincerity with every word. They showed me that she wanted to be with me for who I was. It wasn't like she was out for money because she started out as my superior at work and now we were equals. I'm not the kind of guy that believed in destiny or fate, but whatever was going on pushed me further into a state of confusion. It was a good confusion, if there is such thing. I knew that either of these women could provide me with what I needed mentally, emotionally, and physically. The situation reminded me of my favorite mafia movie, *A Bronx Tale*. Sonny, the mob boss, told Calogero, a young boy that he had taken under his wing, that a great woman only came around once every ten years and you were only allowed three great ones in your lifetime. If I were only allowed three, then there would only be one more to come if I let these get away.

When the conversation slowed down, there was a deafening silence. For about five minutes. Karen and I just sat on my couch and stared at each other. Her eyes begged for me. Before I could speak, tears began to fall. They were not sad tears, but the tears of a woman freed from a serious burden that she had carried inside for quite some time. She excused herself as I sank down into my couch. I could do nothing but gaze at the ceiling and take deep breaths. After about fifteen minutes, Karen hadn't returned from the bathroom. I lifted myself out of the sofa and walked in the room to check on her.

"Karen," I called. "Are you alright?"

She didn't respond. Just as I walked towards the master bathroom, she came out. I was speechless. A vision of loveliness stood before me that would have given sight to the blind. Karen exited the bathroom wearing a red teddy that complimented her beige skin oh so right. She walked towards me and gave me a deep and passionate kiss. As I wrapped one arm around her waist and placed the other on the back of her head, I could feel her body melt into mine. In one kiss, we became one. I gently laid her on the bed and began to kiss her from her neck to her navel. Foreplay was in its beginning stages. I paused and looked at her. I thought about all of the times I'd seen her body. Never had it called out to me the way that it did at that moment. The taste of her body was so addictive. The more I put my lips to it, the more I wanted to taste it. With every caress and kiss, her body trembled. The moment had become spiritual in every way. The more I kissed her, the faster she undressed me. When we were finally skin to skin, she rolled me over on my back and straddled me.

My soldier was at attention and waiting for commands. As Karen looked down at me she reached behind me and began to stroke me up and down indicating that she was ready to receive the special delivery that she had been waiting so long for.

I felt her moist flesh lift up. Before I knew it, she had placed me inside of her and slid down. Upon insertion, she let out a stuttered breath and a soft moan of ecstasy. Slowly she went up and down, taking it all in every motion. I could feel her muscles tighten as she came down. Every time I tried to make an upward motion she would stop me and tell me that for that moment, she was in control. When she was ready for me to take over, she would let me know. I could tell by her actions that she had been sexually starved for quite some time. I was growing impatient and was ready to get into the driver's seat. As the tables were about to turn, Karen switched gears and was out of control. In a matter of moments, her body tightened and she grabbed onto me and begged me not to let her go. She had released an orgasm that shook my apartment like the earthquake that rocked Candlestick Park in San Francisco some years ago.

Our bodies were soaked with sweat and Karen was breathing like she'd just run a marathon. I laid her on her back and spread her legs wide. Her body was still trembling from the aftershocks of her first climax. As I re-entered a familiar territory, I felt her jump as I touched her spot with every stroke. Once in control, I turned Karen every way but loose. Screams of passion rang throughout the silent apartment as I moved in for the kill. Looking at the intense emotion and expressions of ecstasy on her face, I thought about a position a friend had told me about when I was a teenager. He called it the *small package*. The story behind it was that if you ever wanted to make a girl fall in love with you, then this was the position to use. The position consisted of me putting her legs over my shoulders, pressing them towards her, reaching under her to grab her shoulders and pull her towards me in every stroke. Without thinking, that was exactly what I did.

Karen tried to break free, as if she knew the consequences of the position. Eventually she gave in and took it like a big girl. The more I sexed her in this way, the more she moaned and screamed. She reached an orgasm so intense that she broke free from my clutches and rolled over on her side and held onto herself. I could do nothing but lay there and watch as this beautiful woman lay soaked in the essence of me.

When she calmed down, Karen slid over and put her head on my shoulder and ran her finger up and down my chest. To her surprise, my erection was still standing tall. Before I knew it, she was engaged in a mouthful of me. Never had it felt so good. It felt as good as being inside of her. That was a sensation that all men dreamed about. When she was through, she walked into the bathroom and turned on the shower. I followed behind her because I was not ready for it to end. When I walked up behind her, she was looking at me in the mirror with weary, gray eyes.

The next thing I knew, I turned Karen around to face me and lifted her up on to the sink. We were like Lem and Bird from *Soul Food*—minus the panties in my mouth. She wrapped her long legs around my body and held on tight. From this position I felt my climax coming. Every time I tried to pull away she would use her legs to keep me in. I tried and tried to break free but she would not let go. I stopped fighting and released inside of her with a great force that no words could explain. She finally let me go and I sat down on the edge of the tub. I was beat, and could bear to stand no longer.

After the high sexual energy came down, we took a shower together and retired to the bed. I was too tired to turn on the television, so we laid quietly in the dark and basked in the memory of our first sexual encounter. The silence was overwhelming and something had to be said. Before I had the chance to break it, she spoke.

"That was the best experience of my life," she said as she rolled to face me. "My body was long overdue and you gave me exactly what I needed."

"I'm glad it was everything you wanted it to be."

"Believe me, Dré, it was everything and more. If only you knew how long I was waiting for that…especially with you."

There was nothing more I could say. What could any man say after that? The only thing I could do was put my arms around Karen as the two of us drifted off into a deep, coma-like sleep. I just hoped that the morning after would be as pleasant as the night before.

17

Talk of the Town

The next morning, I rolled over and found Karen's side of the bed empty. Where had she gone? I walked into the front room and found her sitting on the couch watching a talk show. The situation seemed so familiar to me. She was doing the same thing Alicia used to do whenever we stayed with each other. Alicia would get out of bed, leaving me undisturbed, to go out and lay on the couch to watch her talk shows. The only difference was Alicia always had breakfast prepared.

"Good morning, sweetie," she said as she noticed me standing in the hallway. "Breakfast is in the kitchen."

This was too much. It was like having two Alicia's—one in Atlanta and one back home. The problem was that, eventually, I was going to have to choose. That was going to be the hard part. These two women never ceased to amaze me.

"You better eat before the food gets cold."

"You are too much," I said walking into the kitchen.

"What do you want to do today, since we are off?"

"Me and the boys are supposed to shoot basketball this morning. After that, the rest of my day is yours."

"That's good because Charlene and I are going to the salon and the spa today after my doctor's appointment. You know…girl stuff."

"What doctor's appointment?"

"Just a check-up. Nothing serious."

"Has your blood pressure been bothering you lately?"

"A little, but it has been nothing unbearable, maybe a headache here and there. Nothing for you to be worrying about."

"Okay, if you say so. Anyway, we should be finished ballin' around five or six. Meet me back here at about seven."

I finished my breakfast and talked to Karen for a little while longer. She and I joked around and talked about ideas for future episodes for the show. In the middle of an idea, someone knocked on the door. I opened up the door to reveal a damn-near mirror image of Karen.

"Is Karen here?"

"Hey, Charlene," Karen said as she stood up and walked to the door. "Come in. Charlene, this is André."

"A pleasure to finally meet you," Charlene said as we shook hands. "I've heard so much about you."

"Like wise. Now, if you ladies will excuse me, I have to get ready to go." I kissed Karen on the cheek and walked into the back to get dressed. I could hear the two women cackle like two schoolgirls at lunchtime. From the sounds of Charlene's reactions, it sounded like Karen was telling her about the night before. All of that was confirmed when I walked back into the room and they got quiet. I kissed Karen again and left.

I arrived at the gym at about 10:30 that morning. I saw J-Rock and the rest of the crew standing out front waiting on me. I gave everybody dap and pounds as I approached.

"What up, Mr. Lover Man?" J-Rock clowned.

"Chillin' man," I answered.

"What the competition look like?"

"Same scrubs as usual," one of my homeboys said. We walked into the gym and called next. While we were stretching and getting warmed up, Jerome brought up a name that I hadn’t heard in a while.

“Deja asked about you last night,” he said as he bent over to touch his toes.

“For real?”

“Yeah. She asks about you all the time. You should come by the club and check her out.”

“I can’t come see her. I got too much goin’ on right now.”

“Like what?”

“I got Karen and Alicia to worry about. I’m tryin' to come to a decision about who I should be with.”

“You got to be the luckiest man in Atlanta. You got in-house coochie, a girl back home, a girl in my building, and one at my club. Not to mention a pro basketball player on your roster.”

“It’s not like that,” I said cutting him off. “I’m just confused. Me and Alicia got a history and Karen is with me every day. Because of Karen, I think I’ve lost Alicia.”

“You’ve been through this same situation with Alicia and ol’ girl in North Carolina.”

“And I lost ol’ girl in North Carolina. I’m

tired of losing girls."

"Life is too short to stress. You need to live life to the fullest. You'll figure it out. Until then, let's ball."

We played basketball for five straight hours. At the end of our reign of victory, I sat down to rest with a towel positioned on my head like a pharaoh's headdress. While I watched the next game, I noticed two familiar faces walk into the gym. It was XXXplosive and White Zin. The two ladies walked over to J-Rock and me and sat down. Deep down in my heart I started to believe that Jerome was a pimp. Everywhere we went together, at least one of his girls would show up. I excused myself and walked into the cardio vascular room to hit the scales. I noticed people pointing and whispering as I walked through. It had slipped my mind that this was the gym where most of the network employees worked out. When I got to the scales, a woman asked me if I was André from Black Reign networks. After I told her that I was and walked away, she leaned over and whispered something to the girl on the exercise bike beside her.

What in the hell was everyone talking about? I didn't think that Karen and I were that obvious. As the notion passed, I thought about our actions at work. If you were an employee of the network, maybe you could have picked up on us. I thought about how we went from casual hi's and byes to hugging and eating lunch together in the cafeteria. Every time you saw one, sooner or later, you saw the other. We had become inseparable. It was cool as long as it was at the network and not all over town. Somehow, I felt that it wasn't going to be like that for long. Karen was the type of woman that wanted everyone to know who her man was.

I tried not to think about it. Time started moving very rapidly. Before I knew it, it was 5:30 and I had to get back to the house to wait on Karen. I left the boys and rode to the house. When I got home, Karen had not been back. I took a shower and prepared my clothes for the evening. I couldn't help but think about what happened at the gym. It seemed like everyone was pointing and whispering about me. I wasn't anyone special. Why me? I was just an average Joe Blow trying to make an honest living. I had been in Atlanta for quite some time, but my newness had not worn off. Karen came in right on time wearing a gold sequined evening gown.

"Aren't you a little over dressed for dinner and dancing?" I asked.

"What are you talking about? You forgot didn't you?"

"About what?"

"Tonight is the network banquet in honor of the show. Didn't Melanie remind you?"

"Melanie was on vacation last week. I thought it was next week. What am I going to do? I haven't picked up my tuxedo."

"I knew you were going to forget. That's why I called the place to confirm the date. Sure enough, you had it wrong. I picked it up yesterday. It's hanging in the closet. Didn't you notice the black hanging bag?"

"I thought it was just another one of my suits."

"André, go change, please, before we are late."

Karen went on to tell me that they were going to unveil the concept of our new show to the press and elite dignitaries of the city. I wanted to die. I knew they were going to ask me to say something, and I had not prepared a thing to say. I guess I had to rely on my gift of gab. That is what I had to fall back on when I gave my initial presentation. This event would introduce us to the city. Knowing Karen like I did, she was going to take this opportunity to let the wondering minds finally get their answer. Not to mention we were going to be sitting at the head table with the Conrad Brothers and the rest of the executive board.

Right before we left the house someone knocked on the door. The network had sent a limousine for us. The driver informed us that we were the Conrad's special guests. We were going to make a grand entrance to the gala, as well as have an article in the Atlanta newspaper about the new show. I felt like a superstar on my way to a big event. On my arm I had the most beautiful woman in Atlanta. I believed that everything happened for a reason. If this was what God had in store for me, then so be it.

When we arrived at the front entrance of the Ritz-Carlton, there were people everywhere. Cameras were flashing, reporters were talking to different people, and we were getting ready to be the center of attention. We stopped, and the driver opened the door for us. I stepped out with all of the confidence in the world. You should have seen the looks on the people's faces when Karen stepped out of the limo. We were the sexiest pair in the place. We walked the red carpet like Morris Chestnut and Sanaa Lathan on our way into the grand ballroom. As we were escorted to our seats, the pointing and whispering began. The same people I saw in the gym were in attendance.

At the start of the banquet, Jonathan Conrad was greeted with healthy applause. He began by welcoming everyone to the event and thanking those who made it possible. Mid-way through his address, he was joined by his brother, Joseph, who was the jokester of the two. He cracked a host of jokes about everything and everybody. He had the entire place in an uproar. I laughed until my sides were hurting. I couldn't laugh like I wanted to because I was sitting in front of everyone—you know how black folks laugh. After Jonathan got the crowd calmed down, he introduced Karen and me to the audience. He gave us an introduction that was out of this world.

"It gives me great pleasure to introduce my two young guns of the network. Karen Union and André Marshall are the reason for this event. I am proud to have them as a part of the Black Reign family. I give to you, Ms. Karen Union." Karen approached the podium to thunderous applause.

"Esteemed colleagues," she began. "It is an honor, as well as a pleasure, to stand before you to introduce the newest project of Black Reign Networks. I cannot take the credit for this project. This new primetime soap opera came from the mind of a great man, a man that I am honored to work with and to have as a part of my life. Mr. André Marshall."

Her words put an end to the wondering of our co-workers. I was stuck. She had just announced to everyone at the network, and a host of Atlanta citizens, that I was her man. I stood up to a loud roar of handclaps. When I approached the podium after my introduction, Karen kissed me on my lips. That kiss sealed everything. We were officially an item in the eyes of the network. It didn't matter to me, because it couldn't have happened with a more perfect woman. Even though Karen was as wonderful as she was, the decision was made for me; and I still had no closure with Alicia. I was not going to give up until things were decided between the both of us.

After I said what I had to say and returned to my seat, Karen kissed me once again. For the remainder of the night Karen and I carried on like we were a couple. We sat at the table feeding each other, wiping the other's mouths with the napkins and other things that only couples would do. The Conrad Brothers were very impressed with our work and were looking forward to the upcoming season in September. Things were going good, but we had a lot of work to do.

The gala came to a close, and Karen and I were on our way out. People were stopping us and congratulating us as if we had just announced an engagement. I didn't know if they were talking about our work or our relationship. Nevertheless, we accepted the gratitude. The limo pulled up and we were on our way back to the Royal Winds. The ride home was just as good as the ride there. Karen and I shared champagne and fruit as we rolled on our way. I wanted to ask her what she meant by what she had said, but I waited until we got to my place. The limo dropped us off and we were home. When we got in the house, we were laughing and playing around. I playfully tackled Karen on the couch and we began to kiss. I interrupted our moment before things got too hot.

"What did you mean when you said that you were honored to have me as a part of your life?" I asked.

"Exactly what I said. You have become a major part of my life and I can't see me living life without you."

"So what are you saying?"

"I want you to be a permanent part of my life. I feel that you and I belong together, and it seems like the public agrees that we are a good couple. Just look at tonight. All eyes were on us. It felt good to have a man like you by my side." I was at a loss for words. I knew she felt strongly about me, but I didn't know she was ready to take it to the next level. It was almost as if she forgot Alicia existed and that she was a part of my life. We finished our kisses and retired for the night. The next day we would be the talk of the town.

The next morning, just as I suspected, we hit the front page of the Atlanta Journal and Constitution. The headline read: *BLACK REIGN'S DYNAMIC DUO.* It was like reading a tabloid. Members of the network had given the paper information that led them to believe we were a couple. They did a good job masking it behind the report of a new show to air in September. Now it was getting ready to get messy. I'm a private person; I don't like a lot of people in my personal life. With the network, the newspaper, and the people of Atlanta fueling Karen's fire that burned for me, choosing which woman I wanted to be with was going to be a helluvah task. Hopefully, the newspaper had put an end to the constant pointing and whispering that I was receiving while around the network.

Just when you thought no one read the newspaper was the time when everybody just happened to stop at the newsstand to pick one up. On my way to work that morning, it seemed like every woman that I had dealt with since I've been in Atlanta called to ask me about Karen. The first one to call was Vanessa, then Liberty, then Natalie—even Deja called. I was quite the hot item that morning. I guess it was true what people say : no woman wants a man that nobody else wants. One thousand questions was the game I played on my way to the network. The best thing about the gala was the fact that everyone at the network now knew that I was one of the big dogs. At the network, if the Conrad Brothers liked you, everybody else liked you. If they didn't, no one cared.

Life was a funny thing at that time. The people who saw me from day to day thought I was the happiest man in the world. They could not see that on the inside, I was dying because of what was going on in my heart. It was like Alicia and Karen were on either side of my heart engaged in an all-out tug-o-war, but no one was winning. No matter how much Karen meant to me, part of me was still with Alicia. I was an emotional wreck, and there was nothing that Oprah or Dr. Phil could do about it. This was something that I had to sort out on my own. I knew where the answers were, but the question in my mind was: Am I willing to accept the answers when I received them? There was only one person who could solve this whole mess and I needed to get in contact with her. If it meant going home, then that's what I had to do. As bad as I did not want to, it was something that had to be done.

Every time I tried to make plans, something came up that pushed my journey to an understanding back a little further. Karen knew why I was going home, but she didn't want to accept it. For two weeks straight I tried to make it back to South Carolina. It just was not happening. At one point I felt like giving up; but giving up would have meant throwing away my past. There were a number of things in my past that I just was not ready to toss aside. One of those things, at one time, meant the world to me. I used to just think about her and get a chill. Now that another had intervened, the feelings have changed. I used to be a happy man. Now I felt as if I was betraying someone. Now I knew what soldiers overseas, separated from their loved ones, go through. Some think with their bodies and human nature rather than using the tool God gave us to make correct decisions concerning life and relationships. I was being found guilty of that crime. In Atlanta, I was viewed as the luckiest man alive. Back home was a woman that had no clue as to what was going on in the ATL. There is a fine line between love and stupidity, and I was walking it like a tightrope walker with no net.

18

Out of Sight, Out of Mind

A person never realizes what he or she has until he or she is about to lose it. It took some old friends to make me realize how deeply rooted the feelings were between Alicia and me. Two weeks after the network banquet, I received a phone call from two of the original members of my crew back in North Carolina, Ty and Eric. They ran into Alicia one weekend when she was home visiting her parents, and she gave them my number. I got excited when they told me that they were going to visit me in Atlanta. They were going to a wedding in Pensacola and planned to stop through on their way back.

One half of the original UE Crew was getting ready to come back together. I didn't think Atlanta was ready for us. It had been more than ten years since I last saw my friends, so I was anxious to see how they had changed. I planned a weekend full of activities, as a good host would. If I knew them like I did, they were definitely going to want to see some women, so I called J-Rock to see which girls he could spare that weekend. He told me that he would take care of everything. With the activities planned and the women waiting in the wings, the only thing I had to do was get rid of Karen for a couple of days. That was going to be the hard part. When she came back from the store, I buttered her up before I told her my plans. When she walked through the door, I greeted her with a warm hug and a kiss. Immediately, Karen felt I was up to something and got suspicious; she felt that I was being a little too nice to her.

"Dré," she said with a strange look on her face, "What are you up to?"

"What makes you think that I'm up to something?"

"Because you are a little too chipper."

"I have some fantastic news. Remember the stories I told you about my crew back in Fayetteville?"

"You mean the UG Posse?"

"That's UE Crew, but yes. Well, my friends, Ty and Eric, are coming to Atlanta this weekend."

"Baby, that's wonderful. We can have so much fun this weekend. I'll call Charlene and Amanda and we can all take them on a tour of the city and we can…"

"Baby? This is going to be a guy weekend. You know..."

"Oh, okay. I guess I'll see what Charlene is doing this weekend."

I knew Karen was disappointed that she could not spend the weekend with my friends and me, but she understood. She actually took it better than I thought she would. I still wanted her to meet them, but as far as hanging out, it would not be a good idea due to us reminiscing about our school days. Alicia's name would be brought up a lot, and I didn't want Karen to feel uncomfortable.

Friday came, and I was as excited as a kid on Christmas Eve. Karen kept telling me to sit down and be still, but I couldn't. At about six-thirty they arrived, and it was old times again. Eric was half-black and half-German, which gave him sort of an olive complexion and exceptionally large ears. He was about my height. I used to clown him about being by favorite Negro-Nazi. Ty, short for Tyrell, had not grown an inch since I last saw him. He will forever be 5'4". Ty also wore the same haircut, which was a low brush cut with probably the same waves from junior high school. My friends hadn't changed a bit. They looked exactly the same as they did in school—just the grown-up versions. From the jewelry and the clothes, I could tell that they had made successes of themselves. Eric and Ty kept going with music after I left, and now they owned two clubs in Fayetteville and were two of the east coast's top promoters of concerts, stage plays, and comedy showcases. After the introductions, Karen left so that we could start our weekend.

"You know it's on, right?" I emphasized.

"Dog, you just don't know how good it is to see you," Ty said. "I almost didn't recognize you. What happened to all the weight?"

"Actually, I don't really know how I lost it. When I moved to South Carolina, the only thing I did was play basketball. It was rough being away from the crew."

"When Alicia told us you were down here doin' it, she wasn't lyin'," Eric added.

"I'm doin' a lil' somethin'."

"Speakin' of Alicia," Ty started. "Who was that?"

"Who, Karen? She is one of the Executive Producers at the network that is working on this new show with me."

"New show?" Eric asked.

"Yes sir. I created an idea for a new primetime soap opera that is a spin-off of one of the shows we were already doing. The owners loved it, and gave us the green light and the budget to put it in the works."

"Congratulations," Ty said, giving me dap.

"Same to you. I never thought any of us would blow up in the industry. But on the real, y'all need to tap this market down here, because it's crazy money to be made."

"That's another reason we came through," Eric began. "NC, SC on up to New York is cool, but we need to get some more of that Dirty South money."

"Say. no more. Tonight we're going to the spot where all the club owners, entertainment agents, and quite a few entertainers go to hang out, and to top it all off, Jerome runs the spot."

"Ya Cousin Jerome, that went to Anne Chestnutt?" Eric inquired. "I ain't seen that dude in a minute."

"What kind of spot is it?" Ty asked.

"The hottest strip club in the ATL; Club Ebony."

We started the night off right with a little Hennessy before we hit the club. We tried not to get too intoxicated because we still had a whole lot of night left. I called J-Rock to let him know that we were on our way through and to see which ladies he had lined up for our personal after party. He informed me that Jada, White Zin and XXXplosive wanted to chill with me and my boys.

The club was bananas when we fell in. J had reserved us a VIP section so that we could sit back and have a good view of everything. Once I surveyed the scene to see who was in attendance, I pointed the people out that Ty and Eric needed to talk to, and they walked off to do their thing. In thirty minutes, they managed to turn our VIP section into a business meeting. Watching them in action reminded me of the Conrad Brothers. They were all about business, regardless of the g-strings that walked around.

At the close of their business meeting and discussions, Eric and Ty were ready to grab the ladies and head to the house. We scooped them up and headed back to the Royal Winds. I wasn't sure whether or not that was a good idea because I did not know where Karen was. Listen to me. I sounded like one of those jelly-backed men that could not stand up to his woman. If Karen was there, she would just have to leave; but to be on the safe side, I called my house phone. If she was there, she would see my name on the Caller ID and pick up the phone. After four rings, my voicemail picked up. Whew! I was in the clear. Once inside the apartment, we continued to dig into the half gallon of Hennessy we had cracked before we went to the club. We also learned that the ladies had their signals crossed, because they thought we were going to pay them for a private party. They knew that I wasn't coming off no money. The only one that was really making a big deal out of it was

White Zin. Jada had wanted to chill with me since before my presentation, so it didn't matter to her. XXXplosive wanted to get at me, too, until she saw Eric and changed her mind. It was always something about mixed dudes with curly hair.

To keep the confusion down, I asked them to leave when White Zin got loud and unruly. The last thing I needed was for someone to knock at my door and see me with strippers. After they left, I apologized for the misunderstanding and told my boys that I would call Natalie and see what was up with her girls for the next night. Over some cold Hen and Coke, we reminisced until Ty fell asleep. Talking one on one with Eric raised a few questions and thoughts in my mind concerning Alicia.

"So," Eric started. "How are things between you and Alicia?"

"To tell you the truth, dog, I don't really know."

"I could tell, because when I ran into her that day at the mall, our conversation about you was very short. It was almost like you did not mean that much to her anymore. I thought you two got things back on track after you and her transferred to the same school and came back together. What happened?"

"Everything was cool until I moved here. The day I arrived Alicia decided to tell me that she loved me."

"Do you love her?"

"That's the tricky part. I know I love her, but I don't know if I'm in love with her."

"I've known you for a long time, Dré. Alicia has been your favorite girl since the fourth grade. The only time things changed was when we met Victoria and her girls at the skating rink. Remember?"

"That's mostly the problem. Alicia is in South Carolina completing her senior year while I'm here meeting some high quality women, like Natalie who plays pro ball for the Atlanta Diamonds."

"The WNBA team?"

"Yup. Then there is Vanessa, and Karen. Karen and I have spent the past few months together trying to get this show on the air. Now she's gone and caught feelings, but the strange thing about it is I'm not trying to suppress them."

"Well, what about Alicia?"

"That's another thing. Alicia unexpectedly popped up after Christmas and found me here with Karen, and Karen was wearing night clothes."

"So, it didn't look like work."

"Exactly." I continued to explain the entire situation to Eric, hoping he could shed some light on what was going on in my life. Being a true friend, he helped me look at everything, Alicia and I had been through since the first day we met on the playground at Westchester Elementary, on to when I met Victoria, and up until Alicia and I came back together in college. I had to fill him in on how things were in college and up until I moved here. Though Eric was a clown, just like me, he was an intelligent guy. He broke it down so smooth and real, that I almost cried.

"It's like this," Eric began. "Alicia has never taken the time to get to know any other guy but you. Technically, you and her have been going together since Westchester. The way you compare other women to her, and I know you do, she does the same thing with men. Believe me when I tell you that she tried to move on, but her allegiance to you is still too strong. I know this because Danielle and I still keep in contact. Danielle was the one that convinced Alicia to tell you how she felt. I know Karen, Natalie and Vanessa are all blazin' females, because I know your taste. Think long and hard before you throw it all away. Now that Alicia had expressed her love for you, she wants you to be the only man in her life. If you reject her, you'll lose her, even as a friend."

I never knew what it was about a brother on Hennessy. He was capable of telling you things that licensed psychologists weren't able to tell you. Eric's words hit me hard and deep. He had been there from day one, so he knew my history with Alicia; I knew he would not steer me wrong or tell me anything but the truth. I deeply thanked my boy for helping me to see the things that he showed me. He read the situation inside and out. Everything he said, I already knew, but did not want to face up to it. Now that it was out in the open, I had to confront it, and the only way to do that was to go back home and talk to Alicia face to face. No matter how tight Karen and I were getting, I had to make sure that I was willing to let everything go between Alicia and me.

Instead of hanging around for the rest of the weekend, as planned, Eric and Ty left the next day due to a situation at one of the clubs they owned. I thanked Eric for his words of wisdom and told them not to wait another ten years before I saw them. All day that Saturday and Sunday, I thought about the things that Eric said to me. I couldn't shake my thoughts free until Karen came over that Sunday evening. Just like that, those thoughts were pushed to the back of my mind. Right then I realized that I was living by the theory of Out of Sight, Out of Mind. When Alicia and I were together, it was all about her, but when Karen came into the picture in Alicia's absence, it became all about her. I knew I had to make a decision. Who would I choose?

19

Homecoming

It had been about two months since Karen announced to the entire city of Atlanta that I was her man. It seemed to me that, living in Atlanta, one experienced a lot of new beginnings. I didn't know what it was, but for the past couple of months, Karen and I had been in total bliss. The show was on its way and we already had half a season's worth of episodes; taping was getting ready to begin.

My mind had been flushed clean and there were no more clouds. Well, maybe one. Even though Karen and I were straight, I still tried to keep in touch with Alicia. I tried to call, but she was never home and did not respond to my messages. When I did manage to catch her, she was always in the middle of something and rushed me off of the phone. I tried not to read too much into it because I remembered how my final semester at school was—though I always managed to make time for her. I started to get the feeling that Alicia and I really said goodbye for the last time that January. Maybe my grandmother was right when she said that a woman could feel when a relationship was going nowhere. I tried not to allow the fact that I was being brushed off affect me, but it was difficult.

Karen was the only thing that kept me sane.

On that January night when Karen's body touched mine, I felt our souls collide and we had been inseparable ever since. I don't see how it happened. I guess it was one of those things that has no explanation for occurrence. Every time you try to question it, your solution comes up blank; then something comes along to justify it. It is often said that when you go looking for love, you don't find it. When you least expect it, love finds you. With Karen, I felt as if I had found it, but we'd only been dealing on that level for a couple of months. We had a connection like no other I'd experienced. The scary thing about it was that it was almost like the connection, Alicia and I once shared. The guys at work said it was destiny and it was meant to be. Jerome said that all of the qualities that I found favor in with Alicia were evident in Karen, and that she was my version of Alicia in Atlanta. That seemed to be the only difference between the two—Alicia was in South Carolina and Karen was tangible to me. He went on to say that if Alicia had come to Atlanta with me when I moved, then none of this would have happened.

I didn't know why I tried to hold on to a long distance relationship that was never established to begin with. When I left, all I knew was that Alicia and I were just close friends. Maybe I failed to realize what type of guy I was, or maybe I was trying to keep Alicia around just in case. I needed to be in female company at all times. That's how it was back home. If I was down, Alicia was right there to pick me up and tell me everything was going to be okay. When I needed my physical needs met, I turned to other women. I never really looked at Alicia in that way, even though she was gorgeous and had a body that wouldn't quit. A lot of people might have thought that we were involved physically because we were so close. We believed that anything physical, other than an occasional kiss, might have changed things between us. I really needed to know why she was avoiding me. Was she just doing this to get me out of her mind, or was she really that busy? It hurt me to know that somewhere on the campus of Franklin Memorial University all of the answers were just walking around. It was time to go home.

Early, one cold, Friday morning, I called Karen and told her I was going to be out of town for a few days because of a family emergency. After she told me that everything was under control at the network, I packed a bag and jumped on I-20 east, South Carolina bound. For four straight hours I drove. The entire time, I prepared myself for the worst. I did not know how I would react if I arrived at the school and Alicia was with another guy, but who was I to talk. Before I went on campus, I stopped by home to see my grandfather. It was so refreshing to see the pride in his eyes when he looked at me. We sat and talked for about an hour.

Within that hour, he managed to fill me in on everything that had happened during my absence. As we talked, I started looking around the house noticing all of the flaws. The ceiling that he had been working on for the past two years, the bathroom floor that was fixed but never recovered, and the living room that was full of all kind of stuff that had no particular place in the house. Inside me a voice reminded me of the promise I made to myself when I was a young boy. I promised myself that if I ever made it, I would put my grandparents in a new house and buy them all of the things they wanted but could never afford. That was exactly what I was going to do.

After we finished our conversation, my grandfather looked at his watch and realized that he had work to do.

"Goodness!" he said. "I got stumps to grind!"

"Dad, when are you going to retire that old stump grindin' machine and pastor full time?"

"Boy, I still got bills to pay. The house, the church, and wit' my car ackin' up, I cain't afford to stop."

"But you always taught me; that in the Bible it says that if you trust in the Lord, he will provide, and he's done just that since we've been in South Carolina."

"The Bible also says to be wise in everything you do."

"Dad," I paused. "You took care of me for all my life and I love you for it. Now it's time for me to do something for you. Every week, you preach and teach your heart out, and every morning you have to go out and keep breakin' your back."

"God has blessed me and you, and I thank 'em every day for lettin' me live to see you make somethin' out ya'self."

"But what is success if you can't share it?"

"Look, I cain't stand here and talk to you all day, I got work to do," he said as he got in his truck.

My grandfather wasn't one for emotional conversations. That's why he cut the conversation short.

"Make sure you go and see your mamma and your brother so she can stop cryin' to me about you not callin' her."

"I will, but first I have a few things to take care of."

"Well, I'll see you later," he paused. "We been in revival all this week. You should try to make a night."

"I'll try."

I watched as my Dad drove off with his machine behind him. I knew right then where I needed to start, but first I had to do what I came here for. When I arrived on campus, classes were changing. Franklin Memorial University was just as I remembered it. Frats and sororities congregated in the same areas in the quad. The breezeways between the two main buildings were full of white people, as usual. I rolled through campus waving and speaking to all of my people. As I drove, I could see the mouths of the gold-diggers begin to water. All of the girls I ever tried to talk to were breaking their necks to speak to me once they found out I was the driver of the luxury SUV that no one had ever seen. Was it me, or was it the Cadillac Escalade? If I knew FMU women like I did…it was probably the Escalade.

When I pulled up in front of Alicia's apartment, I could see people peeking through their blinds when they heard the rumbling of my stereo system. I knocked on her door a couple of times, but there was no answer. Just as I turned to leave, Alicia came out of the adjacent apartment.

"Dré," she said with surprise. "What are you doing here?"

"I'm here because we need to talk. You got a minute?"

"You want to talk here or somewhere else?"

she asked.

“Let’s walk.”

“Let me get my coat.” She walked into her apartment and after about two minutes she came back out. The entire time we walked, there was silence. She could tell by our path that we were going to our spot—the track behind the University Center. When we got to the track and sat down on the bleachers, there was more silence. I stood up and stepped down.

“I guess we don’t have time for each other anymore,” I said as I leaned on the fence.

“What are you talkin’ ‘bout?”

“Not returning my phone calls, rushing me off of the phone, unanswered emails, what’s up with that?”

“You know how senior semester is…”

“Alicia, don’t give me that bullshit. No matter what, we always managed to have time for each other. Be straight up with me. What’s the deal?”

“Dré, don’t go there. Not when I come all the way to Atlanta to surprise you and find you living with Miss Thang.” OUCH!

“Okay… I deserved that, but I thought we

were past that."

Alicia stood up and walked towards me. "André, I care about you, but you gotta get ya head right. I knew somethin' was up when I wanted to make love and you wanted to talk."

Alicia was hitting below the belt, but there was nothing I could say because she was right. At that moment, I realized that Alicia and I were never going to be the friends we once were and I needed to straighten it out before we lost our complete friendship.

"Look," I said as I grabbed her hands. "When we talked that night, we said that we were going to be straight up with each other. Remember?"

"I remember."

"I can't do this anymore. I would rather us be best friends as opposed to us getting into a relationship and it not work and then we lose everything we ever had."

"This has something to do with Karen, doesn't it?"

I said nothing. Alicia's eyes filled with tears as she let go of my hands. "I know I can't be in Atlanta for you right now, but I do love you. Even with me knowing that you can't stay with one woman longer than a couple of months, I still wanted to give it a try. I guess I was stupid to think that things would be different because it was me. You can't play the field all your life, André."

"Alicia, wait." I called as she began to walk away.

"I thought what we had was special," she said as she stopped and turned around. "She may care about you and may even love you, but believe me when I say this: She will never love you as much as I do, and I always will."

I knew that choosing between Alicia and Karen was the hardest decision I would ever make, but my heart told me to choose Karen. I stood and watched as the woman that I thought I loved walked out of my life forever. My best friend and confidant was gone. I walked around the track asking myself how this happened, and why me. My only other tie to the area, besides my grandfather, was severed. That night, I sat in church trying to suppress my feelings and enjoy the service. I could not stop thinking about the fact that I had lost Alicia for the last time. I had to shake her for at least a minute in order to hear what God had given to my grandfather to give to the people. For the next hour he preached under an anointing and power I had never seen before. His sermon came to a close, and the offering was raised. When it was all said and done, my grandfather, pastor, and friend stepped to the podium for the benediction.

"Let the church say Amen," he commanded.

"AMEN!" shouted the congregation.

"I just wanna thank the Lord for bringin' the Prodigal Son home," he laughed. "Is there anything that you would like to say?"

"Giving honor to God, my pastor, saints and friends," I said as I stood up and walked to the front of the church, "this is a great man of God, and words can-not express how much I love him. He has taken care of me for twenty-six years of my life. When I was born, all of his children were grown, but still, he and my grandmother took on a responsibility that was not theirs, and raised me. Through his prayers, God has blessed me and I feel that I can now be a blessing to him." I reached in my pocket and handed him the keys.

"What's this?" he asked.

"Those are the keys to your new Eldorado Cadillac. Burgundy and paid in full."

"Thank the Lord," my grandfather replied and a huge smile spread across his face. My grandfather praised the Lord like never before. The only time I had seen him happier was the day he closed the deal on the church in which we stood. I had finally grown up. For many years people had given to me, and all I could do was take. Selfishness was a bad trait to have, especially if one planned to have any type of serious and healthy relationship.

When I woke up the next morning, I felt so refreshed. It was hard to believe that after the previous day's events, I did not feel like crawling in a hole and lying there to die. Giving up a woman that had been with me my entire life made me realize that I had to come to terms with myself. Regardless of how good my life was going, I had to be real with myself. Alicia and I were not going to survive a long distance relationship. Instead of trying to hold onto something that was not there, I decided to let go and let love take its course.

Before I left town, I went to spend the day with my little brother and my mother, and then I went back to my grandfather's house. After he and I went for a ride in his new car, the time for me to shove off for Atlanta came. My Dad said a prayer while we stood in our front yard, and then I was on my way home. This time the drive was worthwhile. I enjoyed the sights, the music, and the good feeling of a new beginning. Look at me. I was a successful Executive Producer and writer for a major network, and I had a beautiful woman waiting on my return. What more could a man ask for?

When I got into Augusta, I called Karen to let her know that I would be home soon and ask her to choose an outfit for me to wear and for her to be dressed when I arrived. It was time to celebrate. She had no clue what we were celebrating, but she said just that having me back was reason enough. Night had fallen by the time I reached home, and for the first time I could soak myself in the city's beauty. For some reason, things were different now. Cruising down Peachtree Street that night was like a walk on the red carpet at the Oscars. Everyone was looking at me as if they knew how good I felt being there. Now all I needed was to see Karen's beautiful face and I would be satisfied.

20

Two Plus One

Upon my arrival to my place, I was greeted by a familiar voice.

"Hey, stranger," called the voice. "Long time, no see." It was Vanessa.

"Hey, Vanessa," I said as I turned around. "What's up?"

"Don't what's up me! If you were involved with someone, you should have told me."

"The last time I spoke to you, you were on your way out and never called me back. Furthermore, a lot has happened since then."

"Whatever!" Vanessa barked. "Save it. It was nice to meet you, and you have a nice life. I hope she makes you fuckin' happy!" I watched as that stallion galloped down the street and out of my life. I smiled as I walked into my building. The only thing that bothered me was: How did she know that I was involved with someone?

When I arrived at my apartment and opened the door, I saw the most beautiful sight a man could ever see, dream or imagine—Karen Union. She was wearing a very elegant evening gown of royal blue, my favorite color. I didn't know what was more blinding, the sparkle of the diamonds in her ears or her smile. I walked towards her and embraced her as if I had been away for years. Daddy had come home and Mommy was right there to greet me. "Girl, you just don't know how much I missed you," I said as I kissed her on the neck.

"Now stop it," she giggled. "We have reservations, and if we want to make them, let's not start the fire."

"Right, right. There is plenty of time for that, but first I have to get dressed. Did you pick out an outfit for me?"

"It's all laid out on the bed and the shoes are on the floor beside the night stand on your side of the bed."

"You're too good to me."

"I know," she said as she followed me into the bedroom. "How was home?"

"Everything was cool. I bought my grandfather a car, saw my lil' brother and told Alicia that you and me are together." She couldn't understand the last thing because I threw it in right as I started to brush my teeth.

"What was that?"

"I bought my dad a car."

"No, no, the last thing." I motioned for Karen to hold that thought while I finished brushing my teeth.

"I said," I paused to wipe my mouth with a towel. "I called everything off between me and Alicia. It just wasn't working."

"Oh, if that's what you want." She knew damn well that's what she wanted to hear. She was just trying to play it cool.

"I believe it was for the best. Now if you excuse me, I have to take a shower."

"Please do, stinky man," she joked. After my shower, I was getting dressed and Karen came at me with a couple of questions that knocked a pause in the conversation.

"Baby…who are a Vanessa and Liberty?"

"Vanessa is the first person I met when I moved here and Liberty is some girl I gave my number to at the club about two weeks after I got here." I was trying to stress the age of me meeting these women.

"Well, Vanessa stopped by about five minutes before you came in and Liberty left a message for you at work." I walked towards Karen and hugged her.

"Those were two women of my past. You are my present and hopefully my future."

"Okay, but tell your little bitches to stop calling and coming by."

"Jealous?"

"No. Just protecting what is mine."

After I got dressed, we left for Ramon's. Karen and I spent a wonderful night together. Following Ramon's, we went to a new salsa club that opened downtown. We got so lost in the night that we almost forgot that the next day was Sunday and we had to get back on the grind. At about one o'clock that morning we dragged ourselves into the house and readied ourselves for bed. Together we said our prayers and retired. Just as I was about to doze off, Karen shook me.

"Are you asleep?" she asked.

"Almost."

"I've been thinking about this all day and I really don't know how to tell you this."

"Is it good news or bad news?" I asked as I sat up in bed.

"Depends on how you take it."

"Just come out and tell me. We have open lines of communication and…"

"I'm pregnant."

"…if there is something you need to talk about…Huh?"

"I said that I'm pregnant. I took a test after you left because I missed my period. It came out positive." For about five minutes we sat in silence. I didn't know what to say. I was getting ready to be a father.

"André say something."

"Karen this is the happiest night of my life!" I jumped up and danced around in the bed. I ran to the window and began to shout to all that were listening.

"ATL! I'm about to be a father!"

"Dré come in here and stop all of that noise. People are trying to sleep. It is not one hundred percent yet. I have to go to the doctor Monday morning."

"What time do we have to be there?"

"No sir. We don't have to be anywhere. I have to be there at 9:30. You have to be at the studio because the Conrad Brothers are coming for a visit and one of us has to be there."

"Okay, but you come directly to the studio when you find out so we can tell the crew."

"I will. Now go to sleep."

I could not fall asleep right away. Who could sleep after receiving news like that? Finally I was getting ready to fall out of the ranks of being one of the four grandchildren, out of thirteen, on my father's side, that did not have a child. I knew my mother would be happy, because she's wanted to be a grandmother for so long. My little brother, Jason was going to love the idea of being an uncle. My father claimed that he's too young to be a grandfather, but he would get used to it. The only person I was leery about telling was my grandfather. With him, it wouldn't be the fact of the child, it would be the fact that I had the baby out of wedlock. That was going to be the disappointing part. Hopefully all of my other success would help ease this little mistake.

When I got to work on Monday morning I wanted to tell the entire network, but I had to wait until it was confirmed. In my office, I paced back and forth as I did the day I gave my presentation. Twelve o'clock rolled around and Karen walked into my office. It was official. I was a father-to-be. We walked down to the cafeteria and announced the good news to all of our friends. Everyone was happy and excited for us except for a couple of people. It didn't matter to me who cared or didn't. Once the day's hype had settled and Karen and I were back home, reality started to set in very heavily. I was getting ready to be a father—*A Father*. I was twenty-six years old and could barely take care of me, much less be somebody's daddy. I didn't want my nervousness to get the best of me, although it was natural. Karen picked up on my vibe when she heard me fumbling around in the kitchen. I guess the second glass that hit the floor gave it away.

"Are you all right in there, baby?" Karen called to me from the living room.

"I'm cool," I replied as she walked into the kitchen. "They slipped out of my hand."

Karen asked as she took a closer look at the glasses, "How are the glasses slippery when they aren't wet?"

"My hands were wet."

"André stop lying. You're nervous aren't you?

"I told you, I'm cool."

"Then why are you about to drink a glass full of plant food?"

"Plant food!" I said examining the labeled container. "I thought that was green Kool-Aid."

"Go in the room and sit down." By the time I sat down, my hands were shaking, my heart was pounding, and my legs would not stay still. As far as financial status was concerned, I was stable. Was my mental on the right track? I needed answers, but did not know who to call because the only one I ever felt comfortable talking to about a situation of this magnitude was no longer a part of my life. I also did not want my fear to cause me to take flight and leave behind the seed that I had planted. Too many children were already growing up, or grew up, without their fathers—like me. In my father's case, it wasn't his fault.

Besides, I had too much to lose if I did decide to run. My career would have been thrown away, all my hard work would have been in vain, and my dreams would have been shattered. This was going to be one of the greatest achievements of my life. If it meant that much to me, then why was I trippin'? All of this was running through my head too fast, and I needed to ease my mind. I called all the fellas and told them to meet me at our usual sports bar. After I made sure that Karen was cool with me stepping out for a little while, I bounced out to meet the guys. When I arrived, everyone was there except for Zack. Troy later informed me that his lady would not let him out the house. I had not told them why I wanted them to meet me, and after only one round of drinks, they were getting antsy.

"What's the deal, Dré?" Smoke asked. "It's Monday night and we are at the bar. What's the problem?"

"Does it always have to be a reason for brethren to gather with one another and commune?"

"I'm ya cousin," J-Rock interrupted. "And with you talkin' like that, the answer must be yes."

"Okay, Okay, Okay. I have something to tell you." I paused. "Karen's pregnant."

"Dré, you told us that this afternoon in the cafeteria," Troy reminded.

"Yeah and you called me this morning," J-Rock said. "Now for the last time, what is the problem?"

"I don't know if I am ready for fatherhood, just yet." I went on to explain how I was feeling to the fellas. To my surprise, instead of clowning me for feeling like that, they sat, listened very attentively, and even gave me some helpful advice. They told me about their individual experiences that they had when they had their first children. Out of all of the guys that were sitting at the table, I was the only one that was financially stable with my first child on the way. As I listened to them talk, I could also sense the regret in their stories because none of them had the relationships with their children that they wanted. Hearing their accounts made me think that I had to go against the grain and step up to my responsibility. Not saying that they were bad fathers, it was just the fact that none of them was with the mothers of their children. We continued to talk, and the entire time they were discreetly telling me to make sure that Karen and I were tightly bound.

Before I got intoxicated, I called it a night. When I got home, Karen was up watching some movie on Lifetime. She asked as I sat on the couch beside her, "How was your evening?"

"Very enlightening."

"How so?"

"That's not important. What is important is the fact that I want us to be the perfect parents for our child."

"Me too, but nobody's perfect."

"That's true, but I want us to try."

"I know you are nervous. I am, too. Trust me, we'll be okay."

Over the next couple of months Karen and I became closer and closer. She did not move all of the way in with me, but she was damn close. She kept her place because of her mood swings. Whenever she started ranting and raving, I would go there because that was the last place on earth she would look for me. Our friends at work helped to keep us sane. The ladies would take her out to keep her moods balanced, and the guys would take me to the club to keep me from losing my mind. After the baby was born, hopefully Karen would let the baby be the only child in the house. She had become worse than a two-year-old, pouting and whining all night. Now I see why they wanted to throw mama from the train, but it was okay. She was my big baby and I was with her every step of the way.

I had always heard guys talk about getting sick when their wife or their girl was pregnant but I was ridiculous. I couldn't keep anything in my stomach. I was throwing up left and right. To top it all off, I started to gain weight. How was it that I was sick all of the time and Karen wasn't? I was a hot, wicked mess. I remember the first day it hit me. One morning while sitting at my desk, I turned around to get something out of my file cabinet and lost all my breakfast. Bacon and eggs went everywhere. My homeboys at the network gave me hell for the first couple of days until they realized how miserable I was.

21

Bound by Blood

Just because a baby was on its way into the world, we could not stop working. *Matters of the Heart* was in the final stages before taping began, which made it crunch time in more ways than one. Karen and I continued to build our relationship on the strong friendship and working relationship we'd already established. We opened up to each other in ways that I could not believe. For example, Karen started coming into the bathroom while I was trying to handle my business. Now, that took some getting used to. I thought only married people did that.

After enough nerve building, Karen and I broke the news to our parents and families. To our surprise, our parents took the news better than we expected, considering their strong religious beliefs. I guess things are different when you are grown and having a child, as opposed to being a teenager. At the same time we were building our relationship with one another, we also got acquainted with each other's parents. Soon I began calling Mrs. Union "mom." I kept it at Mr. Union when I talked to her father. He and I had a long conversation about marriage one night. He tried to say that he was not pressuring me by saying it was the right thing to do.

Karen and I had talked about it, but came to the conclusion that people didn't marry any more just because they were expecting. We felt no need to rush into anything.

My grandfather was the coolest of them all. The only thing he said to me was: "Well, you know what you have to do." His reaction shocked me—especially with him being my Pastor. He knew that I realized that I had made a mistake and him preaching to me about right and wrong was not going to change what was already done. He just reassured me that we were always going to be in his prayers. As for my father, he was still claiming he was too young to be a grandfather.

When Karen started to develop a little baby pooch, the madness began. She didn't want to lose her figure, so every morning she had me up at the crack of dawn to go walking. She threw all of the junk food away and replaced it with healthy mess. I don't know how I would have survived if it were not for the secret stashes that I had in my office desk and in my car. I never realized how sensitive women were about their weight until the day I was joking around with Karen and said something about her starting to put on pounds.

"Hey, fat face," I joked as I walked into the bedroom.

"What!" Karen shrieked as she ran to the

bathroom mirror. “Am I getting fat for real?”

“No baby, I was just joking.”

“Don’t lie to me André.”

“You’re not, I was just kidding.”

“Well, don’t. It’s bad enough I’m not going to be able to fit into my clothes in a little while. I don’t need you rubbing it in.”

“Baby, you are pregnant. It’s only natural that you put on a few extra pounds.”

“In my family, a few extra pounds is an understatement. All of my mother’s sisters ranged from sizes five to eight before they started having children. Now, they are as big as houses.”

“I’m sure it’s not that bad.”

“You know Crystal from wardrobe?” I nodded my head yes. “They make her look like a size two.”

“Damn!” I paused. “I’m sure you’ll just be all baby.” I walked over to her and turned her around to face me. “Look, you are barely showing.”

“But I’m only three months.”

“As much as we walk and eat healthy, you will be fine.” Karen stood in the mirror for about fifteen minutes examining every aspect of her body from her face to her butt. Now that I thought about it, I had seen some pictures of her aunts, and they were some healthy women. I just prayed that whatever it was that made them gain and hold on to their weight skipped Karen's generation.

Now that we were expecting a baby, I had to change my social ways a little bit. I cut back on going to the club with the crew every weekend to only going maybe twice a month. I couldn't let it go completely because the way Karen's hormones had her out of control sometimes; I would have lost my mind. It was amazing to watch how a sweet and loving woman could get pregnant and turn into a living nightmare. Karen went from being a woman that was difficult to figure out to being an emotional amusement park ride. I never knew what to expect. One morning she came into my office crying and didn't know why. I thought something had happened. Later on that night she told me that it was something that just started while she was sitting at her desk. They were not tears of joy or pain, just tears. She would also get emotional whenever we were out and saw a young girl or a young couple with a newborn baby—or any baby for that matter. She could not resist going up to them to talk baby talk. At night, we used to sing songs to the baby while rubbing Karen's stomach. Sometimes she would tell it a story. You could tell we were getting ready to be new parents in the new millennium because Karen had bought every child-rearing book on the market. The baby books were the only things I was allowed to read except for the newspaper. By the time the baby arrived, I would know more about children than Sigmund Freud and B.F. Skinner combined. I was just glad that Karen had not signed us up for the child birthing classes yet, but I knew they were coming.

My friends clowned me so bad. Some days I would come to work and be fine. Other days, I walked around like a zombie because Karen had kept me up the night before. The road to fatherhood got rougher and rougher as the pregnancy progressed. I had to get out of the house a little more than I was, or I was going to lose it. I used to get J-Rock to call the house and ask me to come pick him up or drop him off at the club because his car was acting up. Even though it was brand new, Karen did not have to know all of that. I didn't go to Club Ebony much before Karen got pregnant. After she started getting self-conscious about her body, every now and then I got the urge to see a thong or two without the basketball poking out in the front. Me going to the Club Ebony was like going to visit friends and family. J had told everyone that I was getting ready to be a father so they wouldn't let me spend any money, regardless of how much I had.

I remember one particular night that I went; temptation was running all up and through the club. Deja had just returned to work after recovering from a car accident. Because I had not seen her in a while, I forgot exactly how fine she was in her pink, velour jogging suit that was zipped up just enough to expose her cleavage. She also had on matching pink and white shell-toed Adidas, pink shades with silver rims, and a pink headband that was surrounded by her curly black hair.

"Hey boo!" she greeted with a huge smile on her face as I walked into the club. "Come here and give me a hug." Deja's body was as soft as cotton as I squeezed tightly.

"How have you been?"

"I feel better now that I'm back. You know bill collectors don't stop collecting just because you can't go to work."

"True indeed."

"When my relief gets here, in about thirty minutes, you have to let me buy you a drink."

"That's what's up."

"Before you go, I have to ask you a question. What's with the jeans?"

"What do you mean?"

"You never wear jeans."

"I just threw on anything I could find and got out of the house. Why, do I look bad?"

"Actually, you still look better than most of the guys that come in here. Anyway, I'll see you in a little while."

"You know where to find me."

"Yes I do, you alcoholic."

"We got jokes," I laughed. "I have a pregnant woman at home. I deserve a drink." After choppin' it up with Deja for a minute, I hooked up with my cousin and chilled out by the bar. One of his bartenders called in sick, so he was running the drinks. We joked around until Deja's relief came, then she and I went off to talk.

"How have you been?" she asked as we walked down the corridor to the office.

"I'm cool."

"I know you must be really excited about being a father."

"Excited and nervous at the same time."

"At least you are still with your woman. The night I told my baby's father I was pregnant was the last night I saw him until the baby was born."

"I didn't know you had a child."

"I told you that the first night we met."

"You did? My bad. So much has happened since then. I'm surprised I still remember my own name."

"Trust me, I can understand that. My little lady will be three next month." Deja and I talked for a while until it started to get late and I had to get home to Karen. Before I left, Deja said some things to me that made me think about what was to come in my life.

"Before you go," she said, stopping me at the door. "Do you remember the night we were alone in here?"

"How could I forget?"

"Since we had not talked too much since then," Deja paused. "I wanted to apologize for that night."

"That's not necessary."

"Yes it is. I just wanted to tell you that I'm sorry for the way I acted that night and for not calling you or keeping in touch with you like I said I would. The only time I did call you was because I saw you with another woman. I was really feeling you and didn't know how to express it. Now it seems that it is too late."

"It does seem that way, doesn't it?"

"I know you have a lot goin' on right now and whether you know it or not, I know more about you than you think I do. Me and J talk about you all the time."

"Is that a good thing or a bad thing?"

"It's a good thing. Speaking as a single mother that went through everything by herself, I just want to tell you that no matter how rough things get, always be there for your woman. She needs you just as much as that child is going to need you. Don't let anything take that away from you, not even you. My daughter's father said that the reason he bailed on me was because he wasn't financially stable. At that time, the money didn't matter. I just needed him there. Now that you and Karen are bound by blood, she should be your everything."

"Thanks Mommy," I said as I hugged her. "I really needed to hear that."

"And don't forget, if there is anything you need to know about taking care of a child and can't get in touch with anybody, don't hesitate to call me. For your sake, do it on the low. I know how women can be."

I never thought that after everything that happened between Deja and me she would ever tell me anything like that. I saw why J-Rock couldn't function without her. Once I went back to the bar to tell my cousin that I was leaving, I said goodbye to the dancers and went home to put my big baby to bed. When we settled in the bed for the night, I put my arms around Karen and held on to her until she fell asleep. Thanks to Deja, I had a better understanding of Karen's need for me.

Now I lay me down to sleep,

I pray the lord, my child to keep.

Because to me, it means so much,

For you to guide us with your touch.

22

Hell in Houston

Around Karen's third or fourth month of pregnancy, and the beginning of the WNBA season, she really started to get under my skin. I started to feel as if my life was falling into ruins. From the day I found out she was carrying my child, I cut off all other females and focused on Karen. There was no Natalie, no Vanessa, no anybody. In everyone's eyes, I had turned into a husband with no ring. I quit seeing and associating with other women, cold turkey, until my urges started to creep up on me. Desire for more female company started to rise, and that was no good because it would lead to exactly that…no good. I was cool until I ran into Deja in the grocery store and thought about that night in the club. On top of that, I thought about Natalie, Vanessa, even the mystery bathtub woman. To this very day, I still don't know her name. Before I completely sold out, I felt that I needed to slide at least one more time.

Opportunity knocked when Karen went with her best friend to a wedding. With the wedding being in Miami, they decided to make it an entire weekend event. As soon as she left, I called the boys to see what the plans were for the evening. Troy and Smoke were going to Club Ebony that night. Zack was sick, and Alex was out of town. I had two choices. I could to go to the strip club or I could call on an old friend or two. If I went with the second choice, the question was: Who would I call? Since Karen and I started getting closer, I lost touch with everyone. Names started floating through my head of the women that I had been in contact with. I managed to narrow it down to four people—Natalie, Vanessa, Liberty, and Shawna.

Karen cut off Vanessa and Liberty. Natalie was upset because I tried to talk to her teammate, and Shawna…I had done nothing to Shawna. I'll call her. I rushed to my room and straight to the closet. In the closet was an old Nike shoebox that held my old cell phone with all of my numbers in it. Hopefully she was in town. The phone rang three times before she finally answered.

"Hello?" she answered.

"Hey, Shawna," I said with relief. "This is Dré"

"Hey! What's up?"

"Nothing much. I was wondering if you were busy this weekend."

"Well, I leave for Houston tonight for a game Sunday."

"Is your man going?"

"Him? Go to a game? Never."

"How about I fly to Houston?"

"Seriously?"

"Yeah. How does that sound?"

"Sounds good to me. We're staying at the Hilton in downtown Houston."

"I'll see you in Texas." It was a done deal. Now all I had to do was call the airport and I was off. I did a little running around before I had to be at the airport. I ran into Vanessa in Phipps Plaza. After our last encounter, I thought she was going to have nothing to say to me. Turns out I was wrong.

"Hey sexy," she said like nothing had ever happened. "What's going on?"

"Not a whole lot, what about you?"

"Nothing really. I was talking about you earlier today."

"To who?"

"Your cousin. He told me that you were the man at Black Reign."

"Something like that."

"You know, André, regardless of whether you are involved with someone or not, we are still friends. I decided not to let jealousy take that away. I'm sorry for how I acted. Can we still be cool?"

"Of course. Besides, how could I forget the first sexy woman I met when I came to Atlanta?"

Vanessa and I continued to talk as we walked around the plaza. It felt good to clear the air between us; besides, she was right. We were still friends. Time moved rapidly and I still had a flight to catch. I left Vanessa and met Troy back at my place so he could drop me off at the airport. On our way there, we stopped to pick up Smoke.

"What's the deal, fellas?" Smoke greeted as he got into the car.

"We gotta drop Dré off at the airport before we go to the club."

"Airport for what? Where in da hell you goin'?"

"I'm going to a basketball game."

"What game?"

"The Diamonds versus the Comets."

"Either you are a true WNBA fan, or this has something to do with the Navigator girl," Smoke replied.

"It has nothing to do with Natalie. It's Shawna."

"The startin' power forward?" Troy asked. I nodded. The two joked around about me being a pimp like my cousin. As they poked fun, I started to wonder if I was doing the right thing. I knew I wasn't, but I'd already set the plan in motion. Before I knew it, I was on my way to Houston, Texas.

When the plane touched down in Houston, a funny feeling came over my entire body. It felt just like the feeling I had when Alicia came knocking at my door and found me in the apartment with Karen. I knew what I was doing was wrong, but it seemed like I was not in control of my actions. Something else was driving my body. I couldn't figure out what it was. Until I did, the only explanation for this trip was pure lust. In so many words it was nothing more than a long distance booty call. It's amazing what men will go through to keep from getting caught up at home.

After making my way to my hotel, which was conveniently located across the street from the Hilton, I called Shawna to let her know where I was. In less than an hour, the Atlanta Diamonds landed in Houston. Thirty minutes after they got to the hotel, Shawna was knocking at my door. She hugged me and then sat down on the couch. For the first half-hour we engaged in small talk as a way of getting reacquainted. Instead of going out, we had room service send up some food. Neither of us wanted to risk being seen, especially with Natalie right across the street and one of other the player's boyfriend in town for the game. He was a friend of Shawna's man.

We were both involved with someone. For at least one weekend, we wanted to be involved with each other. Nothing happened the first night. It was kind of like a getting to know each other session. I don't know why. It wasn't like we were ever going to be involved after this weekend. After Shawna returned to her room, I went down to the bar to have a couple of drinks before I turned in. That was the biggest mistake I could have ever made. I was sitting at the bar sipping on some Hennessy when I saw someone walking into the bar. It was a short woman wearing an Atlanta Diamonds warm-up. It was Natalie. She spotted me as soon as she walked into the room and joined me at the bar.

"What are you doing in Houston?" Natalie asked. I could tell by her face that she was happy to see me.

"I'm here on business for the network," I lied.

"Mind if I sit?"

"Not at all. What are you drinking?"

"Grand Mariner, up" she said to the bartender.

"You ready for the game on Sunday?"

"I'm kind of nervous. You know the Comets are still undefeated."

"Until Sunday." Just like at the Silver Dollar back in Atlanta, Natalie and I had a couple of drinks and shot a few games of pool. We talked and laughed. I could tell that Natalie was troubled by something other than the Sunday's game.

"Are you okay?" I asked as I racked the pool balls.

"Dré, I have a confession."

"About what?"

"About Shawna. A week after our last conversation, she admitted to me that she added more to the story than there really was."

"Why didn't you call me?"

"I was too embarrassed because I had jumped to conclusions. I was really feeling you, but I thought you had nothing more to say to me."

"I thought everything was cool after we talked that night, but you stopped calling and wouldn't return my calls."

Damn. It was all a misunderstanding and now I was here to see the woman that almost caused me to lose a good friend. My feelings immediately changed and I no longer wanted to be involved in any way with Shawna. It was Natalie I really wanted to be with. Telling her wasn't going to be easy, so I didn't tell her right then. Natalie had come back to me, but I didn't know how to get Shawna out of the picture. I didn't care about her feelings or how she was going to take it. The only thing I did know was that I had an entire night to figure it out. Natalie and I returned to my suite. Though we had alcohol in our systems, we didn't get sexual. We got in bed and talked ourselves to sleep. The next morning, Natalie's wake-up call woke us and my Diamond was on her way back to her hotel to get ready for practice. As soon as she walked out of the door, Shawna called to tell me what time she got out of practice and that she wanted to see me for a little while. I told her that I had to handle some business and I would see her when I got back. Hopefully, Natalie wasn't going to say anything to anybody about seeing me before I could get this situation under control. After my conversation with Shawna, sleep pulled me back under. When I woke up again, it was four o' clock in the afternoon. Between the network, Karen, and jet lag, I had missed a lot of sleep.

By the time I woke up completely and got myself together, it was a quarter past five and practice for the Diamonds was over. Twenty minutes after they arrived at the hotel, Natalie called.

"Hey, André," she greeted. "It's Natalie."

"I was waiting for you to call. What's up this evening?"

"Nothing too wild, remember, I have a game tomorrow."

"Let's find a quiet restaurant and have dinner."

"That sounds good to me. I'll be there in about an hour." Time continued to tick and before I knew it, Natalie was at my room. I grabbed my wallet and keys to the Expedition I had rented, and we were gone.

Neither of us had ever been to Houston before, so we tried not to stray too far from the hotel. Nat and I managed to stumble up on a quaint Italian restaurant. It was a glorious time. Because the night was going so well, I felt that it was time for me to come clean, even if it meant ruining the moment. "Now that we are here and everything is going good," I mumbled. "I have a few things to tell you."

"What is it?"

"First of all, I came to Houston for another

reason than the one I told you last night. My intentions were to come here and spend the weekend with Shawna."

"What?"

"Before you get upset, let me explain. Since the last time you and I spoke, a lot of things have changed."

"Like what?"

"Me and Alicia parted ways because of my so-called need to be in the presence of the woman I was with."

"I'm sorry to hear that."

"On top of that, I'm getting ready to be a father."

"By who? Karen?"

"How'd you know?"

"I saw the two of you on the front page of the newspaper. I could tell by the article and the smiles on your faces that you two were more than just co-workers."

"Are you upset?"

"I'm not upset, just a little disappointed."

"If I hurt you, I'm sorry."

"I just got ahead of myself. I was really starting to fall for you. I know we didn't spend that much time together, but it was something special about you. Looking at the relationships of my teammates made me want you even more. Though they were in relationships, only a couple of them were happy. Then I looked at you and saw a brother that had it all together. I was willing to throw caution in the wind and settle down with you before I knew who you were. The only thing that kept me from pressing the issue was the fact that you still had your girl in your life. At first I didn't care about her, but I had to respect your situation. The thing that made me think it was possible was the night we went out with my girl and her husband."

"That was a good night."

"Yes it was. Now it seems like I missed my prince."

"No matter what, you and I are still friends and right now, I need that more than anything. As always, I'm here for you." The rest of the evening was spent reconciling the friendship. We left the restaurant and went back to the hotel for a nightcap. When we got there, we got a shocking surprise. Shawna had managed to get a key to my room and was waiting on my return. When we walked in, there was candlelight, soft music, and I noticed a bottle of champagne. After I turned on the lights, Shawna was lying in the bed wearing a short lavender and lace nightie. I figured it like this: Lingerie from Victoria's Secret…$75. Candles and Slow Jams mix CD… $25. Bottle of champagne…$125. The look on Shawna's face when she saw me and Natalie together... Priceless.

"What the hell is this shit?" Shawna screamed as she leaped from the bed.

"I should be asking you the same question," I replied. "How did you get in here?"

"Never mind how I got in here. Why are you with her?"

"Because he needed someone that was going to keep it real with him and not someone who goes around telling lies just to get what she wants." I stepped back as the two Diamonds collided.

"You always have to be number one, don't you?" Shawna asked Natalie. "Number one draft pick. I don't give a shit about André; I did what I did because of you. Everybody is always talking about Natalie Simms this and Natalie Simms that. Coach is always talking about being like Nat. In my opinion, fuck Nat!"

"Is that what this is all about? I earned my spot on the team because I am what they wanted. The only reason you got on the team during the expansion draft was because Lisa Leslie wouldn't fit under the cap, Dawn Staley tore her ACL and Cheryl Swoops decided to re-sign with Houston. You're not even good enough to be sloppy seconds."

That was the spark that did it. Before I knew it, I watched David and Goliath go toe to toe. Shawna's rage and embarrassment led her to slap Natalie. Though she was out sized, Natalie didn't let Shawna get the best of her. Being from Camden, New Jersey, Nat was straight hood. I tried to pry the women apart, but every attempt failed. The harder I tried to break it up, the harder they fought. Eventually, I managed to get the two of them apart. Shawna stormed from the suite with more than just a bruised ego. Beyond the swelling and the scratches on Shawna's face, she became very ugly to me. Her personality and competitive nature destroyed her outer beauty. I got some ice out of the champagne bucket to put on Nat's face to keep the swelling down.

"I'm sorry." I said trying to console her.

"It's not your fault. It was time for her to face reality. We've been beefin' since day one. I kinda felt it coming, but I didn't think it would get to this. Now I done went and got you involved in this mess."

"I should be the one apologizing to you. If I

hadn't come out here tryna creep, none of this woulda happened."

"Look at it this way…at least we got things straightened out between us." After our conversation, I walked Natalie to her room. I stayed for a little while to make sure she was all right and then I went back to my room. In the aftermath of Mike Tyson and Lennox Lewis II, I sat and thought about a lot of things—my life, my current situation with Karen, and my loss of Alicia. I hadn't been in Atlanta a year, and I already managed to foul up a lot of things, namely my relationship with Alicia. Now I was in a situation that my ethics were forcing me to be in. That weekend told the entire story. If it were not for Karen being pregnant, then who's to say that we would be together? While she was in Miami at a wedding, I ran off to Houston scheming on booty. I had to get it together if I wanted things to work out between me and Karen, if not for us, then for the sake of our child. Only time would tell as my head swelled with blueprints of a new me.

The next day came and I went to see Natalie and The Diamonds commit a first-degree murder of the Houston Comets. On the court, Natalie was as classy as she was off the court. The way she played, one would have never known that anything ever happened last night. Nat dropped thirty-one points, had twelve assists, and ten steals—her first career triple-double. She was a true Diamond. Shawna, on the other hand, let her frustrations get the best of her. She only scored two points and got ejected early in the second half.

That night, I left Houston a little less confused than I was when I arrived. New things were finally starting to click in my mind. All of the years of running wild and dealing with girl after girl made me realize that in order to have a successful relationship, I had to settle with just one. There was no other alternative. Before, I was trying to have sex with every girl I met. If I gained nothing from my trip to Texas, I did gain a true friend in Natalie. Just like Vanessa, Natalie needed a good man in her life, but as much as I wanted to be that man, it couldn't be me.

23

All or Nothing

The average player would have tallied my weekend in Houston; in the loss column. For me, it was a learning experience. As men and women play dog chases cat, a few different outcomes can happen: the dog catches the cat, the cat gets away, and sometimes, the dog chases the cat so much that when he does catch it, he doesn't know what to do with it. In reality, that's all I had been doing was chasing cats. It was a scenario I had been doing since I first got interested in females. You know as well as I do, it had to stop somewhere. On the Sunday night that I returned to Atlanta from my expedition to Houston, my eyes were opened up. I never knew that when a woman said that she had eyes everywhere, she meant it. When I walked into my apartment that night, Karen had a few choice words for me.

"What in the hell were you doing in Houston?" Karen screamed.

"I went to see the Diamonds play the Comets," I said as I tried to keep my cool.

"Why halfway across the country? You

haven't been to a Diamonds game since the season started, but now all of a sudden you want to be a fan."

"Me and the fellas thought that it would be fun to take a road trip."

"See, let me stop you right there. Smoke, Alex and Troy all left messages for you to call them when you got back in town. So try again." Some friends I had. Now I was in a tight situation and I didn't know how to get myself out of it.

"Let me explain."

"You're not going to explain, you're going to listen. I know this is awkward for you. Hell, it's just as awkward for me. This is my first child, same as it is yours. We've already talked about the life that we want to provide for our child, but if you and I don't have a strong enough relationship, how can we expect to provide a stable and loving environment for this baby? I don't want us to be co-parents and I sure as hell don't want to be your *baby mama*. I want to be your world…your everything."

I sat and listened to the future mother of my child chastise me as if I were her child. Be that as it may, everything she was saying was absolutely correct. Karen read me from top to bottom, and I realized that she knew me better than I thought she did. After she finished with me and sent me away, I walked back into my room to take a shower. As the steaming hot water ran down my body, I prayed for it to cleanse me of my ways. The crazy life I was living had to come to an end. All of my lying, sneaking around, and keeping my options open had to stop. Karen had given me a true chin check and I had to come to grips with the fact that whether I wanted it or not, a child was on its way into this world. When my shower was over and I entered the bedroom, Karen was already in bed. I stood in the door and gazed at the woman that was carrying a part of me. It was a part of me that I wanted to watch blossom into a being that was going to be more beautiful and successful than its mother and father. My thoughts were snapped by a sudden sniffle. Why was Karen crying?

"Are you okay?" I asked as I sat down on the bed beside her.

"André," Karen paused. "How do you really feel about me?" Those seven words plucked a nerve in me that caused me to really express to her my true feelings.

"You really want to know how I feel?"

"Yes I do."

"I'm a little confused, as well as a little scared. Since I've been in Atlanta, I've been trying to figure out my reason for being here. All I know is that I gave up the person that meant the most to me in this world before you came along. For a while, I was trying to place the blame on everybody else, but now I realize that the only person to blame for my actions is me. When I went back home and watched Alicia walk out of my life forever, I thought I was going to be okay because I had you here. I was starting to love two women at the same time and I knew that, eventually, I was going to have to choose and I did. I chose to be with you. When you first told me that you were pregnant, I felt that I was the happiest man in the world, but I was crushed. I was trying to cover up the pain that I had deep down inside. Over these past months, you and I have spent so much time together; I thought that you were the one I was destined to be with regardless of my past. You have become a major part of my life in more ways than you will ever know. You are responsible for my success at the network because you believed in me. During the time we spent after the network gave us the go ahead for the new show, you became more to me than just a colleague. You became a friend. Other than Alicia, you are the only person that knows almost everything about me. To answer your question, I care a lot about you and hopefully… I can grow to love you."

Karen sat up in the bed and put her arms around me and hugged me. I could feel her tears running down my back as she cried even more. Somehow I felt that those tears were tears of joy. Maybe this was what she had been waiting to hear. I didn't know. When she finally gathered herself enough to speak, Karen opened up to me that night causing me to look at her in a totally different light.

Karen grew up in University City—which was a suburban area in St. Louis, Missouri. Being from a wealthy family, one would have thought she had it easy. I found that the children of well-off parents had it worse than average kids or project kids. They are put under a tremendous amount of pressure that either drives them to succeed or drives them crazy. In Karen's case, I think it did a little of both.

Daniel Union, son of a white New York lawyer, married Carla Stedman, a young, black girl from Syracuse. Shortly after their wedding, Mr. Union's grandfather passed away, leaving him a large inheritance. Included in the inheritance was an enormous estate in St. Louis and the sum of five hundred thousand dollars. He gathered his belongings and his new bride and headed for the Midwest. Two years later, the Union's brought a baby girl into the world—Karen Elizabeth Union. At the time that Karen was born, her parents were going through pure hell because they were an interracial couple. Through all the ignorance of the time, it made them stronger despite the persecution of their families, mostly his. Growing up, Karen did not know why she never associated with black children. Mr. Union only wanted the best for his child, as any loving father would, but his ways were a little warped. He felt that in order for her to gain acceptance, he had to promote her in his white-washed society. Karen took ballet, etiquette classes, and piano lessons. For the first thirteen years of her life, she was raised to be a white child. It wasn't until her ninth grade year that the school district rezoned, forcing her mostly white high school to further integrate.

Her father wanted to withdraw her and place her in private school because he did not want his daughter to associate with what was by birth, her heritage. Her mother fought and fought until she convinced him to do what was best for Karen and let her be submerged in a diverse culture and associate with children like her. Her transition was not an easy one. She had been a part of her father's white culture for so long; she was socially retarded when it came to being around black students. She knew nothing of black music, fashion, slang, or the dances. Many days Karen came home from school crying because she was teased about being a white girl. Her looks were already one strike against her because she had an extremely light complexion, gray eyes, and straight brown hair. As I learned growing up, kids are going to be kids. If it wasn't for one girl, she would have never learned how to function or survive in a diverse environment. No matter how hard she tried to gain acceptance, she couldn't until she met her best friend to this day, Charlene Graham.

Charlene took Karen under her wing and reprogrammed everything in her mind. Through her newfound friend, Karen learned how to adapt to Black culture. By her senior year in high school, Karen was one of the most popular girls at University City High School. She was Captain of the cheerleading squad, Student Body President and Vice President of the National Honor Society. Her change almost destroyed her father. How could any man want to deny his child their heritage? No matter how much white she had in her, she was still going to be viewed as black.

Mr. Union felt that his dreams for his daughter were being shattered. His plan was for her to attend an Ivy League College and study Law, as he did. He tried to do everything he could do to keep her in his little white society, but you know how teens get when they feel forced to do something they don't want to do. Karen became very rebellious, and her defiance caused her to run down some wrong roads. She tried to do everything opposite of what her father wanted for her. He wanted her to go to Cornell University in Ithaca, New York, but she wanted to attend Clark Atlanta University. He even went so far as to say that if she wanted to attend the college of her choice, then she would have to pay for it by herself. How was a girl that had never worked a day in her life going to pay for college?

After high school graduation, armed with

only determination and a dream, Karen left St. Louis and moved to Austell, Georgia to live with Charlene. Her best friend managed to pull a few strings and get her a job working at the same mortgage company she worked for. When the fall semester came around, Karen didn't have the money to pay tuition, so the start of her college career had to be deferred. Day in and day out, Karen worked many long and hard hours to gain every dollar she could. She worked overtime, double time, and whatever else she could to put money in her pockets. When the spring semester rolled around, she enrolled as a full time student at Clark Atlanta University majoring in Mass Communications with a focus in broadcasting. The fulfilling of her dream was on the road, but far from over.

During her first semester, she met Keith McDowell, a junior at Clark. Keith was the typical upperclassman that preyed on the freshman class. He knew he was attractive, and he used the fact that he was high yellow with good hair to lure women in. Karen took a quick liking to him for the wrong reasons. Keith also had money, and he used that to keep Karen and manipulate her to do everything he wanted. The more money he spent on her, the harder she fell for him. By the end of the semester, she was head over heels in love with Keith.

Blinded by her love, she couldn't see the things that Keith was doing to her. Nothing mattered to her, as long as he was coming home to her. Because of him, she became the laughing stock of Clark Atlanta. Anytime she walked into a room or a building, she would see people giggling and whispering, and she didn't know why. As the relationship (if that's what you want to call it) went further, Keith became verbally and physically abusive. Her love and loyalty would not allow her to leave. There were quite a few days that she wore dark sunglasses to work and class to hide black eyes. No matter how hard Charlene pleaded with Karen to leave him, she wouldn't. Soon she turned her back on her own best friend. Now she had no parents and no friends—just an asshole that she called a boyfriend.

Prior to Keith's graduation, Karen walked into her apartment and found him in bed with another woman. Shakespeare was right when he said: "*hell hath no fury like a woman scorned.*" Karen unleashed all of her anger and pinned up frustrations out on Keith and his mistress, sending the girl to the hospital and Keith out of her life forever. Her eyes were opened, and she realized that she didn't need a man in her life in order to function. Before I came along, she'd dated but couldn't bring herself to get serious with anyone.

After Karen finished telling me that horrid story about her life, I never looked at her the same. I had newfound respect for her. At that moment she issued me an ultimatum that I had no choice but to succumb to. "André," she said, "I care a lot about you, but I refuse to go through that ever again. I'm telling you right now, it's all or nothing. Either you commit to me, because you care about and want to be with me and not just because I am carrying your child, or I can walk out of your life and the only time you will see your child is through the courts." From the look in those gray eyes, I could tell that she meant every word. In my mind I thought about all of the children that grew up without a full family and realized that I didn't want my child to be one of them and have to grow up without me.

"You mean the world to me," I stated, "but if my ways are going to cost me a relationship with my child, then it is you I choose. Understand that it is not going to be easy; I have not been in a committed relationship in a long time, but if you care about me like you say you do, you'll be patient with me."

"All I want from you is love, unconditional."

With those words, I kissed my queen and put her to bed. My mind was racing too much for me to sleep, so I went in the front to watch television. While watching some movie, I saw a commercial for an episode of the Montel Williams Show entitled, "Where Were You?"—A show about single mothers confronting their children's fathers. I didn't want that to ever happen to my child. Because of how I grew up, even though my grandparents gave me all of the love I ever needed, I still wondered what my life would have been like if my parents had stayed together and raised me. That is something I'll never know the answer to. I did know for sure that my child will never have to ask where his or her father is.

24

Choices

Karen and I settled our differences and went to bed. As hard as I tried, I still couldn't fall asleep because of the ultimatum Karen issued me. With one hundred and one thoughts running around in my mind, the thought of Alicia was the most prevalent. Quite a few months had passed and not one word—no email, no phone call, no nothing. I thought we could have at least salvaged a friendship. Alicia was a woman that I practically grew up with. She knew me inside and out. I never would have thought that we would be in this type of situation. True, she and I had a falling out back in junior high, but we were just kids then. When we reunited in college, we vowed that nothing would ever come between our friendship.

The choice Karen gave me was a hard one to swallow. Since I made the decision to let Alicia go, I grew to care for Karen. Many men would have killed to be in my situation. Sometimes I felt as if I didn't want to be in my situation anymore. At that point in my life, I was a successful black man who did not want for anything. Why wasn't I happy? As far as my love life was concerned, I was still a mental and emotional wreck. I had given up Alicia and chosen Karen before I found out that she was pregnant. I should have just chilled out. Since Karen was carrying my baby, I had to make it work; if not for me, then for the sake of our child. I cared about Karen a lot, but it seemed that I needed a little more to seal it.

That next weekend, Smoke invited us to a cookout at his house. Karen and I went because a lot of our friends and colleagues from the network would be attending. With everyone inquiring about the baby, we seemed to be the center of attention. It made me feel good to see Karen's face light up every time someone commented on how beautiful the baby was going to be because of the two of us, or how lucky I was to have a woman like her in my life. Midway through the evening, I found myself engaged in an intense game of Spades with Troy, Smoke and Alex. Troy and I were on the verge of running a strong ten when Karen came out to the patio to see if I needed anything. When the guys saw that take place, that's when the conversation began.

"I gotta tell you, Dré," Smoke said as he threw out a card. "You have got to be the luckiest man alive."

"Why you say that?"

"Every man at Black Reign, including the dudes sittin' at this table, done tried to holla at

Karen. You bring yo pretty ass to the ATL and look at you now… Mr. Karen Union." We all laughed.

"That's true," Alex interrupted. "I tried to holla at her right before you came to the network, but she shot me down before I had a chance to get all my words out. She told me she didn't date and she wasn't ready for a relationship."

"Neither was I," I said. "Karen and I was something that just happened. When I first came here, my focus was on my girl back home."

Smoke asked, "Whatever happened to her?"

"I didn't tell y'all?" They shook their heads no. "At the end of December, Alicia decided to pay me a surprise visit. When she got here, she got a surprise of her own. She found Karen in my apartment with me."

"Doin' da grown people?" Smoke asked.

"No, fool. That was around the time when me and Karen started working on *Matters of the Heart* and was doing most of the writing for it at my place after work."

Alex inquired, "What happened when you tried to explain?"

"Karen and I both assured her that we were just colleagues and that our involvement was strictly professional, but you know how some women are. The situation just didn't look like work."

Troy asked as he racked a book, "Why not?"

"Because when I answered the door I was wearing a pair of basketball shorts and a wife-beater and Karen came from the back in some short night shorts and a T-shirt that Alicia bought me for my birthday last summer."

Alex asked, as he straightened the cards to shuffle, "So what happened then?"

"Karen stayed away for the week that Alicia was in town, but after Alicia left, Karen told me that she had started to develop feelings for me. One thing led to another, and Alicia and I went our separate ways, and now Karen is pregnant."

"I guess the next step is marriage," commented Troy.

"Hold up!" Smoke threw his cards on the table, stood up and held his hand in the air. "I don't allow no cussin' in my house!"

"Sit yo black ass down!" Troy laughed.

"Marriage." I paused for a minute and sorted my hand. "Wow…that's a big step. Karen and I have to be together a lot longer than what we have been if we want that to happen."

We continued to shoot the breeze until the game was over. After the game, I went in to check on Karen. Smoke's lady friend told me that she was in the back bedroom talking to one of her friends from the network. As I walked to the back, nature called and I had to get rid of a little Hennessy. I didn't realize that the bathroom I went into was connected to the bedroom where the two women were talking. I heard Karen's voice through the cracked door as I unzipped my pants. I stopped what I was doing when I picked up on their conversation.

"The question you are not answering is," she said. "Do you love him?"

"I care a lot about André and I do love him. The more we are together; the deeper I fall in love with him."

"Have you told him this?"

"I want to, but not until he shows me that he cares for me because of me, not just because I am carrying his child."

"I can feel you on that, but how is he as a companion?"

"He is wonderful to me. We talk about anything and everything. He treats me like a queen, but I can't help feeling that he's sleeping around on me."

"What makes you think that?"

"I'm going to tell you something in the strictest of confidence."

"I won't say a word."

"I went through a lot with men before André came along. I was fed up and through. On that day when he sat across from me in his first interview, something inside of me told me that I had to have this man."

"What was it about him?"

"André is a gorgeous man. He is educated and sexy, but as far as I was concerned, he was beneath me on the social scale. After I saw his work, I knew that he would be successful at the network and one day he would be on the level that I needed my man to be on. Without flinching I set out to make him mine, and I was going to do it in a way that he couldn't deny me. The fact that he had a felony on his record gave him that bad boy streak that all women like. When he came up with the idea of this new show, I knew that he was going to do big things, and I was not going to let anybody else get to him. The only thing that I regret is lying to him."

“What did you lie about?”

“When the network gave him the green light for the show, I insisted that I be put on as an Executive Producer. I told him that the only way the network would let it happen was if he and I shared the position of Executive Producer. After that, I practically strong armed my way into his life.”

“Wow. That is serious. Are you ever going to tell him?”

“Not right now. I just can’t. I know what I did was wrong, but now that we have this baby coming I don’t want to do anything to make him want to leave me stranded as a single mother.”

“Since you were open with me can I give you my honest opinion?”

“Yes.”

“What’s done is done and you can’t go back and change it. You have to be honest and realize that if he is cheating or has cheated on you, you have to forgive him because neither of you are right in the situation. From what I know of him, he is a good man. Hearing everything you said, I advise you to forget about the past, wipe the slate clean and move forward. Not for you, not for him, but for what is growing inside of you.”

“I love him, but I will not let him disrespect

me."

"I don't think he's that type of man. A lot has happened to him in a short period of time, and if you ask me, the fact that he is still by your side says a lot."

"You're right, but I want him to love me for me and not just because I am carrying his child."

"You can't force him to love you. You just have to let it happen."

I couldn't believe my ears. I've heard of women trapping men, but I never thought that it would happen to me. Never had a woman gone through the lengths that Karen went through to be with me. In a way I was flattered, but on the other hand, I was a little angry. Because of her actions, I lost my best friend. Because I was blinded by other things, I let it happen. I should have remained focused on what I had, instead of looking at the things I could have had. At that point, everything was irrelevant because of my child coming into this world.

Now I had a serious decision to make. In a few months, a child was to be born bearing my blood and my name. If I chose to stay with Karen, then the relationship I dreamed of having with my child could be a healthy one. If I chose otherwise, the child suffered along with me. I had a decision to make, and it had to be made soon because Karen was going to want an answer. It wasn't like I would be unhappy with Karen, despite what I had just heard. She was a good woman—a little twisted, but still good. I just wanted to be sure beyond the shadow of a doubt. That night, as Karen and I rode home, I said nothing. I wanted so badly to call her out on what she said, but I kept it inside. The only thing I could do was occasionally glance at her when she wasn't looking or had her eyes closed. It seemed odd, but by the time we reached our destination, I had made my decision. I helped Karen upstairs and assisted her with getting ready for bed. When Karen fell asleep, I went in the front to watch television. About twenty minutes into the movie, Karen woke up, waddled from the back, and joined me on the couch. The look in her eyes told me that it was now or never.

"Karen," I said, as I turned down the volume. "I care a great deal about you, now so more than ever. It's not just because you are carrying our child, but because you are so wonderful to me. "

"How so?"

"Since day one, you believed in me. You saw something in me that you had to have. At that time it was for the benefit of the network, but now it's grown deeper than that."

"How can you tell?" Karen asked with certain nervousness in her voice.

"Let's just call it a hunch. At this point, the baby doesn't matter. I want to be with you and only you. The baby only adds more joy to the life that you and I already have."

"Oh, Dré!"

"I can't tell you that I love you just yet, but in time I will, as long as you continue to be the woman that you have been this entire time."

"I know you love me, André. I also know it's going to take some time to get it out. I'm willing to be here for as long as it takes, because I know that on the day you tell me you love me, you're going to mean it from the bottom of your heart and from the depths of your soul." Karen embraced me and I felt the bond between us tighten. I don't know what made me finally tell her what I did on that night, but I'm glad I did. That conversation seemed to ease her mind. No longer did she worry about my dealings with Vanessa, Natalie, or anyone else. I was her man and she was my woman, and nothing was going to take that away from us.

25

Reflections

For about a month and a half, I was on Straight Street with Karen. She was happy, and my life was in much better shape. I had not talked to any woman in any manner other than a friendly one. I even cut out going to the clubs with the guys. The only time I saw the fellas outside of the network was at the gym. How much trouble could a man get into while working out? One Thursday, I stopped off at the fitness center to relieve some stress that I had acquired due to Karen's pregnancy and the upcoming show. I started off with a run on the treadmill to get the cardiovascular pumping. While engaged in my run, a woman walked by, that caught my attention. She must have been new because I'd never seen her around the center before. I watched as she walked into the aerobics room and disappeared from my sights. When I completed my run, I walked over to the water fountain so I could peek into the room. She was the instructor.

Everything about her was sexy—the way she moved, her voice, and especially her body. She must have felt me looking at her because she managed to glance at me for a split second. If I was a single man, I would have stepped to her, but I wasn't. I shook her off and walked upstairs to move onto the next part of my workout. First it was bicep curls, and then onto the bench press. After a couple of sets, I rested on the bench with my eyes closed.

"Need a spot?" a voice asked.

I opened up my eyes to see this Aphrodite-like goddess standing above my head and leaning on the weight bar, staring down at me with a pretty grin on her face. This woman was brown-skinned and had stacks like the International House of Pancakes. The workout ensemble she wore showed everything from her washboard abs and thick muscular thighs to the thick print of her lil' woman that pushed through the Lycra shorts she wore. She had her long hair pulled back into a ponytail, brown eyes, and full, sexy lips. You know I had to check her out.

"Hi," she greeted as she extended her hand. "My name Serena."

"I'm Dré, nice to meet you."

"The pleasure's all mine. Listen, I know this sounds a little straight forward, but you are one of the sexiest men that I've seen in a-while."

"Thank you."

"A man like you must have a woman in his life."

"Actually, I do," I said as I laid back on the bench to continue my workout.

"Does she treat you right?"

"I can't complain."

"Does that limit who your friends are?"

"Not at all."

"Since I've been here, I haven't been anywhere, and I was wondering if you could suggest a good club."

"Me and my people go to Club Blaze on Friday nights, and sometimes we go to another spot called Classics."

"Are you going out this weekend?"

"I was thinking about it. It has been a while since I've been out, especially with my lady being pregnant."

"Oh really?"

"Yup. This is my first child."

"Okay. I guess I'll let you get back to your workout. It was nice to meet you and thanks for the suggestions."

I had really turned around in a short time. I

told her everything I could to let her know that I was not available. From the time I moved to Atlanta, to this day, I still haven't been able to figure out what was so special about me. I couldn't figure out why I got so much attention. When I was in South Carolina, women seemed to pay me no attention until I stepped to them.

I got Serena out of my head and completed my workout. Soon I was back home getting ready to enjoy a quiet dinner that Karen had prepared for me. She was quite the gourmet cook. When it came to pastas and sauces, she had it down to a science. Just as I was getting into my meal, my cell phone rang. I didn't recognize the number so I ignored it.

Karen asked as she paused from a fork full of pasta, "Why didn't you answer your phone?"

"I'm trying to eat. Besides, if it's important, they'll leave a message." Just as I was getting those words out of my mouth, my voicemail notification went off. I silenced it and continued to eat.

"Aren't you going to check it?"

"After I eat. Why are you so concerned with me answering my phone?"

"I'm not. It's just that you've never, not answered your phone unless you're asleep."

The phone rang again, bearing the same number. Once again, I ignored it and continued with my meal.

"André, answer the phone."

"Why?" I started to get a little bothered. "I am trying to eat my dinner."

"Are you hiding something?"

"You know what," I started, as I dropped my fork. "We're not getting ready to get into this right now."

"Why are you getting so defensive and upset?"

"Here," I said handing her my cell phone. "If it rings again, you answer it. If it is going to make you feel better, call the number back or check the voicemail. I don't care." I excused myself and walked back into the bedroom and slammed the door. Why was she all of a sudden questioning me, as if she had any place to? I had been nothing but straight up with her, but still she stressed me. Ill thoughts started to cloud my clear judgment and I needed to calm down. Suddenly, my conversation with Serena ran through my mind. I also thought about something that my grandfather told me. He used to say that if you give a woman any reason to question your fidelity, she is going to. From the episode after Houston, I knew Karen had been wondering. All she knew was that I spent the weekend in Texas with another woman. I admitted that to her. What she hadn't seen was me constantly telling women that I had a woman in my life, nor has she heard any of the cussin' outs I've received trying to cut some of those women out of my life.

Karen walked into the room as I was getting out of the shower. She handed me my phone and sat down on the bed. I looked at the phone to see if she had checked the message or called the number back; she hadn't. Maybe she did trust me and I was overreacting.

"Why is Serena calling you?" she asked

"What?"

"Why is Serena from the editing department calling you?"

"I don't know. I met her today while I was at the gym. She is one of the new aerobics instructors."

"How did she get your number?"

"I don't know. I guess she has access to membership records."

"Then why did she call your cell instead of your home phone?"

"Because when I joined, I was still living

with Jerome and I used my cell phone as my primary number." From the look on Karen's face, I could tell that she still was not convinced.

"Are you telling me the truth?"

"We can sit here and argue all night about this. I met Serena while I was working out and told her I had a woman that I was happy with that was carrying my child. She must have accessed the membership records and called. There is nothing I can do about that."

"She has no business using the fitness center's files for her personal use. I should have her fired."

"Baby, it's really not that serious." Why in the world did I say that? Karen then told me of the background between her and Serena. It was obvious that Serena had lied to me when she said that she was new in town. She and Karen used to be close friends before I moved to Atlanta. They would party together every weekend. I found that Serena was the type of woman that had to have every man that was showing interest in someone other than her. When she and Karen became friends, and guys would become interested in Karen, she would do everything that she could to lure their attention towards her. With her being a Black Reign employee, she must have known about our relationship. I guess she had her sights on me.

Judging from Karen's story, the more I rejected her, the more she would pursue me. I believed that it was going to be one of those situations that I was going to have to let my lady handle, and handle it she did. The next time the phone rang bearing that number, Karen answered the phone. Never before had I heard those types of words come out of my angel's mouth. Hopefully, Serena got the message and the situation was over. Boy was I wrong.

That Friday night it was guy's night out, and Karen decided to go out with her girls. As usual, the crew and I were going to Club Blaze. We had no clue where the girls were going. They couldn't do too much of anything with Karen carrying that basketball around in her shirt. At least I didn't have to worry about guys trying to hit on her. As usual, Club Blaze was jumpin'. From the time we walked in the door, the ladies were in full swing. I never understood why there were always more women than men in the club. I had to maintain; I had been doing good. I didn't want to fall off of the wagon. If not I was going to have to go back to those MWA (man-whore's anonymous) meetings. After we made our first round, I remembered that I told Serena that this was where I went on Fridays to party. Hopefully after her talk with Karen on the day before, she wouldn't say anything to me if she was in attendance.

I forgot that Black Reign was taping an

original movie about the origins of hip-hop. That explained the difference in price, and the fact that I saw so many stars walking around. Jermaine Dupri, Method Man, Rakim, Dr. Dre, and a few others were in attendance. Kid Capri and DJ Jazzy Jeff were the guest DJs for the night. No wonder it was fifty dollars to get in the club. All of the stars had the VIP sections and the best tables were occupied. I could see that the gold-diggers were in full lust mode. If Serena did come, hopefully she would focus her attention on someone other than me. Once again, I was wrong. Me and the fellas sat at our table, sipped Hennessy, and talked about people as usual, when they walked by. As I was laughing at Smoke's retarded ass, I saw Serena over Troy's shoulder. I turned to position myself to where she couldn't tell who I was if she did look in our direction.

"What are you doing?" Smoke asked when he noticed me slouch down in my seat.

"I'm trying to keep her from seeing me."

"Her who?" Alex inquired as he indiscreetly looked around.

"The one in the blue dress."

"Dayuuum, Dré!" Smoke shouted. "Why you tryin' to hide from her fine ass?"

"Would you please shut up and stop drawing

attention this way."

"My bad."

Serena was looking for someone, and I hoped like hell that it wasn't me she was searching for. I watched as she walked on and off of the dance floor. She even passed our table a couple of times and didn't look our way once. Either she didn't recognize me or she wasn't looking for me.

Troy asked, "What's the deal with that?"

"I met her yesterday at the gym. We had a conversation. I told her I was with Karen, and she walked off. When I got home, she called and Karen recognized the number and asked me about her. I told her the same thing I just told you. Her and Karen got some old beef between them."

Smoke asked while stirring his drink, "What's that got to do with you?"

"It seems that she tries to go after every man that wants Karen, and now I think she's after me."

Just as I said that, I saw Smoke's eyes look up at someone that was walking up behind me. I prayed that it wasn't Serena. "Hey, Dré," she said as she sat down. "I've been looking all over for you."

I didn't say anything. I got up and walked to the bathroom. When I came out, Serena was waiting for me. I took her aside and explained to her that there was nothing I could do to her or for her due to my allegiance to Karen. She tried to convince me that Karen was no good for me and it was her that I needed in my life. In the middle of one of her sentences, I saw that same look in her eyes that I had just seen on Smoke's face when she walked up behind me. I turned around and looked dead into the eyes of Karen Union. Karen asked with extreme attitude, "What is this, André?"

"What does it look like?" Serena replied when she stepped in front of me.

"Let me tell you something, Bitch. André is my man and there is nothing you can do for him that I can't or haven't already, so why don't you step off." Though she was prim and proper most of the time, Karen was still a black woman with a black woman's attitude.

"Why don't you let André speak for himself, because that's not what he was telling me before you showed up."

"I'm going to tell you this for the last time," Karen said as she rolled her neck and pointed her finger at Serena. "Stay away from my man before shit gets ugly, because right now you are treading on thin ice."

"What can you possibly do to me?" Why did she have to ask that question? Karen reached into her purse and pulled out one of her business cards and handed it to Serena.

"What is this?"

"Just so you know…I am not a writer any more. The Conrad Brothers and I are very close. So I'm not asking you, I'm telling you. Leave my man the fuck alone." Serena retreated into the crowd as Karen and the rest of her posse walked away. I realized that, when it came to me, Karen meant business. She was determined to let nothing come between us ever again, even if it meant she had to pull rank and flex her authority every now and then. I wanted to say something to Karen, but because she was in an ill mood, I left her alone. Around a quarter after two, I watched Karen and her girlfriends leave the club. The guys and I stuck around a little while longer because they wanted to holla at a couple more ladies. The heat mixing with the Hennessy led me outside to wait on the rest of the guys. While I was standing outside of my truck surveying the perimeter, Serena pulled up.

"I thought all you had was a girl," she said putting her car in park. "Didn't know she was your bodyguard, too."

"I guess it be like that sometimes."

"Anyway, I just wanted to tell you good night and hopefully I'll see you at the gym sometimes."

"Okay, whatever."

"And tell Karen that she better hold on tight because if she ever loosens her grip, I might just take you away."

"You can't take something that doesn't want to be taken."

"Don't worry, I'm just that good," she said as she drove off. There went a woman who either had a whole lot of nerve or a death wish. She knew that Karen meant what she said inside the club, but still she wanted to play with fire. Nevertheless, I was going to keep my distance in order to keep anything from popping off.

Five minutes after Serena drove off, the fellas came out of the club following three women. I was ready to go, but being the good friend that I am, I waited patiently on my homeboys. By the looks of things, my night wasn't getting ready to end just yet. Smoke came walking towards me with this look on his face. If I knew Smoke like I did, he was up to no good. Right before he got to the truck, Alex and Troy jumped in the car with the three girls and drove off.

"Come on dog," Smoke said as he opened up the car door. "We gotta follow them."

"What? Follow them where?"

"To an after party, at the Ritz Carlton in Buckhead."

"You have got to be kiddin' me."

"We knew if we rode with you, it wasn't happnin'. That's why Alex and Troy went with them. I know you ain't gone leave your boys hangin'. Are you?" Smoke gave me a Cheshire cat grin.

"The shit I do for y'all. Get in the truck." We followed the girls to the hotel. When we got there and went upstairs, the sixth floor was on swole. I later found out that one of the area's rappers had the entire floor for the night. You should have seen it. There were ten ladies to every one guy. Normally, I would have been cool with those odds. The way my life had been going, it was going to lead to nothing but trouble. It seemed like every room that I walked into had some ill actions taking place. All I wanted to do was chill until they were ready to go. I didn't want to be a part of what was going on. I told Troy I was going downstairs to the bar and for them to call me when they were ready to go. Unfortunately for me, the bar was closed, so I walked into the pool area to relax in one of the lounge chairs.

As I sat poolside, I gazed into the water; for a moment, I thought I was dreaming. I began to see reflections of my life appear on the glassy surface of the water. It went all the way back to the first day I met Alicia in elementary school, then to the day I left to come to Atlanta. The next scenes were the meetings of Vanessa, Natalie, and then Deja. After the sequence of women came my rise at Black Reign. Next was Karen. The next image was the most frightening. I was standing in between Karen and Alicia as they stood back-to-back, ready to face off in a duel with pistols. I watched as the two women took ten paces and turned to fire. The scene got twisted when neither woman fired their weapon, but an arrow came from behind Alicia and pierced Karen in the heart. I ran to catch her as she slumped over. She gasped, mouthed the words "I love you," and then died in my arms.

When I came to my senses, I was breathing heavily and scared to death. What did all of that mean? Had I made the wrong decision by choosing Karen? Maybe it meant that out of all the women that I had come in contact with since I had been in Atlanta, Karen and Alicia were the only ones that were true, and neither one of them wanted to let go. It was up to fate to decide. Now that Alicia was out of the picture, I wondered if Karen was the woman that I was supposed to be with. Only time would tell.

After witnessing that, I had to go. I tried to call each of my friends, but not one of them answered the phone. They were grown men, and they would have to get home the best they knew how. Home was where I needed to be. While in the elevator, I wondered if Karen was still going to be up.

When I walked into the apartment, I saw my baby asleep on the couch. Being that Karen was a light sleeper, she woke up as soon as I she heard the door close.

"Hey, baby," she said groggily. "What time is it?"

"4:30," I said as I put my keys on the end table.

"What took you so long to get home?"

"You know how my boys are. They don't get out much, so when they do, they make the most of it."

"As long as you had a good time."

"It was alright, but I think I am going to let the clubs go for a-while.

"What happened?"

"Nothing happened. I was just thinking, and I realized that I needed to spend a little more quality time with you."

"That's so sweet. Come here." I sat down on the couch beside her and she put her arms around me. This was the beginning of something stronger between Karen and I. When it all boiled down, she and my child were all I had. I leaned back on the arm of the couch and Karen put her head on my chest. We both rubbed her stomach as she sang a little song that her mother used to sing to her when she was a little girl. What more could I ask for? I had a beautiful woman, a great job, and a little one on the way. For the first time in a long while, I realized that I was truly blessed. Luck had nothing to do with any of it.

26

Completion

There comes a time in every man's life when he feels that it has all come together. Believe me when I tell you that it is a beautiful feeling. When it happened to me, it was something indescribable. My journey for completion was exhausting, and quite a few times I felt like giving up and accepting failure. As a strong, independent black man living in America, I could not allow that to happen. I struggled on, and look at me now. I had a successful career that carried high prestige and salary. Along side of me was a very beautiful and successful woman, and on its way into the world was the first of 2.5 children, as required for completion of the *American Dream.*

Once my eyes were opened up, I came to the conclusion that my life, as it existed, was real; because for a minute, I thought I had been dreaming the entire time. Alicia was gone and Karen was getting ready to bring a child into my life. Sometimes it takes your life flashing before you to take heed to your current situation. I'm just thankful that it didn't take a near death experience for me to see things clearly. After going through quite a few new beginnings, I could comfortably say that things finally leveled off. The relationship that Karen and I started building grew to be a healthy one. We were a happy couple on our way to being happy parents. The bond between us tightened more and more each day.

One time, I felt as if it had tightened too much too fast because of a conversation that came up, out of the blue, between Karen and I. "Do you think you could see me as your wife?" she asked.

"Is this a trick question?"

"I'm serious."

"Actually…yes I could."

"What about me; makes you say yes?"

"Because you are beautiful, intelligent, and an all-around phenomenal woman," I replied, then kissed her on the cheek.

"But what if we don't make it to that point? Suppose something happens between us and we part ways."

"Can we not talk about this right now?"

"André, these are things that we should be able to talk about."

"I know, but we should be concentrating on getting the child here first." I was trying to avoid that conversation as much as possible because it was a touchy subject, although I knew what Karen was getting at.

"André," she began. "I don't want to ever lose you."

"I'm not going anywhere."

"Do you promise?"

"As long as you promise never to leave me."

"Only death could ever take me away from you." That was a serious statement for her to make. Karen put the exclamation point on how strongly she felt about me, but I did not know the magnitude of her feelings was that great.

During my day-to-day activities, I could hear Karen's words echoing in my head. It was those same words that helped curb my curiosity about other women. No matter where I went, no woman seemed to draw me near her. My magnet for the opposite sex had finally worn out and lost its pull. A year had passed, and never had I expected my life to be how it was. In my original blueprints for my life, this was the section that would have brought Alicia to Atlanta; and nowhere on the plans was a section that said fatherhood. As a matter of fact, every time the blueprints changed, never was there such a section. Nevertheless, it had been incorporated in the newest plans for my future.

Many men dreamed of walking in the shoes that I was filling, and to tell you the truth, that's all I ever thought it would be for me—a dream. Seemingly insurmountable obstacles had to be overcome to put me in the position I was in. As a teen, I lost my grandmother, and losing her was like losing a piece of me. After that, I obtained a felony that was extremely difficult to shake off until Black Reign gave me the opportunity to prove myself. The love of my life left; came back and then I pushed her away; only this time, I felt like it was for good, and I really couldn't blame her if she never spoke to me again. Through everything, I existed with half a heart and still managed to rise to the top. When I looked at Karen, I only hoped that she would never leave me, but become the woman that I could give all my love to. The way we were going, it seemed that Karen, the baby and I, were destined for a future together. My skepticism and walls of fear that I built around my heart slowly crumbled and allowed me to pull Karen into me and nurture her feelings towards me. She rapidly filled the voids in my heart that were formed by the loss of my grandmother and Alicia.

I never thought that I could impact the lives of others around me the way that I did. As my friends watched the exterior of my relationship with Karen, they began to sluggishly put away their doggish ways. Troy faced up to his fears and told his lady friend that he was involved with, via a long distance relationship that he wanted her in Atlanta with him, because he was ready to take it to the next level. Surprisingly enough, that was the only thing that she had been waiting for Troy to say. Alex proposed to his girlfriend of six years, and she accepted. They hadn't set an exact date, but they did say that they were pushing for late next year. Zack finally gave in and married his fiancé of two years after she issued him an ultimatum similar to the one Karen issued me. Smoke put up a hard and grueling fight, but his girl finally KO'ed him into a commitment. Karen and I were reaching everyone, even my slut of a cousin, J-Rock. Just kidding. As hopeless as he was in the department of love, I knew that somewhere in this vast world that we lived in, there was a woman out there who would finally steal his heart. Maybe one day she would make parole.

My circle of friends was happy, I was happy, and as long as I was happy, Karen was overjoyed. We came to a stage in our relationship where we really needed to look towards the future a little bit. With the critical part of the show out of the way, it was time to disassemble the in-home writing room and turn it into a nursery. Living with a woman before I was married to her, was something that I did not want to do, but it was necessary. With the baby coming and Karen's lease getting ready to end, we made plans for her to move in with me, so we could put away some money to buy a house when my lease terminated.

I felt that I was falling in love with Karen, but I wanted to be a little surer before I expressed it to her. Karen seemed to be suppressing her desire to tell me that she loved me before I told her, but it was okay because we had an understanding of how the other felt. The mutual feelings were evident. Sometimes we would be sitting around the house and I would look at her in a certain way without saying a word. Every time she saw that look on my face, she would reply by saying "me too"—as if that look had told her that I loved her. Maybe it had, but I was not ready to verbally tell her.

Shortly after Zack married Nikki, we took him out to celebrate, since we did not have time to throw him a bachelor party because of *Matters of the Heart*. It was a Friday night in the ATL. We made plans to go to Classics instead of Club Blaze. Though we were all good friends, I had never had the chance to really get close to Zack because he wasn't around that much when we chilled outside of the network. That night, he asked me to pick him up on my way to the club. "What's up, pimpin'," I greeted as he got into the car. "You ready to do this?"

"You know it. I haven't had a drink in almost three weeks."

"Why not?"

"Nikki doesn't like me to drink when I'm

just sittin' around the house because her father was an alcoholic. I guess it bothers her, but it's rough for me, especially on those days when we had a rough one at the network."

"I feel you. Some nights I come home and drink a beer or a little bit of Hennessy. But other than that, is everything cool?"

"I can't complain. Nikki's a good girl, and she's good to me. What about you and Karen?"

"Everything is cool so far. We gettin' mad tight. She's moving in with me after the baby is born."

"That's cool, but be careful."

"Why you say that?"

"Me and Nikki lived together for two years before we finally got married. In the beginning it was lovely, but after a-while, I started to feel trapped."

"How so?"

"It was simple stuff like arguments. Whenever we got into an argument, I was stuck. It wasn't like I could go home or she could leave, because my home was her home; if I did leave, I still had to come back at some time or another. We had a space problem."

"Have you gotten it worked out now?"

"It'll never be completely worked out. A situation like that, you learn to live with and adapt to it."

"True." I tried not to let that deter me from the route that Karen and I were on. I had virtually lived with Karen for the past nine months or so, even though she had her own place. Things were rough through during that period when I was having a dilemma, about which woman I wanted to be with, but overall, Karen and I lived rather well together. Putting that out of my mind, Zack and I proceeded to the club where the rest of the crew was waiting for us.

Why! Why! Why! Out of all nights, this one had to be ladies night. Ladies got in free all night long, making the ratio of women to men about 10 to 1. Odds like that never go in my favor. I tried to convince my crew to leave and go to Club Blaze, but after they saw all of the women going into the building, their mouths started to water. "Calm down, André," I kept telling myself. "It is going to be okay."

Even though I was on the right path with Karen, the path was narrow, especially living in Atlanta. I had to walk slowly and think with the big head instead of the little head. Classic's was in a state of crunkness that I had never seen before.

Frank Ski from V-103 had the party hype. All the mornings I listened to him on the radio before I started listening to the Steve Harvey Morning show, I didn't know he had skills like he did. The night was going smoothly until I ran into an old acquaintance, Liberty Singleton. She was the one that I knew, but never had the chance to get to know. It's something about the "what if..." factor that sometimes causes the demise of a lot of things. I used to sit and think about Liberty and wonder what it would have been like if she and I had taken the time to get to know each other, because when I say she was a winner, it was no understatement.

Liberty spotted me about five minutes after I noticed her. She had this look on her face like she knew who I was but couldn't figure it out. We had only seen each other that one time at Club Ebony. We continued to make eye contact as I stood at the bar waiting for our drinks. She sat at a table with her friends. I figured that she was talking about me to her girls because, they too, started looking in my direction. On my way back to our table, I had to pass theirs. One of Liberty's friends stopped me. "Are you André Marshall?" asked her friend.

"Yes I am."

"Do you remember my girl?"

"I believe so. Your name is Liberty...right?"

"Yes." She answered then smiled.

"Let me drop these drinks off at my table and I'll get with you in a minute." Now what do I do since I had been positively identified? I talked it over with the other four members of my crew, and we asked the ladies to join us. The three sexy women sat with us as we partook in some drinks and friendly conversation. As Troy and Smoke kept the conversation going, I did not say too much. I kind of faded into the background, sipping on my drink. That way, when the liquor started to set in, I would be in a mellow mood and still maintain good judgment.

The thing I liked most about Classics was that the crowd was twenty-five and older, therefore there was not a lot of kill, kill, shoot'em up music played. The DJ mostly smoothed it out with quite a bit of old school hip-hop and R&B, but still maintained a hype crowd. If I knew this particular DJ like I did, he was getting ready to go into his classic ballad set. That set included artists like Luther Vandross, Patti LaBelle and Teddy Pendergrass. Sure enough, he dropped Luther's *If Only for One Night*. One of Liberty's friends squealed, "That is my jay-um." She grabbed Troy and took him out on the dance floor.

Liberty asked, "You wanna dance, Dré?" I followed Liberty through the crowd to the middle of the dance floor. She put her arms around my neck and began to sway her hips to the music. Dancing with Liberty to that old school song reminded me of the night I danced with Kayla to Ready for the World. Usually when men and women slow danced, the woman would rest her head on the man's chest or shoulder, depending on the height and the hairdo. Liberty was about five feet, five inches tall, and with her heels on she and I were eye to eye. It felt a little bit awkward being with her after breaking dates and avoiding her, not to mention the way she found out about Karen. I wanted to say something, or at least offer an apology, but I could not think of a word to say. Following Luther, a song came on that I had not heard in ages. It was Whitney Houston's classic ballad, *Where Do Broken Hearts Go*? At that moment I thought about my first junior high school dance. I danced my first slow dance to that song. The girl I danced with was Alicia. Because of the alcohol, I think, my emotions became very unstable. My nose started to burn, signifying oncoming tears. I let Liberty go without saying a word, made my way off of the dance floor, and went outside.

Zack must have seen me head towards the exit and followed me out into the parking lot. When he caught up with me, I was leaning on the back of my truck looking into the sky as if I was searching for something. "You straight?" he asked.

"I am so confused right now," I answered.

"Confused about what? You should be on top of the world. You got Karen, a successful career, a fat pocket, and you're getting ready to be a father. What's there to be confused about?"

"My life isn't as good as it seems. On the outside everything is cool, but on the inside, its pure hell."

"Dré, trust me. All of that is natural. You've been through so much in a short period of time."

"When I heard that song just now, the only thing I could think about was Alicia. Where is she? Who is she with, and if she is with someone, was he treating her like she was supposed to be treated?"

"From what I know about you and what I've heard about her, I know she meant the world to you. You made the decision to let her go. Now you have to put that behind you and focus on what is going on in your life now."

"But how can I let all those years of friendship and history go; just like that?"

"I know it's hard, but new things are going on in your life, that require you to be fully focused, meaning your child and your relationship with Karen. Clouded judgment has no place in your life right now."

"You're right. I really appreciate that."

"What are friends for, if we can't help each

other out?" Zack and I exchanged *one love* and went back inside the club. Everyone was wondering what happened to me. I told them that I was feeling sick and had to get some air. Once it was determined that I was okay, we continued our night. Talking to Zack helped me relax and realize that I had to overcome my past, no matter how hard it was for me to do. From that night, I battled my inner self something fierce. The harder I fought to gain control, the more difficult the task became. Everything that reminded me of Alicia surfaced—songs, clothes she bought me, little things she used to say, and things that Karen liked that she liked. I managed to push Alicia to the back of my mind, but not completely out. Though she was gone, there were still some memories that I wanted to hang on to, good and bad.

27

Deconstruction

More months went by and Karen got bigger and bigger. Around the close of the eighth month, our little one decided to make her grand entrance into the world ahead of schedule. I remember it like it was yesterday. Karen and I were on the couch watching a movie when all of a sudden she let out a sharp scream. I sprang to my feet and grabbed her. "Baby, it's time," she yelled. "Call Dr. Eason!" I ran around the house like a mad man. I didn't know who was more emotional, Karen or me. I managed to get everything together and we were off to the hospital.

It was excruciating to hear Karen scream in pain, and there was nothing I could do about it. For twenty straight minutes she called me everything she could think of. It felt as if I was driving Richard Pryor to the hospital. Through it all, I was there for her every step of the way. We got to the hospital and the nurses took her to the maternity ward, leaving me to get her registered. After completing that task, I was prepped and taken to the delivery room. I walked into the room just as the nurse was administering Karen's epidural. The sight of the needle alone caused me to become faint. One of the nurses caught me as I was falling to the floor and helped me to a chair. When I came to, I was on oxygen and the doctor was in the room. Things didn't look normal. Karen was not moving, nor was she saying anything. The nurse noticed that I was conscious again and asked me to step into the waiting area with her. When we got there, she told me that Karen was experiencing some complications, but assured me that all of the necessary precautions were being taken to ensure a safe delivery. I could barely think straight. I needed someone to talk to. Who could I call? In all my times of trouble, Alicia was right there, but it had been about nine months since I talked to her. It didn't matter at this point. She was the only one I could turn to.

What was she going to say? Maybe if I just heard her voice, it would give me the strength to see this through. My body went numb as I dialed her number. Every ring seemed five minutes long. After about four rings her voice mail picked up. "Alicia, this is André. I know I'm probably the last person you want to hear from right now, but I have no one else to turn to. Karen is in the delivery room right now giving birth to my child, but she is having complications. I don't know what to do. If you have any feelings left in your heart for me as a friend, please call me back. I need a friend right now." I hung up the phone and dropped my head.

I felt a little guilty because Karen was in

trouble and I turned to another woman for help. It seemed bad, but Alicia was really the only person I felt I could turn to. An hour later, the doctor came out of the room. I could tell by the look on his face that it wasn't good. "Mr. Marshall," he called as he approached. "We have a problem."

"What's the matter? Is it the baby? Did she lose it?" I started to get hysterical.

"Calm down, Mr. Marshall, the baby is fine. It's Ms. Union. Apparently her complications were worse than we thought. She had an aneurysm that led to a stroke. We had to do an emergency C-section on her to deliver the baby. Now she is in a coma."

"Is she going to be okay?"

"Right now, it's hard to tell. The only thing we can do now is wait and see, and hope for the best."

"Where is my child?"

"If you go around to the viewing room, the nurse will meet you there with your new daughter." I was truly thankful that nothing happened to the baby but what about Karen? What was I going to do if something happened to her? I could not raise a daughter by myself. All of this was becoming too much for me.

When I got to the viewing room, there she was. She was the most beautiful thing I had ever laid eyes on. She was an angel with a head full of jet-black hair, with her father's chinky eyes that were gray like her mother's. The nurse motioned for me to come into the room to hold the baby. When she gave me my child, I began to feel warm all over. "Hey little one," I said to my child. "Mommy's going to be alright and we're going to take you to your new home."

"Have you thought of a name for her?" the nurse interrupted.

"Yes Ma'am. Taylor A'reon Marshall." This was the name that Karen and I had chosen because of its meaning. Taylor was Karen's grandmother's first name. She and her Nana were very close. It was hard for Karen to gain acceptance from her father's side of the family because she was a bi-racial child. Nana Taylor loved her regardless. The first time I met Nana Union, she treated me as if I was one of her own. For those reasons, we chose to give our child the name of such a loving woman. As for A'reon, it was Egyptian, meaning *great treasure,* and that is exactly what she was, my greatest treasure.

Taylor was beautiful in every way, but I could not help thinking about the situation that I was going through. I realized that I really loved Karen for who she was. A future was in the works, but what would happen if she did not pull through? Karen had become my all. She was a companion and a business partner. She was a lover as well as a friend. After all of the strife that I went through to make things right between us, I felt that she had to pull through. I didn't want to sound selfish, but there were a lot of unfinished things that I needed her for. The show was in a critical state, we had the baby, and our relationship was just getting to the point we needed it to be in order to move to the next level. Until Karen recovered, I had to maintain for my child. For a week straight I never left her side. Finally, the doctor suggested that I take the baby home. I was a nervous wreck. I did not know how to take care of a child, nor did I have a mother's maternal instinct. This was definitely going to be a challenge. That evening, I loaded up my new baby and went home. It must have taken an hour to go twenty minutes down the road. When I got Taylor home, I held her in my arms and cried. Never before had I seen a more beautiful child. The thing that made her so unique was the fact that she was mine.

Whoever said taking care of a baby was an all day and all night job; was absolutely correct. I had to take maternity leave from work and was not the one that had the baby. It was murder for me being away from the job considering the show was just getting on the air. The Conrad Brothers brought in a producer from *Tryin' Times,* in order to keep the ball rolling. I was glad that they were so understanding and sensitive to my situation. They put me at ease by telling me to take all the time I needed, and that everything would still be there when Karen and I returned. Over the next couple of weeks, one would have thought I had won a shopping spree from the Baby Warehouse the way people brought things for the baby. The network sent a crib, a bassinet and a car seat. Our colleagues brought clothes, pampers, and formula. You name it, Taylor had it. You never know who your real friends are until tragedy strikes. Every night before I went to sleep, I would hold my daughter and say a prayer for her and her mother. I would ask God to keep my daughter safe and to watch over Karen and bring her home to her family.

Life was hard taking care of a newborn without her mother. Three months had passed and Karen was still in the hospital. One time we thought we lost her, but Karen was a fighter. She wasn't going out that easily. The hardest thing for me to do was leave my daughter and go back to work. I was put at ease when Karen's mother flew in from St. Louis to help me take care of the baby. Mrs. Union was more than happy to come take care of her first grandchild.

With Mrs. Union around, it was just like having my grandmother back in my life. When I woke up in the mornings, I had a hot meal, and when I came home in the evenings after work, dinner was waiting and the baby was fine. Regardless of how good things were going, my life was still empty. It was funny because even though Karen was not around, not one female tried to wiggle her way into my life. I guess they respected my situation. The first time I took Taylor to the mall, you would have thought she was a magnet. Out of all of the kids that were in the mall that day, every woman flocked to mine. When we stopped at the Portrait Studio to have our pictures taken, all of the ladies were melting to see a father with his daughter in that way. Usually it was the mother that took the baby for her pictures. Taylor and I were one. She was *Daddy's Lil' Angel* and was spoiled rotten.

Though everything seemed like it was going to be all right, things took a turn for the worse. Three months had passed and Karen was still in the hospital. It was hard to go on without her, but I had no choice. The Conrad Brothers tried to give me as much time as I needed, but without me at the network, the show would not have made it on the air like it was supposed to. One night at about six o' clock, Mrs. Union, the baby, and I were having dinner when the hospital called. I could tell by the look on her face that the situation didn't look good. We hurried off to the hospital. By the time we arrived, it was too late. Karen was gone.

I couldn't believe it. The woman that had mothered my child and helped me to get where I was at the network was no longer in existence. The doctors finally allowed me to see her. It just did not seem fair, but who was I to question God's work? It had to be for the best. As I looked down at my fallen angel, I was at a lost for words. I grabbed her cold hand and talked to her. I knew she was gone, but deep down inside, I knew she could hear everything I said. "The first thing I want to do is tell you thank you. Thank you for being there for me. Thank you for helping me; make a successful man out of myself, and thank you for giving me a beautiful daughter. Most of all, thank you for helping me realize that love really does exist. Even though I never got the chance to tell you before you left, I love you and I always will. I promise that I will do my best to raise Taylor in the image of you. Also to let her know who her mother was, and to let her know that even though you are not around, you will always be with her." I started to cry uncontrollably as the doctor and nurses helped escort me back into the trauma room. I did not know what I was going to do. Only God could give me the strength I needed to carry on and raise my child. When I sat down, Mrs. Union put Taylor in my lap and put her arms around me. For the first time in a while, I felt a mother's genuine love.

After I gathered myself enough to drive, I took Mrs. Union and Taylor back to my apartment. I wasn't ready to go in, so I drove around the city for about an hour. While I drove, thoughts raced through my head at a rate that I could not keep up with. People that passed by me, might have thought that I had gone crazy because I was talking to myself. There was no longer anyone for me to turn to; so who else could I talk to but myself? "Why! Why! Why!" I screamed as I hit the steering wheel. "After everything I went through trying to choose the woman that I thought was right for me and now she is gone. I thought that I was finally on my way to happiness." Tears started to fall from my eyes as I vented. "I always thought that to achieve the things you wanted, you had to take risks sometimes. I took the risk of a lifetime when I chose Karen over Alicia, but now my choice was in vain. I gave up more than ten years of love and friendship because I wasn't willing to maintain a couple hundred miles. I've lost everything." My emotions were getting the best of me, and it became hard to drive. I had to pull over into a parking lot to gather up so I could return home. I sat for about thirty minutes and sobbed over the loss of Karen. Her death opened up a gash in my heart that I thought had healed. The entire situation was in God's hands and he would be the only one that could help me through my pain.

Four days after that sorrowful night, we buried Karen at the Langston Hughes Memorial Cemetery. The funeral was beautiful, and all of our family, friends and colleagues were there. In my time of need, everyone was right there to help me through, but in my mind I felt something or somebody was missing. Through all of the turmoil, I could not manage to figure it out. After the funeral, our families gathered at my place for food and conversation. All of the noise and commotion was a little too much for me. I needed to get a way, at least for a little while. I put Taylor down for a nap and told my grandfather and Mrs. Union that I was going out for a walk. When I got downstairs and exited the building, I made a left and began to walk. I didn't know where I was going, nor did I have a destination in mind. I walked and I walked. Before I realized it, an hour had passed. When I looked around, I realized where I was. I was standing in front of the Deep Blue Jazz Café. This was where Karen and I spent almost every Saturday night listening to jazz and poetry. I peeped through the window and could see the cozy table that we used to sit at and enjoy time together. Such a talented poet and wonderful friend would never occupy that table again.

The scene was getting hard for me to bear. I began to walk back in the direction that I had come from when I noticed a strange car creeping beside me. I couldn't tell who was in the car. As I inconspicuously tried to make out the figure, the window rolled down and through it rolled a familiar voice. The voice asked, "Do you need a ride?"

I could not believe it. Slowly I turned to my left and there she was. The woman I thought I said goodbye to forever. It was Alicia. "Your grandfather told me you were out here somewhere. I guess I found you."

When I climbed into the SUV, I was still in

shock. I could not say a word. Even if I could, I wouldn't have known what to say. "I'm sorry I did not return your call, but I was in Japan on business. My job sent me there for training." Still I sat quietly looking at my lost angel. The only thing I could see or think about was the day, at Franklin Memorial, when I watched her walk out of my life, and now she was right here when I needed her the most. "I'm really glad to see you," I said in a hoarse tone.

"I'm sorry to hear about Karen. I don't know for sure, but did the baby make it?"

"Yes she did. I'm the proud father of a beautiful baby girl."

"What is her name?"

"Taylor A'reon," I said as I smiled and showed her a picture of the two of us. Alicia and I talked the entire way back to my place. She was exactly what I needed to help me get through this time. It might have been too soon to say, but deep inside I felt that I had my friend back.

We arrived at the Royal Winds and went upstairs. The majority of the people were gone. Mr. Union was asleep on the couch; Mrs. Union and my grandfather were sitting at the table talking about church. I introduced Alicia to Mrs. Union. They shook hands and then she hugged my grandfather. After the greetings were exchanged, she and I walked back into the bedroom so that Alicia could see Taylor. "Oh my God!" she said in a soft but excited voice. "She is so beautiful. Can I hold her?"

"Of course you can." I watched as Alicia picked up my daughter and held her close to her heart.

"Where are you staying while you're in town?"

"I'm at the W off of Ashford Dunwoody."

"How long are you going to be here?"

"I was supposed to leave on Monday. After seeing you, we need to talk about some things, but not right now. We'll get to that later." Alicia laid the baby down and we went back to the front with my grandfather and Karen's mother. The four of us sat and talked for hours. It was almost like old times again. My grandfather, Alicia, and I used to sit and converse for God knows how long on Sunday afternoons after church. No matter how things were with Karen and me, these were the times I missed. At one point during the conversation, I thought about my life and how it was one big baseball game and Atlanta was doing the pitching. No matter how hard I swung, I could not connect with a single pitch. Alicia…fastball. Vanessa…knuckle ball. Karen…curveball. Natalie…slider. Now another fastball. This was too much. The scary thing about it was that I didn't know whether or not I could function without someone in my life. In my time of pain, I needed someone to be there for me. For my own sake, I needed to work through this alone, at least for a little while.

The entire time we talked, I couldn't take my eyes off of Alicia and she couldn't take hers off me. It was like we were looking into each other's souls trying to find answers. As much as I wanted to have her back in my life, I felt like it was a no go.

Too much time had passed and we had a lot of catching up to do. Even if we couldn't have a relationship, I at least wanted my friend back. The night grew old and Alicia was getting ready to go back to the hotel. She said her goodbyes and walked towards the door. I followed, wanting so badly to ask her to stay with me, but not with my grandfather and Karen's parents still here. After we got downstairs, we sat in her car and talked for at least another hour. There was something burning inside of me that needed to be released and if I didn't let it go now, it would consume me.

"Alicia," I said as I took a deep breath. "I know we've been apart for a long time and we've had time to grow up as individuals. I want to take this time, while we are together, and apologize."

"There are no apologies necessary," she said cutting me off.

"Please, let me say this. I'm sorry for being selfish. When I left to come here, I didn't take time to look at the big picture. I tried so hard to hold onto something I knew wasn't going to work."

"Dré, please. You and I both knew that we were foolin' ourselves. A country boy in the big city, especially a guy like you."

"What's that supposed to mean?"

"You are a woman's dream. You are fun to be with, you treat the woman you are with at the time like a queen, you're easy to talk to, and if I tell you this last thing, promise me you won't let it go to your head."

"What is it?"

"And you are one of the finest brothers I know. Believe me, I didn't want you to leave, but who was I to stand in your way? Now you're living your dream. You have a successful career and a beautiful daughter. What more do you need?"

I looked her directly into her eyes and said nothing for five minutes. "My friend back," I finally answered.

"I never left you. Even though you didn't choose me to be the woman in your life at the time, I knew deep down that our friendship was still there, and if given the chance, we'd get it back together."

"But what about all that I've put you through? How could you possibly want to be my friend?"

"Do you remember what you told me about a month before you left to come here?"

I thought about it for a minute. "No," I said. "I don't remember."

"Think about it and it will all come clear. We'll talk about it more tomorrow. I have a training class to teach early in the morning."

"How about; we meet for lunch at that Chinese restaurant, two blocks from your hotel. You'll see it when you go back tonight."

"Lunch it is. I'll see you tomorrow." Alicia kissed me on the cheek as I was getting out of the car. I stood as she drove out of sight. What could I have possibly told her before I left? Hopefully it will come to me by our engagement.

I had been through enough for one day, and Mr. Sandman was calling my name. When I got back upstairs, my grandfather had gone to bed and Mrs. Union was still cleaning up. I tried to get her to go to bed, but she said that she just couldn't stop. I thought that I was hurt the most by Karen's death, but I failed to realize that she was the Unions' only child. I said goodnight to her and walked to my study to go to sleep. She stopped me. "André," she paused. “Come here and sit down.”

“Yes Ma’am,” I said as I walked to the table and sat down.

“Tell me the truth. Do you still have strong feelings for Alicia?”

“Honestly, Mrs. Union, I don’t know what I’m feeling.”

“Let me tell you something. I know you still have feelings and a strong attachment to Karen, but now it’s time to face reality. Our baby is gone and there is nothing you or I can do to bring her back. You are a successful black man with a daughter now. With the caliber of your profession, you need someone to help you. Don’t let your foolish pride or wondering how everyone else is going to react, stop you from knowing when you can’t do something by yourself. An opportunity is here, and you need not let it pass you by.”

“I don’t understand,” I said with confusion.

“Take it from a mother. Alicia needs you and you need her. Whether you know it or not, I know the entire situation from start to finish. Karen told me the whole story. Believe me when I tell you; mama knows best. While she’s still in Atlanta, you need to take advantage. God makes things happen for a reason. It’s not going to happen overnight, but it will happen. You just have to let it."

"How can you tell?"

"While all of us were talking earlier, I watched the two of you. You were like two teens in high school, watching each other's every move. I talked to your grandfather about the situation, and he agrees with me one hundred percent. The rest is up to you." How did she know everything I was going through and feeling? I felt as if that was my grandmother talking to me through her, and my grandmother never once steered me wrong.

Tomorrow was a big day and I needed to get some sleep. I hugged Mrs. Union and thanked her as I turned to walk away. "André," she said. "Remember, if you let something go and it comes back, that shows you how strong it was." That was it. Those are the exact words that I told Alicia before I left to come here. I ran back to Mrs. Union and kissed her on the cheek. "Thanks…Mom."

It had all come clear to me now. Alicia was the one I belonged with. Even if it took losing Karen for us to come back together, it was somehow in God's will. I realize things happen for a reason and shouldn't be questioned. Patience will help bring it to the light. Maybe Karen was put here and brought to me to teach me how to love. That night, as I knelt to pray, I thanked him for my child, my grandparents, Mrs. Union and especially Karen.

28

Reconstruction

Even though I had gone to bed late that night, at about 8:30 A.M. my eyes just popped open and there were no signs of sleepiness or fatigue. I felt as if I had been reborn. When I walked into the front room, Mama Union was feeding Taylor. Mr. Union and my grandfather had gone downstairs to load the cars for their journeys home.

"Well, son." said Mrs. Union. "It is time for me to go. If you need me, you know how to get in contact."

"I don't know if I'm ready for this."

"You're ready. You didn't get where you are today not knowing if you are ready or not. You can do it. Remember what I told you last night. Your help is here, you just have to go and get it."

"Yes ma'am." As I said that, the two men came back in laughing.

"Well, André," said Mr. Union. "Take care of my granddaughter and don't be a stranger. Call and let us know how you and the baby are doing, and hopefully you'll come to St. Louis to visit."

"I will, sir."

Mrs. Union stood up and gave me the baby. She hugged me and told me to be strong, if not for myself then for my daughter. She gathered the remainder of her belongings and the two of them were gone. I looked at my grandfather.

"Are you sure you can't stay a little longer?" I asked.

"I would, but I gotta preach outta town tomorrow. I need to be gettin' up the road."

"Thanks for everything, Dad."

"That's what your family is for. Don't worry. Everything gone be alright. You just trust God, and he'll see you through. But for your sake, you need to find a church down here and get in it. Become a member, but rememba, you can always come home."

"I know, thanks." When I hugged my grandfather as he was leaving, I knew that instant that everything was going to be just fine. When he left, I sat down and gazed at my daughter. I was so thankful for her, and because of her, I had to succeed and maintain.

Time began to fly and before I knew it, it was time for me to meet Alicia for lunch. While I was getting Taylor's things together, I started to see what mothers have to go through before they leave the house. I had to make sure she had pampers, wipes, bottles, bibs, extra clothes, and who knows what else. Before I could complete the task of getting all of her belongings together, the doorbell rang. I guess she figured that since I had the baby, Alicia came by with carryout. I wish I had known this before I ran around the house like a maniac. I walked back in the nursery to put Taylor's things away. When I came back in the front, I saw a scene that almost made me cry. Alicia was sitting on the couch holding Taylor. I stood in the hallway and watched her talk to my child. It was amazing. I guess all women have some type of maternal instinct. Taylor looked right at home in Alicia's arms. After about five minutes, she noticed that I was watching her.

"Come and eat before the food gets cold, Daddy," she said as she smiled. I couldn't take my eyes off the two of them. The two ladies that meant the most to me were together and getting along. We started to eat and laugh as if we had never been apart.

"I guess it was that strong," I said as I paused from my fried rice.

"Stronger than you could ever imagine." Alicia knew exactly what I was talking about. "So where do we go from here?"

"I need you in Atlanta, with me."

"I need to be here with you."

"What about your job?"

"Remember when we were talkin' last night?"

"Yeah."

"My job is givin' me a transfer. I can go one of two places, Los Angeles or Atlanta." I could not believe it. Through all of the chaos and storms in my life, I could see my skies brighten. I was given the chance to make things right. "If I choose LA, I fly out in two days. If I stay, I have two weeks to find a place. During those two weeks, my company will pay for my accommodations at the hotel that I'm at."

"Alicia," I paused. "You mean the world to me. There is nothing that I would rather have than the chance for us to regain what we had in school. You know as well as I do that we can't have that if you go all the way to the West Coast."

"So what are you asking me?

"Alicia Burroughs, I ask you for the opportunity to make things right between us, no matter how long it takes. I need you in my life. Please, stay in Atlanta." When Alicia looked into my eyes, she saw true sincerity. She knew that what I was saying was real and straight from the heart. Emotions rose to a high level of intensity, and before I knew it we were locked in a hug that combined our souls once again. Not once did she ask me about my feelings for Karen. It seemed like she knew that the feelings I had for Karen were different than the ones I had for her. She also knew that it was going to take some time for me to get over losing her. Nevertheless, she assured me that no matter how long it took, she was going to be right there for me.

The rest of the day was spent getting our newly found family acquainted. She and I played with Taylor and with each other. I had my friend back, and I refused to let her go ever again. We sat and started brainstorming for our future. Through the course of throwing ideas around, the subject of a house came up. It wasn't a bad idea because of the baby. We needed an office/study and Taylor needed her own room. If we bought a house, we would have a yard for the baby. Most of all, we would be away from the hustle and bustle of the city. There were several outskirt towns where nice houses were available, but it was too early to be making those plans. We had only been back together for a few hours and we were already looking towards the future. It might seem crazy but it felt right.

Night fell and all of the fun and games wound up. Alicia fell asleep on the couch with

Taylor lying on her chest. I stood on the terrace and looked out over the city of Atlanta. At that moment, I offered an apology to the city on behalf of everyone that had ever blamed it for any hardships concerning a relationship. For me, it was a helper. It helped me grow up and become a man. Atlanta also helped teach me about responsibility and real love. I thought about something that my grandfather told me when I was a young boy. He told me that life was like a field mule. If you show weakness it won't respect you, nor will you be able to control it. If you stand firm and let it know that you are in full control, it will be your best friend. That's how I felt about my life at that moment. It started to become my best friend. At first, it was kicking me around. When I realized that it was up to me to control it, things changed. As that thought passed through my mind, two stars twinkled in the distance. I believed that was the city's way of saying that it accepted my apology for the blame it had taken from everyone.

After my conversation with the city was done, I stepped back into the house, covered my two ladies up with a blanket, laid down on the floor below them, and went to sleep the happiest man in the world. The next morning I woke up to the smell of bacon, eggs, and pancakes, just like old times. Alicia was on the couch watching her talk shows as she fed Taylor. My phone rang as I walked into the kitchen to fix my plate. I called from the kitchen, "Could you get that for me?"

"Hello," Alicia answered.

"I'm sorry, I must have the wrong number," said the voice.

"Are you calling for André?"

"Yes I am."

"Hold on a minute," she said putting down the phone. "André, telephone."

"Who is it?"

Picking the phone back up, "May I ask who's calling?"

"This is Natalie."

Handing me the phone, "Natalie."

"Natalie, what's up?" I put my plate on the coffee table.

"Hey, Dré. How've you been?"

"I'm maintaining as best I can." Alicia looked at me.

"Who was that lady that answered the phone?"

"That was Alicia."

"Your friend from back home?"

"The one and only. So, what's up?"

"I was just calling to tell you that I'm sorry I couldn't make the funeral and if you need anything, call me."

"Thanks Nat. I really appreciate that. Can I hit you later? I was just about to eat breakfast." I finished my conversation and hung up the phone to eat.

"Was that Natalie Simms?" Alicia asked sipping her coffee.

"Before you get started, Nat is just my friend."

"Come on Dré, you know me better than that. Our slate has been wiped clean and the past is now the past. We have to get over it, me more so than you. If we are going to finally do this, then I have to trust you. I'm here now, and I don't plan on going anywhere." We finished breakfast and got ready to get out for the day. Since I was still off work, Alicia took the day off so we could go looking for an apartment for her. She could have easily lived with me, but she had this thing about living with a man before marriage and I respected that because I was raised the same way. While we were riding to her hotel for Alicia to pick up a few things, she asked me an array of questions that I didn't mind answering until she asked me that question I wanted to avoid for as long as I could.

"How many people have you slept with since you've been in Atlanta?"

"Huh?"

"If you can huh, you can hear. How many? And before you answer, I want the truth."

"Let me think," I said as engaged in a long pause.

"Damn, André, that many?" she asked jokingly.

"I didn't say anything."

"I know, but anytime a man has to think…"

"Three."

"Negro Please! I know you."

"Honestly."

"Who?"

"Karen, of course, Estacia Morgan…"

"The Actress? Stop lyin'."

"Seriously."

"And who else?"

"I don't know her name."

"So you just got busy wit' a complete stranger."

"Uh huh," I nodded.

"You so nasty," she playfully said.

"What about you?

"One."

"Who?"

"Promise me you won't get mad."

"I promise."

"Patrick."

"Patrick Knight! Gay-Ass Patrick Knight!"

"He is not gay. He's just a pretty boy."

"Pretty gay."

"You mad?"

"Nope."

"Yes you are, because you are the king of the double standard. Remember back in junior high when you started going with Victoria and I started seeing Shawn?"

"Why you bring up old stuff?" Until that

moment, I never realized how beautiful Alicia was inside and out. As she drove, I could do nothing but stare at her. She saw me looking at her, but she said nothing. It was like we were having a mental conversation. After we went to the hotel, we picked up an apartment guide and started our search for the perfect place. For about three hours we rode around various parts of Atlanta until Taylor started getting aggravated, so we took her home. When we got there, I fed Taylor and put her down for her nap, then started going through the guide some more.

"What about the Bridgeford Arms?" Alicia asked.

"No," I said shaking my head. "That's where Jerome lives. It's not a good area."

"But it's not that far from here."

"This is the good side."

"Who else lives there?" Alicia asked as she played devil's advocate.

"What is this, 21 questions?"

"Why are you getting so jumpy? I just asked you a simple question. Is there something you want to tell me? "

"Okay, okay. I'm going to get it all out in the open. Vanessa lives there. She is the first woman I met when I got to Atlanta. She and I got kind of close, but she knows about you. Natalie and Shawna are basketball players for the Atlanta Diamonds. Natalie and I went out a couple of times and she knows about you, too. I didn't deal too much with Shawna. Liberty called from time to time. We never officially went on a date, but we ran into each other at Classics. We met at Club Ebony. Speaking of Club Ebony, I almost had an episode with this girl named Deja that works there."

"A booty girl?"

"No. She runs the door and helps J-Rock with the books."

"Is that all?"

"I think. If I come across somebody else, I'll be sure and let you know."

"Listen, you didn't have to tell me all that, but its good you got it out of your system. I'd hate to have to bust ya ass when they came poppin' up later and you try to hide them or cover them up."

"You think you know me don't you?"

"I know you better than you know yourself."

"This is true. All I ask of you is patience. Everything has happened so fast, and I just want to have a clear head."

"I know it's gonna take some time for you to get your mind right, and I'm with you every step of the way. You have always been my number one guy, and I have always had your back. Why would I stop now?"

29

Into the Soul

A couple weeks after Karen's death, reality set in. My emotions took me on a ride that I was not ready for. I was upset, confused, traumatized, and most of all, hurt. Through it all, I knew that time would work everything out. When Alicia assured me that she was going to stand by me while my wounds healed, she was for real. I was hurt in more ways than I thought. For one, I lost Karen. I did not realize how much I loved her, despite what she'd done to me, until she was gone. The thing that hurt me the most was that I never got the chance to tell her before she passed. Another thing that was hard to deal with was the fact that I had to face Alicia after what I put her through. If it had been the other way around, I don't think I would have been as understanding as she was toward me. Her understanding was one of the things that made her so unique. She had forgiven me for so much. Now that I had her, I felt like I didn't deserve to have her back in my life.

Before Alicia and I jumped into anything, I needed to do some serious soul searching. I wanted to spend every day and night with her, but I couldn't. I felt like I was bouncing from one woman to the next. I needed to take some time to be by myself to sort some things out and refocus my outlook. One night after work, I felt that I had to talk to Alicia about the things I needed to do concerning my life and our future. When Alicia and I sat down to discuss the matter, she took it better than I thought she would. Then again, that was Alicia. "This is a hard thing for me to talk about," I began. "Me and you've been through so many things together that our relationship almost seems supernatural."

"I feel the same way sometimes," she expressed.

"We have withstood some trials and some tests, and now we're back together. I don't really know how to say this, so I'm going to just come out with it."

"What is it?"

"Things are going fine between us, but for my sake and ours, I need a little bit of time to myself. I'm not ready for another relationship yet. It has nothing to do with another woman or anything like that. I just need to clear my head and do some soul searching. I promise you, the outcome will be well worth it."

Alicia looked at me for a good five minutes before she said anything. "I understand," she replied.

"You do?"

"Yes. It would be selfish of me to expect you to jump in a relationship with me after what you've been through, regardless of our past. A lot of time has passed, and you and I have both changed. We know each other, but we need to take time to get reacquainted with each other's changes. I said it before and I'll say it again, and a thousand times more. I love you, André. If you say you need some time to get yourself together so that we can have a solid future…time is what I'll give you. I respect your request because you're thinking along the lines of what is going to benefit us and not just what's gonna benefit you. What woman can argue with that? But remember this…I'm not going to wait forever." Deep in my mind, I knew that she would understand, but something within helped me to go about it the right way instead of just disappearing and hoping she understood. After that night, I set myself on a quest for answers that I needed to help our relationship.

When I said that I needed time to myself, I didn't mean that I was going to stop being with or around Alicia all together. We still spent time together. She helped me with the baby, but at the end of the day we went our separate ways with an occasional overnight visit. Some nights she would keep Taylor for me so I could have complete time to myself. In the beginning, it was hard because I was not used to sleeping alone. Even when I slept alone while Karen was in the hospital, there was the feeling of hope that made it seem like she was still there—not to mention the scent that she had left embedded into my pillows. Every time I closed my eyes, all I could see was her face. That is how I knew that I loved her. Another thing that rang out in my mind was when she told me that only death would take her away from me. It was almost like she knew.

In the beginning, I fell into a deep state of depression. I didn't eat, I couldn't sleep, and I was not my usual self. When my depression started to affect my work, the Conrad Brothers saw it. Joseph suggested that I take a little more time off, but I couldn't. I had already been out for too long. I really need to shake it off for the security of my job. Business was business, and I knew that if I couldn't perform at the level I had been before my loss, the network would bring in somebody that could do the job—even if the show was my idea. Taylor was the only thing that kept me going. I knew that she needed me the most. She was my ray of sunshine peeking through the dark clouds that hovered over me. I knew I had to pull through for her.

For the most part, I stayed confined to my domain, and the only time I left was when I went to work or needed a little break from myself. Alicia understood throughout the entire time. I weighed out a host of things. Among the things I tried to find was the reason that our first relationship did not work. I tried to blame it on the distance, but that was just a cop out. There had to be something else. It was something about me that was not right. I searched and I searched until I found a seam.

I started to mentally playback all of what I could remember of our relationship since day one, and then it came to me. I thought about a conversation that she and I had before I came to Georgia. She told me that in order for me to love someone completely and have a whole relationship, I had to be whole as an individual. When I moved, I had only begun my journey towards completion. For a while, I was weak-minded and I allowed that mindset to take over. That is how Natalie, Vanessa, Deja, and the other women I had dealt with crept into my life. As much as I tried, I could not distinguish the difference between the women that wanted to be friends from the women that wanted to be more than that, so I kept them around thinking that they would weed themselves out.

Karen was a different case because she and I were something that she concocted without me knowing it, and I fell for it. If I had kept our relationship strictly professional, none of this would have ever happened. The plans that Alicia and I had originally made would have already been executed. That thought shifted me to another thought. If I had not gone through what I did and had not met Karen, my life may not have wound up the way that it did. The entire time, I thought Karen and Alicia was almost the same person, but they weren't.

Alicia was a small town girl that was a little naïve in some ways. I was able to get away with a little more with Alicia because we were so close. Alicia was more like me than Karen was. She liked to have a good time, crack jokes, or just sit in the club and talk about everybody that walked by. She was classified as Taye Diggs said it, *Brown Sugar*. Karen was the complete opposite. She was serious most of the time because she was a corporate woman that didn't take anything off of anybody. She couldn't be easily manipulated. I knew that if I was going to be with her, I had to be or act a certain way, and that's what I did. I saw how I changed myself in order to fit into what she liked to call…*her world.*

It might have been cool for a-while, but down the road it might have caused some serious problems when I wasn't able to be myself. I also noticed how being around me caused Karen to change some of her ways. She loosened up after she got comfortable with me, but she was still firm. When we went out, it had to be classy in every way. She didn't like it when I did the things with her that I did with Alicia. I had to be a perfect gentleman at all times. It was a learning process that prepared me for my newfound position on the social scale. Falling in love with Karen was like falling for one of your favorite teachers because she taught me so much.

I never thought that it was possible to love two women at the same time, but it was. I loved both Karen and Alicia, but in two very different ways. Alicia and I carried history and a friendship that Karen and I did not have. Karen helped take the boy out of me and pushed me farther towards manhood. At the same time, I brought a playful side out of Karen that she'd never been introduced to. We were so opposite, but we complimented each other—I was the Yin to her Yang. Looking at it now, it seems that I would have never been ready for Alicia's move to Atlanta if I had not learned the things that being with Karen had taught me. The more I searched within myself, the more the puzzle of Alicia and me came together. I found pieces that were missing and laid them in place. What I was going through, within my mind, was something that I should have taken the time to do before I rushed into things with Karen. There were factors that would not allow it—I guess it is like that sometimes. My soul searching went on for a few months, and just like she said, Alicia was right there.

It was like I had started my last new beginning. As time moved on, the wounds healed one by one. Each day that passed, my heart got stronger. I had taken two parts of me and combined them as one to make me whole. I knew something was happening when Alicia noticed it. The first time she said something was when she, Taylor, and I came in from dinner at Red Lobster one night.

"There's somethin' different about you," she exclaimed.

"Is that a good thing or a bad thing?" I asked.

"It's definitely a good thing. It's almost like you're a different person, but still the same André I've always known. Does that make any sense?"

"It doesn't."

"I can't really explain it. Whatever you have been doin' over these past couple of months is really working for you."

"Thanks, baby. I'm not just doing it for me, I'm doin' it for us."

"I know you are. If I didn't think you were serious, I wouldn't be wastin' my time. Because it's you, I'm cool."

"I gotta be honest with you. When you came back into my life, I didn't feel like I deserved another chance. That's how I know that you love me. I told myself that if you just up and decided that you didn't wanna be with me anymore and walked out on me, I couldn't get upset because I would deserve it."

"For a long time I weighed the situation and came up with some interesting things. You and I both knew that a long distance relationship was not going to work. It hurt like hell when you came home just to tell me that you wanted to be with Karen. After the initial hurt was over, I maintained respect for you because you were man enough to tell me. Not only did you tell me, but you told me face to face. That took a lot of heart. It's qualities like that that make me love you so much."

"I just want you to know that I never meant to hurt you in anyway, because you know I would never do that to you."

"I know." That conversation helped close another wound in my heart. The more answers I found, the more I changed. The more I changed, the tighter Alicia and I became. She could see the changes in me. Thanks to Karen, I had learned a lot of things. Being with her helped pull me out of being the same person all of the time. I learned how to be more like a chameleon—able to adapt to all situations and environments. Our relationship also helped me to look at things outside of the box and see things with a broader outlook. I was more than thankful to have had Karen Union as a part of my life. I was blessed.

As my heart continued to heal, I could see things a lot clearer. Many things that I did in the past became obsolete. Even the women that I added to my life respected my relationship with Alicia. One night, while at the Silver Dollar with J-Rock, I ran into Natalie. By talking to her, I found that she had done some soul searching of her own.

"Is that André Marshall?" she joked as she stepped into the billiard room. "I heard he was the man at Black Reign Networks."

"Hey, girl," I greeted as I hugged her. "It's been a while. How you been?"

"Everything's cool. I'm just glad the season is over."

"And what a way to end it. I am actually friends with a WNBA champion and MVP."

"Hey, I do what I do," she modestly replied.

"Y'all beat the Comets?" J-Rock asked with surprise

"Beat is an understatement," I interjected. "They demolished Houston. You would have never thought that they had won back to back championships. My girl was the showstopper."

"Stop it, Dré. You're gonna make me blush."

"Let me buy you a drink. It's the least I can do."

"Okay. Let me see if you remember my drink."

"C'mon now. I know that Miss Natalie Simms, starting point guard for the Atlanta Diamonds, drinks Hennessy and Coke with Grand Mariner up on the side."

"Very good. I'm impressed."

"I'll go to the bar," J-rock volunteered. "I wanna check out the new bartender."

"She's not your type, Cuz."

"Why you say dat?"

"She got on too many clothes."

"You got jokes," Jerome laughed as he walked off.

"What's been goin' on, Big Time?" she asked, racking the balls to start a new game.

"Not a whole lot. I'm just tryna put things into perspective. Losing Karen was rough, but I'm managing."

"I guess you and Alicia are back together now."

"Kinda sorta. We're back together, but we're not rushing the relationship. A lot of time has passed, and we've both changed. We're just taking time to get to know each other again."

"I feel you on that. After that night in Houston, I had to put some things into perspective myself."

"Really?"

"Yeah. I had to stop wearing my heart on my sleeve because it wasn't good for me."

"What do you mean?"

"When we met, I was really feeling you, but you were already in a relationship. I knew it, but I didn't want to accept it. That's why I acted the way I did when Shawna lied to me. I just couldn't bear to think that I might have lost you even if you weren't mine to lose. I was almost willing to wait until you broke up with Alicia. Then I realized that wasn't fair to you, her, or me. I would have been selling myself short and putting pressure on you at the same time."

"I don't understand."

"I know what kind of woman I am. When I see something I really want, I stop at nothing until I get it. I had to stop and ask myself if I would have been comfortable if someone was doing that to me. The answer that I came up with was no. That's why I put some distance between us after we reconciled our friendship. I told myself that if it was meant to be, it would be."

"I feel you one hundred percent. That incident in Houston almost caused me to lose Karen because she found out about it. It could have been avoided if I would have been thinkin' with my head and not my crotch. The good thing that came out of the weekend was our friendship, and that means a lot to me. I don't want you to think that just because me and Alicia are back together that we can't be friends."

"I need a good friend in my life. Since I don't have one now, you'll do."

"That's cold," I laughed.

Jerome came back with the drinks and the three of us shot pool and joked around for the rest of the night. It felt like old times. I was with my family and my friend. I knew things had really changed when I went by Alicia's place to pick up my daughter. I told her that I ran into Natalie at the sports bar and all she said was: "Really? How is she?" A while back, I would have taken it as a sarcastic remark. Things had changed between Alicia and me. We knew we had to respect and communicate with each other. There was no need to hide anything. When my quest for answers came to a close, Alicia and I started to function as a normal couple again, and things fell into place. I didn't trip about her male friends and colleagues, and she didn't trip about my friends and colleagues of the opposite sex. It was almost like we were back in college again. The only difference was that Alicia was my number one woman, lover, and friend.

30

Home Again

Alicia and I had been back together for a while when she finally got settled in the apartment that she wanted. She was right around the corner in Midtown. Me and Taylor were still in Buckhead. Every day after work, either Alicia or I would pick Taylor up from the daycare center—most of the time it was her because I had some late evenings on the set. We continued to rebuild and strengthen the ties that I thought were severed. As we knew, it was not going to be easy. I realized that I had a lot more to lose than I did before, if feelings of infidelity started to invade my newly developed frame of mind. It was funny because over the time, Alicia managed to meet almost everybody I had been involved with. She met Natalie while she and Taylor were in the mall one Saturday. I was out shooting hoops with the guys. To my surprise, she and Natalie hit it off pretty good and became friends. I was cool with it because Natalie was one of my closest friends in Atlanta that I had not slept with. To top it all off, there was no pressure because she was now in a relationship. This way we could chill and be cool like we used to be with no suspicion.

The way Alicia met Vanessa was kind of funny. We were at J-Rock's place because he wanted to spend some time with his goddaughter. I guess she saw my truck parked out front and figured I was at my cousin's. Just as she knocked on the door, Alicia was coming out of the kitchen and J asked her to answer it. When Alicia opened the door, Vanessa had this strange look on her face because she knew she had seen Alicia's face before—my key chain.

"Is André here?" Vanessa asked.

"Yes he is," Alicia replied stepping to one side. "C'mon in."

"Hey, Vanessa," I nonchalantly spoke.

"What you been up to?" she inquired.

"Nothing but raising my baby girl. I'm sorry, Vanessa, forgive me for being rude. This is Alicia."

"Nice to meet you," Vanessa greeted. "I've heard so much about you." Alicia gave Vanessa the phoniest smile I had ever seen before. After the two ladies exchanged pleasantries, Alicia sat down in the chair behind where I was sitting on the floor. The four of us engaged in small talk for about fifteen minutes, then Vanessa left. Alicia took Taylor into the back to change her diaper.

"So, pimpin'," J-Rock began. "What's your next move?"

"Honestly, cousin, I really don't know. I'm just tryna live one day at a time."

"Look, Dré, I know you and I have our differences about women. You're the settle down type. You've always been Mr. Relationship. Forget about what I might think or what Troy and the rest of your boys might say. You got your girl back, now you need to ride this muthafucka until the wheels fall off."

I couldn't believe that my cousin, being the man-whore that he was, would have ever been more right. That's the thing about Jerome; no matter what I decided or wanted to do, he always had my back. That's what family is for. Alicia and I chilled out for a little while longer so J could spend a little more time with his niece, and then we headed back to my place.

Taylor was asleep when we got her home, so I laid her down. It was still early and I knew she would be up again later on. Alicia and I started watching a movie.

"Alicia," I started. "Something has been on my mind for a couple of weeks."

"What is it?"

"I know we are just getting back together and our relationship is fairly new, but I can't help feeling like something is missing."

"To be honest with you, I been having the same feeling."

We stared at each other for a good minute or two and then...BAM! It hit us. As long as we had known each other and dealt with each other in so many different ways and situations, not once had Alicia and I made love to each other. We had found what we were missing. I leaned towards Alicia as she closed her eyes and accepted my invitation with her lips. Both of our bodies trembled at each other's touch. We were like two young lovers getting ready to make love for the first time. Every kiss became more passionate than the previous one. Alicia and I were on our way to ecstasy. In the middle of a kiss, I pulled away from her and stood up. I reached down for her and pulled her up from the floor. Before we went any further, I put both of my hands on her face. I used my thumb and ran it across the scar she received from her accident. I mouthed the words, "truly beautiful" which caused her to smile. She reached for the bottom of her shirt to take it off, but I stopped her. The pleasure of unwrapping that long awaited gift had to be all mine. Slowly I pulled her Donna Karen over her beautiful body and completely off. Amazement filled my eyes because never before had I seen a more beautiful body. I gently kissed her from her neck to her stomach. I looked up at her as I was coming back up and she was looking down at me with a playful smile. My hands were on a journey around her back to unfasten her bra, but she stopped me. Alicia grabbed my arms and shook her head no.

After she stopped me, she kissed me from my lips to my neck. For every button on my shirt that she undid, she kissed the area that she exposed. The further down she went, the more excited I got. On her way back up, she looked up at me as I did her, bringing both of her hands up my stomach and chest, over my shoulders and down my arms to remove my shirt. Alicia then grabbed my hands and put them around her back as if she was giving me the cue to continue where I left off.

Now her beautiful breasts were fully exposed. My first sexual instinct told me to kiss them but I declined. Instead, I pulled her close to me so that I could feel her skin against mine. Due to our height difference, Alicia's head was right on my chest. She put her ear over my heart as if she was trying to hear what it was saying to her. Apparently, it told her what she wanted to hear because she reached for my belt and then unbuttoned my jeans. With extreme skill, Alicia removed my boxers and jeans at the same time and pushed me on the couch. She stood in front of me as I sat and gave her my undivided attention. I watched as she grabbed the remote and turned on the CD player. *Nothing Even Matters*, by Lauryn Hill and D'Angelo swooned through the speakers. Alicia and I fell in love with the song back in college.

As the music built the mood, she reached for her belt and unbuckled it. Every move she made was in synch with the melody and the beat. She turned her back to me as she unbuttoned her Capri pants. Alicia slid them down as she bent over from the waist to push them to the floor. Seeing this made me want to call *Victoria* and tell her that her *Secret* was well worth the wait. Her fingers slid in between her flesh and the strings of her thong, as I had seen exotic dancers do. The only difference was that I hoped that I was the only man that had the opportunity to see Alicia in this way. The CD switched to the next track as she turned to face me. The song truly described what Alicia was to me—*One in a Million.*

My sultry princess danced for me as she removed the remaining article that stood between ultimate pleasure and me. Though Alicia was only standing about three feet away, when she started walking towards me, my anticipation made it seem like it was taking her forever to get to me. When she arrived at her chosen destination, she straddled me and took me inside of her and went all of the way down. When she stopped, she began to tighten her muscles to match the beat that was playing. If Timbaland only knew how much I appreciated his talent for his beat double up's.

Alicia rocked slowly back and forth, rolling her hips in every motion. Normally, I would have tried to take over, but I was content with her being in control. From her reactions and facial expressions, I could tell that she had been waiting for this moment just as much as I was. I lifted my head up in order to look her in the eyes, but they were closed. I watched as the expressions on her face told the story of how she was feeling. Gently, I made an upward pelvic thrust and I knew I hit her spot because I felt her body jump. I repeated the motion, making her let out soft moans and oohs. I didn't know what Alicia had done to me, but whatever it was brought out the best in me. I stood the both of us up, without pulling out of her, turned around and placed her back on the couch. With one leg over my shoulder and the other one straight between mine, I stroked her slowly. Not once did I have the desire to get out of control and treat her body in any ill manner. I made love to her as if I was holding a rose gently by the petals.

Never did I imagine that we would have ever experienced this action in this way, especially after I watched her walk out of my life on that day back at Franklin Memorial. Our sweaty bodies rubbed against one another causing the heat of passion to fuse our souls together for what I hoped would be for the last time. Over the next two mixed CD's, Alicia and I sexually, mentally and emotionally tied our lives together. In an act of passion we committed to each other all over again.

The last track of our favorite CD came on and really caused an emotional hurricane between the two of us that was far greater than any we had experienced.

From the first piano note of Maxwell's, *This Woman's Work,*" I felt my body temperature rise to another level. All of a sudden I began to think about everything we had been through since the first day we met at Westchester Elementary School. My nose burned and I felt water form in my eyes. Tears began to fall, and because of the emotion, Alicia immediately detected the difference between the sweat and the tears. As I shed tears of joy, I heard her sniffle. Neither of us said a word. I didn't understand at that time, but now I realize that while we were physically making love, we were also mentally making love for the very first time.

As Maxwell came to his climax, we came to ours. I tried to pull out but once again, I was kept in. Alicia and I reached an orgasm in unison that put the final piece of the puzzle in place—Trust. Feeling that we would get to this level and the fact that I was a new father, Alicia was already on birth control. It didn't matter whether she was on it or not, deep down inside, I knew that I would never let her go again. At the end of our sexual explosion, I sat up and then collapsed on the other end of the couch. Like a little girl, Alicia crawled on top of me and laid her head on my chest. Nothing was said by either of us. We just sat in silence with a newfound understanding for each other.

Fifteen minutes passed and the moment was broken by the stirring cry of Taylor. Alicia and I gathered our clothes while I threw on my boxers to go and get my daughter. In Taylor's room there was a picture of Karen that hung over her crib. When I looked down at Taylor, whom had silenced her cries when she noticed my presence, I could see Karen in her little gray eyes. I stood over the crib and gazed at the photograph when Alicia came up behind me and put her arms around my waist.

"You miss her, don't you?" she asked.

"More than you'll ever know," I answered as I leaned down to pick up Taylor.

"You know God works in mysterious ways."

"Yes he does. But you know what? I believe that it was in his plan. He took you away from me and then He sent an angel down to rescue me from my evil ways and to teach me how to love a woman the way he intended for her to be loved so when he brought you back to me, I'd be ready. When he felt that her job was done, he called her home."

"I guess she earned her wings."

"As well as leaving a part of her behind," I said kissing Taylor on the cheek. "Speaking of Karen, the network is having a banquet next Saturday in honor of our two Primetime Emmy nominations for *Matters of the Heart* and to present me with my seat on the Executive Board of Producers. Are you busy?"

"Busy? I wouldn't miss it for the world. I'm there." Alicia stood on her tip toes and kissed me on my cheek. "Well, Boo, I'm going to head to the house. I have a couple of things to do before Monday morning."

The night of the gala came, and Alicia and I were in route to the Ritz-Carlton Buckhead. The occasion had me nervous and anxious at the same time. Other than the night's events, I had something else on my chest that I needed to get off.

"Alicia," I began.

"Yes babe?"

"Before we go any further, I need to tell you something." I turned down the radio. "Sometimes to advance in our lives, we do things that we are not proud of to get where we're trying to go. A couple of months before Karen went into labor, we were at a cookout at Smoke's house. I overheard Karen talking to one of her friends telling her that she used me."

"Used you how?"

"She used her position over me to lure me into her. She had been through so much with men that she would've done anything to get a man who would treat her right. When I told you about how she acted towards me in our first interview, I said it jokingly, but it turned out to be true. Even before we first started working on *Matters of the Heart*, I picked up on a strong vibe coming from her that had nothing to do with business. In the beginning it started off as harmless interactions and flirting. I was up front about you and never hid you from her. I constantly talked about you. I told her about things we used to do together and the way I treated you. I'll never know, but I feel like that's the reason she wanted to get closer to me. Maybe she thought she'd found what she was looking for in a man. As time went on, I became more uncertain about our commitment that was never established. I let my guard down, allowing her to get into my head. That's when she set out to make me more than just a colleague. I fell for it, hook, line and sinker."

"Some women will do what they can to get a man. She saw everything that I see in you, and she couldn't help herself."

"Before you take my side, as you always do, there's something else." I paused for a moment and took a deep breath. "I did the same thing to her."

"You did what?"

"When I realized that Karen had a thing for me, I used it to my advantage to advance my career. I knew that I had what it took to make it, but I needed a foot in the door to get my ideas into the hands of the right people. Karen was tight with the Conrad Brothers and she was on the Executive Board of Producers. I saw that as my opportunity. I felt that if I flirted a little and showed her some attention, it would soften her up enough for me to make my move. I never expected it to go as far as it did. I knew I was playin' a dangerous game, but I didn't see myself retiring from Black Reign as just a writer. I had all intentions on breaking it off with her once I got where I needed to be. I lost focus and let my emotions get involved. Because of this, we started to drift apart, so I latched on to Karen."

"Why didn't you tell me this then?"

"I loved you too much and I didn't want to get you caught up in the mess that I created.

"Wow," Alicia exhaled. "That's deep."

"I'm sorry."

"André Marcellus Marshall, I've loved you since before I knew what love was. We been through hell and high water, and I've always stood right beside you no matter how good or how bad. You are my man, and you will always be my man. You didn't have to tell me all of that, but the fact that you did makes me love you even more. We both agreed that we would wipe the slate clean. Me and you are together now, and that's all that matters to me."

Wow! She took it better than I thought she would. The final burden had been lifted off of my chest. As I inhaled once again, I felt new life. The journey that all men and women set out on from the time they started dating was over. I was back with my soulmate, and I was on my way to one of the biggest nights of my career. When we arrived at the Ritz, the red carpet had been laid out for Black Reign. As we walked into the hotel, I received a host of strange looks. I think it had something to do with the fact that everyone was so used to seeing me with Karen. It was hard for them, at first, to adjust to seeing Alicia on my arm. Many of my colleagues spoke to us, but not one mentioned Karen's name. I must have introduced Alicia to about thirty people before we made it to our table. Joseph Conrad was the first to greet us as we approached the table.

"André," he said as he stood up. "It is so wonderful to see you again."

"Evening Joseph," I greeted as I shook his hand. "Allow me to introduce Alicia Burroughs, a long-time friend."

"It's a pleasure to meet you, Mr. Conrad." Alicia greeted.

"Please, no need for formalities. Call me Joseph. You two are sitting there. Now if you will excuse me, I have to find my brother so we can get this show on the road." We took our seats and spoke to a few more people as Joseph and Jonathan Conrad approached the podium. As usual, Joseph was making jokes and Jonathan was trying to keep him on track.

"Now everyone," Jonathan started. "Before we go any further, I want to take this time to remember one of our colleagues that is no longer with us, Karen Union. Though we had our ups and downs, Karen was a great asset to Black Reign. We managed to steal her from the competition and she rose to the challenge of helping a new network get off the ground. For that, we say thank you to Karen Union. She will be deeply missed. If you will, I'd like to take this time to take a moment of silence for Ms. Union." A silence filled the ballroom as her friends and co-workers paid their respects. "Now to the reason that we've all gathered…Over a year ago, we were having problems within the network and my brother and I called on Karen to help us fix it. With all of the confidence in the world, she rose to the challenge. She brought us a young man with talent, ambition, and passion. The first time I read his work, I was impressed; but I didn't let him know that." The crowd laughed as Jonathan turned and winked at André.

"He is a true example of hard work being its own reward. A little over a year ago, this young man started with us as a writer, and now it is an honor to present him with a seat on our Executive Board of Producers. On top of that, he has given

Black Reign Networks another top-rated show. I look forward to the years to come. Ladies and gentlemen, without further-adieu, it gives me great pleasure to introduce to you, the man responsible for much success, Mr. André Marshall." The room erupted with applause and a standing ovation as I stood and walked to the podium. I stepped to the podium and cleared my throat as the crowd silenced.

"My great colleagues," I began. "I cannot stand here before you tonight and take all of the credit for this occasion. This moment is to be shared with quite a few. Even though *Matters of the Heart* was my idea, it took many people to get it off of the ground and on the air. First and foremost I would like to thank God for instilling in me the talents that I possess. Second of all, this honor goes to the Conrad Brothers, for giving it a chance; to our director, Shane West, and the entire cast and studio crew. The next honoree, who should be standing here beside me, unfortunately, is no longer with us. That person is Karen Union. Karen believed in me and what I could do from the moment I called her that night and ran the idea by her. You have no idea how many hours we spent outside of the network in order to get this project ready to go on the air. Even though she is not here physically, I believe that she is smiling down on us, just as proud as we are. As you all know, she left behind a beautiful baby girl, and I want to thank everyone for being so supportive of us in our time of need. I probably would not have made it through as smoothly as I did without all of your help. The last person I would like to thank is this young lady that is here with me tonight, Miss Alicia Burroughs. I have known this woman since the fourth grade. She has always supported me in everything I have set out to do. Whether I was trying to be a rap star back in junior high school or trying to direct and produce my own plays in college, she was right there for me. I have so much love in my heart for her that I don't know how I survived being away from her for so long. Nevertheless, we are here and we are together. In closing, I'd like to say that I love being a part of the Black Reign family, and I can't see myself happier at another place of employment. So, to the Conrad Brothers, the cast and crew of *Matters of the Heart*, Alicia Burroughs, and Karen Union, I love you all. Thank you." I walked away from the podium to another standing ovation and was greeted by the warmest hug from the woman that I loved more than anything in this world.

The rest of the night we laughed and had a grand time. What more could a man ask for? I had success, a beautiful daughter, and I was finally together with the woman that I truly desired. When all of the festivities came to a close, Alicia and I walked, hand-in-hand, back to the car. "André," she said while putting her arms around me. "Did you honestly think that we would ever come back together like this?"

"Honestly? Alicia, when I watched you walk away from me that day, I thought I had lost you forever."

"If you only knew how miserable I was for the first few weeks. Every time I passed a telephone, I wanted to call you."

"I missed our nightly conversations. They kept me going when I first got here."

"I'm just glad that we settled our differences and are able to move on." Alicia stopped me just as we were approaching my truck and gave me one of the deepest, most passionate kisses she had ever given me. We must have been engaged in that kiss for about five minutes, but it felt like an eternity. "Damn, girl!" I said as I gathered my senses. "I'm really buggin' right now."

"Why?"

"I look at everything that we've been through since we first met. I've put you through so much unnecessary bullshit. I've lied to you, I've treated you bad, and through it all, you forgave me."

"Remember when we came back together in college and we made that promise to never be apart again?"

"Yeah."

"I knew it was going to be hard, but I knew that one day you would realize that I am the only woman you will ever need in your life, as a lover or a friend. You have been and you always will be the only man I'll ever need, want, or desire. Just promise me one thing."

"You name it."

"Promise me that from this day forward, you will never lie to me again."

"No more lies. I promise." We exchanged kisses once again and walked towards the SUV. I opened the door to help Alicia into the vehicle and then took my place on the driver's side. Alicia stopped me as I stuck the key into to the ignition.

"Before we go, I also have a confession to make."

Turning to Alicia, I asked. "What's on your mind?"

"I've always wanted you to be my man. Why do you think I was there for you as much as I was? When your cast walked out on you in college and you had to recast three weeks before opening night, I was there. I supported you, I pushed you, and I helped you through broken relationship after broken relationship because I knew you had what it took to make something out of yourself. When you got the job at Black Reign, I was so excited for you, but I knew that if I let you go to Atlanta without me, somebody else was going to get my man. I've always wanted to be the only woman in your life, but just like you, I didn't want anything to ruin our friendship. That's why I told you that I loved you that night. I knew I had to do something to buy me enough time to get out of school and get to the ATL. From past relationships, I also knew that even though we considered ourselves a couple, you wouldn't be faithful. I accepted it. You're not all to blame for us drifting apart. After Christmas, I started spending time with Patrick to occupy my time, but it backfired. My feelings got involved and he consumed most of my time. A week before you came home to break up with me, I stopped seeing Patrick because my heart knew that it belonged to you. That's why I was crushed that day. I let Patrick go, then I lost you. It hurt more because I allowed myself to get caught up with someone else. Why do you think that I didn't make a big deal out of the women you were with? We were both guilty. I know you went through a mental battle because you wanted to stay faithful to me, and for that I apologize."

"After everything I've done, an apology is not necessary."

"If Karen hadn't died and the two of you were still together, that's something I woulda had to live with for the rest of my life."

"When I left South Carolina, I had a lot of growing up to do. Having you in my life, as more than just my best friend, made me want to give you everything and I knew I couldn't do it as just a writer. I wanted us to live the life we lived in Florence on a larger scale."

"I appreciate that but all I ever wanted from you, money couldn't buy. All I ever wanted was for you to be my man and my man only."

"I guess we did what we had to do and fortunately for us, it all came together."

"By any means necessary."

Thank you for reading Hidden Agenda's by PRINTHOUSE BOOKS; Author; Lorenzo 'El Gee' Gladden. Please leave a review; we would love to know what you think.

PRINTHOUSE BOOKS

Read it, Enjoy it, Tell a Friend!

Atlanta, Ga.

www.PrintHouseBooks.com

www.ingramcontent.com/pod-product-compliance
Lightning Source LLC
Chambersburg PA
CBHW020535060726
47499CB00017B/95

* 9 7 8 0 9 9 1 1 7 1 9 1 0 *